Digressions

A Novel of the Civil War

Clifford E. Schroeder

Beaver's Pond Press, Inc.
Edina, Minnesota

ISBN 1-890676-81-0

Library of Congress Catalog Number: 00-111354

Printed in the United States of America.

03 02 01 00 5 4 3 2 1

This novel is dedicated to my fellow English teachers in the public schools of America

Author's Note

The title of this novel is meant to call attention to the diverse digressions that intrude into the lives of all men and women. Time, circumstance, social upheaval: these touch our life-paths. Robert Frost in his poem, "The Road Not Taken," speaks of this to us. The digressions of our lives become part of our lives.

This novel is, of course, fiction. The towns of Milford and Clearfield, Tennessee, are imaginary, as is the Battle of Little Hilltop. However, the author wishes the reader to know that all other historical events, geographical locations, and technical information have been researched and references to these are accurate.

The characters of this story are also fictional, created by the author's imagination; however, when historical persons are mentioned, such as Phil Sheridan the Union cavalry general, they are presented as authentically as research can determine—even to the naming of Sheridan's favorite horse.

The author is aware of several anachronisms in this novel and pleads simply a creative license in the inclusion of them in this story. These noted anachronisms are:

The Pledge of Allegiance to the Flag of the United States is used, spoken by the spectators at a football game in the story time of 1917. The Pledge was used from before the turn of the century; however, the phrase, "under God," was not, in fact, part of The Pledge until 1953 when it was officially declared part of The Pledge by President Eisenhower.

That phrase was included by the author in The Pledge in the story because its absence might be more startling to the reader than its inclusion, and because today it seems a very natural part of The Pledge.

The Klu Klux Klan dates back to the days of reconstruction after the Civil War, but it was quite inactive by the turn of the century. After WWI, however, its membership grew to its highest totals, and across the nation numerous demonstrations and marches were conducted by them in order to influence public opinion. The incident in the story where the Klan attempts such a demonstration at a football game takes place in 1917 story time predating the actual resurgence of the Klan by perhaps a half dozen years.

The author enjoys using quotes from poetry in this novel. The quotes from and references to the poetry of Robert Frost, Carl Sandburg, Andrew Marvel, John Keats, Edgar Allen Poe, and Emily Dickinson are accurate. In the quotes from "Sonnets From the Portuguese" by Elizabeth Barrett Browning, the author of this novel in quoting from Verse XLIII, deleted some of the lines that did not seem to carry the tone of the scene portrayed.

But it is in regards to the poetry of Matthew Arnold that this author has a confession to make, in that some lines were quoted in this story from Arnold's "Dover Beach" a good seven years in this story time before that poem was published. It seemed to this author to be too good a quote, appropriate for the feeling of the incident, not to use.

Finally the author would call attention to the letter designation of The United States Marine Corps companies in World War I. Marine companies were, in fact, at that time designated by numbers rather than letters. In other respects, the account of the company, part of the 5th Marine Regiment, including the assault of the machine guns by nine men, led by a young lieutenant, is accurate. The use of the title, "F Company" in that episode, and also designating the company in the Confederate Army by that letter, comes from the author's own sentimental connections with F companies of the past.

Clifford E. Schroeder
Grand Rapids, Minnesota, July 10, 2000

Book I

Albers College, Milford, Tennessee
Spring 1917

The Old Professor

Chapter 1

Albers College, Milford, Tennessee
Spring 1917

He was an old man, but that was not what you noticed when you first saw him. You would be aware of his alert appearance, his firm steps, and his erect—almost, but not quite, military—posture. His eyes, too, were blue and alive.

He was perhaps six feet tall, though he appeared taller because of his erect posture. On his face was a full beard and mustache, neatly trimmed; and also on his face from his left eyebrow to left ear, partially covered by the beard, was a faint scar line. His clothes were neat and clean, and on his feet he wore sturdy, brushed boots.

He would appear without fail on the rather vast, rambling college campus grounds every day at midmorning, and always he was accompanied, a few paces ahead of him, by a shy, orange-freckled faced, white setter whom he addressed as Sally. And, of course, the horse, a quite large and handsome, bay thoroughbred; but he led the horse as often as he rode it, and, especially when he was not riding it, the horse would arch its neck and snort and prance about as if it was just now about to run the race of its life.

Usually the man wore no hat, but on rainy days he wore a broad-brimmed canvas hat and slicker, dark brown in color; and on the cooler days of winter he might wear a Western-looking sheepskin coat with some of the shearling showing at the collar. But he rode and walked each morning despite the most inclement weather that this Middle-Southern state had to offer.

Occasionally he appeared again in the late afternoon, but now accompanied only by the setter; and they would walk on the soft gravel paths, over footbridges that spanned the streams, and on trails that meandered across meadows and under huge sycamore trees.

Sally, the setter, soft-stepped her way the usual half dozen paces ahead of him; and, though she sometimes paused to briefly note some interesting deep thicket of blackberry bushes, or to flavor some scent upon the breeze, she did not leave the path. Chasing squirrels or rabbits was quite beneath her dignity.

The grounds were seemingly too large for the grounds and building staff of Albers College to completely control, but the inner radius of the grounds, those nearest the academic buildings, were well kept with grassy stretches and turnouts for benches beneath spreading trees and benches out in the open sunshine, perhaps beside a small stream.

As the old man met students or teachers during his walks, whether on horseback or afoot, he would gravely greet them. To the men he would nod, and now and then speak their name; and, since he wore no hat, to the women he would give a pleasant, informal, somewhat military salute—a hand to his forehead.

The students spoke of him as "the old professor," and when they spoke to him they addressed him as "Professor," not knowing if he had ever really been such. The staff seemed to be more familiar with him, and when they addressed him as "Professor" they did so with utmost respect and the knowledge that he was indeed a professor of literature and that he had taught such subjects at this college for many years, but that also, some years ago. Some of the staff seemed to be on quite familiar terms with him and would not let him pass by without some pleasantries.

When the man stopped to speak with these, the dog, Sally, would stop, step gracefully to the side and lie down, tail outstretched, head resting on paws, and facing the old man.

The students could easily have discovered more about the old man with a few questions of their teachers, and perhaps they did ask, but preferred instead the aura of mystery and romance that seemed part of his presence. Or they could have asked him, but, though he seemed friendly and pleasant, yet he had a reserve to him that did not seem to invite questions about the past.

The students would stop him and ask a question about some novel, perhaps, or about a line of poetry. Sometimes one student stopping would stop a number of others, and some vigorous discussions broke out around the old man. He would be intent; his eyes moving from speaker to speaker, perhaps adding a probing question now and then. Sometimes the discussions would become so lively and draw such numbers, that the entire group, realizing that they were blocking the pathways, would move to a nearby sunny slope of grass and the students would naturally arrange themselves in a semicircle, some seated, some standing, some crouched on one knee. The old professor would find himself in the front of the group looking very much like a teacher, except, of course, that he was flanked on one side by the gentle Sally, and on the other by the ripple-muscled thoroughbred, who would now finally, with bridle reins hanging on the ground, resign himself and meekly allow a dozen hands to stroke his neck or flank.

When the talk ended, the students would say, "Thank you, Professor," sometimes almost in chorus, and they would go on their way. Sally would rise and take her place at the front, and the impatient, stamping thoroughbred would arch his neck and flare his nostrils; and they would be on their way.

On a sunny, spring day with term finals imminent, there would be several dozens of students sitting on the benches, or leaning on an elbow on the grass, studying or putting some final work on papers that were due. Many would greet the old professor as he came by. He seemed to know most of them by name, and not only that, he seemed to be aware of their class work and how they were doing.

"Good morning, Daniel," he would say. "Did you complete your paper on American existentialism? Were you able to get some back up quotes from Emerson?"

"Well, Rebecca," he would say. "And what do you think of our friend Walt Whitman now after studying his poetry for nearly a half year?"

The setter would pause and look at the addressed person, quite confident that important words were being spoken. Thor, the impatient thoroughbred, was not quite so sure.

"Stella," the professor addressed a pretty girl in a sailor-cut dress, "were you able to come up with a topic for your final paper in Early American Novelists class?" She was sitting on a wooden bench quite near the pathway. Perhaps she had planned to be close enough to talk to him as he came by, as he surely would, on his morning walk.

"Yes, Professor, I think I have," she said. "I'm thinking of writing on how unreliable so many of those writers were in their depiction of the American Indian, and how they shifted their opinions seemingly without reason."

"That just might do," said the professor after a short pause. "Yes, I think that might do quite well for Professor Anderson's class."

Stella's face brightened. She leaped to her feet. "Here," she said, "I've already started a list of the critics that I might quote."

"Hmm," said the old professor as he scanned the list. "Yes. Yes. Good, and add to that Twain's essay titled 'Cooper's Literary Offenses.' You'll find it in the library, of course; and you'll enjoy reading it. It's one of his best."

"Oh, thanks," said Stella with a bright smile and a touch on his arm.

The old professor smiled warmly in return, and, with his customary salute, continued on his way led by the setter and followed by the horse.

On very rainy mornings there would by less traffic on the grounds, of course. There would be several students carrying umbrellas hurrying between buildings, or a teacher headed for a midmorning class. Covered delivery drays pulled by big, clopping horses might follow the service roads to the backs of buildings where supplies were hurriedly delivered by men who tried to keep their cargo as dry as possible—foods to the cafeteria, or boxes to the library.

Such rainy weather did not deter the professor and his entourage. They would follow their usual route along the paths. Sally, looking a little bedraggled and forlorn in the slanting downpour, would step daintily around standing puddles. When she looked up at the old man, she was not questioning why they were doing this, but rather making a comment on the situation like, "It sure is raining, isn't it, boss?"

The professor would say, "Good girl, Sally."

Thor, the big thoroughbred, if anything, looked even more magnificent in the rain. Water would be running in rivulets off the muscles of his glistening rump and neck, and on cooler days his breath was visible as he snorted and pranced along.

The old professor, either riding or walking in the rain, seemed content. His face and collar were well protected by a broad-brimmed hat, and he looked out from under that brim at the dripping trees and at the foggy lowlands with keen interest. If there were some deer half hidden under the trees, Sally, without pausing, would point briefly in their direction, and the man would say, "I see them, Sally. Look at that young one. What big eyes!" And Sally would look a half grin back over her shoulder as they went on.

Each morning, too, the ice wagon would roll up the gravelly service drive pulled by two proud, black Percheron horses. The wagon would stop behind the college cafeteria and two burly men with leather aprons would struggle up the steps with great blocks of dripping ice.

Thor could never ignore the other horses, and to all of them, he would roll his eyes, blow through his flaring nostrils, and generally let everyone in the vicinity know just how superior he felt to these mere horses that pulled wagons. His knees came a bit higher, and he pranced in the anticipated pleasure of running these other horses into the ground.

The old professor would tolerantly pet his flaming steed on the neck and sympathize with his friend. "I know, old fellow, I know," he would say. "We all have our dreams, and yours is to run like the wind."

Thor would quiet down and perhaps nuzzle at the man's coat pocket. Sally would turn back and stand beside the old man and for a few moments the three would be a tableau—a picture of comradely contentment.

"And what are your dreams, Sally?" said the old man, though he knew the answer. Sally would lift her head and nose to look the man in the face and slowly wag her feathery tail.

"Of course, of course," said the man. "Quail, and plenty of them. Perhaps a broken covey scattered through hedgerows and small openings; and the chance to work downwind from them and patiently point each bird for your not so gifted friends."

The man knelt on one knee and placed the palm of his right hand under the soft muzzle of the dog. Thor lowered his majestic head and the man stroked the velvety nose. "I share your dreams, my friends. I wish I could defy gravity and time, and glory in the workings of my body. I wish I could feel more of life by more acute senses. And I have my own dreams too."

On a beautiful, mellow day, the man would stop at a bench at the farthest boundary of the grounds. The bridle reins would be dropped to the ground. He would take from the saddlebags a well-wrapped canteen of hot tea, a unit of nesting cups, and a cloth bag of biscuits. Then he would seat himself on the bench, pour himself a cup of tea, and offer one biscuit each to the horse and dog. Any passerby would be welcomed to the tea and biscuits—and many accepted. A half-hour of talk and companionship would ensue.

The bench overlooked part of a rushing stream. Across the stream were high bluffs, some sheer rock cliffs, and beyond that the deepening green V of a forested valley. Just beyond the bluffs a misty trail of vapor floated upwards; and just barely audible was the rumble of water pounding over rocks and drumming on the rock shelf below.

On days that no other person shared his tea, the old man would take a small book or a magazine from his coat pocket, and read poetry to Sally and Thor—and to any latecomer that arrived after he had started reading. By their rapt attention, it was quite obvious that both Sally and Thor deeply appreciated poetry, and they would be rewarded for their good taste in literature by another biscuit each.

One day he extracted a new book titled *Mountain Interval* and read the first poem in it to Sally and Thor. Some passerby stopped to listen and he read it again. "'Two roads diverged in a yellow wood,'" he read and continued to carefully read the account of the traveler who had chosen the trail that was "grassy and wanted wear." He read through to the end, "'and I—I took the one less traveled by, and that has made all the difference.'"

He paused and looked at his audience—all quiet—all eyes on him. He cleared his throat. "This is good," he said. "This is the truth." He nodded his head and turned to the front cover of the book. "This one, this Robert Frost—he shows much promise."

"Thank you for the tea, Professor," each student said, bringing him their cups. "And thanks for the reading," added a lithe, golden-haired girl. "We've got to hurry to get to class." The students hurried down the paths, some turning to wave farewell after they had gone a little distance. The old professor gravely saluted them in return.

On days when the air was warm and pungent with the smell of spring's blossoms, the old man would often walk by some couples who were sitting quite close together on some secluded bench. "Good morning, David," he would nod to the young man. Both young people would be looking at him, perhaps slightly embarrassed, but still holding hands. The old professor would smile and make some innocuous remark. "It's a rare and beautiful morning," he might say, and go on his way.

When the old man was out of sight, David said, "How did he know my name? I've never talked to him before."

"I told him your name last time I talked to him," said the girl. "I think he's nice."

Passing near one of the academic buildings, the science building, the old professor came upon a young man sitting on the ground, back against one of the spreading elms that shaded the building. The young man was deep in concentration in the book he held in his hands, but when he heard the sound of Thor's hooves on the path, he looked up.

He leaped to his feet. "Oh, Hi, Professor," he smiled and came toward the trio, a well-muscled, smooth-moving, young man. "I'm studying for my chemistry final," he said, showing the book to the professor. "I'm going to make it, too, this time."

"I know you are, Harold," said the professor. "I know you are."

The two men looked at each other, both obviously enjoying the meeting. "I saw you run the quarter mile in the track meet yesterday afternoon, Harold," said the professor. "You have my congratulations on a well-run race, and on the win."

"Thanks," said Harold. "You know, Professor, for the first time in that race yesterday, I felt as if I was really into it—my mind and body working together in some sort of harmony. When I needed that burst the last fifty yards, it just came automatically it seemed. I didn't have to tell myself to go. I was just along for the ride. You know what I mean, Professor?"

"Yes, I think I do," the professor nodded as he keenly looked Harold in the face. "I thought I saw that in you as I watched you run. It's a beautiful thing to experience."

"It was great," said Harold, his face flushed, perhaps from reliving the exciting race, and perhaps a little embarrassed for seeming immodest about his win.

Impulsively, Harold reached out to grasp the professor's hand. "Thanks for everything, Professor," he said. "Thanks very much for everything. I'm going to graduate in June, and I'm not sure I could have made it without your help." When he saw some flush of emotion touch the old man's face, he felt he could have thrown his arms around the professor and hugged him.

The professor cleared his throat. "I'm tremendously proud of you, Harold," he said. "The right stuff was in you all along. If I helped to bring it out, I'm more than happy."

As the professor turned toward the horse, Harold stopped him with a hand on his sleeve. "I've got one more thing to say while I have this chance," he said. He looked around. No one else was nearby. "When you talked to me two years ago," Harold continued, "and you asked me if I was cheating on that test; and I wouldn't admit it, but I am admitting it now. But I haven't since then. When I waited and waited, and you didn't turn me in, I knew you believed I was worth a second chance." He looked the old professor full in the face. "You believed in me, and I learned to believe in myself. Thanks, Professor."

There happened then, a moment of clarity—a moment when two people looked at each other, and measured each other's worth, and approved of what they saw. There was, in that bright moment, a mutual sense of humanness, a feeling that did not regard age or gender or social status as a basis of measurement. It was a moment of greatness in the human race.

At that moment Thor thrust his regal head between the two men, and both reached to smooth his velvety nose. "What a horse," said Harold.

"I've one more thing before I go," said the professor. He reached into the saddlebags and brought out a new book. "Here," he said, "is a book of poetry by a young fellow named Carl Sandburg. I remember last time we read poetry you complained that poetry was too light, not down to earth enough. Well, this may change your mind."

Harold took the book and read the title. *Chicago Poems*, he read. "All right. I'll try it," he said. "And I'll take care of the book for you."

"Oh, no," the professor said, "if you like the poetry, the book is yours to keep. If you don't like it, return it, of course; but I rather think you'll appreciate these poems, especially the first one titled 'Chicago.'"

Sally, anticipating the moment, had already stationed herself a few paces up the path, and now, at a last nod from the professor, they continued on their way, the old man feeling good, walking briskly. Harold watched the departing group until they disappeared around the bend in the trail. Then he looked at the new, blue book in his hand, carefully put it in his coat pocket, and, picking up the chemistry book, he seated himself at the foot of the tree and continued studying.

Chapter 2

Autumn 1917

On a windy, autumn afternoon, a Saturday, the college football team played host to their most intense rivals, Slippery Rock Institute, a football team from a neighboring state. The occasion also marked the traditional celebration of homecoming for alumni. The air was chill enough so that fans wore coats or sweaters and carried, perhaps, a blanket to wrap around themselves when they weren't on their feet cheering on their team.

The play on the gridiron was intense, staying mostly in mid-field as neither team seemed to be able to break the other's defense. Suddenly, when most of the fans, and perhaps the players themselves—their faces streaked with sweat and dirt, their helmetless hair tousled and hanging over their eyes, their jerseys grass-stained, and their legs aching with bruises—would have settled for a tie; the home team, using a deceptive reverse play, was able to get the ball inside Slippery Rock's ten-yard line. From there, by dint of determined efforts, they were able to score the five-point touchdown. And thus the game ended.

The fans swarmed onto the field after the game and clapped their players on their backs. The players, after they had huddled and had given their opponents fifteen big cheers, shook hands all around. It was a day of good cheer, shared even by the losing players who felt they had played their best.

The old professor had watched the game from one end zone where he sat astride Thor, the added elevation of the horse giving him a vantage point he might not have had in the stands. When the play progressed to the opposite end of the field, he would raise a pair of field glasses and study the play through them. Some of the spectators, their eyes straying from the action on the field, would be slightly startled by the picture of what might have been a cavalry officer directing his troops on a field of battle.

The professor thoroughly enjoyed the game, especially seeing some students of his acquaintance doing well on the field; and when Pug Swenson ran the reverse that led to the winning score, the old professor raised his arm in salute to the play.

After the game the professor lingered, a little reluctant to leave the scene of success. The fans, brightly colored in their attire, swirled onto the campus much like the autumn leaves swirled in playful eddies by the wind. There were cheery greetings everywhere, students greeting their parents, alumni greeting each other after long separations—a motley of students, parents, alumni, and teachers, some still in the bleachers, some yet on the playing field, and some beginning to drift toward the buildings of the adjacent campus. The old man had just thought that he would bring Thor to the college stables and return for some talk with students, past and present, at the informal tea get-togethers that each department was sponsoring, when the entire casual scene changed.

Perhaps some cloud had just obscured the sun; perhaps the autumn wind felt colder. People began moving back toward the bleachers saying, "What is it?" "What's going on?"

There seemed to be a preponderance of white on the field in front of the bleachers; and as people came closer, some stepping back up in the stands, some crowding in from the end zones, it was indeed clear—there was a group of white-clad figures, perhaps a dozen, though no one counted, in a semicircle facing the crowd. Many of the figures were holding their white-draped arms up as if in salute, or in entreaty for the crowd to silence and listen. In the middle of the half circle stood a more imposing figure, possibly because he held a large bullhorn in his hands and was beginning to address his audience. But what caused the most gasps of surprise, and perhaps of fear, was that each of the white figures was also topped by a tall, cone-shaped headdress with dark, round eye holes.

"Please, your attention, please," the bullhorn man was saying, but he need not have asked, for the spectators were shocked into silence. A few people moved to get a better view, but for the most part, there was an expectant stillness.

The speaker seemed satisfied with the crowd's attention, and he spoke in ringing tones. "My fellow citizens," he said. "We are your neighbors. We live in this fair community in this great state. We also have children attending these schools and this college. We have businesses in this community, and we go to church beside you each Sunday."

He spread his arms out to include his fellow white-robed figures. "We are a group of concerned citizens who have banded together in order to preserve the honor and integrity of this, our beloved Albers College."

The speaker, a bulky man, discernible despite the loose, white robe, seemed to gather himself together for a dramatic statement. He paused, then continued: "It has come to our attention that this college plans to admit, and may already have admitted, students from Jewish background."

He paused again, then waved a hand to encompass the campus of the school. "Jews within our midst," he said, "planning and scheming to take over just as they have been doing for centuries all over the world. Jews!" he spat out, "and probably Catholics, too. And where, I ask you, will our children go to school when they have taken over? Where? Yes, to state-run schools run by atheists and skeptics."

He doubled a fist and shook it in the air. "Here!" he shouted. "We have to stop them here. We must make the dean and the board of directors sit up and listen when we come in with our just and unanimous demands."

He lowered his voice to a deep, menacing tone. "And now," he said urgently, "now just when we are most vulnerable, just as our country is engaged in a great war against the Huns, just as some of our very own students are fighting over there to preserve the purity of places like this; they sneak in. They sneak in and..."

The speaker became aware of the fact that his audience was no longer looking at him. They seemed to be looking over his head, past him. He raised his megaphone in a desperate attempt to bring their attention back to him, when he became aware of the thump of hooves on grass behind him and the loud blowing of breath through flaring nostrils. It was Thor.

It was Thor, not galloping, just stepping briskly, each front leg raised high, then thumped on the ground. In the saddle, sitting ramrod straight, was the old professor, the front of his hat, set straight on his head, flaring up just a little from the wind.

The burly speaker turned just in time to be brushed aside by the massive chest of Thor, who somehow managed not to step on him; but he did completely demolish the megaphone which could not have been deliberate, but almost seemed so, with blows from his front hooves. Thor wheeled in a circle, scattering the other white-robed figures, then he faced the bleachers, stamping and blowing, arching his long neck in obvious pride and dignity.

The professor did not need a megaphone. Perhaps his higher elevation put him in closer proximity to his listeners. They had no difficulty hearing him.

"Friends of Albers College," he said. "Friends and students and alumni of Albers College. You have listened to a speech and seen a demonstration by people who do not have the courage to show you their faces." Here the old professor swept the hat from his head with something of a flourish.

"How much weight shall we put to opinions expressed by people who do not dare to show their faces as they speak? How insidious is it for them to bring the fear and dislike of the enemy we are fighting in Europe and try to plant that fear here on this campus?

"Instead of fear and hatred, we should think of trust and respect. Yes, changes come to our country, to our lives, and perhaps even here to Albers College, but do we have to fear such changes?

"Why should we fear diversity in our community and in our school? Diversity can make us stronger if we let it. Yes, there will probably be Jewish students here, and likely Catholics, too, and someday, when we are ready for it, black students will study here beside the other students.

"After all, we already have had students from a half dozen countries across the seas; and they have given us more understanding and respect for others.

"We cannot allow blind prejudice, nor ignorance, nor self-interests to rule our thinking. Understanding is what we must strive for. The war in Europe will be over one day, and we must not allow hatred and fear to determine how we make peace.

"Yes, we have former students who are now on the battlefields of Europe, and we knew them when they were here as students; and knowing them, we believe they would not want us to breed more hate and prejudice here, at the college they loved. We believe they are putting their lives at risk in the name of honor and justice and peace in this world. To believe otherwise would be to desecrate their sacrifice—and a few have made the supreme sacrifice."

The old professor paused, seemingly searching in mind what direction to go. The people in the bleachers and on the field around him were quiet and thoughtful. They seemed to sense that they were witnesses to an epic event—a beginning of something—something to hold on to in their memories. In years to come, they seemed to be saying within themselves, they would be able to say, "I was there. I heard it. I saw it. I was there."

To those who remembered the scene afterwards, the panorama was a gripping one. In the middle was an erect man on a bold horse; in the stands were the people, their coats and hats now and then fluttering in the wind, and people crowded in from the end zones; and the scattered white-robed men, but none making any gesture or voicing any opposition; the leaves drifting from the trees, and through the trees, just visible, some flags waving in the wind on the campus. And on the edge of the football field, well out of harm's way, sat a silky, smooth-coated, white dog with orange spots on its face.

"With your permission," said the professor, "I would like to dedicate what we have here today—this football game, this gathering of students and friends of Albers College—I would like to dedicate it to the memory of former students who have given their lives in the great war in Europe. They will never be able to return to this or any homecoming. We owe it to them, to remember what they died for."

People were beginning to stand up if they were seated. Men were removing their hats. Women clutched their scarves around them. Children, near their parents, were silent, all looking at the figure on horseback before them.

When all was silent, the professor, looking over the heads of his listeners, as if he were reading from a scroll in sky, said:

"John Marcus Andrews, Class of 1916, Ensign, United States Navy.

"Henry Adam Goodwin, Class of 1915, Captain, United States Army.

"Margaret Colleen Bell, Class of 1913, Nurse, American Field Services.

"Harold Robert Banner, Class of 1917, Lieutenant, United States Army."

There was complete silence. Some stood with their heads bowed. Some looked off across the campus. Though there was no movement among them, yet they seemed to draw closer together. All of them, including the man on the horse—the horse which stood quietly now, and even seemed to bow his proud neck—were caught up in a deep, stirring emotion.

After a long, quiet moment, Thor stirred, stamped an impatient front hoof, shook his head; and the spell was broken. People looked up, looked at the professor. What to do now? The professor, too, felt the need for some concluding, closing action.

The professor raised his arm, pointed to the campus. "There through the trees," he said, "you can see our country's flag flying high and free. Let us turn in that direction and speak the Pledge of Allegiance together."

Thor wheeled majestically in the indicated direction. In the stands the people turned, removed hats, placed hands over hearts. In the end zones on the field, the people turned and faced the distant, fluttering stars and stripes. In the ensuing movements and stirrings, the white-robed men quickly disappeared behind the stands. No one even seemed to notice their presence or their going.

When the professor began the words of the pledge, he was quickly joined by the voices of perhaps a thousand others. "I pledge allegiance to the flag...of the United States of America...and to the republic for which it stands...one nation under God, indivisible...with liberty and justice for all."

The professor placed his hat back on his head and snapped a sharp, military salute—a salute that would have done a West Point cadet proud—toward the flag. The people stirred and began moving toward the campus. Thor turned sharply on rear legs and cantered briskly to the center of the field, turned left and high stepped the length of the field. Thor, a natural showman, knew he was on parade, in review. Sally, leading the procession, had to quicken her pace—but did so with dignity—to keep ahead of the prancing thoroughbred.

At the end of the field they turned onto a well-used trail that brought them quickly to the college stables on the outskirts of the college grounds. The professor dismounted, threw the reins over Thor's head and led him into his stall. He removed bridle and saddle, carrying them into the tack room, and returned with a rough sack. He began to rub down the horse, and Thor, anticipating the pleasure of the rub, leaned against him.

The stable hand, a student earning part of his expenses in pleasant work, came up with a measure of oats. "I heard we won the football game, Professor," he said.

"It was a fine game, Robert," said the professor. "I'm sorry you couldn't be there."

"That's all right," said the young man. "I could hear the cheering. How was Thor?"

"Thor?" said the professor. "Thor was fine. He was superb. He deserves a little extra oats—not much extra. We don't want him more spoiled than he is now, but today, definitely, an extra measure of oats."

Thor, his rub down finished, looked regally around at his two slaves. He braced himself, and the professor, knowing what was coming, moved a pace back; and Thor shook himself, his skin, his tail, his neck and ears—shook himself as briskly as a dog coming out of water. Then he blew through flaring nostrils, blubbering his lips and began in on the oats in his feed box.

Chapter 3

The old professor brushed off his trousers, lightly buffed his low boots, and removed the heavy coat he was wearing. He hung the coat in a locker from which he took another dressier, somewhat longer-cut coat, and put it on. He tied a blue ribbon tie around the collar of his shirt. He looked at his face in a small mirror inside the locker door, combed his wavy, gray-brown hair, brushed his short-trimmed beard and mustache, took a final hitch to the lapels of his coat, and turned to go.

"Oh, just a minute, Sally," he said. "The ladies will be all dressed up. I want you to look nice." He brushed and combed Sally's hair and long ears until they were glossy. "Very, very nice," he complimented. Sally put her nose in the air, stuck out her chest, and walked elegantly out the door with the old man.

They followed a well-used path that led them to the main commons and the First Academic Building. It was late afternoon, but many people strolled along the paths, talking, greeting acquaintances, stopping in groups, and going up and down the broad steps that led to the open doors of each of the buildings that faced the main commons.

At the steps, Sally quickly moved back to walk beside the professor. They entered the broad, open doors, and at a nod from the professor, Sally found a quiet corner of the hallway and lay down. She sighed deeply and laid her squarish head on her paws, eyes alert, following the professor as he moved among the people.

Soon he had a napkin in one hand and a cup of tea, served to him by a member of the English faculty, in the other. Many of those present, both older and young, seemed to know him, and they moved toward him, greeting him and were greeted in return. It seemed, in fact, that the hallways grew more crowded when he arrived, as some people drifted in from other hallways and other departments. Most who spoke to him mentioned some aspect of the football game to which he responded with pleasure. A few made reference to the event after the game, to which he nodded his acceptance, but made no response.

When an animated discussion broke out between some past Albers College students about the lines of a particular poem, he was able to, his blue eyes alive, quote the poem line for line, and his listeners readily acknowledged his authority on the subject. He quoted Andrew Marvel, the author of the poem in question:

> *"But at my back I always hear*
> *Time's winged chariot hurrying near;*
> *And yonder all before us lie*
> *Deserts of vast eternity."*

Only at one time did his reserved composure falter briefly. He was standing, tea cup in hand, when a young woman pushed through the people around him, threw her slim arms around his neck, and pulled him down to where she could kiss his cheek. There were tears in her eyes, and she was quite oblivious to the fact that the old professor had deftly managed to keep his tea cup out of the way, and, in fact, had not spilled a drop.

"Thank you so much for what you did this afternoon at the football game, Professor," she said. "Harold Banner was my brother. He thought a great deal of you. When they sent back his effects from France, your poetry book was in them. I know he would have been pleased by that ceremony this afternoon."

"And I thought a great deal of Harold," said the professor. "I'm tremendously sorry, Susan."

"I know, and thank you," said the girl. "My parents and I were in the stands, and what you did helped us understand and accept that Harold is gone." She pulled his head down once more for a teary kiss before she released him. "Thank you," she said. She looked him in the face, and they shook hands; and she turned and quietly made her way back through the crowded hallway.

The old professor looked after her and was able to, quite unobtrusively, touch his tea napkin to his eyes and wipe away some stubborn tears.

The talk in the hallway picked up again and presently the dean of students himself approached the professor. The dean was a tall, vigorous man. He shook hands with the professor.

"We're glad you could make it here," said the dean.

"It's my pleasure," said the professor.

"I understand you enjoyed the football game," said the dean.

"That I did, and very much so," the professor smiled.

The dean lowered his voice. "I want to tell you how appropriately you acted in the incident after the game," he said. "You have my and the board of directors' sincere appreciation."

The professor nodded. "I was happy to be of service," he said.

After the dean left, the professor looked around for Sally. She was still in the corner of the hallway, where she was patiently enduring the rather sticky affections of several children. She had gravely accepted half a piece of cake from one, and had carefully licked clean the sticky fingers of another. Now a toddler was giving her a choking hug around the neck, and her eyes were pleading to the professor for some relief.

At a nod from the professor she stood up shedding youngsters like a dog shedding puppies. She walked carefully a few steps, then when the last child let go, she hurried, happy, alert, feathery tail wagging, to the professor.

The two walked out the door and down the broad steps together. At the bottom, Sally, slightly ahead, paused and looked back at the professor. He briefly indicated with his arm the direction they would take, and they soon disappeared from view down the winding pathway.

Chapter 4

Their path took them past the stables, where they waved to Thor who was so busy prancing and showing up the other horses before an appreciative audience lined up at the rail that he did not notice them. The professor was amused, and commented to Sally, "I know he is so vain, but he's got a big heart." Sally agreed.

After they passed the stables their path began to incline upward, and presently they stepped up on a gravel trail wide enough for a team of horses and a wagon. Again they walked up toward a fold in the side of the low, tree-covered mountain before them. The distance from the campus was not great, perhaps a mile, and both walked briskly, quite used to this exertion and, also, quite enjoying it.

They turned in at a small, low roofed cottage that was built of logs and was tucked in under the trees. The professor opened the unlocked door, but paused to look back down the hillside up which he had come.

The lowering, evening sun was casting long shadows across the valley below. Below him, the professor could just make out Thor still wheeling and cavorting in the paddock. Beyond that, slightly to the left was the football field, the stands now dim shadows. And adjacent to the field, and to the professor's right, was the wooded knoll that was the campus of Albers College. Some of the red tile roofs of the larger buildings showed through the trees, catching the evening sun, and one speck of color showed the flag at the top of its mast, still fluttering in the breeze.

Beyond the college grounds, on into the valley, was the small city of Milford. A river, sometimes visible in the distance, ran the length of the valley through the center of the town; and several steel-girdered bridges could be seen spanning the river.A few stores and businesses were clustered on the level near the river, but one building, a three-story brick taller than the others, the hotel, dominated the business section. Dwellings had climbed partly up the side of the facing mountain slope.Trees were scattered throughout, and a few streets were visible through their foliage.The trees themselves were brilliant in fall colors highlighted by the evening sun.

The old man held the door open for Sally and they entered.The living room which they entered was the entire front of the cottage and was spacious, perhaps twenty feet square, but it was dominated by a massive rock wall and fireplace that was the center inside wall. To the left of the stone wall was a door that led to a bedroom and bathroom.To the right of the wall was a similar door opening to a kitchen and pantry.The lower half of all the walls of the living room was covered by book shelves that were filled with books. These bookshelves extended to the bottom of the windows—two large, square windows on each side of the entry door. Between the windows were hung paintings, some almost as large as the space between the windows, and others smaller. Most of the paintings depicted some outdoor scene or wild creature. On the mantle of the fireplace was a curious assortment of items: a long, slightly curved officer's saber, a round object perhaps five or six inches in diameter that could have been an old artillery cannon ball, some colorful stones that gleamed with quartz flecks, and two quite small, faded photographs, one of a handsome woman and the other of a pretty, young girl in a green-tinted dress.

Overhead on the ceiling ran massive, hand-hewn timbers, purloins that ran the length of the house.These were supported by the rock fireplace in the middle and continued on to the other rooms. These overhead beams were dark with smoke and time, but they expressed the strength of age and time by their presence.

In the center of the room was a rustic, plank table, in the middle of which stood a mantle lamp with a tall, glass chimney and white glass shade. At each end of the table was a comfortable wooden captain's chair; and it was quite apparent that one chair was used for writing and reading, books—one open—papers, pens and an inkwell cluttered that end of the table. On the table before the chair at the other end was a place mat and a folded napkin—a place to eat meals.

Sally went directly to the rug before the fireplace and lay down, luxuriously stretching her legs and curling her toes. The professor went to the fireplace and opened its two iron doors, swinging them wide, and allowing out the radiant warmth of a low fire. The professor swung a small, black iron pot that hung on a hinged hook over the fire and lifting the lid, stirred the contents. Steam and a rich aroma wafted out, and Sally lifted her head in appreciation.

"That's our supper, Sally," said the professor. "Partridge stew. Smells good, looks good, and I believe it will taste good. But let's get comfortable first."

He went into the bedroom and reappeared presently wearing a heavy flannel robe that went below his knees, and wool socks and soft moccasins. He was drying his hands on a towel, which he draped over his shoulder and went into the kitchen. He came back with two blue enamel bowls, a spoon, and a partial loaf of dark bread tucked under his arm. He filled the two bowls with the succulent stew and set one on the floor and one on the table.

Sally had looked at the bowl set on the floor, but she did not get up. "That's still quite hot, Sally," said the professor. "Better give it a few minutes." He set the bread on a cutting board on the table and lay beside it an opened clasp knife, ancient, worn, but with an exceedingly keen edge.

From a sideboard the professor produced a glass and a quart jar of amber liquid. He poured a finger of the whiskey into the glass and stood, his back to the fire, sipping slowly. Presently he stooped down, touched the bowl of stew on the floor and said, "It's just right now, girl." Sally came and daintily ate, and the professor seated himself at the table and ate his supper.

The sun had set. Under the trees the shadows of dusk deepened. The air was cooling quickly, but inside the cabin, with the glow of the flames of the fireplace on their faces, the man and his dog felt at peace with their world.

Chapter 5

On a morning, after the professor had completed his tour of the college grounds, he turned the reins of Thor's bridle around the hitching rail in front of the college administration building. "Wait for me, Sally," he said, and Sally found a grassy spot and lay down.

The professor went up the steps, through the front doors, and turned into the comptroller's office. A middle-aged woman rose from a desk behind the counter and greeted him. "Good morning, Professor," she said.

"Good morning, Miss Hattie," returned the professor. "How are you?"

"I'm just fine, Professor," she replied. "My goodness, are you getting younger? You look quite fit. It's not fair," she continued. "The rest of us are getting older, and you persist in getting younger." She smiled and brushed his hand where it rested on the counter.

"It's talking to cheerful people like you that keeps me young," said the professor. His smile was warm. "I've come to add some funds to the Elizabeth Barrett Browning Scholarship Fund." He took an envelope from his breast pocket and lay it on the counter. "I believe there are four hundred dollars in there."

"Of course," said Miss Hattie. She counted the bills and wrote out a receipt. "Since you are here, and you are one of the directors of the fund, would you like to go over the account book and approve the expenditures that have been made?"

The professor nodded and carefully scanned the ledger that she opened before him on the counter, running a finger down the expense column: "Tuition," "Dormitory Room," "Cafeteria Meals," "Clothing Allowance," "Textbooks." When he came to the heading titled, "Reading Books and Materials," he stopped, tapped a finger on the item and looked pleased. "Good, good," he murmured. "She's getting the idea."

He carefully initialed each item and, closing the ledger, he handed it back to Miss Hattie. "It all seems to be in good order," he said. "Thank you, Miss Hattie. And a good day to you."

Miss Hattie held the ledger in her hands as she watched, a warm smile on her face, the professor step out the door and walk down the hallway.

Outside the watchful Sally got up as the professor came out the door and the drowsing Thor roused himself to arch his neck—large eyes wide, ears perked—and watch the professor as he came down the steps. "Ready to go?" spoke the professor as he gathered up the reins and swung up on Thor. "Let's see if we have any mail." They headed toward the student union building which also housed the post office, Thor carefully walking, from habit, around some of the lower branches that would have swept the professor from the saddle.

"A letter for you, Professor," said the man behind the grilled window at the small post office. He handed out a thin, gray envelope.

"Thank you, Henry," said the professor. "Letters are always welcome." He looked at the return address, and smiled at the bold handwriting. "Ah, Alexandra," he said. He seated himself at one of the small writing desks in the lobby and with a sharp knife from his pocket, he slit open the top flap. He extracted the single, handwritten page, unfolded it and read:

Dear Captain Greyson,

It has been some time since we last corresponded, so I hope things are well with you. Of course, both of us are getting on in years, so we must expect some difficulties.

As a matter of fact, this letter is somewhat related to age, since I am writing to inform you that I have retired from my teaching position. I would have, perhaps, continued on, but a very capable person applied for a teaching position here at Stuart Mills Institute. I seized the opportunity and turned my duties over to him.

As I thought over the forty-seven satisfying years that I have worked here helping people of my race get an education that would give them a better life, I could not help reflecting on the fact that—now more than a half century ago—you were instrumental in starting me in this direction. If it weren't for you, I wouldn't be here. Thank you for that.

I know you did it in memory of the person we both loved, but that does not make it any less generous on your part.

I sometimes long for the warmer climes of my birthplace, but I will remain here in Illinois where I can live my quiet life without the age-old battles of my race. My pension is small, but adequate for my life style so do not concern yourself for me on that account.

I remain as always, your faithful friend,
Alexandra Barrett

The professor folded the letter and thoughtfully placed it back into its envelope. Something of a sigh escaped him, and he remained seated at the desk a few minutes longer looking at the letter in his hand, or perhaps not looking at anything in particular. Finally, he placed the letter in his coat pocket and returned outside.

"Well, my friends," he said to Sally and Thor who looked up as he approached, "let us go to our warm and comfortable homes and see about some lunch." He undid Thor's reins from the hitching rail. "If you don't mind, my friend, I will walk beside you for a ways." The trio headed for the stables and home.

Chapter 6

On a warm, fall day—the glorious sort of day that everyone exulted in because they knew winter's sterner weather was surely soon to come—it seemed to the professor that almost the entire student body must be outside on the grounds. Students were everywhere, walking in pairs, sitting on the benches, grouped in the sun on the grass. It amused the professor to think of the obvious excuses that would be given for skipped classes, for tardy arrivals, and for unfinished assignments.

He greeted students warmly, individually and groups, and the students seemed more willing than usual to stop and talk. Finally the professor's walk was stopped entirely by a rather large group of students that had gathered at a sunny turnoff from the path.

After "good mornings" and "beautiful day, isn't it?' the students looked at each other, friendly, casual; one of the students spoke up. "Professor," he said, "some of us are worried about the war. We wonder just what is right and what is wrong in a supposedly civilized world that can arrange to shoot at each other on a battlefield."

"Yes," put in a pert, red-haired girl. "Here we are in the twentieth century, and we're still acting the same as they did in the middle ages."

"They called those the Dark Ages," said another. "What about these times?"

The first speaker, Paul Osborne, a senior, spoke up again. "Professor, some of us were at the football game a few weeks ago. We heard what you said there. You sounded so confident about your statements, and most of us probably agreed with your sentiments—but how do we know if we are right? How do you know you're right, Professor?" He smiled deprecatingly. "We don't mean to put you on the spot, Professor, but what do you think?"

The professor looked at Paul and at the students around him. "That's all right, Paul," he said. "When you make public statements, you should be put on the spot to back them up. That's what I was trying to do to those people who started that demonstration. I usually prefer to stay out of the limelight."

The professor looked gravely at the students and they at him. There were many questions in their eyes. The professor dropped Thor's reins on the ground and moved forward toward the students. Sally had already lay down at the edge of the group near a seated girl from whom Sally was pretty sure she would get an occasional stroke on the head. More of the students seated themselves, and the professor put one knee on the ground and leaned forward, arms on the forward bent knee. He felt that what he was going to say was more important than anything he had ever said in a classroom, or perhaps, more important than anything he had ever said in his life.

"First, I have to tell you," he said, "that just because I am old doesn't mean I know all the answers. If anything, my long experiences have taught me that some questions in life may never be answered, or that answers change according to time and circumstance. But perhaps mainly, I have come to believe that I must always continue to search for answers. And sometimes I have learned that the search for truth is the answer itself. I feel I must believe in the search."

He paused. He knew they wanted more. He wondered if he had any answers for them. "But along the way, we want and need some guidelines, and I would be betraying the good life I have had if I could not at least say to you what has worked for me as I looked for the right and truth of things of life."

He paused again and looked at the faces before him. He had the sudden impression that he was looking the future in the face. Thoughtfully he continued. "Believe in beauty," he said. "Look for beauty in life around you—and within yourselves—learn to recognize it in all its various forms. See it, watch it, feel it within your soul, touch it, recognize it, honor it. If you can touch beauty, you will also touch truth.

"Keats said it quite well in his poem. I'm sure you've heard these lines from 'Ode on a Grecian Urn,' but I will quote them as best I can. '*Beauty is truth, truth beauty—that is all we know on earth, and all we need to know.*'"

Many of the students nodded. Most of them were upperclassmen—and women—and they had had classic poetry in their literature classes. They had struggled enough with poetry of Keats, Shelley, Byron, Wordsworth, and Blake to know that meanings were not always obvious.

After a thoughtful pause, the professor continued. "What are some of the examples of beauty around us? Let's consider some obvious ones—a mother holding a child in her arms and feeding it. Beauty. And the opposite is a picture of a child crying, hungry; and the mother, because of some social conditions, is unable to take of care of her child—war, famine, injustice, greed. We must strive to make it possible for the first to happen, and we must abhor the conditions that allow the opposite to happen.

"Or let's look at another example that may be something we can all identify with—a classroom of students. Let's suppose that the students in the classroom represent all the various racial, ethnic, and religious backgrounds that compose our country. Now which image has a beauty to it—the students intermingled, friendly to each other, united in a common cause of learning; or a classroom in which each sect forms its own group, sits by itself, is angry and suspicious of the other groups? In my opinion we must strongly oppose any forces that actually promote the ugliness of hatred in our society."

The professor paused again, looked at his audience, perhaps waiting for questions. When none were forthcoming he went on with his comments. "Believe in beauty," he said again. "I believe this principle of beauty can be applied to all aspects of our lives—in how we treat each other, in how we view and treat nature, in how we recognize the value and beauty of aesthetics in our lives.

"And each of us has some beauty within ourselves. All right. Let's look at it in its simplest, but by no means complete, form—our physical appearance. Some among us have more of the traditionally accepted forms of beauty—and that is not to be deplored—we appreciate that beauty. But look at the person next to you for a moment. Notice their bright eyes, their pert noses, their strong cheekbones, a curl of their hair, a graceful turn of their hands. None of us is without some of that beauty."

He smiled at his students, and they smiled back at him. Then briefly, they looked shyly, a little embarrassed, at each other. There was a murmur of talk among them, then a sort of easy, comfortable settling among them. Even Sally got in on the individual beauty exercise. The girl that sat beside her, stroking her ears, bent down to look her in the eyes, and Sally was able to get in one quick lick on her face before the girl retreated.

"Those are the quite obvious aspects of each individual's beauty," the professor said. "But the deeper beauty is within, and that can be seen in how we live our lives—with honor, with dignity, with generosity to people around us. It shows in the courage we have to stand up against adversity, and in how we stand up for our principles—and in the respect we show for this earth we live on, and for all its inhabitants."

"But how does the war fit in this?" asked the golden-haired girl. "There can't be anything more ugly than a war, and yet some of us have friends—good friends in it." There was a little catch in her voice, but she bravely went on. "I have a very good friend over there, and he is a kind and gentle person. I can't think of him as ugly."

The professor shook his head slowly and looked at the girl kindly. "I know of whom you speak, Lisbeth, and no, he is not ugly. I know him to be a unique individual with many good qualities. I don't believe it is the individuals that get caught up in a war that are ugly; but the greed and intolerance that precipitate wars that are very ugly."

"Is it possible for there to be beauty somehow within a war?" asked Lisbeth. "I don't mean the shooting and things, but the way some sacrifice for others in a war?"

"I believe that is true, Lisbeth," said the professor. "Margaret Bell, a graduate of this school, was a nurse working in a field hospital when a long-range artillery shell exploded and killed her. Certainly the work she was doing, and the sacrifice she made, was of beauty. I believe that."

Lisbeth nodded her head and seemed to accept the professor's statements, but she looked troubled, concerned. "I'm still worried that a war can be so ugly, that it can mar something that is beautiful—can change people that are in it."

"I understand what you are saying," said the professor, "but I don't know the answer." He looked at the students—his friends—quietly. "We must strive for beauty," he said.

After a long, thoughtful silence, one of the students who had not spoken before said, "Professor, we heard that you were in the War Between the States—the Civil War. Is that true? We heard that the scar on your face is from that war. Were you there?" Everyone looked at the professor, waiting for his answer.

The professor seemed to deliberately compose his face. He reached up and touched the scar on the left side of his face. He briefly shut his eyes, then opened them. "Yes," he said sadly, "yes, I was there." He nodded his head slowly. "That was a half century ago, and I was there. And that war was as ugly as anything can be." He paused and shut his eyes, and the students barely heard him say, "But in the midst of that war, I was touched by something so beautiful that I will remember it until my last breath."

The group was silent as the professor turned back toward the horse. Each of them felt that they had learned something—something worthwhile. Lisbeth touched the professor's arm and he turned toward her. "Thanks, Professor," she said. "Thanks so much." There were tears in Lisbeth's eyes as she spoke, and she was surprised, as she looked in the professor's face, to see that the professor also had tears in his eyes.

Chapter 7

Lisbeth hurried from the professor and the discussion group, taking all the short cuts in the paths that led to the main college buildings. She had a 10:45 class, and now that the discussion had ended, she meant to get there on time. If the professor had gone on talking to the group, she would have been quite happy to accept a tardy to class, or even skip it altogether, because she was very interested in the topic of the discussion. But now she intended to get to class, and, what's more, stop in at the student union building and check her mailbox. Her feet fairly flew along the path, and the hem of her dress fluttered around her ankles.

It had been almost two weeks since the last letter; and though she had waited longer at other times, she was very hopeful. Lisbeth ran up the steps of the student building. At the door, a fellow classmate held the door for her.

"After you, Lisbeth," the student said. "I see you are in a hurry."

"Thanks, Harvey," said Lisbeth. "I'll see you in class."

Lisbeth's mailbox, No. 206, was just slightly above her eye level, and she stood on tip toes to see into it. Her heart leaped as she saw the familiar flimsy, gray-white envelope, and in a second she had it in her hands eagerly scanning the return address. Of course, it was from him, and she knew immediately that she would save it to read later in the privacy of her room—where she could laugh or weep as the words of the letter touched her.

Lisbeth tucked the letter into the pages of a book, and started for class; but then a terrible thought came to her. Wouldn't it be awful if this letter, which had already come thousands of miles by ship and train, should fall out of her book and get lost? It needed a more secure place than the book, and Lisbeth, with a quick look around her, quickly unbuttoned the top buttons of her blouse and tucked the letter into her bosom. She rebuttoned the large buttons, quickly picked up her books, and, with a flash of ankles, she skipped down the steps toward American literature class in the First Academy Building.

After class, at noon lunchtime, Lisbeth, with her canvas book bag slung over one shoulder, pushed a tray along the food line in the cafeteria. She selected one piece of roasted chicken, a green salad, a glass of milk, and a gingersnap cookie.

The senior student who punched her food ticket complained. "Lisbeth," he said, "you're a growing girl. You need more than that to eat."

"I didn't think you noticed," said Lisbeth. "But really, this is plenty for me, and it's all such healthy food too."

"That's our mission," said the senior dramatically. "We here who sweat and slave in the cafeteria, strive to keep you healthy."

"I'm deeply indebted to you," said Lisbeth with a smile. She carried her tray to a table by a window where she could watch the sun shine through the trees, some of which were beginning to look bare of their leaves.

She carefully propped a book up on the napkin holder, just behind her tray so she could read as she ate her meal. She read: *"Because I could not stop for death..."*

"Hi, Lisbeth. Could we sit with you?" It was Kathryn, the girl from across the hallway at the dormitory. Two other girls were following her.

"Of course," said Lisbeth. She closed the poetry book and set it aside.

"Have you met Helen and Julia?" asked Kathryn. "They are both freshmen this year."

"Hello," said Lisbeth. "I think I've seen both of you in natural science class."

"That's right; I've seen you there," said either Helen or Julia. "You usually sit up front. I try to sit in the back so I won't get called on in class." The three newcomers seated themselves at the table. They talked as they ate—talked of friends, of football games, of classes, and of studying.

"What were you trying to study just now when we interrupted you?" asked Kathryn, pointing to the book that Lisbeth had put aside.

"Emily Dickinson," replied Lisbeth, with perhaps something of a frown. "I guess I like her poetry, and some of the imagery she puts together is neat, but I do wish she would pick at least a few cheerful topics."

Kathryn nodded her head. Helen and Julia just listened. Kathryn said, "Maybe it's because of the way she lived, the secluded life she had."

Lisbeth agreed, "That must be part of it. I can't believe anyone would choose to live as a recluse. Yet she was able to see a great deal of life, and write with insight. But I do wish she could have lived a happier life, and written some happy poetry."

"Maybe, if you see life as it really is," said either Helen or Julia, "it's difficult to live a happy life."

Lisbeth nodded. That's pretty good insight for a freshman, she thought. "So how do you like this school?" asked Lisbeth of the two freshmen. She was beginning to see the two girls as individuals. Helen had bright eyes and a ready smile. Both girls were brunettes, but Julia tossed her head back often as if it were covering her face. She looked directly at you when you talked to her, and Lisbeth liked that.

"Oh, I really like it," said Julia, "and Helen does too. Don't you?" looking up at her friend.

"I like it too," said Helen, "but both of us are a little homesick. We're roommates and that helps, but we're really looking forward to Parent's Day next weekend when both our folks are coming." She and Julia smiled at each other.

Kathryn agreed. "It's nice when they come," she said. "Mine are coming up all the way from Atlanta. Even though I'm supposed to be a big, worldly sophomore, I'm glad they're coming."

All around them students were talking. There were the sounds of silverware, of chairs scraping, of trays being set down. The cheerful voice of the senior punching tickets at the end of the food line could be heard as he greeted everyone by name. One corner of the room by two big windows was supposedly set aside for staff use, but many of the staff ate at student's tables, sometimes continuing discussions that had begun in the previous class.

It was a cheery scene, yet in those moments Lisbeth felt a deep loneliness. She looked down at her plate, studiously picking at the last of the salad with her fork. When she looked up, all three girls were looking at her with sympathy. Do I always let my feelings show? thought Lisbeth. She smiled.

"Lisbeth," said Kathryn, "I'm sorry we sounded so happy about our parents coming. I guess yours aren't coming?"

"No," said Lisbeth. "It's okay." The girls continued to look at her quietly, for the moment stopping their eating. Lisbeth took a deep breath. "Now don't feel extra sorry for me or anything, but I may as well tell you, my mother died four years ago when I was still in high school. She was older than most moms since she was almost forty when I was born. And my father died when I was quite small. He built and repaired big farm wagons and there was an accident with some horses."

"We're really sorry," said Kathryn, and Helen and Julia shook their heads in agreement. "It sounds like maybe you don't have any brothers or sisters either."

"No, I don't," said Lisbeth, "nor grandparents either. They dated back to the War Between the States, and they would have been quite old by now." She smiled brightly, perhaps a little forced. "So you see, I'm all alone in the world, but really, I get along fine. The closest relatives I have that I know of are like second cousins, and sometimes I miss that, but then sometimes I think I'm lucky too."

Lisbeth stopped. The sympathy on the faces of her listeners was clear. Quickly Kathryn leaned forward. "Listen," she said. "Come to the Parent's Day dinner with me and my family on Saturday evening. Please come. It will give you a chance to dress up, and I know my parents would like to meet you. You'll come, won't you?"

"That sounds like fun," said Lisbeth. "I'll come. You're sure your parents won't mind?"

"Of course not," said Kathryn. "I'm really glad you'll come."

They finished their meal, Lisbeth eating the fresh gingersnap cookie for dessert, and the talk went back to the more usual topics that college girls talk about. Just as they were ready to pick up their trays and leave, Helen stopped them. "I don't like to bring up the subject again, Lisbeth, but how do you manage without a family—without some older person to go to for advice? It just seems too difficult to me."

Lisbeth thought for a moment. "Well," she said, "I do miss it because I find myself drawn to older people, like teachers on the faculty here—and, oh yes, do any of you know the old professor—the one that has that pretty dog and that beautiful horse? Well, I talk to him quite a bit, and he always listens. Once in a while he gives me some advice if I really ask for it, but mainly he just listens and, I think, understands. Actually, he is one of my favorite old people. I sometimes think, if I had a grandfather, I'd like him to be like that."

Chapter 8

All day Lisbeth had been very aware of the letter she was carrying buttoned up in her blouse. More than once she had been tempted to excuse herself from the company she was in, or from a class session, and go to some private place to read it. But she only touched it through her blouse several times to feel it crinkle. Fortunately, the belt of her dress was snug against her slim waist so there was no chance of it falling through.

Finally her afternoon class was over, and she hurried along the leaf-strewn paths toward the women's dormitory. She ran up the flight of stairs to the second floor and opened the unlocked door—no one locked their dorm rooms. Her roommate had a late afternoon class and Lisbeth enjoyed the privacy of having the room to herself for a couple hours, especially now that she had a letter to read.

She opened the window sash so some fresh, autumn air could come in, stacked her books on her sturdy, wooden desk, hung her short coat in the closet—enjoying the anticipation of the letter to be read. When she knew she could wait no longer, she undid the belt of her skirt and stepped out of it as it fell to the floor. The letter obligingly slipped from under her blouse and dropped soundlessly on the skirt.

"Oh," breathed Lisbeth, and with a quick stoop, picked up the letter and leaped onto her bed, sitting cross-legged, but with her petticoat tucked over her knees. She examined the letter envelope in great detail. Was there a way to tell from the outside what it said inside? She held it up to the light from the window. There must be at least two or three pages in there—and written on both sides probably, too.

She read the address again: "Miss Lisbeth Hammond, Sophomore Class, Box 206, Albers College, Milford, Tennessee." Then she read the small writing on the return address: "Lt. Peter Morgan, F Company, 2nd Battalion, 5th Marines, FPO New York, New York."

Finally, with a quickening of her heart, she carefully tore off the narrow end of the envelope, and, blowing her breath into the end of the held-up envelope, billowed the sides out just enough so she could reach in with forefinger and thumb and extract the precious letter.

When she read the salutation: "My dear Lisbeth," quick tears almost blinded her—tears of relief—he was still all right—tears of joy—he still loved her—tears of intense emotions condensed into the words of a letter.

She read the lines of the letter carefully—all three pages on both sides—her feelings ebbing and flowing through her as she read his words. She imagined him sitting at some rough wood table, wearing his heavy, green marine uniform, a steel helmet on his head.

She smiled when he wrote of the first bath they had in almost two months and how good it felt to be clean. She wept just a little when he described how lonely he was for her and for home. She was proud of him when, reading between the lines, she could tell how proud he was of his men, and how they respected him. She laughed with delight when he told how he was able to outwit regimental supply and get an extra ration of food for his company. He did not write of the dreadful things that he must be seeing and experiencing, and she knew he did not write of such things because he did not want her to know; but Lisbeth had read enough war reports in the papers to have some idea of what it must be like.

Near the end of the letter, Lisbeth both smiled and wept as he quoted some lines from the poetry of Elizabeth Barrett Browning: "*How do I love thee? Let me count the ways.*" From there he wrote lines of his own in which he praised her "golden, sun bright hair," her "eyes of sea-deep blue," her laugh "as delightful as a lark's song," and her hands that were "like two swans."

"All my love and devotion, Peter," he signed at the end of the letter, and Lisbeth, holding the pages of the letter to her lips, closing her eyes, her heart seeming to burst, wondered how love could be both so painful and so joyful at the same time.

"I do love you," she murmured, and then, "Please, God, let him come back to me;" and she studied his picture on her desk: eyes looking directly at her, just the hint of a smile at the corners of his mouth, strong jaw line with high cheekbones. He wore his uniform with bright lieutenants' bars on the shoulders and the marine emblem on the collar.

Then she tucked the letter into the drawer of her desk—she would read it again before she went to bed—washed her face in a basin of cool water, and got dressed to go to the evening meal at the students' building. Students were expected to dress up for the evening meal, men to wear coat and tie, and women to wear good dresses. Lisbeth put on a frilly, white blouse, a long, dark blue skirt, and a red belt around her waist.

She looked at herself in the mirror and liked what she saw, but she looked again and decided something around her neck would look good. From a dresser drawer she took an old, but elegant, gold chain and heart-shaped locket and clasped it around her neck. The locket, passed on to her from her mother, was her favorite, but she had never been able to identify either the initials on both sides of the outside, or the small, quaint, old-fashioned portraits that faced each other on the inside.

She had studied both pictures many times. The woman was strikingly beautiful with light colored ringlets falling to her shoulders. Her face showed wide-set eyes and high cheekbones. She wore a low-necked dress, and just visible was a small, heart-shaped locket around her neck on a chain.

Lisbeth knew the picture was not of her mother, but it did look vaguely familiar, possibly because she had looked at it so many times.

The man's picture was not as clear, perhaps from age, but Lisbeth had decided he was good-looking with deep eyes, straight nose, and a strong chin—although the latter was partially covered by a trim beard and neat mustache. He wore what seemed to be a uniform with some insignia on the shoulders.

Lisbeth let the locket hang around her neck, and it came to just above the neckline of her dress. She quickly brushed her hair, and with a last glance at the picture on her desk, she went out the door.

Chapter 9

Parents' Day celebration was held late in the fall when school authorities judged that the new freshmen students would be settled into a routine of classes, dormitory life, and new friendships so they would no longer be so desperately homesick that their parents would be upset. The event was always successful for the students because assignments had been lessened so they could spend time with their parents, and for the parents who were proud to see their sons and daughters taking on new roles in their lives. Usually the parents would come away from the event quite confident that their sons and daughters were in good hands at Albers College.

The small city of Milford was happy to be involved in the celebration. There were welcome banners hung at street intersections in the business district, and many business establishments went out of their way to accommodate the increased trade of visitors. The one hotel in town could not accommodate all the visiting parents so the Chamber of Commerce had organized some of the private homes to take in visitors for bed and breakfast. The livery stable established regular hourly runs to the college campus from town and return. Buggies and single harness horses were available for those who wanted to see more of the mountain and valley scenery, but most parents spent the main day, Saturday, on the college campus.

Special arrangements and events had been planned for the day. In the morning, parents could roam through the academic buildings where faculty staff were supposedly working in their offices, but in reality were there to be pleasant and courteous and answer questions from the parents about their student sons and daughters.

Or they might follow the many footpaths of the large college grounds and see the clear water running in the streams, admire the large, old trees; and finally at the farthermost lookout point, marvel at the deep valley that stretched out between the hazy, blue mounts. All the paths circled back to the buildings, so it was not possible to get lost, and besides, parents were usually accompanied by their student son or daughter who knew the paths well. They might, as they strolled these paths, chance to meet a white dog with orange spots followed by an old man leading a magnificent horse. The old man would greet them courteously and go on his way.

At noon the parents could eat in the cafeteria with their student sons or daughters, and though they felt self-conscious pushing a tray along the food line, it was a cheerful event. The sun shone in through the tall windows brightening the entire scene.

In the afternoon there was, of course, the football game to go to; and after that the visitors were free to visit the horse stables, or inspect the construction of a building that was coming along nicely—a field house for winter and indoor athletics.

But the main event of the Parents' Day celebration was the banquet on Saturday night. For this the large sliding doors between the cafeteria and the student lounge had been pushed back to form a room large enough to accommodate all the students and their visitors. The tables were arranged in a large semicircle facing a small stage at the front. There were few speeches made other than the dean of students welcoming the parents, but before the meal, which was served family style, the student orchestra played several numbers.

A faculty staff member, and perhaps their spouse, had been assigned to act as host at each of the tables; and as there were not enough staff to supply one to each of the many tables, other people connected with the college in some way had been asked to fill in. That is why, when Lisbeth and her friend, Kathryn and her parents, entered the room, they saw the old professor seated at a table near the stage.

Lisbeth was feeling light and cheery, glad that she had come with Kathryn and her parents. "Oh, let's try to find places at the Professor's table," she exclaimed. "He always has some interesting topics to talk about. Although," she added with a side glance at her friends, "he can get carried away with poetry."

"I like poetry," said Kathryn's mother, and they headed for the professor's table. The professor stood up when they arrived. He shook Mr. Marlow's hand firmly, and took each of the lady's hand and bowed slightly. When lastly he took Lisbeth's hand, he seemed, for a moment, to be unable to speak. Lisbeth heard him take in his breath sharply, and as she looked in his eyes, she wasn't sure if she saw delight or some deep pain. The instant of emotion passed, and the professor said, "Lisbeth, you look particularly lovely tonight."

Lisbeth did look lovely. She wore a long dress with a princess waist, a dress that looked a little more old-fashioned than was the style of the time. It had a low enough neckline to show some bare back and shoulders and an elegant neck. Lisbeth had piled her tawny, blond hair high and held it up with combs, but enough stray curls and strands escaped to give her a devil-may-care look. Around her neck was, again, the beautiful, old, golden locket and chain.

Conversation did not lag as bowls of food were passed around the table. White-shirted waiters, actually students that were earning part of their tuition, hurried back and forth between kitchen and the tables distributing bowls of steaming food.

"Did we meet you on the grounds this morning leading a horse?" asked Mrs. Marlow seated just to the professor's left.

"Yes, I believe I remember you," said the professor. "I walk there most mornings."

"I like your horse," said Lisbeth, "but he is so full of energy, he frightens me a little. It's your beautiful, gentle dog that I love."

The professor nodded, accepting the compliments for his friends. Lisbeth was seated just around the corner of the table, and the locket around her neck drew his eyes. Finally, when he knew she would be embarrassed if he looked at it once more, he simply said, "I very much admire the locket around your neck, Lisbeth. Is it something that has been in the family?"

Lisbeth reached up to her neck and looped the chain and locket through her fingers. She looked down at it, the stray curls of her hair falling around her face as she moved her head. "It's a favorite of mine," she said. "But I don't think I know the whole story of it. My mother passed it on to me before she died, and I think it's quite old because it's worn in some places. The initials on the back and front are smoothed out, but they are still readable."

"They aren't your mother's then?" the professor asked.

"Oh, no," said Lisbeth. "I think the locket is much older than that, and I really don't think she knew whose initials they were because I'm sure she would have told me. The initials are," she read first one side, then the other, "E.B." and "A.G."

Lisbeth looked up and smiled. "They don't match the names of anyone in the family that I know of, but I assume they are the initials of the two people whose portraits are inside." Lisbeth made as if to unclasp the chain. "Would you like to see the pictures of the man and woman inside?"

"Oh, no, no." The professor seemed startled. "I couldn't do that." He paused. Lisbeth was looking at him keenly. "It's a beautiful locket," he said.

"Yes, I think it is," said Lisbeth, "and I don't even know if it is real gold."

"Oh, it's gold all right," said the professor quietly. "Yes, it is gold."

The banquet proceeded on its course. After the meal, while everyone was served coffee or tea to drink and a piece of cake from a large cake that had written on the frosting, "Albers College, 1851 to 1917," the college glee club sang on the stage. At first they sang songs that quieted everyone down. "*Oh, Shenandoah, I long to see you*," they sang. After that they sang, "*Over there, over there, Oh the Yanks are coming*," and even though it was a spirited song, it sobered people as they thought of the Great War, as it was now being called, in Europe; and by now very few families were not affected by that war.

But the glee club brought their spirits up again with a lively rendition of "Dixie," and they got the entire assemblage to join in on one verse. "*Oh, I wish I were in the land of cotton. Old times there are not forgotten. Look away, look away, Dixie Land.*"

The evening was over. Chairs were pushed back as people shook hands and wished each other well. At the door, gentlemen were helping put coats and scarves on the ladies, as the outside air was chilly. The dean stood at the door warmly greeting as many as he could. "Thank you for helping, Professor," said the dean.

"It was my pleasure," said the professor. He was helping the Marlow party with their coats.

"We didn't get to talk about poetry," said Mrs. Marlow. "I heard that you can get quite carried away with poetry." She looked at Lisbeth with a smile.

The professor also looked at Lisbeth with a twinkle in his eye. "Yes," he said, "I must confess that is one of my failings. But people are very patient with me, and I do believe sometimes they goad me on." He smiled again.

"Professor," said the dean, "it's quite dark out. Would you want me to send one of the students here to walk home with you?"

"Thanks, but not necessary," said the professor. "Sally is waiting for me at the stables, and she is easy to follow in the dark. Actually, the way is so familiar to me after all these years, I believe I could walk it blindfolded." With a tip of his hat to Lisbeth and the Marlow family, and a good night nod to the dean, the old professor stepped out the door, walking briskly and confidently into the night.

Chapter 10

On a very cool, late spring, midmorning, the old professor, taking his usual walk on the grounds, was surprised to see Lisbeth coming toward him on the path. She had on a long coat with a scarf around her neck. Her hands were deep in the pockets of her coat, and she was walking with her head down so that she didn't notice the professor until she was almost on him.

"Oh!" she exclaimed, looking up, and the professor saw there were bright tears in her eyes. Sally stopped; the professor stopped, and Thor stopped. For a moment Lisbeth and the professor looked at each other, then the professor dropped Thor's reins, stepped forward and put his arms around Lisbeth. She almost seemed to collapse against him, and as he held her up, the professor realized she was shaking.

Lisbeth looked up at the professor with a tear-streaked face. "I don't think it's true," she said. "It can't be true, but then I think, what if it is true."

The professor waited. The distress he felt at Lisbeth's obvious pain was just now too deep to be expressed in words. He relaxed his hold on Lisbeth as she seemed to gain strength and be able to stand by herself again.

"I know I'm not making sense," said Lisbeth. "But I was too upset to go to class this morning." She paused and said, "You know I have a boyfriend, Peter Morgan. He's with the marines in France."

The professor nodded, keeping his face calm. He was beginning to get some idea of the turmoil that Lisbeth was going through.

"I read the newspapers this morning," said Lisbeth. "And there is some big battle over there—Belleau Wood. The accounts even mentioned Peter's company—that F Company had a lot of casualties." Lisbeth shook her head in misery. "I just can't help thinking about it." Finally Lisbeth gave up trying to be strong. She put her head against the old professor's chest and sobbed—long, racking sobs that shook her body.

After a few minutes Lisbeth's sobs came to a stop and she looked up, a weak smile through her tears. "Thanks for letting me talk to you," she said.

The professor looked up the pathways in both directions. "We seem to have this place to ourselves just now," he said, "and you don't seem ready to go back to class. Suppose we sit here on this bench for a bit—and you can either talk, or cry if you wish, until you feel a bit better."

"I'd like that," said Lisbeth.

The professor got a poncho out of Thor's saddlebags and spread it over the wet bench. Lisbeth sat down, and the professor sat beside her, stretching his legs out before him. The two sat in friendly silence for several minutes.

"Tell me about your friend, Peter," said the professor. "I believe I met him once when he came to visit you last school year, and I was impressed by him, but I don't know much about him."

Lisbeth smiled. She knew she could talk about Peter. "He's from my hometown, Clearfield," she said. "He was three years ahead of me in high school. He played football, and he was captain of the basketball team. I was surprised he asked me to the prom his senior year.

"When he went off to VMI, you know, the Virginia Military Institute, we started writing. After that we dated each summer, and we became good friends. Then when I was just finishing my senior year in high school; and trying to figure out some way to go to college the next fall, I got a letter from the college here suggesting I apply for their Elizabeth Barrett Browning scholarship. I was so thrilled to get it because, you know, Peter was very protective of me since I didn't have a family, and I don't know if he would have gone back to VMI for his senior year if I hadn't some place to go."

Lisbeth turned a bright smile at the professor. "It feels so good to talk to someone; and I know you are on the board that directs that scholarship, and I haven't said thank you in person. Thank you very much."

"Your thanks are accepted," said the professor. "And you did write us a very nice thank you letter when you got it. I knew then we had picked the right student for the scholarship, and now I'm sure of it. Your grades and your work here have proved that."

"I want to do well," said Lisbeth. "Peter did so well at VMI. He was high in his class, and he was very proud when he was able to get a commission as a second lieutenant in the marine corps. You can't believe how handsome he is in the dress uniform with the red stripe down the trousers." Lisbeth blushed a little through the tear streaks and the eager smile on her face.

"Am I talking too much?" asked Lisbeth. "Just stop me. Right now I can't seem to stop myself."

The professor waved his hand in dismissal of such a possibility. "If you are comfortable talking," he said, "I can listen for a long time."

"Well, there isn't much more to tell," said Lisbeth. "Peter went to some officer training that summer at Quantico, Virginia, and I got to see him once. Then he went to the 5th Marines in North Carolina, and very quickly they were overseas. I know it is something he would want to experience," said Lisbeth. "He is a bit of a daredevil—I guess you have to be, to be a marine."

Lisbeth looked earnestly in the professor's face. "I suppose I don't have to tell you that I think he is very nice."

Lisbeth was quiet for a moment; then in a subdued voice she said, "I think I love him."

The professor nodded. "Yes, I think you do," he said. "I can understand your concerns. I also read the newspaper accounts of the battle. It sounded as if the 5th Marines saw a lot of action, and it's not over yet."

"That's why it's difficult for me," sighed Lisbeth. "Just yesterday I got a letter from him that he wrote six weeks ago, and this big battle, Belleau Wood, started just three or four days ago. I don't know if he is hurt, or even dead." She paused, her emotions choking her. "And if he is, I'll keep getting letters from him for the next two months." She shook her head sadly. "I don't know if I can stand it."

The professor listened quietly, sympathy in his eyes. He didn't know what he could say to help her face such a painful situation, but he felt he had to do something.

Lisbeth leaned back, put her head on the back rest of the bench. She reached over and took the professor's hand. "I haven't talked like this to anyone till now," she said. "It's too difficult. And besides, I don't think most of my friends here would understand. They're just not involved like I am."

Lisbeth continued. "Maybe it wouldn't be so hard if my mother was still here. My father died when I was quite young. I think she would have understood what I feel like now. I wish I had someone to confide in, maybe even a grandfather—someone like you." Lisbeth smiled. "I feel better now, but I know I'll start to worry again."

Lisbeth and the professor stood up facing each other; their look was one of mutual friendship. The professor thoughtfully folded the poncho and put it in the saddlebag. Sally got up and stretched. As the professor took up Thor's reins, he turned to face Lisbeth. She saw some sort of determination in his face as if he had reached some decision.

"Lisbeth," he said, and paused. "Lisbeth," he said again. "You still have that gold locket that I've seen you wear?"

"Why, yes," said Lisbeth, puzzled. "I still have it." She looked keenly at the professor. He still seemed hesitant. What was he driving at?

"I know something of that particular locket's past," said the professor, "and it relates directly to your need for the support of a family in difficult times." He reached out both hands and gently held her shoulders. He looked directly into her blue eyes. "But I think rather than tell you about it now, and perhaps cause questions and confusion in your mind about whether what I say is true, let's meet after supper this evening; and I will put what I have before you, and you can decide for yourself what would be good for you."

"All right," said Lisbeth slowly, looking into the professor's eyes. In them there was a kindness that Lisbeth could almost feel.

"I don't mean to be overly dramatic, but I'll be much more able to answer your questions later. Let's meet at the faculty lounge in the Old Main Building at, let's say, six o'clock—and bring the locket."

The professor gave Lisbeth the briefest of hugs, turned back to the dog and horse, and was off in the direction of the stables.

A Digression to a Battlefield of the Great War
Belleau Wood, France
June 16, 1918

The marines of Fox Company, 2nd Battalion, 5th Regiment, left their frontline positions at midnight, relieved by a battalion of French army soldiers who looked wide-eyed and frightened to find themselves in battle. The marines, fatigued after thirteen days of pitched battle, picked up their Springfield rifles, their Hotchkiss machine guns, their field packs and walked out into the darkness—a darkness still alive, however, with screaming artillery shells, whiffling mortar shells, enfilading machine gun bullets, and, at irregular intervals, bright, eye-dazzling star shells and floating parachute flares.

Only half as many marines walked out as had walked in thirteen days before. They had walked through the Belleau Woods and across the wheat fields into the chattering death of German machine guns. They had charged the machine gun nests that ringed all around them and silenced them. They had crouched in quickly dug, shallow, foxholes and withstood the pounding of precise German artillery barrages, and with bayonet and rifle, they had thrown back the confident German army and stopped their seemingly relentless march to Paris.

The marines had done themselves proudly, had on occasion fought with an elan that approached artistry. They had screamed their battle cries into the teeth of battle-hell; and the Germans had named them "devildogs" in their dispatches, and the world had called them "darlings" on the front pages of their newspapers.

The French government and its generals, who would never quite understand the marines—a corps of fighting men who would not admit to having the word "retreat" in their vocabulary—were reluctantly grateful to the marines for stopping the German advance in their homeland, and awarded the Croix de Guerre to the men of the 5th Marine Regiment.

"Your platoon had the most casualties," Captain Willis told Lieutenant Peter Morgan. "You've earned the right to lead the way out of here."

And Lieutenant Peter Morgan, with ears still ringing from a near artillery burst, with a bloody bandage inside the torn left shoulder of his shirt, led the way followed by his weary marines—nineteen of the original forty-two. Sergeant Barker, gunnery sergeant of Fox Company, walked beside him.

The column of men was silent except for an occasional exasperated curse as a man stumbled, in the dark, into the man in front of him, or stumbled on the uneven ground.

"We've got to figure some way we can see the man in front of us in the dark, Gunny," said Lieutenant Morgan. "Maybe a white patch or something on the back of each man's shirt."

"Might work," said the gunny. "I don't know why the brass insists on a night relief anyway. As soon as the Frenchies open up with their Chauchat machine guns, the Germans will know from the sound it's not our Hotchkiss guns, and they'll know they've got the French army in front of them, and not marines."

"What then?" asked the lieutenant.

"If you're asking me," said the sergeant, "the Germans will try a small probe, and them Frenchies will run. This is probably the same outfit that retreated down our right flank when we took that first German charge. You mark my words, Lieutenant. When we come back up on line, we'll have to take this line back. Them Frenchies is going to run."

The lieutenant glumly agreed. "You're probably right, Sergeant. I didn't like the look in their eyes. The young officer I turned over my section of the line to looked scared stiff. He couldn't have been more than eighteen years old—why do they commission them that young? Anyway, he was shocked as hell when I talked to him in French. I suppose he thought we were all barbarians."

They walked in silence for a time, the lieutenant peering ahead, trying to make out the way. "I'm glad you're up here with me, Gunny. Don't we follow this path till we come to the farm trail that joins the road to Chateau-Thierry?"

"Right, Lieutenant," said Sergeant Barker. "Don't worry. I know the way." Ahead of them the sky lit up, followed shortly by the rumble of heavy artillery as a battery of 155 mm. howitzers, perhaps a quarter mile away, sent a barrage of shells toward the German trenches.

A second barrage followed the first, the flash of fire from the cannon muzzles briefly lighting the faces of the men, and Peter smiled to think that he and his men were so conditioned to the sounds of survival that they would barely blink at these outgoing blasts fired practically in their faces, but let one solitary incoming shell whistle in the sky toward them, and they would "hit the deck"—in marine jargon—in that split second between the shell's sound and its actual explosion.

They turned on to the farm wagon trail and the walking was easier, but they still had a distance to go; and Lieutenant Morgan, as he so often did when his mind was fluctuating between facing a present reality and a yearning for an escape to a dreamy existence, thought of Lisbeth. Lisbeth of the golden hair, the blue, blue eyes, and the bright smile. Lisbeth of the slender arms, slim waist, and long legs. Lisbeth of the poetic mind, of the deep, challenging thoughts, of the perceptive insight. Lisbeth with nine freckles on her very pretty nose.

Peter dreamed of holding out his arms as Lisbeth ran toward him. He dreamed of holding her in his arms and lifting her off her feet and swinging her around. He dreamed of holding her hand and walking with her, both barefoot, on a soft, sand beach somewhere, feeling the warm sand between their toes, while waves lapped at the shore in a peaceful, quiet rhythm.

"I love you, Lisbeth," said Peter in his mind, then turned quickly to look at Sergeant Barker to see if perchance he had spoken those words aloud. Sergeant Barker walked steadily along beside him in that rhythmic walk that conserves energy—the walk of long distance walkers—the walk of marine infantrymen. If the lieutenant had spoken aloud, and if the sergeant had heard him, there was no acknowledgment.

The lieutenant looked back at the men following him. There was enough pale light in the east to be able to see the forms of the double column of men that followed him. They were tired, as he was tired, but their walk was not a head-down walk of defeat. They walked with weariness, but with resolve—with purpose. They had done their job. In thirteen days they had done what no army had been able to do, stop the Hun drive to Paris. Perhaps they had saved the world from a Prussian master race. If so, the cost may have been worthwhile. Though, thought the lieutenant, I'll never forget Charlie Ironshell.

Charlie Ironshell, full-blooded Sioux warrior from South Dakota. Sergeant Ironshell, 2nd Platoon Sergeant. In his heart the lieutenant knew that much of the courage that had carried him through this ordeal, he had drawn from the example of Sergeant Charlie Ironshell.

"Take off that fancy Sam Browne belt, Lieutenant," the sergeant had said. "The German snipers will spot you as an officer right off."

"I don't think I'm supposed to take it off," said the lieutenant.

"You can't always fight a war by the book," said the sergeant.

Together on that first day, they had led the platoon through the woods of Belleau. Together they had led them across the open wheat fields beyond the woods, machine gun bullets clipping the wheat stalks in front of them.

And then the entire company was stalled by a German machine gun nest on the 2nd Platoon's right flank.

"Pick a detail of men, and take those guns," came the message from Captain Willis.

"I'll go," said Sergeant Ironshell.

"We'll both go," said Lieutenant Morgan.

They took the seven men that were left from the 1st Squad, and the nine of them tried a flank assault under the cover of fire by the remainder of the platoon.

It was a series of short sprints across the open fields and diving for cover—for any sort of cover, a shallow depression in the ground, a rock, a shell hole, and, now and then, the bodies of fallen comrades.

The lieutenant had lost his helmet. Sweat streaked his face. The .45 pistol in his hand was hot to the touch. He was lying on his back in a shallow plow furrow, reloading the pistol, very aware of the bullets that snapped the air over him.

Sergeant Ironshell, on his stomach behind a small heap of rocks, his helmet aslant over one eye, grinned at him, white teeth gleaming in the dusky face. "Did you have this much fun playing football at VMI, Lieutenant?" he asked.

They were twenty yards from the machine guns—there were actually two guns spaced a few yards apart. It had cost two men to get this far. "We'll have to rush them from here," said the lieutenant, laying, for the moment, the heavy pistol flat on his chest.

"Great tactical thinking, Lieutenant," said the sergeant, with a sardonic grin.

"You take the gun over there on the left," said the lieutenant. "I'll take this one on the right." He found he was having trouble speaking. His breath came in short gasps. For a moment, he thought, we're not getting out of this alive. A brief panic seized him. Could he charge the machine guns when the time came? And here was this damn Indian pretending he was playing some sort of game. He opened his eyes to see the Indian smiling at him, no longer laughing, but still smiling—smiling in sympathy, in understanding, in comradeship.

"I'm with you, Lieutenant," said the sergeant.

"Where are Jones and Edson and the others? Will they follow us?" asked the lieutenant.

"Hell, yes," said the sergeant. "They're marines. Besides," he added, "as my ancestors would say, it is a good day to die."

"All right," said the lieutenant. "We'll throw the grenades, then it's over the top as soon as we hear them go off."

"Hey, give me them grenades," said the sergeant. "You may have played football, but I was the pitcher of the James Valley baseball team. I threw only strikes."

Peter Morgan watched as Charlie Ironshell took the grenades and stood up in a crouch. He watched him, as if in slow motion, he pulled the pin from the first grenade and threw it. He watched him pull the second grenade's pin and throw it before the first grenade exploded.

He watched Charlie Ironshell, Sioux warrior, sergeant of the marines, wave his rifle in a forward motion and call, looking back to the men, "Come on, you. You want to live forever?"

And they sprang to their feet and charged the guns—the guns that were firing, at point blank range, bullets at them—bullets that stitched across the charging men—bullets that cut down three men before they had taken a dozen steps—bullets that spun the lieutenant around, one of them slamming through his left shoulder, neatly puncturing the shoulder strap of his fancy Sam Browne belt—and bullets that cut down the sergeant as he leaped over the barrel of the gun on the left.

The lieutenant on his knees, was firing the .45, shot after shot, down into the machine gun emplacement. Were the Germans in there raising their arms in surrender, or in surprise? There was no time to ask questions. He pulled the trigger of the pistol till it would fire no more.

Silence.

A ringing in his ears. Sweat running into his eyes.

The lieutenant looked around. He saw two of his men still with their rifles at the ready, looking down into the gun pits. He saw the sergeant, his body draped across the barrel of the left machine gun. He looked down the sloping field and at the still forms of five men scattered along the way they had come.

And he felt a deep throbbing in his left shoulder, but reaching up his right hand, and finding the Colt .45 still in that hand, and having to holster it before he could reach again; and then thinking, I'm shot, but it doesn't hurt. It can't be too bad.

Lieutenant Peter Morgan, walking a dozen days later on the Chateau-Thierry road in the early dawn, put a hand to the pack strap on his left shoulder and tugged on it to ease the ache. "Damn," he said.

"You okay, Lieutenant?" asked Sergeant Barker.

"I'll make it," said the lieutenant.

"I saw the dispatch go in," said the sergeant. "They recommended you for the Silver Star."

"I don't know if I rate it," said the lieutenant. "If I do, then Ironshell should get the Congressional."

"Agreed," said Sergeant Barker, "but I have a feeling it wouldn't make a damn bit of difference to him. He counted coup before he died, and he died as a warrior wants to die."

They were on a level road now and had been walking for six hours. They were coming abreast an army unit that was lined up for morning chow in a field beside the road. The soldiers in the chow line stared at the marching men. Up and down the double column of marines walking down the road, there was a straightening of shoulders, heads held higher, a quickening of the pace till the formation was almost in step. They were marines coming back from battle, bloodied, yes, but not in spirit. They had met the enemy, and with courage had upheld the long, splendid tradition of the corps, and they were proud of it.

Esprit de corps—they all felt it, and Lieutenant Morgan looked over at Sergeant Barker. "Damn," he said, and smiled.

When the column had nearly passed by the soldiers in the chow line, one soldier called, "What outfit is that?"

A platoon sergeant at the tail end of the column answered, "What outfit is this? I'll tell you what outfit this is. It's the best goddamn fighting outfit in the world. This is the 5th Marines."

By midmorning they had reached their destination, a spacious hayfield, the grass trampled flat, but clean. The men spaced themselves out in long lines by squads, platoons, companies, battalions, and regiment, and stretched out on the comforting grass and slept. At noontime there would be hot food for them, and later there would be the long awaited mail call, but for now, they were content to sleep.

Behind them, scarcely a hundred yards away, three batteries of heavy artillery belched fire and thunder over their heads, but that did not disturb the sleep, and perhaps the dreams, of the tired men of the 5th Marine Regiment.

Peter Morgan, too, stretched out on the grass, a field pack under his head for a pillow, felt the warm sun on his face. Through half closed eyes he could see blue and yellow flowers at the edge of the field along the hedgerows. He believed he could smell the fragrance of the blossoms, and it smelled good. A meadow lark on some invisible perch along the hedgerow, burst into song in praise of the day. Peter shut his eyes and began to compose a letter in his mind to Lisbeth. "Dear Lisbeth," he began. "Today, by the sight and smell of flowers, and by the song of a bird, and by my memories of you, I am reminded of how much beauty there is in the world."

Book II

Central Tennessee
Fall 1861

The Lieutenant

Chapter 1
Central Tennessee 1861

Lieutenant Andrew Greyson, graduate of West Point, until recently a professor of literature at Albers College in Milford, Tennessee, was riding west to report for duty with the Confederate Army of Tennessee, commanded by General Braxton Bragg. Accompanied by another lieutenant, a sergeant and two enlisted privates, he had ridden hard for five days from Milford, making small camps at night to rest the horses. Food for themselves they had been able to get from helpful folks in villages along the way.

Andrew Greyson rode in thoughtful silence, though the other lieutenant would have talked incessantly if he had listened. Andrew most often rode ahead, a tallish six-foot man who held his head up and looked about himself alertly, wearing a gray coat with a gray cape in the cool mornings and evenings. He wore a gray felt hat with gold officers' braid around the crown; a long, slightly curved saber hung from his belt, though he often strapped that to his saddlebags. The tall, cavalry boots he wore and the gray coat and cape were new, items he had quickly gotten made to order when he knew he would be leaving soon for a long campaign.

As he rode the long hours, he pondered the situation he was in and what had brought him there. He knew he was not a staunch supporter of the secessionist movement, and as a matter of personal conscience he was opposed to any form of slavery. Yet he felt strongly about the goodness of life in the southern states and wished there were other ways to solve its problems than military conflict.

Of course, his years spent as a student at the United States Military Academy at West Point, New York, and the subsequent several years in military service, had made him something of an expert in military affairs; yet, he did not consider himself even mildly militant. Was there some boyish thrill of adventure that had sent him on this course?

Andrew considered another possibility as to why he had agreed to accept a commission in the Confederate Army. There was, of course, the unspoken expectation that anyone of his age—twenty-nine—would take part in this armed conflict. After all, their homeland was being invaded by a ruthless army. Andrew felt that single reason may have pushed him to the brink. But deep in his heart, he knew that there might be another significant cause for his action, and that was a lingering boredom in his marriage to Anne.

Anne Shipley, a well-to-do Methodist minister's daughter, intrigued Andrew during his senior year at West Point with her quiet, demure manner. Unfortunately, he had realized within months of their marriage, which occurred after his military service and his acceptance of the professorship at Albers College, that what he had seen as shyness was in reality a coldness and reservedness that baffled him. There had been no children in nearly five years of marriage.

When they had arrived at Albers College, Anne had quickly settled into a quiet, subdued life of social teas and church activities. That wasn't the way Andrew had seen their future life, and their companionship gradually became separate ways. Anne hadn't seemed at all upset by his announcement that he would be leaving for the army. There had been no emotional concerns, no teary farewells—just calm, cool acceptance. And on the final morning, Andrew had ridden off into the cool dawn, turning once to wave, then closed his mind to some of the past.

Chapter 2

Midmorning of the sixth day they arrived near Clearfield to find it nearly surrounded by Federal forces. Andrew had taken his big Navy Colt .44 out of his saddlebags and strapped it on his belt, and the others had nervously seen to their weapons. They cautiously, after asking what directions they could, picked their way through a swamp on the south side of the city. Even there they were nearly shot at by a Confederate outpost that mistook them for a Federal scouting party. Once in the city, they asked directions from the first military man they met, and since they were reporting to different units, Andrew Greyson rode on alone.

Andrew rode through almost the entire small city in his search for the 11th Volunteer Regiment, and it was apparent that a real clash between infantry troops had not yet happened. There were no barricades, no burnings. In fact, most of the city's residents were still in their homes going about their every day business. Washed clothes hung on clothes lines; people casually walked the streets, and in the small park beside the river that flowed through town, mothers were pushing baby carriages.

Most business establishments seemed to be open for business, and Andrew stopped at a small shop and bought a small piece of cheese and an apple to eat. Leaning against the hitching rail, he shared his apple with his horse as he watched freight wagons pulled by horses roll up the dusty main street. A few horsemen rode by, and, now and then, small groups of very orderly soldiers walked by.

But throughout the city, wherever open grounds were available—sometimes in spacious front yards of large homes, or in backyard orchards—they were covered by rows of white tents with soldiers beside them, or in formation in front of them.

Lieutenant Greyson stopped his horse near a group of four junior officers who were taking a morning break from the training of their men. In the background were several companies of troops, relaxed but staying in ranks. Andrew already knew where to locate his regiment, but was curious as to the military situation. He swung off his horse and approached the officers leading his horse. Greetings were friendly and respectful.

"I'm reporting to the 11th Regiment this morning," Andrew said. The men nodded.

"This is the 18th Regiment," said a boyish-looking lieutenant wearing a militia uniform.

"I'm just in from the eastern part of the state," Andrew said. "What is the situation here? It doesn't look like people are very concerned."

"Nope," drawled another lieutenant. "We all figure the Feds don't really want this place. There's nothing here for them 'cept maybe a couple warehouses of grain for their horses."

Andrew listened, accepted the offer of a cup of coffee. The young lieutenant called back to one of the large tents behind him. "Cookie," he called, "another cup of Java here."

"Yessir," from inside the tent, and presently a large, grubby man strolled out with a steaming black cup of heavenly smelling coffee. "Here you are, Lieutenant." He handed the tin cup to Andrew.

"Thank you," said Andrew. He sipped the hot coffee appreciatively. He shook his head. "This is the best I've had for quite a few days," he said.

"So what is the 11th like?" asked Andrew. "I don't know much about them. I know that the CO is Colonel Biddell."

"He's a charger," said the drawling lieutenant. "If we try to break out of here, he'll have his regiment lead the way. Actually," he went on, "we've got three regiments in here—almost a division; and we're supposed to be up at Fort Donelson up on the Cumberland River. That's where the big fight is shaping up. But we got delayed here, and first thing you know there's two divisions out there blocking our move."

"Your regiment is blocking the Feds from coming into the city," said another officer, older looking. "Since you're new, they'll probably put you in charge of a company that's likely to see first action."

"Everyone pretty much agrees that they don't want the city. But that can change," said the drawling lieutenant. "If Grant suddenly wants his two divisions to help at Fort Donelson, they could move in and try to take us out before they go."

"Let 'em come," said the young lieutenant. "We'll take care of them, is what we'll do."

"Thanks for the coffee and the information," said Andrew. "If that coffee is any indication, you have a good regiment." He waved as he turned his horse to go.

"Take care," from the young lieutenant.

"Remember, don't volunteer for any of Biddell's wild schemes," said the drawling lieutenant.

For the first time since he had made the decision to become part of this war, Andrew began to feel involved. The last days at the college, and at home with his wife, Anne; and even the ride west had seemed casual. Now as he saw the formations of soldiers, saw the regimental pennants flying from staffs, could almost feel the presence of an enemy force just over the near horizon, he felt he had become part of it all.

Muddy from slogging through the swamp, dirty and unshaven, but still riding his large, bay horse easily and carrying himself erect, Lieutenant Greyson reported to the commanding officer of the 11th Volunteer Regiment, Colonel Forrest Biddell. After asking numerous directions, he had located the colonel's command post situated on a large estate near the northeast edge of the city. A large, undamaged Southern plantation-style home dominated the grounds. The front lawn of the house was occupied by a four-gun battery of small, short range, twelve-pounder cannon. The two dozen, or so, artillery men lounging around their guns, did not bother to pay heed to a mere lieutenant. For colonels and generals, coming and going to the command post, they could come smartly to attention, but for a dusty, dirty lieutenant leading a horse that had obviously traveled hard, they merely looked.

"Bring in any mail, Lieutenant?" one indolent soldier called, and Andrew Greyson pointed to his horse's saddlebags. He did have, in fact, a large packet of letters, but they were all for the men in this army that were from the eastern Tennessee area around Milford.

When he had known where he would report to, he had put a notice at several public places in town offering to carry letters from the families to their men. Quite likely, every family that had a brother, son, husband, or father in the Army of Tennessee had sent a letter. It was not an opportunity to pass by as such chance couriers were almost the only way that letters were exchanged between the battlefields and home.

Chapter 3

Dismounting and leading his horse, Andrew quickly realized that the command post was not in the house, which the family still occupied, but in the spacious stables in the rear. He followed the worn pathway around the house, wrapped the reins of the bay horse around the hitching post, and tried to dust some of the travel dust from his clothes. He took special pains in wiping and polishing his boots; then slapping the dust from his hat, he headed for the open stable door.

The private beside the door saluted. "Good morning, Lieutenant," he said.

Andrew returned the salute, and realized that he had quickly again picked up the almost automatic salute that he had performed so often at the academy and in later service. He put his head through the door, knocked on the door trim and entered. "Lieutenant Greyson reporting, sir," he said.

The three men leaning over a plank table looked up. Another man, a captain, was seated at a small table to the side writing. He got up and came toward Andrew. "You're Lieutenant Greyson?" he asked.

"Yes, sir," replied Andrew.

The captain turned to the colonel, the shortest of the four men and said, "Sir, this is Lieutenant Greyson." He went back to his table and began leafing through some of the papers there.

Colonel Forrest Biddell, a short, wiry and energetic man, sat down in a chair behind the plank table. "Come in, Lieutenant," he said. "And stand at ease."

Andrew walked the few paces to the front of the table. He took off his hat and waited. All three men were eyeing him, but he kept his eyes on the colonel.

"West Point graduate?" asked the colonel.

"Yes, sir," replied Andrew. "Class of '54."

The colonel pulled a stubby pipe from a pocket and began filling it. He did this seemingly without taking his eyes off Andrew. He tamped the tobacco down with his thumb, and before he could look for a match, one of the majors held one for him. "And what have you done since '54?" asked the colonel, blue clouds of smoke in front of his face.

"I spent three years in Colonel Sheridan's battalion at Camp Buckner, sir," said Andrew. "Then I was separated from the army and have been a college professor since."

"Hmm," said the colonel, blowing more blue smoke. He looked over at the captain. "Adjutant," he said, "have we got anything on this man?"

"Yes, sir," said the captain, handing the colonel several sheets of paper. "We couldn't, of course, get any records from Washington or the Point, but I've gotten a few opinions from a few classmates that are here, and also, as it happens, from several of his instructors at West Point." The captain smiled and made a joke. "I sent a courier to get an opinion from Sheridan, but he wouldn't oblige us."

"Some day we may just run into him and then he will have to oblige us," said the colonel, scanning the papers that the captain had handed him.

"Hmm," said the colonel. "One of your instructors remembers you doing very well in small unit tactics."

"Ah, yes, sir," said Andrew. "I enjoyed that class. As a matter of fact, that is pretty much what I trained for when I was with Sheridan—small unit movements, advancing under cover of dark, tactics for fighting Indians—things like that." Andrew decided to try a little humor of his own. "I believe Sheridan would give me a good report, sir."

The colonel looked up and fixed Andrew with a steely eye. He did not smile, or frown. "Hmm," he said. "And what's this," he pointed at the papers. "A classmate of yours remembers some stunt you pulled off during some night maneuvers in a small unit tactics class. Tell me about that."

Andrew hesitated. He remembered exactly what the stunt was, and still enjoyed the memory of it; but he wasn't sure the colonel would approve. Might as well be forthright, he thought, and said, "Yes, sir. Well, sir, we were in some simulated battles in the hills just to the north of West Point, and I was appointed company commander by the instructor. He told me my mission was to take a rather steep hill just to our front—that I should get the company ready and to take it in the morning." Andrew paused. The colonel, the two majors, and the captain were looking intently at him.

Andrew continued. "Well, sir, the 'enemy' on the hill was made up of some of the cadre and some of the instructors, and I didn't think we had much of a chance using orthodox methods. And," Andrew said, "since the instructor had told me to attack in the morning, but not what time in the morning, I figured that meant any time after twelve o'clock."

By now Andrew could see keen interest in Colonel Biddell's eyes, so encouraged, he went on with his story. "Just after midnight we moved out—I guess there were about two hundred of us. I had them wrap pieces of blanket around their boots, and wrap rifles in cloth, and anything else that would make noise. I ordered no talking at all—just follow the man in front of you—don't lag. Well, sir, everybody got into the spirit of it, and we were lucky to have just a little moonlight. We circled three or four miles behind the hill and came up the back side. We got there about four in the morning, and I had everyone just sit down around the 'enemy' camp in a big circle—just sit and wait for them to wake up." Andrew smiled. He could still remember the satisfaction he had felt, the chagrined surprise of the instructors as they woke up, the complaints that he hadn't followed the rules.

The colonel was smiling now, and Andrew was somewhat relieved. The colonel was obviously amused and pleased about something. "I'd say that was neatly done, Lieutenant," he said, and looked at one of the majors. "What do you think, Major Stone?"

"Oh, yes, sir," said Major Stone.

The colonel stood up and reached a hand over the table to shake Andrew's hand. "This is Major Stone, my operations officer, and this is Major Hardesty, my intelligence officer—and this is Captain Sanders, my adjutant. Now Lieutenant Greyson, we may just have a special operation for you."

Colonel Biddell looked Andrew straight in the eye—though he did have to look up a little. And Andrew, though he had just met the colonel, felt a confidence in him. He returned the colonel's look and though he may have felt some hesitation in the prospect of danger, that was quickly brushed aside by the surge of elation that all adventurers must feel. "Yes, sir," said Andrew.

The colonel nodded. "All right. Come around the table here, and we'll fill you in on the situation on this map. Captain Sanders, have the private at the door bring us some coffee, if you will."

Andrew moved around the table and looked at the map. Maps were something he had always taken a special interest in, and he was good at reading them. The map before him was an enlarged sketch of the city of Clearfield and the area around it. Roads, hills, valleys, streams, wooded areas, farms, all showed clearly on the map. Andrew knew immediately what the situation depicted on the map was, but he followed carefully and nodded as Major Hardesty, the intelligence officer, briefed him, pointing out locations of Confederate units and the believed locations of Union forces.

At that point the colonel stopped them. "Now that you see the situation, Lieutenant," he said, "what stands out?"

Andrew studied the map carefully. He saw the river leading into the town; he saw the open farm lands and orchards that would aid an advancing army, but his eyes kept coming back to a small hill that, according to numbers on the map, rose about three hundred feet above the surrounding terrain. He put his finger on the hill on the map. "This," he said. "This hilltop controls the entry to the city. It overlooks the river; with a small cannon it could stop anything coming down it. And it also overlooks this main road and open fields leading into town."

As Andrew talked and as he noted the salient features of the map, he became more sure of his observations. Almost automatically he began to look for the ways and means of taking the hill. What roads were nearby? What ravines and valleys would provide concealment for an invading force? The enemy was certain to have units in the open fields, but here were some draws coming up from the river. Obviously you couldn't just walk up the front; they would be observed long before they were in effective rifle range.

Andrew looked up to see an amused look on the colonel's face. Sudden realization hit him. "Is that the special operation? Taking that hill?" The cups of coffee arrived, and though he sipped the hot coffee carefully out of the tin cup, his mind was already moving ahead, planning, considering possible routes, surmising what equipment would be needed.

Colonel Biddell and the two majors were filling Andrew in on the military situation around Clearfield, and he was slightly amused at how readily they spoke to him as an equal, asking for his opinions. "The situation here has been relatively static," Major Hardesty was saying. "The objective for our forces was to probe for a break out so we could join Bragg's army at Fort Donelson; and, incidentally, keep two Union divisions occupied so they won't join the assault on Fort Henry and Fort Donelson. We assume the enemy's objective was to keep us bottled up without invading the city and taking casualties they can't afford."

Major Hardesty was pointing to the points on the map as he talked. "However," he said, "we think their mood has changed in the last few days. We think they have gotten orders from Grant to do as much damage to our forces here as they can, and then get those two divisions up to Donelson." Hardesty pointed to a point up river from Clearfield. "We have a report that they are building some rafts here. They could transport supplies right to the edge of the city."

Major Stone pointed to the northeast edge of the city and to the orchards and farmlands adjacent. "They are shifting their regiments in this direction," he said. "This is their best invasion access into the city—happens to be right in front of our 11th Regiment."

"That is why this hill is more important than ever," Hardesty pointed again at the small hilltop that they had previously been talking about. "This hilltop, as we said before, could affect both the river and this clear area. We need control of that hill." He tapped his finger tip on the map for emphasis.

"What do we know about what is on this hill?" asked Andrew. He felt more and more committed.

"We don't think they have more than a hundred—a hundred fifty at most—men on that hill," said Major Hardesty. "That's a small area, not room for a lot of troops; and we don't think they have any thought that we would take, or even try to take, that hill. From their vantage, it doesn't seem so important. The hill overlooks the routes into the city, rather than the city itself."

Andrew sipped his coffee, cold by now, and saw Colonel Biddell looking at him, a shrewd look in his eyes. "Lieutenant," said the colonel, "if you don't volunteer for this operation, I'm going to order you to go, so you may as well be a hero and volunteer."

"Yes, sir," said Andrew.

"And how do you think you'll be under fire?" asked the colonel.

"I've never been under actual fire," said Andrew facing the colonel quietly, "but I have had responsibility under stress. I think I have the fear of a normal man, but I am confident that I can handle myself under fire. There's too much at stake in a mission such as this, to give way to personal concerns," he added.

"As for that," said the colonel, "very few of us in the army have been under fire. A few officers and NCO's are veterans of the Mexican War, but very few of those were in pitched battle. Yes, I think you are right. We all have to prove ourselves at the moment itself."

In his heart Andrew knew he was already committed to the operation, and he felt a thrill to the danger, to the adventure. What's more, he believed the mission was possible. He believed he could pull it off. The possibility of failure was no longer a factor in his mind.

"Now that you've volunteered," said the colonel, "we're going to give you command of F Company, 2nd Battalion." The colonel looked at his adjutant. "Write out the orders for that," he said. "Also pass the word for the entire regiment that any soldier who wants to get in on a special operation—a dangerous operation, you had perhaps better add—to report to regimental sergeant major. F Company is a good company," Colonel Biddell said to Andrew. "Their CO is laid up with some flu bug. The exec is a young lieutenant a few years younger than you. We'll beef up the size of the company with some of these volunteers—hopefully, some of the experienced veterans will step forward—by now they should all be bored silly with this stalemate we are in—and it should be a first rate company."

The colonel paused, and Andrew said, "Yes, sir." To tell the truth he was feeling a little light-headed. A little more than a week ago he was teaching literature to a classroom of college students—an occupation he thoroughly enjoyed—but just now he had no desire to be back there.

The colonel rapped the tobacco out of his pipe on the dirt floor and stepped on the ashes. He said, "We'll have the soldier outside the door take you to your company, but start working on a plan of operations for our hill. Major Stone will work with you on that, and he will coordinate with intelligence and supply. You'll have the final say on any volunteers that show up. If you think they won't fit in, send them back to their home unit."

The colonel looked at his intelligence officer. "How much time do you think we have before they move against us, Major? Four or five days?" The major nodded. "That's short, Lieutenant, but that's the way it is. Let's say, we have to move in four days."

"Yes, sir," said Andrew again, and started edging for the door when the colonel stopped him.

"Lieutenant Greyson," said the colonel. "I was sorry to hear about your father's death at Bull Run. He was an able officer and a gentleman. I served under him at Arlington quite a few years ago. That was after your mother had passed away, and you were off at prep school. My condolences, sir."

Andrew paused. The reminder of his father's recent death in the first battle of the war, and the obviously well meant sympathy of the colonel touched him. But before he could respond with a thank you, Colonel Biddell waved him on his way.

Chapter 4

Guided by the private soldier, Andrew found F Company encamped in a small hay field on the outer perimeter of the regiment. The company—some hundred and sixty men—was lined up for evening meal at the mess tent, mess kits in hand. They went in one door of the tent and came out the other end with a utensil filled with a steaming bean and pork stew.

As Andrew came up leading his bay horse, he was greeted by curious but respectful looks. He suspected that by now word had already reached the company that their new commanding officer was on the way. He never underestimated the speed and accuracy of military rumors.

A wide bear of a man, who walked with a slight limp, detached himself from the end of the line and came toward Lieutenant Greyson. He was older than most of the men there, and on his arms were the stripes of a first sergeant. Andrew perceived at once that chance had dealt him an ace. Two things about this man impressed Andrew. One was that this man, who could pull rank among enlisted men, was at the end of the chow line, making sure the men were fed before he ate. And second, the man was striding toward him with a purposeful, dignified walk, his eyes directly on the lieutenant. Here was a man, thought Andrew, who believes in his own worth, who could lead by example.

Andrew remembered a conversation he had had with his father, who, when knowing he would soon be in the Confederate Army, had ridden west to Andrew's college in Eastern Tennessee to pay a visit to his son. As they had discussed the prospects of the upcoming war, and the relative merits of the opposing armies, his father had said, "One area we aren't going to match the Union Army in is in the senior sergeants ranks. These Southern boys are going to be great soldiers, but we're going to have to promote sergeants out of the ranks, and most of them won't want it—it won't be healthy for one thing. Their pals in the ranks just aren't going to stand for being bossed by someone they think is no better than themselves. Southern life just doesn't have that brawling, city-bred Irishman or Cockney that will lead physically and mentally—and the North has them. They are tough men who don't have the education or the desire to be commissioned officers; they enjoy their beer and fights too much, but they know how to make men fight. And you know, Andrew, armies need officers and they need privates, but it's the sergeants that make it work."

The sergeant saluted as he came near. "I'm Sergeant O'Donal, sir," he said. "You'll be Lieutenant Greyson?"

"That's right, Sergeant," said Andrew returning the salute.

"I'll have one of the men take your horse," said the sergeant. "And if you've not eaten, the stew looks good."

"Let the men finish eating before you call one," said Andrew. "This gives me a good chance to look them over."

The men, with their full bowls of stew and a piece of bread, sat on the ground, or on crates, or leaned against the mess wagon in groups to eat their evening meal. From the looks he got, Andrew knew he was the topic of most of the discussion, and he wondered just what impression he was making. He consciously stood erect and looked back at the men, his eyes ranging from group to group. The men looked clean and capable. Spirits seemed reasonably high. Their uniforms, though not all standard issue, were in good shape.

"And where are the officers, Sergeant?" he asked.

"Well, sir, mostly they eat at the regimental officers' mess," said Sergeant O'Donal. "We have four lieutenants, besides yourself, sir. If you're wanting to see them this evening, we'll have to send a messenger over for them—though," he added, "the word of your arrival will probably be talked of there."

Andrew nodded. "The company looks in shape, Sergeant, and I assume much credit for that goes to you. I'm ready for some food now, and perhaps while we eat, I can meet some of the other NCO's."

At the early morning formation of the troops the next day, Lieutenant Andrew Greyson took the report from First Sergeant O'Donal. "All present or accounted for, sir," said the sergeant.

"Can you give me a breakdown of that, Sergeant?" said Andrew.

"Yes, sir," said the sergeant. "We have two men at regimental aid station, Privates Harrison and Nevers. One has a broken arm, sir, and the other was severely bitten by a swarm of bees yesterday." There was the slightest ripple of amusement in the ranks which the sergeant quickly quelled with one dark look. The sergeant looked back at Lieutenant Greyson. "Private Johnson is on liberty to visit a brother in the 18th Regiment, sir. He is due back at noon today."

"Thank you, Sergeant," said Andrew. "Have the men stand at ease. I have a few words for them."

"Yes, sir." The sergeant saluted, turned to face the troops and barked out the "at ease" order. The men relaxed, standing in place, a low murmur of voices and some shuffling sounds. But they kept their attention on Lieutenant Greyson, their new commanding officer. They knew, from experience, how important it was to get to know their commanding officer. He was the one man that largely determined what their daily lives would be like, how intense the training, how much leisure time they would have, how well they would be fed; and perhaps the most important of all, how expertly they would be used in battle. There was some middle ground, but commanding officers were either despised or revered.

Most soldiers liked to have a character for a commanding officer, someone flamboyant enough to ignore flying bullets, who defied death; or, on a less crucial note, flaunted regulations, particularly if it meant some benefit for the troops.

Loyalty is a two-way situation in the military, and Andrew knew this as he faced his men that morning. He had had experience with the military, of his own and of his father's, and he knew that to get extraordinary performance from these men, he had to provide extraordinary leadership. That meant facing the same hardships and dangers as they did, expecting the best from them and himself; and at the critical time in battle, show a fearlessness that would bring them back from giving in to their fears.

Lieutenant Greyson waited while Sergeant O'Donal saluted him, about-faced and quick-stepped to the end of the last rank of troops. Andrew waited another half-minute for emphasis, then spoke up so everyone could hear him. "Men of F Company," he said, "I am Lieutenant Greyson, your new commanding officer. In the brief time that I've observed you, I can see that you are a good outfit. For that I am glad because the first task I am going to ask of you will be an unusual and a difficult one. For now, I won't say more than that, except that each of you should make sure that all your equipment is in good repair; that your boots are in good shape, and that your rifles are clean and ready. Be ready to move out within a couple of days." Andrew looked over his company, and they, for their part, looked steadily at him. "Men, we have the opportunity to make a bold strike for our cause, and I know you will do yourselves proudly." He paused.

"Sergeant."

"Yes, sir." Sergeant O'Donal came forward.

"Dismiss the men for morning chow. But directly after the meal I want you to meet with me and the officers at the smokehouse. And, Sergeant, we need a trooper that is something of an artist—one who could copy a map well. Bring him to the meeting. Also, some of the men, or at least one, should be a local from right around this area. Bring him, or them, to the meeting also."

"Yes, sir," said the sergeant.

"Let's meet in, say, an hour." Andrew turned and went back to where his officers were grouped, four lieutenants who had awakened this morning to find the company under the command of a new officer. All the lieutenants looked a little sleepy, and Andrew thought that they probably didn't usually get up in time for morning formation.

Though not eager, the four men seemed respectful, and they stood straight and saluted as Andrew came up to them. "Good morning," said Andrew, returning the salute. The salute from the lieutenants, the same rank as Andrew, meant simply that they were acknowledging him as the commanding officer.

One of the lieutenants, the short, stocky one, stepped forward. "I'm Lieutenant Taylor," he said, "the executive officer." He introduced the other three officers as Andrew shook hands with them and looked each man over. Generally, Andrew was pleased with what he saw. Having come through the military academy and having observed numerous men of this rank and age, Andrew felt these were above average. Each of them carried himself well and looked him in the eyes.

Lieutenant Taylor, the executive officer, was a graduate of West Point and a native of Virginia. Two years junior to Andrew in rank, he did not seem to resent the fact that Andrew was stepping out of civilian life to take over a company that he might well command himself.

Lieutenant Schyler was a militia officer, very young. He was obviously trying to grow a mustache to perhaps add dignity to his position as an officer. For all his youth and eagerness, he did not seem to be too overwhelmed by Andrew and the other officers. Lieutenant Schyler was in charge of the 3rd platoon of the company.

Lieutenant Hadley was tall and the oldest of the officers there, several years older than Andrew. He, too, was a militia officer, having gotten his rank either through political appointment or by election by his troops before he left his hometown. He spoke softly, but confidently, and Andrew thought he could have been a school teacher or a lawyer before the war. He commanded the 2nd platoon of the company in which were a number of men from his hometown, all natives of Tennessee.

Lieutenant Meeks had the 1st platoon of the company under his command. He had been a student at Virginia Military Institute and had been immediately granted a lieutenant's commission when the war broke out, even though he was still a year from graduation. He looked serious and totally capable as a leader.

"Gentlemen, I'm happy to make your acquaintance," said Andrew. "I'm going to suggest that since we are all the same rank, we dispense with the usual military formalities. Let's call each other by our given names, unless, of course, we are in the presence of troops. Now I trust my stepping in to take command here doesn't distress any of you too much. I think I can assure you that, though I am just now out of civilian life, I have served under Lee at the military academy and under Sheridan in the field.

"Our company has been selected for a special operation that I'm sure will appeal to all of you once it is explained to you. Meet in an hour at my quarters, the smokehouse, but for mow, let's get some coffee and whatever else the cooks have for us."

Chapter 5

The company's encampment was on some rolling pastureland that was next to the main yard of the estate they were on. Spread out on the grass of the pasture in neat, straight rows, were the fifty-some, white tents of the company. The number of men to each tent depended on the rank of the occupants. Five or six privates shared one tent, four corporals shared a tent; but at the sergeant rank, only two or three shared a tent. On the near side of the ranks of tents were two larger, white tents, the cook tent and a supply tent. On this cool morning, smoke issued from the smoke stack that came out of the cook tent, and steam came off the tubs of hot water where the men would rinse their mess kits.

Cooks have always held a special status in the military; they are pretty well left alone as long as they get the job done, and though they grumble about getting up early and cleaning up the equipment, most of them develop a great pride in their ability to provide tasty food for their units. Of a particular challenge to good cooks was to provide something hot to drink when either the weather or battle conditions were most adverse.

The cook sergeant of F Company was quite typical of all army cooks. A large man with tattoos decorating both bare arms, he had a loud voice that got immediate obedience from his four cook's helpers and that intoned a scathing remark to any enlisted man that dared criticize the food he was being served. If an officer looked askance at, perhaps, a large kettle of stew, Sergeant Grant would pick up a large kitchen utensil, a long-handled stirring spoon, and standing belligerently by his steaming kettle he would say, "Yes, sir, Lieutenant, sir, what did you think was wrong with the stew, sir?"

Company officers quickly learned the value of a good cook and the positive effect on the morale of the troops, and would give the cook free rein in his own domain, the cook tent. On the other hand, they dared not boast too loudly to other regimental officers about the culinary talents of their cook, or they would soon lose him to the higher-ranking officers of regimental headquarters.

In the case of Sergeant Grant, newcomers to his kitchen were often shocked by the contrast between his good food and the vulgar language with which he described it, or, for that matter, all his verbal communications. As the men passed through his tent getting their rations of hot food, the sergeant would stand behind his steaming kettles and offer personal remarks to various individuals. Newly arrived privates dared hardly look at him. "Smile when you eat that food, Private," he would snarl, and they would smile, believing that Sergeant Grant's authority was at least as great as the commanding officer's.

"Grant?" someone would ask him. "Are you related to…?"

"Yeah, you heard of another Grant?" the sergeant would glower. "I never heard of him."

Lieutenant Greyson sat on a plank and sawhorse table finishing breakfast with some strong coffee. When Sergeant Grant came out of the cook tent and stood nearby, Andrew thought some compliments were in order. "Good coffee, Sergeant," Andrew said, raising his tin cup.

The sergeant grudgingly accepted the praise, then said, "You know, sir, we don't get as much coffee as we could use. I have to add stuff to it, like roasted acorns and roasted grains—grind them up to make the coffee go farther."

"Well, in that case," said Andrew, "it's excellent coffee."

Sergeant Grant finally smiled.

Chapter 6

Andrew finished his coffee and walked up the slope to the smokehouse. Several small buildings were within the perimeter of F Company's assigned area. The company officers had taken over a tool shed with a wooden floor for their quarters, and Andrew had moved into the quarters of the previous company commander, a sturdily built smokehouse.

This small building, perhaps twelve by twelve, had not been used for some time, but it still smelled pleasantly of smoke and spices. The small building had two levels, the lower of which was built of large field stones and was sunk halfway into the ground. A small, three-step ladder led down, and Andrew had his sleeping cot there. The upper level had a three-step ladder going up to it, had a plank floor, and, since it had much more light than the lower level, this is where Andrew planned to carry out his administrative duties for F Company. He had a table made of boards where he could write, and a canvas chair to sit on. His equipment, saddle for his horse, saddlebags, canteens, canvas pack, saber, revolver and belt; these all hung on the walls behind the table. It was a good place to live and work, and Andrew was pleased with it.

As Andrew arrived at the smokehouse and opened the narrow door, he could see the officers approaching from their quarters; and down toward the camp, he could see Sergeant O'Donal coming toward him with three privates following him.

The sergeant arrived and indicated one of the men. "This is Private Calloway, sir. Says he can draw all right."

Calloway was a slightly built young man. He stepped forward. "Yes, sir," he said. "I was studying to be an architect at the state college when the war started. I've had some drafting classes."

"I think you're the man for the job I have in mind," said Andrew. "Wait down by the cook tent, and we'll be heading to regiment soon."

"Yes, sir." Private Calloway set off briskly.

"And these two," O'Donal swept a hand to the remaining two men, "are local boys, farm boys from around here. I had to borrow this one, Private Hatfield, from B Company. Apparently these two grew up with each other and have been in some scrapes together before they got patriotic and joined the army." The two boys—they seemed too young to be called men—stood together, grinning. Both had dark eyes and black hair. Even at attention, they had the slouching ease of a wild animal. The sergeant went on. "Private Clarkson, here, got transferred to this company because the two of them was raising so much dickens together. 'Course they never got caught, but everybody knew who was doin' it. Sergeant Stanfield, the first sergeant in B Company, said he couldn't stand them anymore, so I took one as a favor." Sergeant O'Donal shook his head. "Now it looks like I got both of 'em." The two boys smiled broadly.

"Now get them silly grins off your faces," said Sergeant O'Donal, "and listen to the lieutenant."

"Yes, suh," said the two in unison, and the smiles left their lips, but remained in their eyes.

"And they claim they aren't related." Sergeant O'Donal spread his hands out, palms up, to show that he believed this to be another of their pranks. But there was no doubt, from the way he was presenting the situation, that despite their reputations, he liked the two men.

Andrew eyed the two soldiers for a moment, and they looked back at him, looking a little more serious than before, but not much. "Do you know this country around here, especially north of town?" asked Andrew, waving an arm to the north.

The two looked at each other, merriment in their eyes. "Yes, we knows it," replied Private Hatfield.

"I's bawn on the river up tha'," said Clarkson.

"Would you know your way in the dark?" asked Andrew.

"I knows it best in the da'k. Then no one kin see ya'," said Hatfield.

"It has probably changed some with the Union Army in there," said Andrew.

"Not much, it hain't," countered Clarkson. He confronted Lieutenant Greyson's questioning look. "I been back, suh. I been back to see if my mam is okay." He smiled gleefully. "They han't even found our cabin yit."

Andrew chose to ignore this statement that obviously disclosed a serious breach of military duty, but Sergeant O'Donal thought things had gone a little too far. "Stand at attention when you talk to the lieutenant, Clarkson. You too, Hatfield, and say sir when you answer him."

"Yes, suh," said the two, standing in as much attention as their supple bodies seemed to be able to. Andrew was reminded of some swamp animals he had encountered, a mink perhaps, or an otter. Their black eyes looked at him, black hair hanging over eyes. Both boys, he perceived, were too young to shave. He had, at first, considered taking only one guide, but these two seemed to work as a team, fishing and hunting as they must have done in the hilly country up river.

He decided one more question was in order. "Do you know the hilltop about a mile up river?" he asked. "The tallest one with the steep ridge running down to the river?"

"Yes, suh," said Hatfield. "That's Old Man Scroggins' hill. He had a still on tha' till that army come. He's way back in the hills now."

Andrew turned to Sergeant O'Donal. "Keep these men off duty for the morning, Sergeant. Make sure they have good walking boots. Be ready to move out shortly after the noon meal." He looked at Hatfield and Clarkson. "You won't be taking your rifles, but you might want to make sure the rest of your gear is in shape. I'll see you later."

Both men touched their foreheads with their right hands in a motion that could loosely be described as a salute. Andrew returned the salute, though he was surprised they had remembered to salute. The two young soldiers left talking excitedly together, obviously believing they would be going on some sort of lark.

"They may be young, but I think they are good at what they do," said Sergeant O'Donal. "You'll have to keep an eye on them."

"That's so," agreed Andrew. "But you can help me keep an eye on them. You'll be going with us."

The four company lieutenants had been waiting at the smokehouse door, pretending not to listen to Lieutenant Greyson's questioning of the two privates. But they had heard enough to start drawing conclusions, so when Andrew turned toward them, they looked at him eagerly.

"You're probably right in what you are thinking," said Andrew. "Colonel Biddell fears the Union Army is getting ready to move on Clearfield, and he wants control of the hilltop north of here on the river. F Company has the job of taking it."

"Wow!" said Lieutenant Meeks.

Andrew went on to explain his plans. "Sergeant O'Donal and I and two scouts are going in there this afternoon and coming out tonight. The idea is to plan some sort of route in, and come out after dark so we'll have an idea of how it looks at night. Your jobs back here are to get the company ready to go. You've got until tomorrow night." He explained what he wanted. Every man with fifty rounds of ammunition and two canteens of water. "We could be cut off up there for a few days," he said. "Check the foot gear of every soldier," he emphasized. "They have got to be able to walk without lagging."

Then he went into more particular and unique details. He wanted a white cloth about six inches square sewn on the back of every soldier's jacket. "So they can see the man ahead of them in the dark." He wanted each man to have two sections of blanket about three feet square with cords to tie them around his feet. "We won't tie them on till we get close," he said, "but that could make the difference in surprising them. And that element of surprise is going to be important." He wanted each man to check his personal equipment and pack to be sure nothing clicked or rattled as he walked.

Andrew turned to his executive officer, Lieutenant Taylor. "You can draw all the extra materials at regimental supply. Colonel Biddell will authorize it." He smiled. "If you draw better blankets than what the men have, might as well keep those and cut up their old ones.

"Any questions?" Andrew asked and waited. He looked at the officers and at Sergeant O'Donal. He saw interest and eagerness. No one seemed to be holding back, for which he was glad. He felt it very important that his officers express optimism and confidence to the men.

"Are we taking any horses?" asked Lieutenant Hadley, the second platoon leader.

"At this time, I don't think so," said Andrew. "After I've scouted out the route, I may change that. I've been trying to think of a way for Sergeant Grant to get a few days' supply of food in with us, and some pack horses would do it; but I'll wait and see what the terrain looks like."

Around them the company was stirring with activity. Down the slope the soldiers were in and around their tents taking care of personal business, straightening out their bed rolls, brushing their clothes, cleaning rifles. In a half hour they would be in formation again and be assigned their day's duties. They would be pleased to learn that today it would not be the usual marching drills or clean up details. Their commanding officer had other plans for them.

Lieutenant Greyson turned back to his officers. "What you have to get done today," he said, "is get the white patches sewed on and the blanket pads for their boots worked out. They'll have to practice to see what works best. Then this evening, just after dark, I want the entire company out for a dress rehearsal. The sergeant and I won't be back yet, so it will be up to you." The officers nodded.

"Take them out for a hike carrying the equipment they actually will carry later; work out any kinks. Go long enough so they'll have a good idea of what it will be like. Practice trying on the boot pads in the dark. And above all, enforce a no-talking discipline. They have got to realize how important that is. Distribute your sergeants and corporals through the ranks so they can keep them under control, and threaten them with three days sentry duty if they make any noise."

Andrew looked directly at his officers. Look them right in the eye, he thought. Get a commitment from each of them. That's the only way we can make this work. And they did return his steady gaze: Lieutenant Taylor, Lieutenant Hadley, Lieutenant Meeks, and Lieutenant Schyler; and, of course, Sergeant O'Donal.

Watching the scene around him, looking at these men whose lives were now inextricably woven into his, knowing that this afternoon and tonight he would be in enemy-held territory with a wily, old sergeant and two, semi-outlaw, young men; feeling all this, Andrew felt a thrill pass through him. He grinned, suddenly at the men around him, a gleam in his eyes. "I don't know about you," he said to them, "but this is a real challenge, and I'm looking forward to it. I know there's danger involved, but it is also a chance to pull off an unusual feat, and I don't mind telling you that I'm going to be glad to be able to say that I was part of it. You don't get many chances like this in a lifetime."

"You can count on me," said Lieutenant Hadley.

"Me, too," from Lieutenant Taylor.

"This is what I came in the army for," said Lieutenant Meeks.

"I'm with you," said Lieutenant Schyler.

"How about you, Sergeant?" asked Andrew.

"Sir, I wouldn't miss it," said Sergeant O'Donal.

Chapter 7

By midmorning, Andrew and Sergeant O'Donal, with Private Calloway in tow, were headed for 11th Regimental headquarters. At first he had intended to bring his two young scouts also, but decided against doing so because he wasn't sure what impression they would make on the colonel and his staff. Andrew couldn't quite see the rather dignified officers and the two backwoods boys around the same table and map conversing together. Besides, he had an impression that whatever maps the boys were familiar with were in their heads.

As they walked by the battery of cannon in the front yard of the mansion, Andrew stopped, a thoughtful look in his eyes. "Have you ever worked with artillery, Sergeant?" he asked. "How mobile do you suppose those cannon are?"

Sergeant O'Donal looked at the cannon, and he looked at Lieutenant Greyson. "I know what you are thinking," he said. "Let's find out."

They walked across the grass to where a sergeant was watching two privates polishing the black tube of a twelve-pounder cannon. The sergeant, a red scarf around his neck, greeted them cheerfully. "Morning, Lieutenant. Morning, O'Donal. I see you are interested in my pretty guns."

"The lieutenant and I were wondering," said Sergeant O'Donal, "how heavy are these cannon? Can those guns be separated from the carriage and packed on horseback, for instance?"

"Could they be fired from some sort of smaller frame, like ships' cannon are fired?" asked Lieutenant Greyson.

The sergeant turned and thoughtfully considered his prize guns. "These tubes without the carriage wheels weigh 212 pounds. The range of these babies is 860 yards. These guns are supposed to be mobile; that's why they're called mountain guns. I've never fired them off of their regular mounts, but I guess it's possible," he said. "In order to fire these guns with any accuracy, you have to support the tubes in three places, sort of like a tripod. You support them on each side of their pivot shafts, and in the back you support them at whatever elevation you want to fire them."

The sergeant walked over and patted one of the gleaming guns. "Yes, sir, I think it could be done. It wouldn't be real precise, but they could be fired from some sort of ground mount."

Andrew and Sergeant O'Donal grinned at each other. "It's just a thought," said Andrew. "At this point it's just hypothetical."

"If you've got some sort of action planned," said the sergeant, "let me in on it. I'm bored stiff keeping these guns looking pretty on this damn lawn in front of this house. Haven't fired a shot in over four months. It's no way to fight a war. The name is Sergeant Holbrook, sir. They call me Brookie."

Andrew was intrigued. The possibility of having some artillery support for this maneuver made it seem more likely to succeed, not in the assault, but in defense of the hilltop after it was taken. "You believe, then, Sergeant, that a gun like this could be carried on the back of a horse or a mule?"

"Yes, sir," said Sergeant Holbrook. "We would need pack saddles. They've got those at regimental supply. This gun is not that heavy. Hell, sir, I'd carry it myself if it gave me a chance to get out of here."

Andrew nodded, the possibilities seeming better all the time. He said, "I appreciate your offer, Sergeant. Could you, in any spare time today, do a little rough planning on just what sort of portable carriage would be needed to support this gun while it is fired? Make some drawings with measurements. If this becomes a reality, we'll have to move fast, and I'll go through channels to get you into the operation. But for now, it's strictly unofficial."

"Yes, sir," said the sergeant. "Yes, sir. The name is Holbrook, sir. Sergeant Holbrook, A Battery, Mountain Artillery Group, attached to the 11th Regiment, sir."

"Right, Sergeant," said Andrew as he and O'Donal turned to go on toward the stables, the command post of the 11th Regiment.

"It might work," said Sergeant O'Donal.

"It would be a real asset once we got it up on the hill, to hold off a large assault."

At the command post they found Major Hardesty, and Andrew quickly briefed him in on the scouting patrol that he was planning for later in the day and into the night. They were looking at the large map as they spoke. "I don't want to walk right through the middle of them," Andrew said. "I'm planning to swing east, perhaps on this trail, here," he traced the trail with his finger, "and come in from the back side of the hill. I've got two local boys who know this country well. They should be a big help."

The major nodded, looking at the map. "All right," he said. "That seems a good plan. Fill us in on what you find out when you get back. I'll let the colonel know what's going on. I have to add that we are getting anxious about time. They've been shifting troops toward the east over here, and bringing them in closer. They could move any day."

"If things go according to plan," said Andrew, "I'll be back tomorrow morning from scouting out a route, and we'll finish getting the company ready and move out the night after next, two days from now. I think that is the earliest we could get everything ready."

The major nodded. "All right. Now if you need any materials, any supplies, any special equipment, let me know and I'll authorize you to draw them at regimental supply."

"Yes, sir," said Andrew. "I'm sure there will be some special requests. I sent some of my company officers over there this morning to get some white cloth and some extra blankets. And I need a copy of the north half of this map. I brought along a draftsman to copy it for me, if you will allow it, and we were hoping to get some suitable paper and pen from you to do so."

"No problem," said Major Hardesty. "Send him in."

Private Calloway came in a bit timidly, but when he saw what was to be done, he leaned his rifle against the table and began to draw and trace the map. "I can do this, sir," he said.

"We need only this top half of the map, and only on this side of the river." Andrew traced with his hand the perimeters of the map he needed. He noted that once Calloway set the pen to paper, he was confident and sure in what he was doing.

"When you're finished with the map, Calloway, make sure the first sergeant gets it."

The private, intent on his work, barely glanced up. "Yes, sir," and he continued his careful drawing.

"Sir," said Andrew, addressing Major Hardesty, "I'll report to you tomorrow. Good day, sir." Lieutenant Greyson and Sergeant O'Donal headed back for F Company.

Chapter 8

Late in the afternoon the scouting party was on its way. They passed through their own units, pausing at the last outpost to warn them that they would be returning in the darkness of early morning, and headed east in a long sweep that Andrew hoped would be outside the lines and camps of most of the Union Army. The two privates, Hatfield and Clarkson, led the way, perhaps fifty yards ahead of the lieutenant and the sergeant. Hatfield and Clarkson still thought it a lark, though they didn't understand why they had to take such an indirect route to get to where they were going. They felt they could easily pass through the entire Union Army undetected by following ravines and deeper woods. Andrew explained the need for a route over which they could bring an entire company of men in the dark; and the two boys, conferring together, had set off, Andrew carefully marking on his map the trails and crossings he believed they were traveling on.

The only firearm in the group was carried by Andrew; his big Navy Colt .44 caliber revolver was in a holster on his belt. Andrew had insisted that rifles be left behind since the last thing in the world they wanted was to alert the enemy by gunshots in any way. The two hill boys seemed to understand, but with quick smiles, white teeth flashing, they quietly strapped what appeared to be razor-sharp Bowie knives to their belts. The sergeant had also produced a similar knife from his kit and belted it; and Andrew had taken a few minutes to sharpen a favorite clasp knife that he carried in his pocket.

They wore their uniforms, blue mostly, but in many places dirty enough so that the color hardly showed. Andrew's uniform was the cleanest, and he thought it might be a good idea to deliberately rub dirt on it. No one wore a heavy coat. They had ten or so miles to cover, and, though the season was cool, the activity would keep them warm. Andrew and the sergeant wore visored forage caps, but each of the scouts had a handkerchief tied, headband fashion, around his head. Andrew thought they might pass for desperados or buccaneers, but only if one did not notice the laughter in their eyes and the smiles on their faces.

As they entered the woods, Andrew noted a change in the attitudes of the two boys. They slouched, almost glided, along, their eyes alert, looking ahead and to the sides, communicating with each other with a look, a set of the head, or hand gestures. Andrew could see that they were in their natural element.

Andrew could sense his own body becoming more alive, eyes and ears more sensitive. He became aware of where he was placing his feet, whether they would snap a twig or leave a track in the sand or soft earth. He was aware of Sergeant O'Donal behind him, moving smoothly along despite his slight limp.

They were following a grassy wagon trail that twisted and twined as it followed the very hilly terrain. It would follow a small valley, then go around the end of a ridge into another valley. Most of the time they were surrounded by trees, but on occasion the trail climbed up the nose of a ridge and then for several hundred yards they would follow the very rocky ridge line until it again dropped into a valley.

On one of the higher ridges, Andrew stopped and scanned the countryside below with his field glasses. Off to the northwest he could see the hilltop that was their objective. He could see the seam that the river made in the hills though he could see no water. In one meadow he could see white tents, but most of the Union forces, he realized, were hidden in the trees. However, telltale smoke trails rose from here and there among the trees that would indicate the location of company kitchens such as their own. Andrew trained his glasses at length on the hilltop, since that was the bit of terrain most interesting to him, but it was too far off to see any movements there.

Gradually, the direction they were going became northeast and then north. When the wagon trail they had been following veered east, the two scouts stopped and conferred with each other briefly. Even at the distance Andrew was from them, perhaps thirty yards, he could tell that their conversation was carried on mainly by hand gestures. He wondered briefly what trade these boys had grown up into. Was it something illegal? Very likely. Moonshine whisky running? Trapping or hunting out of season or on posted lands? Robbery? Whatever it was, they had learned well the lessons of survival in their own element.

The lieutenant and the sergeant had stopped in place when the scouts stopped. Now Clarkson pointed into the forest, and Hatfield motioned them forward. They were quickly swallowed into the tree, and as the lieutenant's eyes became accustomed to the deeper shadows of the trees, he saw that the scouts had waited for them and were now moving only ten or so yards ahead of the sergeant and himself. They seemed to be following a vague trail, perhaps a deer path, that to Andrew seemed almost nonexistent, but that seemed unhesitatingly clear to the scouts ahead. Andrew, following, kept an eye on his scouts, but found also that he was watching the shadows ahead, a darker clump of trees, the next dip and turn in the trail. But it seemed to Andrew that it was his ears that had become acutely sensitive. He found he was listening for sounds beyond the woods' noise, the trees whispering, small birds calling. It seemed he was listening for silences as well as sounds—silences that would be foreign to the woods, that were out of place. He could almost feel his ears flexing, about the front, the sides, and even the back. He had seen deer use their ears in such manner, swiveling them in all directions, and he almost put his hand up to see if his ears had grown larger.

Their direction of travel was still north, and Andrew had been carefully marking his map. At first, whenever he had stopped to look at his map or compass, he had signaled ahead for his scouts to stop also, but he soon noticed that they were so aware of his presence behind them that they stopped almost at the same time he did. It pleased Andrew immensely that he had lucked out with such apparently efficient guides.

On the map Andrew could see that they had been following the higher ridges that roughly paralleled the river, but at a distance of more than a mile. Occasional ravines dropped off to the west that drained toward the river. Andrew was trying to keep a perspective on where they were in relation to the hilltop when the scouts ahead, with a wave of a hand, turned sharply off the trail to the left. They were at the head of a deep hollow, and there in the blue distance was their hilltop.

Andrew stopped and signaled ahead for the scouts to return. They pulled off the trail behind a screening thicket of laurel brush. There they sat on the ground, resting, and looked at each other in conspiratorial silence. They were obviously pleased with their progress so far.

"We've come almost four miles," said Andrew in a low voice. "From here on, as soon as we get to the bottom of this hollow, we have to expect to be in very close to the enemy." He turned to Hatfield and Clarkson. "I'd like to stay away from any main trails or roads along which they would likely have their camps." Hatfield and Clarkson looked at each other and smiled. No problem, they seemed to say.

"We cin do that," said Hatfield, "but we cross one good wagon trail, maybe one more good trail." He looked to Clarkson, who nodded agreement.

"All right," said Andrew. "Let's be careful when we get close to them. And we should go slow from here on, a little closer together. I want to get to the bottom of the hilltop, where I can judge some sort of approach up to the top. But the main idea is, don't get seen, even if we have to crawl the last half mile."

Everyone nodded, and Andrew, looking at the sergeant and the two privates and down the valley they were going to cross, felt his pulse quicken. They would be in the midst of the enemy shortly, depending on their own wit and stealth for success of their mission; and possibly, for their lives. The most dangerous game, thought Andrew, man against man.

Chapter 9

They lay back and rested. They had traveled for more than two hours at a steady pace. They drank water from canteens and stashed them under brush and leaves to be picked up on their way back. They had two hours until dusk, and by that time they hoped to be at the foot of the hilltop.

"If you run into some soldiers and can't avoid them," said Andrew to Hatfield and Clarkson, "make some conversation. Ask them what outfit they are from. Tell them you are from the 1st Kentucky Regiment, or whichever one they are not. There are a few boys in those regiments that talk just about the same as you do. Tell them you got to wandering around and got lost, and now you're in a sweat to get back to your regiment."

Andrew paused. The prospect of getting caught by the enemy had not dampened the spirit of Hatfield or Clarkson. Perhaps, thought Andrew, they considered such a happening as not even remotely possible. A person had to admire such irrepressible good humor. As for himself, Andrew realized, with his smart uniform, there was no possibility of faking his identity.

"If you get caught and they take you to some officers for questioning," said Andrew, "tell them basically the truth. I don't want you getting shot as a spy. Tell them you sneaked off from your regiment to come back to visit your mother. That, as I understand, could easily be the truth."

Clarkson smiled broadly; Hatfield did the same. "Well, suh, we could stop in and see her," said Clarkson. "She's just one holler over."

"Some other time, perhaps," said Andrew. The two boys smiled delightedly as if this was a promise of something they could do together in the near future.

The trail, when they again started on their way, was exceedingly steep, and as Andrew followed his two guides, he considered whether horses could come down it without making considerable noise. They seemed to be plunging directly to the bottom of the valley with no switchbacks. Logically, Andrew knew, it was easier going downhill than climbing uphill, but he realized, as at each step his foot pushed forward in his boot, and as his bent leg had to absorb the shock of his weight on each step, that there wasn't that much difference.

Presently, Andrew became aware of the sound of trickling water; and by the time their trail reached near the floor of the valley, the running water, having been joined by other rivulets, was a real stream. The sound of the water cut off somewhat their ability to hear sounds, but it also masked their own traveling sounds. Andrew thought that perhaps, in that respect, the traveler had the advantage. He wondered if his scouts had chosen this path for that reason.

They followed a path along the north side of the stream for a time and then crossed the stream, almost keeping their boots dry by stepping from rock to rock, and followed a path on the other side.

Abruptly, the forward scouts left the stream side and, by hand gestures, indicated that they were skirting around an encampment. Almost at the same time, Andrew smelled smoke and food cooking and the general unsavory smell of wet wool, moldy blankets, and unwashed humans. He turned around and exchanged looks with the sergeant, who nodded and wrinkled his nose. He turned back to the scouts and imitated their style of moving only in the shadows, never crossing an opening.

He was worried about how he was going to be able to get his company past here without alerting sentries. All the time he was listening, watching. He caught a glimpse of some tents through an opening in the trees, and then the answer came to him. He would take his company right through the middle of the camp as if they belonged there. Any challenges by sentries would be explained in hushed whispers about some secret night maneuvers. The soldiers asleep in their tents, secure in knowing they were well behind the front most units, would not rouse easily from their sleep.

Presently they were on the stream-side path again and getting quite close to the hilltop. The two scouts were stopped in some brush that screened them from an opening ahead, and Andrew, checking his map, saw that they were on the edge of a major wagon road, a rutted trail that crossed the stream with a shallow ford. The scouts signaled that they would check out the vicinity, and each went in opposite directions along the edge of the road. Andrew and the sergeant settled into a clump of bushes to wait, sitting back to back. The rest felt good to tired muscles.

As they waited, Andrew studied the map. The stream, whose water they could hear, flowed on below the north side of the hilltop with its banks becoming steeper, and it flowed into the river at the foot of the hilltop. The road that crossed the stream here went on to the south toward Clearfield. Andrew reasoned that there must be Union forces camped in both directions along it, and he became anxious for the scouts to return. He nudged the sergeant and, turning quietly around, showed him where they were on the map and the layout of the land.

The sergeant nodded, and at that moment they both heard voices. Peering through the bushes, both of them now lying on the ground, they saw a scraggly column of troops come up the road from the south. There were perhaps twenty men, and they carried shovels instead of rifles over their shoulders. A late working party, reasoned Andrew, coming back from repairing some section of the road, or from digging some sort of fortifications facing Clearfield.

The men with the shovels were sweaty and tired, and they straggled into the stream, held their canteens down in the water to refill them, and splashed and rubbed their faces with the water.

Andrew and the sergeant lay quietly in the brush. The fact that none of the troops carried rifles told him how secure these military units felt from any sort of Confederate advance. The foray of F Company to capture the hilltop two nights from now stood a good chance of being a total surprise.

Presently a corporal, himself also in the water, said something. Andrew clearly heard him say, "Let's go, men. They won't keep supper forever." With a few grumbling remarks, the men came out of the water, their boots and the bottoms of their trousers soaked, and they headed north along the road.

"Let's keep our men out of the water," whispered Andrew to the sergeant. "Keep their feet and boots dry. Better walking, and they may have to live with those boots on for several days." The sergeant nodded agreement. Andrew was about to say more when they heard hoof beats on the road, and as they watched intently, two horsemen, a full colonel and a captain, came by riding at a cantor. They were followed at a short distance by two privates, also on horseback, rifles carried across their backs with slings.

When the horsemen were by, Andrew murmured to Sergeant O'Donal, "A colonel—that means there is at least a regiment nearby." He thoughtfully added, "There's no sentry at this crossing now, but I think we better assume they may have one here after dark, or possibly a walking sentry that walks up and down this road. We don't want to be detected at this point, if possible. Another half hour toward the hilltop and we could just charge ahead and count on the confusion to help us. But I think once we have the company over this road, our next obstacle will be the actual sentries from the hilltop itself, and by then we will have the momentum. We won't be stopped."

Chapter 10

Evening was coming on. The shadows were getting longer. A coolness was settling over the valley. A slight mist from the stream settled on the grass and bushes. There was no more traffic on the road.

Suddenly Andrew became aware of the figure of a man stopped in a crouch, smiling at him, not ten feet from his side. Of course, it was Hatfield. Andrew shook his head. The woods' skill of these two boys continued to amaze him.

Hatfield crawled over to him and sat down, drawing his knees up. He was still grinning, pretending that he hadn't just sneaked up on his commanding officer. He surprised Andrew by offering a salute, or at least it resembled a salute in that the right hand touched the forehead.

"You don't salute in the field," said Sergeant O'Donal, "and anyway, you don't salute when you're sitting down."

Hatfield took these criticisms of his military demeanor in good humor and went on to say, "I'd like to report, suh, that they is two camps, each about the size of 'ar company, in this direction." He pointed south, the way he had come. "They is camped on the big open fields where they 'usta grow cotton. Also, on the other side of the fields, I seen some big guns, suh. And they eats no betta' than us."

Andrew looked sharply, and Private Hatfield grinned. "Yes, suh. I done loaned me a cup and mess kit from a tent and got in they chow line. They'd beans an' pork. One of they sergeants chewed me out fer not carryin' my gun, suh, ever'where I goes." To Andrew's disapproving look, he explained, "I was hungry, suh."

Andrew exchanged an amused look with Sergeant O'Donal. He knew he should reprimand Hatfield for risking exposure of the scouting party, but he also knew that such audaciousness was just the spirit with which the whole operation had to be carried out to have success.

Andrew had glimpsed Clarkson across the stream a few minutes before, and now Clarkson showed up on this side of the stream, his boots dry. "Two logs across the crick," he answered Andrew's inquiring looks. He pointed downstream across the road. "'bout fifty yards down tha'r."

"What else did you see?" asked Andrew.

"A big camp," said Clarkson. "Some bigger tents with flags flyin' over 'em. And a lot of big guns, suh, cannons. And I knows why us hain't seen more peoples on this road. I heard 'n officer reaming out a corporal for letting his soljers use this road. They is 'sposed to keep it clear fer artillery to move in a hurry." He nodded his head wisely. "I knows one more thing, suh. We dasn't come back through here ta'night on 'ar way back. They's going to be special sentries here 'cause they is practicin' movin' they big guns after dark. Just fer ta'night, though, we gonna' have ta' go 'round."

"You overheard all this, Clarkson?" asked Andrew. "How close did you get?" He had the feeling that perhaps he did not want to know the answer to that question.

"Well, suh, I hung 'round the outside of camp fer a spell, 'n then I seen my chance to borra' a coat 'n a rifle 'n I walks 'round and listens. Good rifle. I'd a liked ta' kept it."

"I don't suppose you got into their chow line?" asked Andrew.

"No, suh," said Clarkson. "They was havin' beans and pork an' I gets 'nuf of that in ar' chow line. But I heard this sergeant gettin' together a special sentry an' guard duty, and I bitched to one of them soljers 'bout extra duty an' he tol' me what they was doin'."

"You both did a good job," said Andrew, "but we can't take any more chances of being detected. We've got to get going here. We have to get to the bottom of the hilltop, or as close as we can without getting seen, and then we have to get out of here."

They crossed the road quickly, one by one, even though, from what they knew now, there did not seem to be any immediate danger. They followed the stream-side trail on the south side of the stream for perhaps a quarter mile. At that point it was joined by another more used trail from the south, and, as the valley walls were getting steeper, the combined trail began angling up the hill. There was no doubt that they must be nearing the limit of how close they could get undetected.

Lieutenant Andrew Greyson went ahead with Hatfield while Sergeant O'Donal and Clarkson pulled off the trail to wait. Andrew and Hatfield proceeded cautiously, Andrew only ten feet behind his scout. Hatfield moved along the trail smoothly and quietly, and Andrew followed. Both men were utterly intent on their surroundings, and, of course, especially on what lay ahead.

Hatfield saw some movement ahead, and with a quick motion of his hand to Andrew, they both melted off the trail. Standing behind a screen of leaves and bushes, concentrating on the trail ahead, they were just able to make out the shoulders and head of a sentry about a hundred yards away.

Hatfield questioned, "Closer?"

"Yes," Andrew affirmed. "I need to get close enough to make sure this trail goes up to the hilltop and that it doesn't have any side trails that will mislead us in the dark."

Hatfield nodded that he understood, and after a pause, they moved carefully up the hill, off the trail in the trees and underbrush. The going was not easy, but Andrew managed to keep close to Hatfield. Presently Hatfield, looking back, made a motion with his hands that the trail forked, one trail going up toward the top of the hill, the other forking right. The sentry they had seen earlier appeared to be just at the fork of the trails. Satisfied that the main trail ran directly to the top of the hill, Andrew and Hatfield followed along beside the right fork. It ran along just below the brow of the hill for fifty yards, then turned up to the top of the hill. Another sentry was stationed at the turn, and Andrew and Hatfield stopped and retreated slowly, carefully, back in the direction they had come.

They joined the sergeant and Clarkson, and Andrew explained the situation. "Both trails lead to the top of the hill," said Andrew. "We'll divide the company there and rush up the hill from these two trails. There will be some shooting with the sentries there, but I believe by then we are within less than a hundred yards of the hilltop, and with surprise in our favor, we can be up there with very few casualties."

The sergeant agreed. Hatfield and Clarkson relaxed off to one side, satisfied that they had done their job. "We'll wait until dark now," said Andrew. "It will be safer, and also it will give us a sense of how it will be to move F Company in the dark." Satisfied, they moved farther from the trail into some deeply shadowed brush, and Andrew, for one, lay back on the ground, resting, thinking through his plans, and waiting for the dark.

Chapter 11

Darkness came quickly in the deep ravine they were in. One moment there was light to see, evening birds calling; and the next they could barely distinguish each other's faces, and there was only an occasional, sleepy chirp from some bird deep in the trees.

Just at dusk they heard the sound of night sentries marching up. From the pauses they made along the way, it seemed that a sentry was being posted about every fifty yards. They could hear the instructions the sergeant of the guard was giving the sentry being posted at the stream crossing. "How am I going to know a Confederate spy if I see one, Sergeant?" they heard the sentry ask.

"Nobody is supposed to be here except the artillery that will come through," replied the sergeant. "Don't stop them. But if someone else comes wandering along, stop them and call the corporal of the guard. Let him handle it."

"Okay, Sergeant," they could hear the young soldier say, as the sergeant walked back the way he had come. After that they heard the sentry walk back and forth, pausing at intervals. Once they heard him talking to himself. Andrew thought he heard him say, "Damn, I wish I was back in Ohio."

When it was completely dark, Lieutenant Greyson got to his feet and stretched. The rest had been good. He felt ready to complete the patrol and return to Clearfield and F Company. The others stood up, stretched, adjusted their clothing, ready to go. Andrew felt a word of caution was necessary.

"We've come this far," he said. "Let's not get careless and lose what we've gained. We have to stay off the road until we are past the sentries. I'm concerned about making a lot of noise thrashing through the brush in the dark." He looked around himself, just barely able to see their faces.

"They is paths 'long most of the way," said Clarkson. "I knows where they is. Sometimes it weren't safe ta' walk this road even in daytime—if they was someone after you."

"That's good, Clarkson," said Andrew. "Now don't go too fast. We don't want to get separated in the dark."

"Yes, suh," said Clarkson. "I'll go 'head and Hattie kin bring up the rear. We sho' don' want ta' lose you, Lieutenant." Even in the dark, Andrew could see Clarkson's teeth gleaming in a smile.

"All right," said Andrew. "You all set, Sergeant?"

"I'm ready," said Sergeant O'Donal. "But I sure never thought I'd put my life in the hands of young squirts like these two."

The patrol started out, Clarkson leading and Hatfield at the rear. They crossed the stream on two logs laid side by side and headed north. Once they started, Andrew found that his eyes adjusted somewhat to the dark so that he could just make out the moving figure of Clarkson ahead of him. He quickly learned to stay just enough back so that any branches that were brushed aside ahead of him would not catch him in the face. He could hear Sergeant O'Donal breathing behind him, and he heard an occasional footstep, but in all, he thought they were moving quietly enough so they would not be detected. Perhaps, he thought, if the sentries do hear something, they will think it some night animal making its way through the brush.

Twice on the trek north, Clarkson ahead signaled for a stop, and then proceeded with added stealth. Each time Andrew was able to, with concentrated effort, sense the signals that had alerted Clarkson—the scuffle of a sentry's feet on gravel or the moving shadow on the edge of the road—but he realized that without his scout alerting him, he would have been much closer to danger before he sensed it. He wondered again at the extraordinary skills of these two hill boys, and he was thankful that he had them with him.

Once as they circled a large encampment and began to move eastward, Andrew heard the plaintive notes of taps being played by some bugler. Playing taps in a combat area, thought Andrew. They must think they are in garrison or something.

Now their route became distinctly eastward; the path seemed to be generally climbing; the sides of the valleys seemed closer. They seemed to be quite out of the proximity of any Union camps. The pace of their walk increased as if Clarkson up ahead knew exactly where they were going, which he probably did, thought Andrew. Then suddenly Clarkson stopped, waiting for him and the others.

"It's steep here," Clarkson whispered softly. "But they's vines along the sides to hold to." He went ahead. Andrew followed.

They were seemingly climbing a narrow pathway, steep and rocky underfoot. The larger rocks seemed to be placed just in the right place for a foot to step and use as a step, as in a stairway. Holding on to the vines on both sides, Andrew climbed up perhaps a hundred steps. He could hear Sergeant O'Donal behind him, and he could feel his tug on the vines.

Presently, all four men were gathered at the top, catching their breath. "Just at the head a' this ravine, this path joins the path we took on ar' way down," said Clarkson. "But we is goin' right by my maw's house. We could jus' stop by. I knows we kin get some cool spring water an' maybe some cornbread with molasses."

"All right," said Andrew. "I can see why no one can find your house. How come you live back in here?"

"Oh, we likes it that way," said Clarkson. "Follow me."

They followed Clarkson, walking more easily now that they seemed well out of any danger. Andrew heard Clarkson ahead stop walking. He also stopped as he heard a two-note whistle repeated twice by Clarkson. They all listened. After a pause there was an answering whistle from up ahead.

"Come on," said Clarkson. "It's all right."

Andrew started walking in the darkness with the others, then almost stopped in momentary fright when they were met by what seemed to be a group of small ghosts with luminous eyes. The newcomers quickly identified themselves with slowly wagging tails and moist, curious noses—a pack of friendly, silent hound dogs that padded about them all, checking them out.

How eerie, thought Andrew, that they don't bark. Then he realized that they had probably been carefully taught not to bark so as not to give away the location of this hidden home in this tucked away canyon. He patted as many heads as were offered by the welcoming hounds.

Ahead of them, a dim light appeared in a doorway, held aloft by a shadowy figure, and shortly they were stepping up on a low porch in front of a cabin. Andrew watched as Clarkson hugged the figure with the lantern, a girl by her young, low, contralto voice. He heard the dogs settling down under the porch, and then the girl was urging them into the door.

The first thing Andrew saw as he stepped into a low-ceilinged room and the light was turned up, was a row of small boys standing in front of a ladder that apparently led to a sleeping loft. They were in shirt tails and nightshirts, three of them with sleep-tangled hair, the littlest one rubbing his eyes. "Is that you, Danny?" the little one asked. "Who is them?"

Andrew smiled at the children, small and appealing as they were, and hoped he did not appear too fearsome to Clarkson's younger brothers. He turned to greet the girl, wondering a little where she fit in, perhaps an older sister of Clarkson's or a girlfriend?

She had turned from stirring up the fire in the fireplace and was contemplating Andrew and his men. "Hello, Hattie," she said to Hatfield, and with a graceful half curtsey to Andrew and the sergeant, she said, "You are welcome here."

She had flashing dark eyes in a heart-shaped face with smooth olive skin. Long black hair was done up partly in a bun, but much of it fell about her face and shoulders like a tangled mane. She was wearing a flannel nightgown that did nothing to hide an astonishingly good figure, and even her bare feet seemed exotically formed.

After a long pause, in which it was obvious that Andrew was somewhat taken back by this beautiful woman, he removed his hat and said, "I'm Lieutenant Greyson and this is Sergeant O'Donal. It's very nice to meet Daniel's little brothers and his sister."

In that instant Andrew realized he had made a mistake. He felt his face flush in embarrassment. The woman before him was no girl; she could be any age from twenty-five to forty-five, but she was clearly no girl—no sister of Clarkson's. There was considerable amusement on her face as she looked at him.

"Oh, excuse me, ma'am," Andrew stumbled over his words. "I thought you were—I was assuming—you are just so..." Where do I go from here, thought Andrew. Was truth the best way?

"You are a very beautiful woman," said Andrew simply.

She accepted his compliment with, again, a half curtsey. "Thank you," she said. Andrew still felt stunned, and at that moment light dawned on a puzzled Clarkson who had been watching.

"Suh, Lieutenant, suh," Clarkson leaped in. "I don' have a sister, suh. This is my mom."

Andrew's feet were back on the ground. He stepped forward and took her hand—a slender, pretty hand, he could not help noticing. "I'm really very pleased to meet you. You have a beautiful home." Andrew's gaze went around the room, taking in the warm hearth, the snug log walls, the neat kitchen, and the row of sleepy, little boys. "It's easy to see, now, why Daniel wants to come home at...ah...different times."

"Thank you," she said again, her smile open and friendly. "It's nice meeting you. I hope you can stay for something to drink and eat." She busied herself in the kitchen, then said over her shoulder, "Danny, pull up another chair to the table, and then run out and get a pitcher of fresh spring water."

They sat at the rough-hewn table and drank cold spring water and ate warm cornbread. They knew they had to leave soon in order to get back to F Company, but this was a pleasant interlude. Before the end of their short stay, the smallest sleepy boy had crawled into Andrew's lap and fallen asleep with Andrew carefully taking his food and drink so as not to disturb the sleeping child.

Before they left, Andrew carried the boy up into the loft and tucked him into bed. He wondered how much the appealing little boy would remember when he woke in the morning. Would he think it all a dream?

Andrew himself wondered if his life and home at Milford would have been different if such a small boy had been part of it. But looking down from the top of the loft ladder as he prepared to come down to the warm scene below, he realized the difference was not particularly children, but the presence of a person such as this graceful, beautiful woman who brought life and love to wherever she was. Andrew watched her briefly as she put an arm around her eldest son, touched Hatfield's face with her hand. Here was a person who transformed the world around her to goodness and beauty. Andrew felt a deep longing for such a life.

He waited a moment longer at the top of the ladder, savoring the scene below. I could be very happy in such a place, he thought. For the first time in many days he thought of his wife, Anne, and he realized that her life of teas and social events would not, by any stretch of imagination, fit into this warm, snug cabin.

Close on the heels of such thoughts came a resolve on Andrew's part that a life such as this, with a woman such as this one, was something worth fighting for, a life that would fill the deep emptiness inside him. After the war, he thought, I'm going to have something like this. He looked once more, imprinting the feeling of this place on his soul, then he threw a leg over the ladder top and stepped down.

"Thank you so much, Mrs. Clarkson," said Andrew at the door. He felt he would have liked to embrace her. "This short time has meant a great deal to me."

She looked him appraisingly in the eyes. "Come back when you can, but please don't give away this secluded place."

"It would be nice to come back at a more peaceful time," said Andrew. "I'll take care of Danny and Hattie as well as I can. They certainly have taken good care of me on this patrol. Thank you for everything."

They left into the darkness, and when Andrew looked back he could see her figure in the doorway dimly lit by the light from inside the cabin.

Hatfield led the way as they climbed up and out of the back of the canyon. The steep trail, the darkness, the overhanging trees and brush, the need to stay in contact with each other, kept them close together. It was a strenuous climb. Andrew could feel the strain on the muscles in his legs. He breathed through his mouth to get as much oxygen into his body as possible. It's good, he thought, that we don't have to take F Company up, or down, this steep trail.

When they reached the top, they stopped to take a breather. Some tiredness was setting into all of them. Even the irrepressible Hatfield and Clarkson were quiet. In two hours they would be back into friendly lines. Andrew hoped the practice night hike by the company had done as well as this patrol. Although they could not relax their vigilance completely, the chance that they would encounter enemy forces was very small. Nobody goes on night patrols, thought Andrew with a grim smile, except us.

The remainder of the walk back was, indeed, easier. For one thing, Andrew had gotten a feel of the country, and he felt he would have been able to find the way back without the guides. The success of the patrol also buoyed him along. Yet, his mind was racing with the preparations for the operation of the entire company just two nights hence. Now and then, as he thought of a detail, he related it to Sergeant O'Donal in a low voice. Finally, just as the first pink light showed in the eastern horizon behind them, they walked tiredly into their company encampment.

At the company kitchen, where Sergeant Grant was just beginning the fires for breakfast, they got some coffee. "Let the two boys sleep till noon, Sergeant," Andrew told Sergeant O'Donal. "We need them fresh for tomorrow night. Better get some rest yourself, and let me sleep for about three hours, and then we'll get to work."

"Yes, sir," said O'Donal. Andrew went up to his quarters in the smokehouse, stumbled down the short stairway to his bed below, shedding clothes and boots as he went, and fell into a deep sleep.

Chapter 12

A day and a half later, F Company left its encampment in good spirits. The soldiers were glad to be on the move after months of garrison-type duty. Though sentry duty and close order drill was a safer life than assaulting a hilltop, these soldiers, as all soldiers before and after them, had come to fight, and they would not feel fulfilled unless they did. They were apprehensive, and some were frightened of what lay ahead, but they covered their fears by disparaging comments about each other, by teasing remarks aimed at the younger soldiers, and by grim jokes.

They joked that the white patches on the back of their coats were targets for the enemy if they turned and ran. They joked that once they got the enemy used to seeing the patches on the back of their coats, they could sew them on the front and the enemy would think they were retreating when they were really advancing. Laughter and talk rippled up and down the double line of soldiers; and the sergeants and officers let them talk, knowing they would have to enforce silence when they got closer.

Hatfield and Clarkson led the column, light and good-natured as ever, but with a more mature air about them as they accepted their roles and responsibilities as leaders of other men. As word of their part in the night patrol had spread, they had, as first, enjoyed the attention and respect of their fellow soldiers; but being of a shy nature, each was happy to be back on the trail instead of the center of attention.

Lieutenant Meek's 1st Platoon was first in the column. Each man carried a blanket roll over his shoulder in which were rolled an extra shirt and a few small personal items. Each man carried his rifle and fifty rounds of ammunition. Tucked into each soldier's belt were two square pieces of blanket material. In a small pack, also hanging from his belt, was a piece of flat bread, a pouch of dried fruit, and a piece of cooked, salted meat wrapped in wax paper—a day's ration of food. Each man carried two canteens of water slung over his shoulders by straps.

Lieutenant Andrew Greyson was in the rear of 1st Platoon. At this position, he felt he could both control the actions of the front platoon and also the 2nd Platoon led by Lieutenant Hadley which followed him, and by messenger, he could keep in touch with 3rd Platoon led by Lieutenant Schyler which brought up the rear.

Andrew felt that communications with his various elements were essential to the success of the operation, and to achieve this, he and Sergeant O'Donal had selected six messengers. Two of these messengers were with him, doggedly following behind him; one was with each of the three platoon lieutenants, and one was with Sergeant O'Donal at the tail end of the column.

The messengers had been chosen for their youth and running ability and for their ability to repeat verbatim, short messages. They carried no rifles or anything that would impede their ability to get somewhere fast.

In between the second and third platoons was a strange column made up of six mules and their accompanying attendants. The first two mules carried in pack saddles Mess Sergeant Grant's essential cooking pots and as much food for the company as could be packed. Sergeant Grant, himself, led the first mule, whom he had already named Ulysses, and wondered at the strange fate that had brought him so close to the front ranks of battle. The sergeant had declined to carry a rifle, but carried in his belt a meat cleaver with which he claimed more accuracy than with a rifle.

Behind Grant's two mules were four mules carrying two twelve-pounder artillery tubes, two wooden ground-mounts for them, four cases of gun powder, and thirty cannon ammunition in crates. The four mules carried between them almost a thousand pounds, and Sergeant Holbrook, who led this column of mules and eight artillerymen, had selected the four strongest and sturdiest Tennessee mules he could find. Brookie was in high spirits, determined to make his role and the role of the artillery, his mules and men, a successful one for the operation.

After 3rd Platoon, which followed the cavalcade of mules, came Sergeant O'Donal, his broad smile gleaming through his mustache and beard. He carried a rifle with a shortened barrel for, as he put it, close-in fighting. And with O'Donal was a squad of fourteen men that had volunteered from other companies in the regiment. They were all seasoned veterans, and Lieutenant Greyson and Sergeant O'Donal had decided they could best be used as a flying emergency squad that would be brought as quickly as possible to any point that seemed threatened.

And so F Company was on its way to strike a blow for the Confederate cause by seizing and holding the Little Hilltop and preventing the Union Army from entering Clearfield. Most of the men in that column felt pride in being selected for this operation, felt that F Company was the best infantry company in the whole damn Confederate Army, or the Union Army, for that matter. Of course, many also felt some apprehension about their personal fate in this battle, but were, for the most part, determined to make their own effort count. Lieutenant Andrew Greyson also felt these emotions, but was much too busy thinking and planning ahead to give much time to these thoughts.

At the place where the column left the wagon trail and entered the forest, the column slowed down as it divided into a single file, and Andrew felt a boyish thrill run through him. If I pull this off, he thought, I'll always remember it. The next thought he had was, maybe I'll be a hero; but since that was not the way he comfortably thought of himself, he quickly put that thought aside for one that expressed a hope that this would be a worthwhile endeavor for the cause, for the men in the company, and for himself.

The column of men fell silent as they entered the trees, partly because they were under strict orders to do so; but more because the darkness in the forest was mysterious and oppressing. They moved more slowly now, each man watching the white patch on the back of the man ahead of him. Andrew was satisfied with the pace the scouts were setting so he made no changes, but he was concerned with how the mules were doing.

The instructions to Sergeants Grant and Holbrook were that if they had difficulty, to allow 3rd Platoon to pass through them, meanwhile sending word ahead. If such a situation arose, Lieutenant Greyson would send one of the scouts back to lead the mule caravan along at their own pace. More likely, thought Andrew, those mules are more sure-footed than we are, and no message was sent up from the rear. At any rate, Andrew had decided that once they began the ascent and assault on Little Hilltop, he would hold the mules and their loads back until the hilltop was taken.

At the top of the steep draw, where they would turn down into the valley, Lieutenant Greyson sent word ahead and back to stop for a short break. The men were to readjust all equipment so that nothing would rattle or be lost in the descent. The artillery, particularly, would probably need retightening on the pack saddles. The men were to take some drinks from their canteens, but with the idea that the two canteens each carried would probably have to last two days.

Once these orders had been issued, Andrew sat on the side of the trail and leaned back against a tree trunk. He made himself relax, knowing that some tense times were ahead, and he would need to be fit and alert. He drank briefly from his canteen, then shut his eyes and let his mind go blank.

Half thoughts drifted in and out of his mind. He wondered how his students at the college were doing, and images came to mind—images of himself leading a class in discussion, himself working with individual students, himself exchanging ideas with sharp, young minds, and himself helping students see what the study of literature and writing could do for their lives. As Andrew thought of these things, he realized that that was what he wanted to return to after the war, a satisfying life as an English professor.

I'm a better teacher than a soldier, he thought. I can do more good teaching young students than I can winning battles. He vowed that if he got back, he would be a very good teacher.

He thought briefly of his father, a lonely man after his wife had died, but a good officer and gentleman until he died at the Battle of Bull Run in Virginia.

Also he thought of Anne, his own wife, and he wondered if he would, or rather could, go back to her at this war's end.

Finally, he thought of the Confederate cause, and he sadly realized what he had felt as soon as President Lincoln had rejected South Carolina's bid for succession, that the South could not win the war. It had the spirit and devotion, he thought, but it does not have the resources for a drawn-out war. But we must make Lincoln and the United States realize, he thought, that we are a force to be reckoned with, that our lifestyle, our interests must be considered.

Andrew opened his eyes. Around him men were stirring, low murmur of talk. Time to get back at this war, he thought. Time to get back to this battle, this hilltop to be taken; time for F Company to prove itself.

"Saddle up," he passed the word. "Move out."

The descent down into the valley was steep and, in the dark, hazardous. A slip and a fall by a man could mean bringing down other men with him. It would mean confusion and noise. The soldiers had been thoroughly made aware of the danger of making noise, and Andrew was pleased that everyone seemed to be making a strong effort to be as quiet as possible. Entering enemy territory certainly made them aware of the risks of making noise, he thought.

How would the heavily laden mules fare on the steep trail? He passed word up to Lieutenant Meeks of 1st Platoon that they should cross the stream at the floor of the valley and just far enough on the other side to allow room for the following units, and to stop there and wait. He stepped off the trail to let 2nd Platoon pass him, and he waited for the mules.

The mules were doing remarkably well, he saw. They were leaning back on their rear haunches, front legs straight out, in a sort of controlled slide at times. But they seemed very aware of where they put their feet; more so than a man, thought Andrew. Perhaps large four-footed animals develop such a sense, he thought, because, after all, they very seldom see their feet as a man does.

Andrew silently greeted Sergeants Grant and Holbrook as they went by. Then he fell in line behind Sergeant O'Donal. He thumped O'Donal on the shoulder, signaling that he was pleased with the progress so far. Sergeant O'Donal answered with a barely audible grunt.

When all the units were down and across the stream and halted, Lieutenant Greyson walked through the column thumping as many men as he could on the back as he went by. He wished he could speak to them, give them some words of praise and of encouragement, but silence was now of utmost importance. The rustle of the men moving about and the occasional thump as they adjusted their equipment was all the noise they could afford. There was no way of knowing if the Union forces had outposts out here.

The men were doing what they had practiced the previous nights in the dark, tying the blanket padding onto their boots. Even the mules had the paddings wrapped securely around their hooves. From here on, the operation had been rehearsed: the silent walk through the enemy camp, crossing the road after a reconnaissance, if necessary silencing any sentries, and silently approaching the accesses to Little Hilltop. After dividing into two assault groups, 1st Platoon would go up the right fork of the trail, 2nd Platoon up the left fork; and 3rd Platoon stay at the fork in reserve, protecting the supplies and cannon carried by the mules, and ready to reinforce either of the two assaults that faltered.

These plans ran through Andrew's mind as he walked among the men of F Company. He had gone over them in detail with his officers and NCOs, but he wished he could emphasize once more how important it was to press the charge up the hill once it had begun. To falter or retreat would be chaotic in the dark. It would be tragic for his men. They must press the assault and succeed.

"Move out," the whispered command came down the line, and each man picked his way as quietly as possible, taking care to keep watch on the white patch on the man ahead of him. Back in his command position between 1st and 2nd Platoons, Andrew felt they were committed.

Chapter 13

The order of march had changed slightly. The plan here called for Sergeant O'Donal and his scout brigade to lead the way, behind Clarkson and Hatfield, of course, until the assault on the hilltop began. Their mission was to handle all sentries or chance encounters with enemy soldiers. Don't kill them unless necessary, were Lieutenant Greyson's orders. Take them, gagged so they could not alarm anyone, along with us. The idea was that a missing sentry in the morning would provide more confusion than a dead one. If the Union forces did not know from where or when they had come, it might well delay any moves they would make to retake Little Hilltop. Any such delay would help them get established on the hilltop to meet an attack.

Andrew reasoned that even if they encountered sentries, the advantage was still with his F Company. All armies, past and present, send their youngest, least experienced soldiers to do sentry duty, Andrew knew. It had always been so. The scout brigade should have little trouble handling them.

Andrew pictured Hatfield and Clarkson moving down the trail ahead, sure-footed and competent in the dark. He wondered if the two scouts were as carefree as they had been on the scouting trip now that the purpose was more serious, and he had to admit that they were probably still enjoying themselves immensely.

The column halted briefly, and waited silently before the encampment that the scouting party had noted. Sure enough, after a half hour's wait, two prisoners were brought back and put in custody of the rear rank of 1st Platoon. Both young soldiers were securely gagged and frightened. Coming close in the dark, Andrew could sense their fear. One soldier was cut on the arm, a wound that was quickly bound up, and they became part of the column under the charge of two soldiers from 1st Platoon.

Andrew took each prisoner by the arm and explained, by gestures, that they must cooperate, must not cause a disturbance, or dire consequences would be theirs. He got an agreeing nod from each of them, and the column proceeded on its way.

It was spooky walking through the Union camp. They stayed beside the stream to allow the flowing water noise to cover, as much as possible, the moving noises they made. Off to their left stretched the white tents vaguely visible in the dark. Toward the center of the encampment, perhaps a hundred yards away, an open fire was burning, throwing flickering lights on the tents and wagons around it. Andrew figured it was probably where the night's guard was located, and he hoped his column would be long gone before the time to change the guard came, and the two sentries would be discovered missing.

But even if they were missed, Andrew believed the first assumption the corporal of the guard would make would be that the two young soldiers were off sleeping somewhere, a fairly common fault of tired, young sentries, and a general alarm would not be raised.

Against the flickering fire, some figures could be seen, perhaps talking, or having coffee, waiting out the night and their time of guard duty.

When his section of the column had passed out of the encampment, Andrew listened for any sounds of their discovery as the rear of the column, especially the section with the mules, passed through the camp. None came, and Andrew had to admit that he himself could not hear the padded footsteps of the men more than twenty or thirty feet from him.

At the road crossing the column halted again while silent road blocks were sent in each direction to stop any chance enemy that might be coming down the dark road as the column crossed it. These road blocks were Sergeant O'Donal's brigade, and all but two, who Andrew kept near himself in readiness for a particular task ahead, were to fall in at the tail of the column as the column finished the crossing. They would be ready to be called up for any emergency that occurred during the actual assault.

And the assault now was imminent. Lieutenant Greyson had taken advantage of the halted column at the road to work his way to the head of the column where he could be sure that each element at least started in the right direction up the correct route.

Very shortly, the head of the column came to the halted scouts, Clarkson and Hatfield. Up ahead, they indicated, were the fork in the trail and a possible sentry. Now it began.

All the next moves had been thoroughly briefed and rehearsed by the people involved. Andrew touched the arms of the two brigade scouts he had with him, and indicated the likely location of the sentry ahead. The scouts knew their job well. After a wait, perhaps a half hour, Andrew thought he heard some sounds ahead, but no outcry—no alarm. Wait some more, and in a short while the brigade scouts came back. They nodded their heads; mission accomplished.

Andrew took a deep breath. All the preparations of the last days were to be put into practice now. He put nagging thoughts of possible disasters out of his mind. This was the test—the test of himself as a leader, and of his men as men of purpose and of courage.

"Lieutenant Meeks, 1st Platoon," Andrew whispered fiercely. "Go!" He grasped Meeks' arm firmly and sent him forward, Clarkson leading the column. Each man, as they came by Lieutenant Greyson, got a thump of encouragement. This was no time for easy pats on the back. This was time for action. The last man of 1st Platoon disappeared in the darkness of the right fork, the white patch on his back wavering out of sight.

The 2nd Platoon came briskly up and Andrew sent them up the left fork with similar encouragement, Hatfield guiding at the lead. The reserve 3rd Platoon, the mules with their cargo, and the detachment of brigade scouts stopped at the trail fork, waiting for Lieutenant Greyson's assessment of how the battle was going and for orders from him.

Andrew also waited at the fork and stood with Sergeant O'Donal and Lieutenant Taylor, his executive officer. Also, nearby were Sergeants Holbrook and Grant. Any moment now they should hear the first shots, the shouts of determined men, the commands of the officers.

Any cannon they have, thought Andrew, has got to be facing the front. They'll have to turn them completely around before they could be made to bear on the attackers from the rear of the hill.

He thought, the longer there are no shots, the farther up the slope we will be, the closer to our objective, the hilltop.

He thought again, pray God, we don't shoot each other in the dark. The men are in column, not front facing ranks as they are used to being. It would be easy for shots to strike our own men. But it's a risk we have to take.

Suddenly, and startlingly, a shot rang in the silence from the left, one shot only. Andrew thought, that shot was fired in this direction from the sound of it, though it's hard to tell in this valley. It must have been the sentry's shot. There were no answering shots. They must have overrun the outpost, Andrew thought. But surely, the firing will start soon.

Almost as he thought it, the firing started on the right, first three sporadic shots, then a volley of shots that echoed in the night. Andrew believed he could hear shouts from that direction. The firing on the right continued at short intervals, usually a small volley of three or four shots, as a target appeared, thought Andrew. Still no more shots from the left.

"All right," said Lieutenant Greyson aloud to the men around him. "We can assume the surprise factor is now over. I believe we should follow up both attacks. Sergeant O'Donal, you take your scouts up the left fork and join up with the second platoon. Lieutenant Schyler, you take your platoon up the right fork. I will accompany you. Be careful of firing since the first troops you see should be friendly."

He turned to the sergeants with the mules. "Wait here for a half hour," he said, "then proceed up the right fork. I believe that is the most direct route to the top. Come forward cautiously so you don't overrun the assault. I don't want you staying here any longer than necessary because any reinforcements they send will probably come up this trail. We hope to make good use of what you have on those mules.

"You're a little bit out on a limb here, Lieutenant Taylor. Stay back here with the artillery and the supplies, then bring them up in as careful and orderly a manner as you can. If we have the hilltop secured, I'll be there to direct you where to set up. If the action is still heavy, hold back just behind our troops."

"Yes, sir," said Lieutenant Taylor. "I understand."

There was a flurry of shots from the left just them. "Good luck," said Andrew to Sergeant O'Donal. "Sounds like action ahead."

"Yes, sir," said the sergeant. "We're on our way." His men and he hurried up the left fork. The time for silence was over.

Chapter 14

"Let's go," said Andrew to Lieutenant Schyler. "I want to be in the lead here so I can get an idea of what's happening up there."

Andrew and Lieutenant Schyler led the forty-five men of 3rd Platoon up the right fork of the trail. They moved as quickly as they could despite overhanging branches, the steepness, and the almost invisibility of the trail. A ragged volley of shots sounded ahead, and one bullet whizzed over their heads, clipping the branches of the trees. Everyone ducked even though, of course, the bullet was long gone by. When a rocket flare arched into the sky ahead, they stopped momentarily, but Andrew, realizing they could move more quickly by its light on the trail, urged them to follow him.

"Let's move," he called back as he hurried forward.

The shots ahead had died down to just an occasional shot when they caught up to the rear men of the first platoon. 1st Platoon had advanced far enough so that they had reached what could be called the brow of the hilltop, but now they were stopped, most of them down on the ground, sheltered from enemy fire by downed trees on the ground.

Andrew found Lieutenant Meeks crouched behind a large tree trunk. "We've taken a few hits," said Meeks. "I've got three wounded men down in that little dip, and I think there were several more hit back down the trail. I've got the men reloading, and we'll be ready for another run at them."

"All right. Listen," said Andrew. "It's time to broaden our assault from just this trail head. I'll get the 3rd Platoon into line behind you. We'll spread out and come through your men and cover this whole front of the hill. When we are by you, get your men into line and follow us. Hold your fire until you are caught up to us if we are pinned down, but I intend to have the men fix bayonets and charge right to the top."

"All right!" said Lieutenant Meeks, eyes gleaming. "Let's go!"

"Don't pause at the top of the hill if you have the momentum," said Andrew. "Sweep right on down the front slope and take the artillery guns there."

"Will do," said Meeks.

It took some time for Andrew and Lieutenant Schyler to get 3rd Platoon in line with an interval of perhaps a dozen feet between each of the men. There was a lull in the shooting with only an occasional shot fired in their direction. This is good, thought Andrew. The men will get used to some shots fired at them. But he knew that when the time came for the charge, he would have to lead them. At the moment he was too busy, amidst the confusion of the darkness, getting the men organized, to consider the possible consequences to himself.

Finally, with his face whipped by unseen branches as he had hurried up and down the lines, with his clothes damp from sweat from his exertions, with his shirt sleeve torn, Andrew met with Lieutenant Schyler at the center of the line. He remembered thinking, this is not bravery. This is not courage. This just has to be done.

He drew his saber with a flourish and struck it against a nearby tree. It rang like a bell in the darkness, and Andrew could feel the eyes of the men on him.

"Men of F Company," Andrew called out. "Fix bayonets." Up and down the line, Andrew could hear the rasp of bayonets coming out of scabbards and the clicks as they were attached to the rifles.

"Men of F Company, are you ready?" A cheer, a throaty, menacing cheer, came up from the lines. A few rebel yells—then an intense silence.

"Men of F Company, follow me!" With a cry, Andrew started up the slope. Behind him the men followed, yelling and cheering. "Let's go!" shouted Andrew over his shoulder.

Later Andrew learned that half the men of 1st Platoon, caught up in the spirit of the charge, had joined the men of 3rd Platoon. As they came over the brow of the hill a steady, disciplined fire met them. Andrew knew they were taking some hits. But he also knew that there would be more casualties if they stopped. Now was the time to seize their goal.

And so quickly they were in the enemy camp—some white tents, piles of equipment, men leaping from behind trees to fire at them. Men went down from bullets, or were knocked down by rifle butts. Some simply fell as they fired their rifles and turned to run. The two forces came together in a jumbled confusion of cries and curses. About the only way it was possible to tell who was on which side was by the direction they faced, Andrew's F Company facing up the hill, and the enemy facing them. But for brief moments, confusion reigned.

Very soon there were no more shots fired—all the rifles were empty. Then came only the sounds of scuffles, the cries of alarm, the thud of contact. Andrew felt his men were carrying the fray, as the conflict moved over the top of the hill and down the beginning of the slope on the other side.

"The guns! Get the guns!" shouted Andrew, sprinting for the cannon on the front slope of the hill. He saw that several of the cannon, which had been pointed down the hill, had been turned around and were now aimed up the hill. In several more minutes, Andrew realized, he and his men would have faced deadly grape shot from the muzzles of those guns.

Accompanied by two men, one with a red headband, Andrew raced for the guns, leaping over the trails of the first cannon into the gun pit. Two cannoneers, unarmed, ran down the hill, but the third, a bulky man, picked up a rifle that was leaning against the trail. He brought it up as Andrew leaped in, and Andrew felt the rush of the bullet go by his face. The next instant he was slashing at the man's arm with his saber, as the bulky man swung the bayoneted rifle at Andrew's head. The two men that had followed Andrew leaped in to help him, and the man went backwards over the gun trails.

"You all right, Lieutenant, suh?" asked the man with the headband, and Andrew realized it was Clarkson.

"I'm all right," said Andrew. He put his hand to the left side of his face and felt some blood, and his head was ringing, but he thought he felt all right. He looked for his saber and was surprised to find he was still holding it in his right hand.

"I'm staying with you, Lieutenant," said Clarkson as he busily reloaded his rifle.

"All right," said Andrew. "Let me just look around and see what's going on." Some of the earliest of dawn's twilight was just lighting up the sky. Andrew could see that the hilltop and the cannon were theirs. From the left side of the hill he could see men of 2nd Platoon arriving. Men were milling about on the hilltop. A few were helping wounded comrades on the ground.

"Lieutenant Meeks," called Andrew. "Lieutenant Schyler, Lieutenant Hadley, get your men organized into a defensive perimeter. We've got the hill and we sure as hell aren't going to give it up to some counterattack just now."

"Yes, sir." Andrew, still sitting on the trail of the cannon, could see the three officers hastily carrying out his orders.

"Sergeant O'Donal," called Andrew. "Are you here?"

"Yes, sir, Lieutenant." Sergeant O'Donal hurried over from the left. "You all right, Lieutenant?"

"I'm fine," said Andrew. "I feel great. We did it, by God, we took the hill, Sergeant." He stood up and shook hands with O'Donal. They grinned at each other. "Now take your scouts and go down this right trail and bring up Brookie and Grant with the mules. They may need some help."

"Yes, sir," said O'Donal and hurried off. A stroke of luck, thought Andrew, that I have this small unit of capable men that can take care of details that need to be taken care of.

As the light of dawn came to Little Hilltop, the chaos had been turned into some order. Grant and his kitchen were set up in a small grove of protecting trees just on the down slope of the east side of the hill. Already he had started a fire with the intention of serving something warm and filling.

The wounded were made as comfortable as possible just off from Grant's kitchen. A canvas tarp had been stretched between trees for a roof to protect them from sun or rain. There were eighteen Confederate soldiers with bullet or bayonet wounds, one with a broken leg, and three with what seemed to be head concussions—they were dazed and had severe head pains. Andrew asked for volunteers and had assigned two men to nurse and aid the wounded.

Also in the improvised aid station were two Union soldiers that were too injured to walk. The half dozen Union soldiers that were wounded, but could walk, and the two prisoners taken earlier,

Andrew had sent down the hill to find their own way back to their units. They had left down the south slope which had a wagon trail coming up it. They were bandaged, bloody, and frightened, but grateful to be allowed to leave.

The eleven dead had been wrapped in their own blankets and placed neatly at the very top of the hill on the west side. It was here, where the slope dropped off swiftly to the river, that Andrew planned to have them buried, in ground least likely to be the site of future fighting. Andrew had put off the burial and service until mid-morning, hoping that by then they could determine what the enemy's next actions against them would be.

Lying side by side with the Confederate dead were five dead Union soldiers. They, too, would be buried. Before the Union walking wounded had left, Andrew had insisted they identify their dead comrades and carry their names back with them to be reported to their own units.

Sergeant Brookie's two cannon had been set up on the north side of the hill, the side up which F Company had attacked. Sergeant Brookie viewed the captured four Union cannon with glee. "Holy smoke!" he said. "I've got me a six-gun battery. Just wish I had more ammo," he grumbled after looking over the supplies of the captured guns.

"These twelve-pounders have more range than our light cannon," he said, "even though they both fire a twelve-pound projectile. What do you think, Lieutenant? Shall I put two of them to cover the river, and two to cover the open fields to the east?"

"Good planning," said Lieutenant Greyson. "Keep their positions flexible enough so that we can fire down the south slope if an attack comes from that direction. I rather think you will have earned your red artillery sash by the time this action is over."

"You'd think they'd have left us more ammunition," growled Brookie. He made each of his six cannoneers a gun chief, then asked for volunteers to man the cannons.

"Take three men to add to each gun crew," said Andrew. "I know that's not a full gun crew, but it will have to do. Where will you be?"

"I'll be where I'm needed," said Brookie.

The infantry platoons had each been assigned a sector of the hilltop to defend. The men were busy under the direction of their officers and were getting tree trunks into position for bulwarks. Behind the bulwarks they were digging shallow pits from which to fire their rifles.

"You can cut any trees you need to," said Andrew as he walked the perimeter to see how the work was going. "As a matter of fact, cut as many trees to your front as you have to, to get a field of fire. Don't leave anything out there for them to use as cover as they come up." That went for the south and the east slope. The north slope was a dense woods, impossible to clear, and the west slope fell steeply down to the river.

"Sergeant Holbrook in artillery brought up some axes and saws. You can borrow them. He's got some good shovels, too, that were left behind by the Union troops."

Just at daybreak, at sunrise, Sergeant Grant, his kitchen steaming with the good smell of coffee and his pots bubbling with hot porridge, came to Lieutenant Greyson. "I brung this," he said, holding out a large Confederate flag. "We ought to let them know we done it."

"Absolutely," said Andrew, delighted. "Let's fly this from the tallest tree on this hilltop."

A skinny soldier volunteered to climb the tree, and shucking his boots, and with a hatchet tied to his belt, he shinnied up the tree like a monkey. He chopped the top branches from the tree to make a bare flag pole, and taking the flag from inside his shirt, he tied it in place to wave slowly in the early morning breeze.

It was a touching moment, everyone looking up at the stars and bars of the Confederate flag. During the intense hours of the assault they had thought only of their own survival and their loyalty to the men around them. Now with their flag catching the early rays of the sun, they remembered their cause and why they had come here.

A ragged cheer came from the men, but it was muted, and Andrew thought, they are like me, a little too emotional to be able to cheer at a moment like this.

The moment passed, and the men came in shifts, leaving some always on watch, to the kitchen for their coffee and cooked cereal.

Andrew stood at the top of the hill with a tin cup of coffee in his hand, tired, dirty, but proud. Coffee had never tasted so good.

Chapter 15

The days and nights that followed were a confusion of alarms, of rushing to throw back an assault, of tiredness, of sleeplessness. When Andrew thought of those days afterwards, even several years later when he revisited and walked over the scene, he could not clearly remember the sequence of events, or, in many cases, the details of the events themselves.

Before the burial service was over, there was a small probing attack from the south slope of the hill. It was quickly repulsed, but it added one more wounded to their aid station. The small attacks continued at intervals during the day, and though F Company was able to avoid any more injury, and likely inflicted some wounds on their attackers, the outcome of such a watchful day was that no one got any rest, Andrew least of all. Sergeant Brookie was all for using his cannons to blast the attackers off the hill, but Andrew cautioned him to wait, to save their cannon ammunition for when it would be the difference between staying on the hilltop or losing it.

Just before dusk, a dozen cannonballs landed on the hilltop, obviously fired from the open fields to the east. One of the explosions tore down the canvas that Sergeant Grant had stretched over his field kitchen, causing him to swear profusely and threaten revenge on all cannoneers.

Again, Andrew cautioned Sergeant Brookie. "Let's hold our fire, Brookie," Andrew said. "We haven't got enough ammunition to win a cannon duel. You'll have plenty of action before this is over."

Brookie agreed, but made the rounds of his guns to be sure they were ready to be fired if needed during the night defenses.

The men stayed at their posts all night with the orders from Andrew, passed on down through the platoon lieutenants, that half the men stay awake. He had sent out no sentry outposts. "I'm afraid we'd just lose our sentries to the enemy out there," he explained to Sergeant O'Donal. "We've got good fields of fire from our lines. Let's let them come in range and then we'll cut them down."

Sergeant O'Donal's scout brigade was kept in the center of camp so they would be able to rush to any point along the defenses that were overly threatened. They had only lost one of their number to wounds so far, but Andrew felt that they would be the difference in the skirmishes to come, and that they would pay a severe price in casualties.

Just after dusk, Andrew stopped in at the aid station and was sobered by the fact that three of the eighteen wounded had died. More burial services in the morning, he thought, dreading it. But overall, he did not have time to dwell on the negative aspects of this operation. He had too many details to concern himself with. He would lean back against a tree trunk during a quiet time, almost doze off, and some detail that he had to see about would occur to him and he would be off to see about it.

There were no serious assaults against the hilltop during the night. Twice, shots were fired down the hillside by the men, but when there was no returning fire, Andrew had to assume that his men had fired at sounds of animals or of the wind. Several hours after midnight he passed the word that only five men in each platoon need stay awake while the remainder could sleep in place. He felt that, tired as the men were, many of them were falling asleep anyway, and this way they could change off.

Andrew, himself, was finally convinced by Sergeant Grant to take a rest, and he lay down on the ground, pulled his hat over his face, and was instantly asleep. Sergeant Grant threw a blanket over him and said quietly, "We're going to need you in the morning."

Chapter 16

The smell of coffee awakened Andrew. He opened his eyes and sat up, leaning his back against a tree trunk. When Sergeant Grant handed him a cup of steaming coffee, he said, "Don't you ever sleep, Sergeant?"

"I get my rest," Grant said.

"Good coffee," said Andrew. He felt that at this early morning, just before light, he could take a few moments to get ready for the coming day. The sky had just the beginning of light in it, and cool mists were swirling up from the river. Sleeping just some ways off were two figures, both with red headbands, curled up, clutching rifles between their knees, sleeping as peacefully as if they were at home in bed. Hatfield and Clarkson, thought Andrew. They are at home anywhere. Their clothing and faces were streaked with dirt, but their faces wore the angelic looks of innocents. Andrew noticed for the first time that Hatfield's left arm was bloodied and bandaged.

He thought of his own wound and put a hand up to the left side of his face to feel crusted blood.

"You look pretty rough, Lieutenant," said Grant. "I'll clean that cut for you with warm water."

"Let's not waste the water until we know we can," said Andrew. "This cut isn't serious."

"It may improve your looks at that," said Sergeant Grant. He handed Andrew a tin plate on which was a cornmeal biscuit covered with gravy. "Eat this, Lieutenant," he said. "You're going to be too busy to eat later."

"I suspect you're right," said Andrew. "And this is good food. Smartest thing I did was bring you along. This food will perk up the troops."

As Andrew ate, he sent his runners to tell the officers to assemble at the field kitchen; and by the time he finished the food, they had all arrived, the executive officer, Lieutenant Taylor, and the platoon officers, Lieutenants Meeks, Schyler and Hadley. Also present were Sergeant O'Donal of the scouts and Sergeant Holbrook from the artillery.

When they gathered around him, each with a cup of coffee and Andrew with a fresh cup, Andrew said, "I have a notion today will be our biggest test yet. They sent up those little probing attacks yesterday, and now they realize we have a sizable force up here. And they are going to have had a chance to think things over and realize that we can put a real kink in any plans they have to move on the city. And, when we fire on them with our cannon, which I believe we'll have to do today, they will realize they have to take this hilltop back. I believe by this afternoon we can expect a full scale attack. We'll beat them back, and they'll come at us again in the morning."

Andrew looked around at his men, and they watched him, serious, earnest expressions on their faces. "I can't read their minds," said Andrew, "but that's what I'd do if I were them. If we can beat them back tomorrow, by then we can be looking for some help from the regiment, certainly by the following morning. I'm not saying the regiment can get to us, but they can divert enough attention by trying to get to us so that we can hold up here.

"That's the situation the way I see it," said Andrew. "Our big problems are going to be shortage of ammunition, so tell your men to make their shots count; and we're going to need water by tomorrow, but we'll solve that when we come to it.

"Tell your men they've done an excellent job so far, which they have, and don't give them any reason not to be optimistic about our situation."

Andrew looked around. "Any questions? Any comments?" He paused. "If there are none, let's get the men here to the kitchen in shifts to eat before full daylight comes, then let's get ready for a busy day."

The sun was rising and tendrils of mist were drifting up from the valleys below as Lieutenant Greyson walked around the hilltop inspecting the defenses of his embattled company. He talked to as many of the men as he could, speaking words of encouragement;

although, he thought to himself, I'm not exactly a picture of inspiration. There were dirt and blood on his face, he knew, and his clothes were muddied and torn. But he walked with vigor and confidence, and, he reflected, he felt surprisingly alert and ready for what lay ahead. The several hours of sleep seemed to have thoroughly rested him, and his mind was busily going over what he might do as possible situations arose.

He had turned his saber over to Sergeant Grant for safe keeping, and the sergeant, with a flair for the melodramatic, had promptly tied a line to the handle of the saber and hoisted it aloft, just below their flag, as a symbol of their fighting spirit. Many of the tired men, as they watched it go up, raised their own rifles in salute.

Andrew had on his belt the big Navy Colt revolver that had been his father's. He knew that his main task was not to fire bullets at the enemy, could not, in fact, allow himself to be distracted by doing so. His role would be, as it had been, to keep an overall sense of what was happening, and to give appropriate orders.

His last stop as he surveyed his positions on the hilltop was at the aid station. Both of the soldiers who had volunteered to work at the station were dead tired. Andrew realized how frustrating their task must be—to take care of wounded men without having the means to do so. Another wounded soldier had died overnight, the aids having placed him to the side with a blanket over him.

"If we could just have water to wash their wounds with," pleaded Corporal Jamison.

Lieutenant Greyson made a quick decision. "Get a gallon of warm water from Sergeant Grant," he said. "I'll let him know he is to give you some. Make it go as far as you can. We have to get water tonight, probably from the river."

"Thanks," said the corporal, and Andrew made a vow that if he was ever again in a similar operation he would make care of the wounded a high priority.

As Andrew headed back toward the center of the hilltop, marked by two, large, fallen trees that he was beginning to call his command post, Private Clarkson came alongside of him. Clarkson was plainly worried. His usual laughing eyes were dark and troubled.

"It's my friend, Hattie, suh," he told Andrew. "His arm's gittin' bad, suh. He knows they cin't do nothin' for him."

Andrew stopped and looked at Clarkson. "What can we do?" he asked, more in sympathy than expecting any reply.

Private Clarkson considered. "With your permission, suh, I'd take him ta' my ma. She's good at curin' ailments. I know she could he'p him, suh."

"You could get through?" Andrew asked Clarkson.

"Thet's no problem, suh," replied Clarkson. "With this mawnin' fog an' all, I'd git by. I could be back this afta'noon."

Andrew stopped and considered. He would lose the efforts of Clarkson on a day when every man would count. But then, he thought, this type of fighting isn't his strong suit anyway. And after seeing the plight of the wounded at the aid station, there seemed little doubt that Hatfield would be better off in the care of the gentle, competent woman that Andrew had met in the cabin tucked back in the deep hollow.

"All right," said Andrew. "Take him to your ma. Go carefully, and don't come back until after dark this evening. That would be safer, I believe." Andrew reached out a hand and touched Clarkson on the shoulder. He realized he had come to like this boy. He thought, if I could, I'd tell him to stay away until this battle was over.

"If you can," said Andrew, "bring us back some water, something we can use to ease the wounded."

"I'll come back, suh," said Clarkson. His spirits were lifted. He knew his friend would be all right. "Thank ya', suh." And Clarkson saluted, the salute such a playful, friendly, unmilitary thing that Andrew almost laughed.

Clarkson hurried off, and in a minute Andrew, watching from the hilltop, saw him leave two rifles with Sergeant Grant at the mess kitchen and slip down through the lines with the arm-bandaged Hatfield following him.

On the hilltop, Sergeant O'Donal pointed out with pride the lookout platform his scouts had built thirty feet up a tree. A rough rope ladder hung down from the lookout that resembled the crow's nest of a sailing ship.

"A great idea," commended Andrew, looking up at the man presently on duty. "What can you see from up there?" he asked.

"Not much, just now, sir," replied the lookout. "There's a lot of fog down in the valleys and over the river." The lookout had his rifle with him and could presumably help a great deal in any upcoming fire fight. He would, of course, also be very vulnerable up there with no cover.

Andrew took his field glasses from around his neck and handed them to Sergeant O'Donal. "Pass these up to him, Sergeant," he said. "He can make better use of them than I can down here." The lookout received the field glasses and immediately put them to use, peering through the mists.

"Take a break, Lieutenant," said Sergeant O'Donal, indicating one of the fallen logs as a place to be seated. "It could be a long day."

"That it could be," agreed Andrew, seating himself and stretching out his legs. "I'm immensely pleased with what your scout brigade has done, Sergeant," Andrew said. "They have been a great help. And I'm sorry we lost the one."

Sergeant O'Donal nodded. Though dirty and thirsty, his eyes were alert. He perhaps could not say he was enjoying himself, yet he knew that at this time he was at the place where he wanted to be.

"I'm going to give you an additional duty, Sergeant," said Andrew. "I'm going to ask you to keep a very accurate list of names of the men we lose and the names of the men that are wounded. The outcome of this battle is very much in doubt, and if things go against us, the survivors could be few. We owe it to the families of the men who die here to be notified of the heroism that their men faced up to here. I'd like to be sure such a list gets back to regiment."

"Will do, sir," said Sergeant O'Donal. "I'll leave the list with Sergeant Grant. He's got about the best chance of coming through this as anyone."

All around them, on the hilltop, in the lines of defenses around the edges, at the six cannon, men were cleaning their weapons and getting their personal equipment in order. Everyone seemed to accept that this would indeed be a very active day.

Lieutenant Greyson's and Sergeant O'Donal's conversation was interrupted by the lookout over their heads. "I think I see something out there, Sergeant," the private called down. "The fog is clearing up down in the valley, and I think I see movement down there."

"Look carefully," called Andrew. "Just what is it you see?" He looked off down the valley himself, hoping to see what the lookout above him was reporting.

"Yes, sir," said the private. He continued to train the glasses on the valley below. Suddenly he stopped and leaned forward. "Hold it," he called. "Sir, there's thousands of men down there. I see flags, sir, and horses. I can't count them, sir."

Lieutenant Greyson sprang for the rope ladder and scrambled up it. Once up in the crow's nest, he searched the valley and the open fields in it with the field glasses. A low whistle, and then a shouted command, "Sergeant Brookie," he called. "Sergeant Brookie, you're about to get all the firing you want. Get your guns trained on the valley below—all of them. No, wait. Keep two of them aimed at the river."

"Yes, sir," shouted Sergeant Holbrook, leaping up from where he was resting by one of the cannon. "All right, my boys. Move smartly now. Lean into that trail and let's pivot this gun so it aims right down that slope."

The artillery men sprang into action, the new volunteers as willing as any. Four guns were quickly swivelled around to the east.

"Range is about eight hundred yards," called Lieutenant Greyson, still watching the Union forces gathering in the open cotton fields in the valley. "Fire a round when ready, and I'll give you a correction."

"Yes, sir," cried Brookie, and a cannon boomed in the cool morning air.

Andrew, watching through the glasses, saw it land in line, but a hundred yards short of the fields. He saw a burst of the ball as it smashed into a tree in the valley below. "Add a hundred yards," called Andrew, "and you'll be in the midst of them."

"On the way," called Brookie, as two cannon roared simultaneously. The other two cannons fired immediately after, and Andrew saw four bursts almost directly in the center of the fields filled with soldiers.

"You're on to them, Sergeant," Andrew called grimly. "Fire as many rounds as you can afford. You'll never have a better target."

The effects of the cannonading below were devastating. In his glasses, Andrew could see the damage and the confusion. At least a regiment bunched up down there, he thought. Soldiers were running to escape the incoming rounds. Officers were wheeling their horses about, sabers flashing over their heads, as they tried to keep some sort of order. Four more cannon balls whizzed into the valley.

Andrew shook his head grimly as he saw the carnage below. "Keep it up, Sergeant," he called. "Shift your guns about ten degrees to the northeast." Another volley of shots rang out from the four cannon. And then another. After two more volleys, Andrew held up his hand. "That's enough, Sergeant," he called. "We've cleared them out of the field. Let's save our ammunition."

They must have been staging up for a march on Clearfield, Andrew thought. *Now that they know they can't do that without taking many casualties, they may realize that they have to take this hill and clear us out of here. Time to get ready, as ready as we can get.*

"Keep a good watch," Andrew said to the lookout as he crawled down the rope ladder. "And keep a sharp watch for troops coming up against us up this south slope. Any advance warning you can give us will help."

"Yes, sir," said the lookout. "I'll do my best, sir."

Remembering the intelligence reports about the Union forces building rafts on which to come down the river, Lieutenant Greyson hurried the fifty yards over to the two smaller guns, still facing the river. "Keep alert for rafts coming down the river," he admonished the two gun crews. "If the reports are correct, there may be some coming. When they come, concentrate your fire on the lead raft. If you can break it up, it may cause problems for the following rafts."

Eagerly, the cannoneers looked up the river, the prospect of shooting at a target in the water firing up their excitement. Sergeant Holbrook came over from the other four guns to supervise, and just as he arrived on the scene, one of the cannoneers, standing as high as he could on the black barrel of his gun, pointed his arm upstream. "Here they come," he shouted.

When Sergeant Holbrook saw that each of the two lead rafts carried an artillery piece, he flashed a grin at Andrew. "Damn, I'm glad you let me come," he chortled. "What artillery man ever had the chance to sink some cannons!"

Brookie stepped into the gunner's spot on one of his mountain twelve-pounders. "Let me aim this thing," he said. "Let's take him just as he comes into that turn where it narrows—both guns at once. Then reload quickly, my lads, and fire at the second raft as it comes into the same spot." He rubbed his hands together. "What a chance," he cried. "Now get ready, my boys."

The rafts continued to come. There seemed to be four of them. Andrew could see that each of the two leading rafts carried an artillery piece, about as many men as would compose a gun crew, and two spans of horses. He could see that the plans of the Union assault on Clearfield had been to get these guns up close in a hurry to fire on the town. A good plan, he thought, but we're here to stop them.

It seemed as if Sergeant Holbrook was waiting too long to give the command to fire, and Andrew was almost ready to himself order them to fire, when Brookie cried, "Fire!"

The cannons boomed, and before those rounds had landed, while they were still in flight, the gun crew was scrambling to swab out the barrel, reload it with powder and ball, and be ready for the next volley. At that moment, the first two shots landed—landed almost dead center on the leading raft. It was much too close to miss.

The raft split in half as a geyser of water shot up. The cannon on the raft slid into the water and sank, and immediately there were four horses in the water swimming in the current amidst the bobbing heads of the artillerymen and the floating logs breaking off the raft.

The men in the second raft had quickly divined what was in store for them, and Andrew saw several of them dive over the side before the rounds landed. The effect of these shots was equally dramatic, the cannon lumbering to the edge of the raft as it tilted and plunged into the water with a splash.

The men on the hilltop cheered and whistled. Sergeant Holbrook's grimy face was wreathed in smiles. He shook his head in sheer wonder at the spectacle. "It's a first, and probably a last," he declared.

The gun crews on the cannon on the hilltop had been somewhat slower in reloading amidst all the celebrating, but the need to be ready to fire was gone. The infantry men who crowded the decks of the remaining two rafts were taking no chances. They were going over the sides into the water in a hurry, so by the time these rafts reached the target point, they were empty. Andrew and Sergeant Holbrook decided not to waste any precious ammunition on the empty rafts.

Chapter 17

And so began perhaps the most hectic day of Andrew's life. From that time on, they were almost continually under some kind of attack. Some cannon shells landed on their position very quickly, causing more casualties for the aid station; and by noon they were driving back assaults by enemy forces, first on the south slope, then on the northeast slope; and finally, at times, assaults on both sides at once. Sergeant O'Donal's scouts rushed to reinforce various segments of the defensive line as they were threatened. More exposed than the men dug in behind some bulwarks, they began to take casualties until they were down to eight men, including the sergeant. The lookout in the crow's nest was wounded but refused to come down, even when Andrew ordered him to do so. "By God, sir, I'm staying," he told his commanding officer.

Andrew himself was exposed to considerable fire as he hurried to various elements of his command as the situation required it. Late in the afternoon, as a new threat faced the 1st Platoon defending the south slope, Andrew drew his revolver and called to O'Donal's scouts to follow him. "Come on, boys. One more time," he cried as he ran toward the action.

Heavy rifle fire was coming from the Union forces coming up the south slope. The return fire from 1st Platoon was steady, but subdued. The men had already been advised to make each shot count—the supplies of ammunition were running low.

As Andrew ran, he felt a blow to his right side and thought he had tripped over a log he was leaping over. He tumbled to the ground, but, rolling with his momentum, he came up on his feet and continued to lead the charge. It was only when the action was over, when the enemy had been driven back again, that, as he was attempting to holster his revolver, he became aware of the fact that the holster had been torn from his belt and that his right side and leg were covered with sticky blood.

"What's this?" Andrew asked, putting the revolver in his left hand and placing his right hand over the torn and bloodied clothes on his side. He still could not quite comprehend that he had been shot—could not quite remember when it had happened.

"Better let me have a look at that," said Sergeant O'Donal. He pushed Andrew to a seat on a log while he explored the wound.

Andrew, suddenly feeling quite light-headed, looked at the sergeant. "I think I'm all right, Sergeant," he said.

O'Donal paid him no heed. "Grant," he shouted to the mess sergeant. "Get me a long bandage—a towel or a shirt."

With surprisingly gentle hands, Sergeant O'Donal pulled Andrew's shirt out of the way and cleaned the wound as best he could. He wrapped the bandage snugly around Andrew's middle. "It may be mostly a flesh wound, Lieutenant," he said. "The ball came out the other side, and the blood is mostly bright red. I don't think it went into any organs."

"Uh huh," said Andrew groggily. "Just give me a minute to catch my breath." He pulled his ragged clothes over the bandaged wound and buckled his belt as tightly as he dared over it. Then he stood up on his feet and declared himself ready to carry on.

He looked at the officers and men gathered around him and smiled grimly. "Well, gentlemen," he said. "We still have the hilltop, and dusk is coming. I believe we'll get a little rest at dark."

Night came quickly under a cloudy sky. Lieutenant Greyson met with his officers and staff NCOs at Sergeant Grant's kitchen. Missing from the meeting was the executive officer, Lieutenant Taylor, who was at the aid station with a serious wound high in the chest. Lieutenant Meeks of the 1st Platoon had a bandaged shoulder, and his platoon sergeant was limping from a leg wound. The officers and sergeants were quiet in the darkness waiting for Andrew to speak.

"How many casualties have we taken?" Andrew asked Sergeant O'Donal.

"Twenty-three dead today," said the sergeant. "Another sixteen wounded to the aid station, and we've lost track of the wounded who go on fighting, like yourself, sir."

"All right," said Andrew. "We're still at almost two-thirds strength. No burials tomorrow. We'll put that off until the day after. I'm thinking that tomorrow we'll be very busy. Give as many of your men as you can a chance to sleep."

"Any chance of relief or reinforcements from the regiment?" asked Lieutenant Hadley.

"If we can hold out tomorrow," said Andrew, "I think we can look for something by evening or the next morning."

The officers and men nodded their heads grimly. They knew there was no way of knowing when help would come, or if it was even possible for help to get through.

"Another thing," said Andrew, "redistribute the ammunition within your own platoons. You've probably already done so, but if one man has twenty rounds and another has five, even it out. I'll count on you platoon sergeants to do that."

The sergeants nodded, and several said, "Yes, sir." Sergeant James, the 1st Platoon sergeant, said, "Some of my men are prying some of the Union balls out of trees and reshaping them with their knives to fit our rifles."

Andrew smiled at that. "Now that's the sort of attitude that will get us through this," he said. He looked at Sergeant Holbrook. "How is the artillery doing?"

"We've got one of the two damaged ones back in operation," said Brookie, "and the other one with the broken carriage will be operational by morning. We're building a ground mount for it. It won't be very mobile, but it will shoot where it's pointed at."

"Good work, Brookie," said Andrew. "I know you're running low on ammunition, too. Now as for where we use what we have, let's face three cannon down the south slope, two to the north slope, and keep one of the bigger ones pointed at the open field to the east. Throw a shell in there once in a while just to keep them guessing, especially if they start massing some troops in there. But your main job tomorrow will be to help us keep this hilltop. I think we can forget about any more raft attempts along the river. At any rate, we don't have the ammunition left to stop them there."

In the quiet darkness, Andrew sensed the mood of the men around him. They were quiet, but determined. Some were standing facing him; he could barely see their dim outlines in the darkness. Some few were sitting on convenient logs, and some were resting on one knee on the ground. Andrew himself was very tired and perhaps would have preferred to sit down, but he felt it was right to stand, showing his determination to go on with the fight.

Andrew sensed a movement in the darkness, heard a slight footstep to his right down the slope. "Who is it?" he asked.

"It's me, suh, Danny Clarkson." It was Private Clarkson coming toward the group with a strange, bulky, cumbersome pack silhouetted on his back. He came up to Andrew and swung the pack off his back, setting it on the ground. A clinking sound came from the pack.

"I brung Hattie to my ma, suh," Clarkson said. "He will get better now."

"How did you get in through our lines?" asked Andrew. "I didn't hear anyone challenge you."

"I come through quiet, suh," said Clarkson. "I didn' wanta' get shot. And I brung you somethin' that my ma says 'oud be good fer the wounded." He reached down into the pack and drew out an object. In the dim, almost no light, Andrew could see that it glinted like glass.

"It's whiskey, suh," said Clarkson. "Not ta' drink, but ta' pour on the wounds—fer a defectant."

"Whiskey?" Andrew said. "Disinfectant?"

"Yes, suh," said Clarkson. "My ma says to pour it on the wound, but put a clean cloth on it so it soaks fer a spell—mehbe a half hour. She says it kills the infection. I also brung as many clean cloths fer bandages as we had."

"I believe it may work," said Andrew, knowing that he was smiling. "I believe it will help. Sergeant Grant, take charge of this supply of disinfectant and see that it's properly administered to the wounded."

"Yes, sir," said Grant. "And one thing, sir. As soon as this meeting is over, I expect you down at the aid station so we can treat your wounds."

After a slight pause, Andrew said, "I'll be there, Sergeant." To Clarkson he said, "We're very grateful to your mother. We'll thank her when we can."

"Yes, suh," said Clarkson.

"We've got one more job for you tonight, Clarkson," said Andrew. "We're sending a detail for water down to the river. I'd like to have you guide them."

"I cin do thet, suh," said Clarkson.

"I know you can," said Andrew, "and we're counting on you. We're desperately in need of water. Sergeant O'Donal, get a detail of volunteers to go after the water—say eight men. Too many and I think they may be detected. If it goes well, we can go a second time."

"Yes, sir," said the sergeant. "There will be plenty of volunteers, figuring they'll get a good drink of water while they're down at the river."

"We best go now while it's darkest," said Clarkson. "In a bit the moon comes up."

"All right. See to it," said Andrew. "Good luck." The sergeant and the private moved off into the darkness. Andrew turned back to the assembled officers and men. "That will be all for tonight, gentlemen. See to whatever details you have to tonight, then get some rest. When the water arrives, we'll divide it fairly so each platoon gets a share. If you have any questions, I'll be at the aid station, and after that I'll get some rest."

The group dispersed quietly into the darkness.

Chapter 18

After getting his side wound treated with a whiskey poultice at the aid station—and he had to admit it felt better—Andrew found a place near Sergeant Grant's field kitchen where he could sit on a log and lean back against a tree. He leaned his head back against the tree and closed his eyes for a moment, slowly allowing the swirling thoughts in his mind to settle down.

He tried to think of other, less turbulent, aspects of his life: his life as an English professor at a college, his father who had died for the same cause for which he was now risking his life. Was this right? he thought. He let his mind go quiet for a time and thought, yes, I am where I belong, no matter the outcome.

And he thought of his wife, Anne. He tried to picture her as she was when he had left, and found he could hardly picture her face. He visualized himself telling her the story of what was happening here. It didn't seem real. She probably would not understand what was going on here and why he had to be here.

After a moment he opened his eyes and leaned forward. From a coat pocket he took a short candle and carefully lit the wick. In the quiet air it burned steadily, a small light in the dark night. Andrew took a note pad from the breast pocket of his coat and slowly began to write:

Dear Anne,

It is quite dark tonight with just a few stars beginning to show. The barest edge of the moon is just coming over the eastern horizon.

I have had a very busy few days, and they have made me consider what my life has been and what it could be in the future. Of course, at this time I am not sure if I will survive this conflict, but I must tell you

> *that I do not plan to return to you if I survive.*
>
> *I regret very much that we did not have any children. Perhaps they could have drawn us together. At any rate, I do not blame you, and I hope...*

Andrew' eyes closed as he leaned his head and shoulders back against the tree, and he slept. The note pad slipped from his hand to the ground. The small candle sputtered in its pool of wax and flickered out.

Sometime during the night Andrew was aware of someone standing near him. Without opening his eyes he said, "Is that you, Sergeant?"

"Yes, sir," said Sergeant O'Donal. "We've got some water, about two cups per man. I took the liberty, sir, of sending a second detail for more water after the first came back. They got through all right, but ran into a Union patrol. We got away in the dark, but I think they have beefed up their patrol down along the river's edge. I don't think we can get any more water."

"All right, Sergeant. You did well." Andrew opened his eyes finally to see the bulky shadow of his first sergeant near. There was enough moonlight now to make out his bearded face. The sergeant was holding a canteen cup toward him.

"You can probably use this," said the sergeant. "This is half your ration. Sergeant Grant has another cup for you when you wish."

"Thanks," said Andrew, reaching for the canteen cup of water. He hadn't realized how thirsty he was until the thought of drinking some water reminded him of it. He put the cup to his lips, then paused. "Have all the men got their rations?" he asked.

"Yes, sir," said Sergeant O'Donal. "They all had two cups, the same as you."

The water tasted of river and swamp, but it felt life-giving as he drank it. He drank slowly, holding the water in his mouth before he swallowed it. He emptied the cup and handed it back to O'Donal, and tried not to think of the second cup that he would have later. He felt somewhat feverish and supposed it was because of the wound in his side.

"Better get some rest, Sergeant," Andrew said. "We'll have a busy day tomorrow."

"Yes, sir, Lieutenant," said Sergeant O'Donal. He turned away. Andrew slid slowly off the log and curled up as warmly as he could with his back against the log. And he slept again.

Chapter 19

At first light, Lieutenant Greyson was up and walking around the perimeter of defense that circled the hilltop. At each platoon either the sergeant or the lieutenant walked with him. Many men on the line were still asleep in their positions, and Andrew thought, let them sleep. They'll wake up soon enough.

One of the men asked, "Are we gettin' any water today, Lieutenant?" and Andrew assured him there would be an attempt to get some that evening.

At the 1st Platoon positions Andrew motioned to a small rise above the rest of the hilltop just behind the positions of the men. He said to Lieutenant Meeks, "Put one of your sharpshooters up on that rise. He'll be shooting over the heads of the men in front of him, but he could get some effective shooting from there."

Lieutenant Meeks looked it over. "I think you're right, sir. I'll do it right away." He turned to his sergeant. "Put Jeb Stringer up there," he said. "See if you can get him a couple extra rounds of ammunition. Have him roll together a couple logs so he has something to shoot from."

The two lieutenants walked on together. "You think it's going to be rough today?" asked Meeks.

"Yes, I think so," said Andrew. "If they want to take Clearfield, they have to take this hilltop. They could do it by waiting us out, but they don't know that. Why they would want to take Clearfield, I don't know. Their real objectives are Fort Henry and Fort Donelson up north. Maybe they figure they've got our 11th Regiment isolated so why not eliminate us. But if it costs them too much in men, perhaps they would just leave us and join Buell's army up north."

As Andrew turned to go, he turned and shook Lieutenant Meeks' hand and said, "Good luck today. You've done a fine job with this platoon. They've taken the brunt of the attacks and done well. I'd move the 3rd Platoon in here, but your men know these positions"

"Thanks, sir," said Lieutenant Meeks. "I don't think my men would leave their positions now. They've gotten real proud of themselves and what they've done." The officers parted with a mutual wave of their hands.

Andrew headed for the aid station where the two tired volunteers were doing what they could for the wounded. The corporal came over to him and said, "I think this whiskey on the wounds works some, sir. At least it cleans them better than just water, and we haven't got any of that left."

Andrew nodded. "Good," he said. "I appreciate the work you and Private Coates are doing. Keep your rifles nearby in case things go badly today."

"Yes, sir," said the corporal.

At the company kitchen, Sergeant Grant greeted Andrew. "I've put together a hot grain porridge with what water we had. It's just moist enough to go down." He handed Andrew the cup of water that had been saved for him, and when Andrew made to pour the water in the kettle of porridge, Sergeant Grant quickly stepped in front of him. "No, sir," he said. "That water is for you. We all need you today, so drink it. And when you've got it down, I'm going to give your side wound another whiskey treatment."

Andrew drank his water and accepted the treatment of his wound. The side was stiff, and he had to carry his revolver on his left side in its ragged holster, but the wound did not seem to be infected. As he sat down on the log he noticed his note pad on the ground at his feet. He picked it up and thoughtfully tore off the front page and threw it in the fire. Then he put the notebook in his pocket.

Lieutenant Greyson stationed himself at the base of the lookout tree at the top of the hill. He reloaded the spent chambers of his revolver, carefully ramming each ball home and placing caps on the tips for the hammer to strike. As he worked, he talked to Private Calahan who was in the crow's nest above him. "Let me know the minute you see, or even hear something," said Andrew.

"If we have some warning, we may be able to shift our men to meet the attack."

"Aye, aye, sir," said Private Calahan.

"What was that?" asked Andrew.

"Oh, sorry, sir. I was in the Union Navy for a spell. I guess sittin' up here in the crow's nest 'minded me of that."

"I imagine right now you wish you were back in the navy," said Andrew.

"No, sir," said Private Calahan. "When someone is shootin' at me, I like to dig a hole in the ground, and you can't do that on a ship."

"That's true," said Andrew, and thought, you can't dig a hole when you're up in a tree either.

"I'll keep a good watch," said Private Calahan.

The first attack took them by surprise. A bullet whizzed by Andrew and struck the tree over his head with a thud. A dozen or so Union soldiers were clambering over the steep brow of the hill above the river, a difficult spot where Andrew had not expected an attack and had not used any of his men to guard.

"Get that officer in that tree!" shouted a Union soldier, and shots struck the tree all around Private Calahan, who flattened himself sideways behind the trunk of the tree.

"I'm no officer, damn ya'," he screamed and angrily fired back. Andrew carefully aimed and fired his newly loaded revolver, and, indeed, the Union foray lasted only minutes as F Company lines on both sides of the hill were able to fire directly at them. Andrew knelt down behind the tree so that he would not be in the line of fire from his own men. The raid was quickly over. The enemy fled, leaving behind a number of wounded.

"Are you all right up there, Calahan?" asked Andrew.

"Yes, sir," said Private Calahan. "Damn them. They thought I was an officer." He fumed on about ignorant Yankee soldiers as he reloaded his muzzle-loading rifle. Below him, Andrew was again loading his revolver.

A drop of red blood fell on Andrew's hand, and he looked up. "You're wounded up there," he said.

"No, sir, just a touch," said Calahan.

"You better come down. I'll get a replacement for you," Andrew said.

"No, sir," said Calahan emphatically. "I'm not coming down, sir. It's just a touch on my arm. One of them damn Yankees got a lucky shot at me."

Lieutenant Greyson looked Private Calahan over, and Private Calahan glared back at him. "All right," said Andrew. "If you can do the job, stay up there."

Mollified Private Calahan said, "Yes, sir," but he couldn't resist muttering, "Lousy shots. Ever' one of 'em had a shot at me—me up in a tree, fer Cripe's sakes, an' they couldn't hit me. This ain't nothin'," he said as he was wrapping a large handkerchief around his upper arm. "You really can't call this a hit. It ain't nothin'."

Andrew reloaded his revolver, thinking as he did so of the shortage of ammunition that his men had. Another few raids like that, he thought, and we will be down to bayonets. At what point do I surrender and try to save lives? he thought. And was there any hope of help from the regiment? With little food, no water, and limited ammunition, we can't last much longer.

"Keep a watch up there, Calahan, and shout out the minute you see or hear anything. I'm going to check the lines, but call out and I'll hear you."

"Aye, aye, sir," said Private Calahan.

Andrew walked the perimeter of his defense, encouraging the men as he went. "If they want this hill, make them pay," he said. "Make every shot count. This is Tennessee land," he said. "This is our home. Let's fight for it."

He felt strangely light-headed as he walked. He hoped he was not feverish from his wound, and thought, more likely it was from lack of water. Or perhaps it was from the exhilaration of the moment. As he went by the flag tree, he lowered his saber from its height and strapped it around his waist. "I may need this," he said to Sergeant Grant. Sergeant Grant nodded grimly.

A shout from the lookout. "Lieutenant! Sir! I can hear people down the south hill. Lots of 'em!"

"All right, Calahan. Now do you hear anything from the north?" Andrew asked.

Calahan turned and concentrated on listening in that direction. "No, sir," he shouted. "They're all down the south side, sir."

Lieutenant Greyson made a quick decision, one that he hoped was the right one and one that he hoped he would not regret. He hurried to the 2nd Platoon line on the north side of the hill. To Lieutenant Hadley he said, "Get half of your men over to back up the 1st Platoon on the south side. They're coming up that side now, and I think we can make it hot for them."

"Yes, sir," said Lieutenant Hadley, and he quickly counted off every other man and rushed them to the south side. Andrew followed, realizing that if he were wrong—if the enemy also came up the north side, the company was doomed.

"Brookie, have you got your guns loaded with canister?" he called.

"That I have, Lieutenant," called Sergeant Holbrook.

"All right," answered Andrew. "Fire when you have proper targets. Use your judgement. This won't be the last attack today."

"My Napoleons are ready," said Sergeant Holbrook, patting the gun beside which he was standing. He seemed quite cheerful.

"Here they come!" shouted Private Calahan up in the tree.

Lieutenant Greyson was walking back and forth behind his line of men, his saber in his right hand. He was about to say, hold your fire, men, when a shot rang out from the far end of the line. There was a moment's silence, then a nervous, young voice called out, "That was me, sir. Sorry, sir."

"That's all right, son," Andrew called back. "Just reload and make the next one count."

"Yes, sir," the boy's voice called back.

A thin line of skirmishers was just showing through the trees. The main attack, Andrew knew, would be about a hundred yards behind them. "Hold your fire, men, until you have a good target. Then make your shots count." To Sergeant Holbrook and the artillery he said, "Don't waste your ammo on this skirmish line. Wait for the main attack." And to Sergeant O'Donal he said, "Keep an eye on the guns. We don't want those taken."

"Yes, sir," said the sergeant. His group of scouts was down to seven men, but they still remained an effective force.

And the battle was on.

Chapter 20

The first line of Union skirmishers was quickly stopped by the disciplined fire that F Company fired from behind their improvised bulwarks. The main attack carried almost to the Confederate line, stopped finally by the accurate shooting of the Southern hill country men who had been shooting since they were young; and by the devastating canister shot of Holbrook's Napoleon twelve-pounders. One gun, in particular, Holbrook had placed slightly forward of the line, and had turned so it fired along the front of the line; and it proved especially effective. So much so, that a detachment of Union soldiers made directly for it with the intent of capturing it, but they were beaten back by a charge of O'Donal's scouts.

There was a lull. In the almost ear-ringing silence, F Company looked around, almost surprised to find itself still alive. There were wounded and dead, but they had fought back a determined attack by a force that clearly outnumbered them. They reloaded their guns and tried not to think of how thirsty they were. "That'll show 'em," they said. "We showed 'em how to shoot, by Gol."

Andrew walked the line with Lieutenant Meeks at his side, shifting some men around to fill any gaps. To Lieutenant Schyler of the 3rd Platoon, he said, "This end of your line got into the shooting, but be ready to bring your other end over this way if the Yankees come up the same slope—and I think they will. They think they've given us enough casualties here to weaken us. I think somebody down there has got an order to take this hill no matter how many casualties they take, and we've got to make it hot for them."

"Yes, sir," said Lieutenant Schyler. He sat down suddenly on a nearby log, and Andrew realized he was shaking.

"I don't know if I can do this," said Lieutenant Schyler. He put his hands over his face and shook his head.

Andrew looked at him quietly for a moment. "Okay," he said. "We're all scared—some more than others. It's nothing to be ashamed of. But we're here and you've got forty men and boys counting on you. They are looking to you, and they need you to tell them what to do. They are good men who believe in what they are doing. Show them you believe in them." Andrew paused and looked Lieutenant Schyler in the eyes. "Think you can do that?"

Schyler took a deep breath. "Yes, sir, I think I can."

"All right," said Andrew. He shook Lieutenant Schyler's hand. "After this is over, we'll have a drink together."

As Andrew came by the end of the 1st Platoon's line, he asked about Jeremy Nathan, the boy who had fired the early shot. He found the boy sitting with his back to a tree, his long rifle across his knees. "Are you all right?" asked Andrew.

"A'hm all right," said Jeremy. "But my best pal ain't." He pointed to a blanket-covered figure laid behind a log. "Me and him jined together." He was serious—a boy that had suddenly grown old.

Andrew wished he could say the right words. "I'm sorry," he said.

"A'hm all right," repeated Jeremy, "but my best pal ain't."

Andrew looked to an old veteran that was on the line beside Jeremy. The veteran jerked his thumb at the boy. "He's a cool one," he said. "He took his shots right along with the rest of us, never flinched." He nodded his head. "I'll look after him, sir."

Out in front of the lines, among the trees and brush where Union soldiers had fallen, were a number of Confederate soldiers. Andrew knew what they were doing—looking for canteens of water and for ammunition. In some cases they were bringing back the rifles and ammunition of the fallen soldiers, and they were gleefully waving aloft the few canteens of water.

"Make sure that water is shared," said Andrew to Lieutenant Meeks.

Lieutenant Meeks nodded. "I've got my sergeants in control of it," he said. "They've got instructions to drop everything and come back to the lines as soon as anything begins to happen."

A furious fusillade of shots interrupted them on the north side of the hill. Andrew ran toward the shots. "Keep your men in line there until we find out what we have here," he shouted back to Lieutenant Meeks. "Come on," he called to Sergeant O'Donal's scouts, but they were already running with him.

The number of shots was already dying down, and O'Donal's men were only able to get off a few shots at the retreating force, disappearing in the trees.

"I believe it was just a small raiding party," said Lieutenant Hadley to Andrew. "The trees are so thick they were close in before we realized they were there. My men did well." He looked proudly down the line where his soldiers, realizing the immediate action was over, were laughing and calling back and forth. They had taken no casualties.

"You're right. They did well," said Andrew. "I agree with you that it was a small raid. The terrain on this side is too rugged for large numbers of troops. I think we'll be getting another large attack on the south side soon, and we'll count on your men here to keep any surprise party off our backs."

"Right," said Lieutenant Hadley.

Andrew passed under the lookout tree on his way back to the south slope. "Any sign of anything yet, Calahan?" he asked. He noticed that Calahan had a bandage on his head now, besides the one on his arm. "You're hurt, Calahan?"

"Naw," retorted Calahan. "Them Yankees are the worst shots I ever seen. These are just nicks. They ain't really hits. Jeez, I'm up here in a tree and they can't even hit me."

Andrew waited. "You know, sir," said Calahan, looking through the field glasses, "I think they're startin' to get together at the bottom of the hill. I cin see some flags down there. But there's also somethin' goin' on towards town. I don't know if it's them or us."

"We could use a little help from the regiment," said Andrew.

"I hope they bring water," said Calahan. "We cin take care of these damn Yankees by ourselves, but I could sure use a drink of water."

Calahan was studying the bottom of the hill through the glasses. "Here they come," he said grimly. "Here they come agin', sir."

"All right," said Andrew. "Take care of yourself up there." He hurried off for the line. Sergeant Holbrook looked up expectantly. "They're on the way," Andrew said. "You and your men have done great, Brookie. Help us out again."

"It's been a pleasure, sir," said the sergeant.

"Your men all back from in front of the line?" Andrew asked Lieutenant Meeks.

"Yes, and we're ready," replied the lieutenant.

The line of blue-uniformed skirmishers came up the hill. Andrew was surprised that they continued to send skirmishers up when they already knew where the Confederate lines were. It's a waste of men, thought Andrew. Nevertheless, the skirmishers came up and broke into a running charge as they got near.

"Stand your ground," shouted Andrew, as the sight of the charging soldiers was unnerving. "Now, fire!"

Some of the skirmishers made it almost to the Confederate bulwarks before they were cut down, or veered off, running for the cover of the trees to the sides. At the point between the 3rd and the 1st Platoons a half dozen Union soldiers broke though the line. O'Donal's scouts again were able to anticipate the break and were there to drive them back. It had been a close-in battle with bayonets and empty rifles used as clubs.

"Where's Jeremy?" asked Andrew, looking around quickly. He knew there wasn't much time before the main attack. Then he saw Jeremy lying beside the blanket-covered figure of his "best pal." Jeremy's eyes were closed, but he opened them when he heard Lieutenant Greyson's voice asking for him.

"I done my best," Jeremy said weakly, and he closed his eyes.

"I'm sure you did," said Andrew and walked over, kneeled down, and put his hand on Jeremy's head. "Rest easy, now," he said.

Chapter 21

From the line Andrew heard shouts of "They're acomin'," and "Tarnation, but there's lots of 'em!" Indeed it seemed a relentless sea of blue was moving toward them up the south slope. They seemed to flow around the trees and other obstacles like a stream. Here and there, sabers flashed in the sun as officers, some mounted on horseback, encouraged their troops forward. Bright guidon flags waved aloft on poles. "They's too many," said a veteran in front of Andrew. The line of Confederate soldiers fell silent as they sensed their fate moving up the hillside to meet them.

The Union troops were perhaps a hundred yards away. Already their shouts and cries could be heard. And then came the shouted commands from the officers, "Double time, double time," and the mass of attacking troops broke into a running charge up the hill.

Andrew's heart quailed within him, but he knew it was disastrous for his troops to run. With a shout, he vaulted over the logs in front of the men, and raising his saber above his head, he walked back and forth in front of the line exhorting his men. "Stand fast, men. Stand fast. Pick your targets carefully, men. We can stop them. Just hold your ground."

By now some shots were coming up the hill, and Andrew felt one bullet pluck at his sleeve. It was time for F Company to fire back, and he was in their line of fire. With a flourish, he raised his saber once more, and bringing in down, point down, he drove it into the ground. "F Company!" he shouted. "No enemy comes beyond this sword. This is where we stand!"

Andrew leaped back over the logs, and F Company rose as one man to greet him. Waving their rifles in the air, they shouted and screamed. Rebel yells split the air. "Fire when ready!" shouted Andrew, and at that moment Sergeant Holbrook's twelve-pounders roared. The battle was joined.

Most of the Confederate soldiers had more than one rifle, the extras being either the rifle of a fallen comrade, or a captured enemy rifle. These rifles were all loaded and placed within reach. Andrew was glad to see his men, for the most part, calmly taking aim and firing; then picking up the spare rifle to continue the fire fight. The smoke and roar of the cannon fire, the cracks of the rifle shots, and the shouts of the men made the scene seem like something from another world. The first wave of attackers were repulsed, and then the second wave was stopped. But when Andrew saw the third wave advancing through the din and smoke, he called to Lieutenant Hadley on the north side of the hill. "Bring your men up here on the double, Hadley! We'll have to take a chance and leave that side open."

When Lieutenant Hadley and about twenty men joined Andrew near the top of the hill, Andrew quickly divided them into two teams. "I'll take one team. You take the other," he said to Lieutenant Hadley. "Watch for where they might break through our lines and rush in to stop the gap."

"Yes, sir," gasped Lieutenant Hadley, panting from being out of breath and from the excitement.

At that moment the line of attackers appeared out of the smoke, and the rifle fire increased. To one side the cannons roared, and Andrew, seeing a formation of enemy nearing the guns, said, "Follow me, men." With revolver in hand, Andrew led the rush down to join O'Donal's scouts, now down to four men, in defending the guns.

"Continue to fire the cannons," shouted Andrew to Sergeant Holbrook. "We've got to keep them firing. We'll take care of these bushwhackers coming in."

"All right, Lieutenant," Brookie said, calmly continuing to direct the loading and firing of his cannon in the midst of bullets whizzing by him. "Fire!" he shouted and two cannons roared, sending deadly canister grape shot into the enemy ranks. "Load!" was the next command. "Ready!" and "Fire!" More shot on the way.

Andrew saw some blue-coated soldiers coming toward them from the side through the drifting smoke. "All right, men," he shouted. "Aim and fire." He carefully fired five successive shots from his revolver, holding back on the sixth one, knowing it was his last shot until there was opportunity to reload.

The rifle fire from his own men beside him was steady and relentless. Most of the blue soldiers coming toward them ran for cover. The few that did not were cut down by the accurate firing of Andrew's men. In the excitement of the moment, it did not seem real to Andrew that they were killing human beings.

The enemy foray on the guns had been thwarted. "Stay here with the artillery," Andrew told the men he had brought. "You're in charge, Corporal. Defend these guns."

"Yes, sir," said the corporal, a bespectacled young man. "We'll hold 'em, sar."

"How's the ammo holding out, Brookie?" asked Andrew.

"I'm down to a half dozen canister shells, and then I'll use ball or shell, whatever I've got," replied Sergeant Holbrook. "It's not as effective, but maybe it will scare them." He laughed shortly. "It's been a good shoot."

Andrew ran for the section of the line where the fighting seemed to be the heaviest. A point of trees and brush ran close to the Confederate line and here a group of Union soldiers had established themselves and were putting deadly fire into the defenders. Lieutenant Hadley's section was already backing up that part of the line, but bullets were pouring in, pinning down the Confederate soldiers behind the logs.

Something had to be done, realized Andrew, or the entire defense could collapse. "Come on!" he shouted to Lieutenant Hadley, "Bring your men."

They followed Andrew as he led them to one of the mountain howitzer cannons that they had brought up the hill on mule back. "We're going to manhandle this gun and aim it at that point of trees," Andrew told the gun crew. "What sort of ammunition have you got?"

"We're out of canister, but we've got a dozen time-fused shells," said the gun corporal.

A dozen men turned the gun in the direction indicated by Lieutenant Greyson. At that point the gun corporal took over and aimed the gun. "Load!" he shouted. One of the loaders, carrying the shell, grunted, sank to his knees, but carefully handed the shell to his partner before he clutched his shoulder, a red stain spreading through his shirt.

"Don't wait for me," he said to no one in particular as he crawled out from in front of the gun.

"Fire!" ordered the gun corporal, and the gun leaped back as the first shell was on the way. The shell exploded on target. Andrew saw a tree crumple to the ground from the impact.

"Right on," said Andrew. "Give them more of the same." The rifle fire from that point of trees stopped at once as the riflemen there realized they were under artillery fire. "Send five more shells in there, then keep the gun aimed there, and be ready to fire if necessary," Andrew ordered.

"Yes, sir," said the gun corporal. "Load...Ready...Fire!" Another shell was on its way.

Lieutenant Greyson walked to the approximate center of his line of soldiers, trying as he went to see through the gunpowder smoke, trying to determine how the battle was going. Behind him the cannon fired four more shots; then after a pause, fired twice more. To Andrew's right front the guns of Sergeant Holbrook roared in unison, then fell silent. All up and down the line the rifle fire sputtered, and died down. There was only an occasional shot from the far end of the line, and that, too, fell silent.

An erie silence fell over the battleground. The smoke from the cannons firing and from the rifles of both sides hung low over the ground like a gray ceiling. Down the slope where the rifles of the Union soldiers had been firing, eddies of smoke drifted through the trees. The trees directly in front of the Confederate line had been blasted by cannon fire, and branches and trunks hung crazily to the ground.

Most of the soldiers of F Company stayed lying on the ground, still in the positions from which they had been firing. Slowly they stirred, but they did not look directly at each other. There was no celebrating. Each of them had been afraid during these times, but had stood his ground—had not run, either because of a sense of loyalty to his fellow soldier, or because of a fear of being called a coward, or because some strange mixture of fear and courage that could not be explained.

None of them had, at this moment of trial, thought or remembered that he was doing this for a cause or for a country. They had found themselves on a little hilltop in Tennessee with a rifle in their hands, with an enemy charging up the hill at them; and they had met the test of what a man does when he is faced with likely death. All their lives would be changed by what had happened on that hilltop that morning.

Slowly they got up from the ground, and they remembered their wounded and dying comrades. They tried to help them, to make them comfortable, gave them the little water that was salvaged from captured canteens to drink. There was no more room at the aid station. The wounded were carefully helped to a hollow spot on the ground, or behind a log. The dead were carried back from the lines and laid out in rows, in as dignified a manner as possible.

Chapter 22

Andrew toured the line again. At the southeast end of the line, where 3rd Platoon had doubled up their men to stop the Union charge, Andrew found Lieutenant Schyler dead.

"He led the charge against the breakthrough," said Sergeant Reiners, the 3rd Platoon sergeant. "We followed him. He's the bravest man I've ever seen."

"Yes, he was," said Andrew. "He was a brave man. You're in charge of the 3rd Platoon, Sergeant."

The 1st Platoon in the middle of the line had taken many casualties. "I've got less that half left," said Lieutenant Meeks. "And that's counting the walking wounded." Meeks did not ask what he had been thinking. How are we going to stop another Union attack?

Lieutenant Hadley's 2nd Platoon, who had missed most of the first attacks because they were on the north side of the hill, had more than made up for that lack of action. Because they had been moving around during the battle, not behind some sort of fortifications, their losses were almost as heavy as 1st Platoon's.

"Send two men back to the north side as a listening post," said Andrew to Lieutenant Hadley. "Their job is to let us know if anyone is coming up that side."

"Yes, sir," said Lieutenant Hadley. He did not ask what he was thinking. What are we to do if an attack comes up that side?

"Integrate the remainder of your men with the 1st Platoon on the line here," said Andrew.

At the west end of the line Lieutenant Greyson talked to Sergeant Holbrook. "What have you got left in ammunition?" asked Andrew.

For once Brookie was subdued. "We've got six rounds left between these four guns," he said. "And it's all solid cannon balls. I understand the mountain howitzers up there have four rounds left. That's all we've got." Brookie threw out his hands. "I'd have the men scoop up rocks and fire them out of the cannons, but we don't have any powder either."

Sergeant O'Donal met Andrew as he walked up the hill. "I haven't been able to keep an accurate list of the dead," he said. "I've got my men out now getting as many names as we can before the next attack. I'm down to three men plus myself."

As they walked under the lookout tree, Andrew looked up. "Calahan's dead," said Sergeant O'Donal. "He wouldn't come down even when he knew he was finished. Had to send a man up there to get him, and he had tied himself up there."

Andrew nodded. "That sounds like Calahan," he said.

"Shall I put a replacement up there?" asked the sergeant.

Andrew paused. "No," he said. "We'll know when they're coming."

They were greeted by a weary Sergeant Grant at his kitchen. Wounded men were everywhere, wherever there was a level spot for them to lie. Sergeant Grant shook his head. "There's a lot of brave boys here," he said.

"I know," said Andrew. He went from man to man among the wounded, touching a hand here, calling as many of them as he could by name. "You did a finc job today," he said. "We're very proud of you."

On his way out, Andrew drew Sergeant Grant aside. In a low voice he said, "Sergeant, we may need a white flag. Have you got anything here that would do?"

Sergeant Grant looked around. "We've used everything for bandages. No, wait. There's my apron. Not very white anymore, and with some blood on it. But perhaps that is appropriate. All right, Lieutenant, I'll tie it to a pole of some sort and bring it down to you."

"Thanks, Sergeant," said Andrew. He shook his head sadly. "We may have gone as long as we can. It may be that from here on it would be a waste of life." He headed back toward the center of the line.

As he came near the line, one of the soldiers came up to him. "Here's your sword, Lieutenant. It's got a nick or two from bullets, but it stood right there through the whole fight. One of them Yankees was just ready to grab it when I got him. I wasn't going to let them get your sword, sir."

"Thanks very much," said Andrew, accepting the saber. He looked at it, but he didn't really see it. He was still trying to come to grips with the question of surrender. Was it something that was put up for a vote? And the majority rules? Or was it something he had to decide on his own? Or was it something that just happens because it is inevitable? The fact that he had thought of getting a surrender flag ready showed that he had already accepted the possibility of it. But would these proud Southern volunteer soldiers accept it? Andrew looked up and down the line of defense. F Company was getting ready for the next attack. Here and there men were improving the fortifications in front of them. Some soldiers were loading their rifles and carefully setting them within reach. Sergeant Holbrook had removed the twelve-pound cannon balls from his ammunition, and, using the powder left, he was preparing to fire a bag of rocks placed in the tubes of the cannons on top of the powder. The soldiers looked purposeful and confident.

How can we surrender ground that we have paid such a dear price for? thought Andrew. Or have we already completed our mission by diverting attacks from the town and by inflicting the casualties that we did? All we can do is be prepared and see what develops. Perhaps I won't have to make such a decision, thought Andrew.

The cloudy, foggy morning had turned into a bright, clear midday. There was still no sign of rescue by their home regiment, and slowly all hope of such an occurrence was abandoned. F Company would have to survive on its own, and it felt a fierce pride in itself. "The hell with the regiment," they said. "We don't need them. We'll take care of the whole damn Union Army."

They knew, after seeing how many troops had attacked up the hill toward them, that it didn't make much sense for the regiment to risk its troops to rescue the one lost company on the hilltop. It was tough, but that's the way it is sometimes. After all, this was war.

Early in the afternoon, movement was seen down in the valley in front of the south slope, and it soon became apparent that this was the biggest attack yet. Rank upon rank of infantry was coming up the hill toward the embattled F Company. This time there were no skirmishers, just a mass of blue coming toward them.

Lieutenant Greyson and the men of F Company who had survived should have felt helpless and overwhelmed by this force that was set out to destroy them. But strangely they were not. Instead, a recklessness seemed to take hold of them. First there were catcalls from the ends of the lines, then wild rebel yells as individuals leaped to their feet, waving their rifles over their heads, daring the attackers to come closer. "You bring enuf' this time?" they called. "Hell, we eats this many for breakfast."

Some of the soldiers got up on the mounds of dirt and logs in front of them and danced a jig to show how unimpressed they were by the oncoming horde. So far, neither side had fired a shot.

Andrew found himself carried along with his men in this spirit of wild abandonment. He shouted with the rest, and with a strange sensation of watching himself from outside himself, he vaulted over the log fortifications and stood defiantly in the open.

"Come on up," he yelled. "You'll meet the best company of fighting men in the world."

"Yah!" the men cheered.

"If you don't come up, we'll have to come down and get you," shouted Andrew.

"Yah!" cheered F Company.

A ragged volley of shots spattered against the bulwarks and trees in front of F Company, bringing a fresh chorus of hoots and catcalls. "My, my, they is getting just a little peeved," the soldiers said. "Look at all them purty soljers. Does you suppose they lets them carry real guns!"

F Company had not fired a shot. The range was a bit too long to be effective, and they did not have bullets to spare. Another spattering of bullets was fired from the advancing ranks, and Andrew, fearing some of his soldiers would waste ammunition, called out, "Hold your fire, men. We'll have plenty of shooting when they get closer."

He was about to turn and climb back over the row of fortifications when he saw a curious happening in the Union troops below him. Several horsemen were riding at a gallop from the rear, and

Andrew realized they must be officers in control of their troops and not some additional threat to his men. However, the riders were waving their arms and shouting something to their troops, who had stopped and were watching the riders, seemingly perplexed by the happenings.

Finally Andrew could make out what the officers were shouting. "Break off!" they were ordering their men. "Turn back!"

The blue-coated troops milled about, more disorganized in retreat than in attack. One disgruntled soldier fired a last, random shot up the hill before he shouldered his weapon and turned with the rest. Slowly the mass of soldiers diminished as they made their way down the hill.

F Company watched and puzzled. What sort of maneuver was this? They stood up on their fortifications and some of the artillery men stood up on their guns to get a better view. Sergeant O'Donal climbed up the ladder of the lookout tree—Calahan's domain—and scanned the lower valleys with the field glasses. There was no doubt; the enemy was leaving the field of battle.

"They're leaving the staging area," reported Sergeant O'Donal. "They're heading north up the road at quick time."

"Any sign of our regiment after them?" asked Andrew.

"No," said O'Donal. He swung the glasses northward up the valley. "They're really pulling out, Lieutenant. They're not just leaving this field. They're leaving the country."

"I'll be damned," said Andrew.

It was late afternoon before elements of the 11th Regiment came up the hill to find F Company still dazed, not only, perhaps, by the developments of the last few hours; but also by the events of the past few days. F Company hadn't done much since the Union Army elements had left the battlefield on the south slope of the Little Hilltop. The soldiers had gotten some water from canteens that hadn't been picked up previously. They had tried to make their own wounded more comfortable, and they had made a weak attempt to bury their dead. But they were out of energy—they were burned out. When the relieving units from the 11th Regiment brought water and took over the task of caring for wounded and burying the dead, F Company was relieved to step aside and watch.

Andrew was exhausted. He found a suitable log to sit on and leaned back against a tree. He sipped slowly from a canteen cup of water and willed his mind to stop thinking. Vivid flashes of some of the happenings of the recent days flickered through his mind. He tried not to think about whether he had made the right decisions at crucial times during these last days.

"You all right, Lieutenant?" It was Sergeant Grant, himself, looking haggard, but sympathetic.

"Yes, I think so, Sergeant. I hope I did the right thing for these men." Andrew shook his head slowly. "They are the bravest of men."

"You needn't doubt yourself, Lieutenant," said the sergeant. "You did right by them. They'll tell the story of this battle for the rest of their lives, and when they mention you—and they will—they will speak of you with respect and admiration."

"Well, yes," said Andrew, standing up and stretching tired muscles, "but there's things to be done here, and besides, I look rather silly wearing both a saber and a revolver on my left side."

An army private came up the slope leading a saddled horse. "Are you Lieutenant Greyson?" he asked, saluting.

"I am," said Andrew, returning the salute.

"Sir," said the private, "Colonel Biddell sent the horse so you could ride back to Clearfield."

"That's a fine-looking horse," said Andrew, "and I appreciate the colonel's consideration, but I am walking back to Clearfield with my men."

A Digression into the Future
The United States Military Academy
West Point, New York 1872

Andrew Greyson attended the reunion of his graduating class at West Point. It was twenty years since they had marched across the parade field, the Plain, at the academy, and then come front and center to receive their diplomas and their commissions as second lieutenants in the United States Army. Their commissioning papers, signed by the President of the United States, declared them to be "an Officer and a Gentleman."

Andrew had graduated in the middle ranking of his class, and was known more for his spurts of brilliance rather than steady persistence. He played wing on the lacrosse team, and though he had not played the sport before he entered the academy, he was a natural for the game and was the team's leading scorer his junior and senior years.

He had grown up with horses and rode well; and would have chosen the cavalry as his branch of service, but all the billets for cavalry were taken by the time his ranking number came up, so he became an infantry officer when he left the academy.

Andrew had known almost from the beginning that he would not make the army his career, but that choice had been taken away from him as the army scaled down its size in the post-Mexican War years.

Now sitting at a table in the Officer's Club on post with old classmates, Andrew realized that only two of his former circle of friends from academy days were still in uniform. Promotions being slow after the War Between the States, both wore the gold oak leaves of a major on their collars.

"You were in the Confederate Army?" asked Thompson, now an attorney in New York City.

"That's right," replied Andrew easily. He was the only graduate from his company that had served in the Confederate cause, but any harsh feeling had long been put aside. Andrew thought that sometimes, though people talked about loyalty to country, perhaps loyalty to the long, gray line of the West Point Military Academy was as strong as, or perhaps even stronger than, loyalty to country. At any rate, this particular reunion had been specifically planned to ease any resentments left over from graduates fighting on opposite sides during the war.

"Greyson, I understand you were at the Little Hilltop battle in Tennessee." It was one of the majors speaking.

"I was there," said Andrew.

"You mean we might have been shooting at each other?" said Jim Michaels from the end of the table. "I was there with the 33rd Ohio Infantry."

"And I was there, too," said the other uniformed major, Tom Chaney. "We heard afterward that you were in command up on that hill. I didn't realize you were so short of officers that you had captains commanding battalions."

"I was a lieutenant at the time," said Andrew.

"My word!" exclaimed Chaney. "Lieutenants commanding battalions! And we knew you had artillery up there, and reinforcements from the 11th Tennessee Regiment."

Andrew smiled. He was glad there was no longer any animosity between them. They could share these experiences of the war, and with participants from both sides present, perhaps gain a more objective view of those happenings. Even Allens, half way down the table, with an empty right sleeve, looked interested.

"Actually," said Andrew, "that was just a company up there, F Company of the 11th Tennessee Volunteer Regiment. About a hundred and fifty men. We packed up two mountain howitzer cannons, and, of course, we captured some of your Napoleons already up there."

"Now wait a minute," said Chaney. "We sent two regimental attacks up that hill. You mean to say you stopped us with just a company? How did you have your troops deployed?"

And suddenly they were all back in tactics class at the academy, trying to solve the ever challenging problems of deploying forces on an imaginary battlefield. Except that this one was not imaginary. It had actually happened. And some of those present now, had been present then. Very quickly the tablecloth became a map as Andrew and Chaney sketched in the features of the Little Hilltop terrain. The men at the table stood up and crowded around, each seeing in his own mind the battle. Men from other tables came to see what was going on and stayed to offer their opinions.

"Cadet Greyson, I see you are still causing turmoil wherever you are." An older gentleman in the uniform of a full colonel was standing at Andrew's elbow.

Andrew turned. "Professor Howell, sir." He wasn't sure if he should salute or shake hands, but the professor settled that by putting out his hand. They shook hands warmly.

"I heard rumors about what you did there in Tennessee, and even though you were wearing another uniform, I was proud of having been your teacher," said Colonel Howell.

At that point the other once-cadets noticed the presence of their past teacher among them. "Good evening, sir," and "Would you join us, sir," and "This is like old times, sir. Would you critique the tactics used at this Little Hilltop battle, sir?"

Another pitcher of ale was delivered to the table, along with fresh glasses for the newcomers. More officers from other tables crowded around. The tablecloth with the sketched map was removed from the table and pinned to the wall so all could see.

"Now, Cadet Greyson, would you mark in the locations of your defensive lines and your artillery?" said Professor Howell.

"Yes, sir," said Andrew and marked in each platoon of F Company and the cannons. He had always been a careful draftsman, and his marks were neat and precise. He marked in his lookout tree, the aid station, and the company kitchen.

"Why are these two cannon facing the river?" asked the professor. He had picked up a large serving spoon and was using it as a pointer.

"Well, sir," said Andrew, "our intelligence had reported large rafts being built up river, so we took the precaution of placing two of our six cannons there. I might add, sir, that I had a sergeant that was an artillery expert. He managed to sink two rafts with artillery and horses on them."

"Damn you, Greyson," came a good-natured voice from the back of the crowd. "Those were my guns you sank." Amid the laughter the voice added, "I'm happy to report we lost no horses, and the men needed baths rather badly." More laughter.

Another voice, that of Thompson the attorney from New York, spoke up. "What I want to know is, how did you get to the hilltop in the first place? We found some mule tracks along the stream, but how did you get a battalion of troops up there?"

Professor Howell handed the pointer-spoon to Andrew, who traced the route of F Company's night march. "My sergeant and I did a reconnaissance of it a couple nights prior, along with the help of two local boys who knew the area well." Andrew smiled at the memory of Clarkson and Hatfield. "We swung all the way around, came down from the hills along this stream, and up the back side of the Little Hilltop."

"Right through our camps?" This was not a question from the speaker, but rather an exclamation.

"It seems to me this is similar to an escapade you pulled while you were a cadet here," said Professor Howell. He shook his head. "I should have let them expel you then. I told them you were a creative tactician and you would do great things some day. Course, I didn't say for whose side." He smiled.

"And you stopped our division with a company," Major Chaney said with grudging respect. "I can tell you, you got General McCarron so upset, we'd be there today still trying to take that hill if we hadn't gotten orders from Grant."

"What's that?" said Andrew. "Orders from Grant? Is that why you left the battlefield that third day?"

"Absolutely," responded Chaney. "That was actually the second order from Grant that stopped us. The first one was a suggestion that Clearfield was not of strategic importance, and the second one was a direct order to get our division to Fort Donelson as soon as possible. McCarron finally took the hint. We rode out in front of the troops to turn them around."

Andrew sighed. In his mind he saw the scene again, and felt the mixed emotions of the day. "I know," he said. "I don't mind telling you how relieved we were to see you break off. We could not have stopped you again." He paused. "I had a white flag ready."

There was a moment of silence from the men in the room as they looked at Andrew and began to get a sense of what had happened on the Little Hilltop in Tennessee about ten years ago.

Andrew cleared his throat. "Gentlemen," he said as he raised his glass of ale. "You will do me a great honor if you will drink to the courage of the men of F Company and to the fine quality of the Southern soldier."

And at West Point, New York, ten years after the war had ended, men of both the Union Army and of the Confederate Army, did just that.

Book III

Clearfield, Tennessee
Late Fall 1861

The Captain and Elisabeth

Chapter 1
Clearfield, Tennessee 1862

On a sunny afternoon, Lieutenant Andrew Greyson stood with a drink in his hand on the lower terrace of the elaborate house of Franklin Turnwell, mayor of Clearfield. Uniforms were much in evidence; Mayor Turnwell, himself, was in the uniform of a militia colonel. Also very much in evidence at this social party, which flowed from the large hall of the house onto the veranda and down the terrace, were the ladies of the city, dressed in bright, eye-catching gowns—swirling skirts, narrow waists, high bosoms, and bare shoulders.

The men gathered into groups talking of little other than the war; then they would look about, get another drink, and sally forth to pay respects to the ladies. Those men that were military wore full officer uniforms, the gray Confederate coat with bright buttons and rank insignia, gray trousers with the yellow leg stripe; and most wore their sabers buckled to their waist.

Bright voices, light laughter—it was a panorama of color and gaiety. There was a small orchestra and a harpsichord on the veranda that played at intervals, and later in the afternoon they were to play waltzes so there could be dancing.

This was the first social event since the Union Army had arrived outside the city, so those invited made the most of it. It was also being held somewhat as a celebration of the repulsion of those forces from outside their city—a salute to the military in general, and to honor individuals who had conducted themselves with special courage and heroism.

As a lieutenant, Andrew Greyson found himself very much in the minority. There were a few other lieutenants, possibly those that were from the more auspicious families of Southern society, but there were many more captains and above, staff grade officers. Andrew, more often than not, found himself standing on the edge of the group of officers he happened to be near; and although he was treated with deference for the remarkable feat he had accomplished, and though his opinion was courteously asked for, he usually spoke briefly and rather quietly.

At first Andrew had been disconcerted when those he met, both ladies and men, had seemed to stare at his face overlong, till he realized they were merely looking at what was still, though no longer bandaged, a rather angry, red scar that ran along his left cheekbone on to the top of his left ear, a bayonet thrust that had come quite close. "You can just grow your beard over this and no one will notice," the surgeon who had dressed the wound had rather cheerfully said to him. "Though, of course," the doctor had added, "most soldiers would give a great deal for a badge of courage like this."

The doctor had been more concerned about Andrew's other wound; a rifle ball had passed through the fleshy part of his right side at the waist. The wound had been lanced out, cauterized, and bandaged, but he could feel the stiffness of it when he walked, and there was some bleeding when he changed the dressing.

In fact, the latter wound was the reason Andrew did not wear his saber as it would have aggravated the wound as it swung at his side. Andrew's gray coat was neat and unscathed, as he had left that behind when they had gone on the special operation. However, he had had to replace his trousers which had been torn by the bullet that had caused the wound, and had also suffered the brunt of three days of living in the field in battle conditions. The only tailor shop in town had been able to produce a pair of trousers that fit, though their color was a dark gray rather than the usual Confederate light gray; but with the yellow stripes from his old trousers sewed on their seams, they looked appropriate. Andrew wore them tucked into his tall cavalry boots—boots of such good quality, Andrew had found, that once cleaned and polished they looked almost as fine as before the assault on the hilltop.

Earlier in the afternoon, with all the guests gathered in the large ballroom of the house, Andrew had realized why he had been invited to this event. Colonel Forrest Biddell had called him to the center of the room and said, "I'm sure that by now all of you have heard of the heroic exploits of Lieutenant Greyson. You know that he led a company of gallant Southern soldiers, at night, through enemy held territory, stormed a strategically important hilltop, routed the enemy; and then for three days and three nights he and his men held that salient against fierce and determined charges. When on the third day the Union forces relented, and we were able to go to the relief of F Company, we found them to be without food or water since the previous day, down to less than a half dozen rounds per man, and only four cannon shot left. Half of the men still fighting had wounds both minor and major, sixty-two brave soldiers had given their lives, and the company was still in fighting spirit."

Andrew had been looking at the faces of the people around him with some self-consciousness. The front rows of people were mainly the ladies with an occasional man standing beside his lady. The men, military and civilian alike, stood in the back ranks. Andrew felt warm and pleased at seeing the friendliness in their eyes, although it would have to be said that many of the military men were also quite envious of his exploits.

The mayor of the town, Militia Colonel Turnwell, also spoke and said, "Speaking in my role as mayor, we would like to express our debt of gratitude for the bravery of men like Lieutenant Greyson."

It was just as the mayor finished speaking that Andrew felt a strong impulse to turn his head and look at the flight of broad, railed stairs that swept up the side of the room to the balcony above. Someone was coming down the stairs, but at that moment Colonel Biddell was reaching out to shake Andrew's hand, and Andrew realized that the colonel was saying something to him. "...recommended promotion to captain for Lieutenant Greyson," the colonel said. "I'm sure General Bragg will approve that promotion when he gets our official reports of the operations here. Congratulations, Captain Greyson."

Andrew shook the colonel's hand, accepting the congratulations and the slight applause that came from the people gathered in the ballroom. Finally he turned his head toward the stairs and saw no one and wondered why he had felt it was important to look in that direction. He was thankful that there was nothing more required of him than a "Thank you, sir."

Andrew slowly made his way through the people toward the large doors that opened to the veranda, slightly favoring the stiffness in his right side. Men shook his hand heartily, leaving no doubt of the admiration for what he had accomplished. Ladies also seemed eager to meet him, holding out their hands to him, which Andrew would take, then bow slightly toward them. He wondered how many times he said, thank you. He noted that most of the men called him Lieutenant, while most of the women called him Captain Greyson. He realized that within himself, he could continue to be a lieutenant, perhaps until he had lived the life of a captain long enough to get used to it. He did not mind the attentions of these friendly people, but he was not quite at ease with them and did not particularly like to talk about himself. He allowed his eyes to roam over the guests that were now spilling out the wide swinging double doors onto the veranda and wondered if there was any person here with whom he could talk about poetry.

Eventually Andrew collected a drink from the large punch bowl on a table in the veranda and made his way down to the lower terrace where he patiently spent the afternoon listening to fellow officers discuss tactics, watching the very pretty ladies walk by, and generally appreciating the warm sunshine and the relief, for one day, from his duties as an infantry company commander.

Chapter 2

He was looking up at the moment that she came through the door, a slender woman wearing a royal blue dress, the full skirt flowing as she walked across the veranda. She had a profusion of golden curls that covered her head like a shimmering halo and hung down to her bare shoulders. She walked proudly, head up, arms swinging slightly. She seemed to look over the people on the veranda, then she looked down toward the terrace.

Andrew did not take his eyes off her. He had the impression he was seeing a vision, something ethereal. The thought came to him that he had once seen a deer step out of the woods just like that, graceful, poetry in motion, alert and poised. Though Andrew was too distant to tell, he knew that her eyes were a deep blue.

When, as her eyes swept across the terrace and the officers grouped there, she seemed to be looking directly at him, Andrew did not drop his gaze. He felt somewhat transfixed, as if it were not remotely possible that he could look away from her. And it did seem as if her gaze lingered on him before it moved on. Andrew realized he had been holding his breath.

She was accompanied by a roundish man in civilian clothes, and they walked across to the top of the terrace. The round man seemed to be talking earnestly to her, and though she would occasionally glance at him, she did not seem to be answering him.

She sat down gracefully on one of the slatted benches at the edge of the terrace, and apparently sent the round man off for a drink for he hurried in that direction. He was detained, however, by Mayor Turnwell who seemed to have a number of points to make. The round man was smiling, bobbing his head as he listened to the mayor.

It was at that point that Andrew found himself walking steadily across the terrace to the veranda where he got a small glass of punch from the black attendant there, and walked back toward the golden girl. She watched him approach, a calm expression on her face.

"Is this what you were waiting for?" asked Andrew extending the drink toward her.

"Yes," she said accepting the glass. "Thank you." She remained seated looking expectantly up at him, and, yes, her eyes were blue—very, very blue.

"I'm Lieutenant Andrew Greyson," he said.

"I thought you were a captain," she said. "Aren't you a captain?"

"Well...sort of," Andrew smiled. "I'm not really...ah...particular." She continued to quietly look him in the face. For a moment he thought she was looking at the scar on his face, but then he realized she was looking directly into his eyes. Deep blue eyes with some incredibly long eyelashes—at that moment the intrepid Andrew Greyson knew that the situation was somewhat out of his hands.

Just at the point where Andrew feared he would have to turn and retreat, she smiled and held out her hand. "I'm Elisabeth Barrett," she said. "I'm pleased to meet you, Captain Greyson."

Andrew took her hand in his, bowed, and almost forgot to let go of her hand. "At your service, miss," he said.

Andrew was startled when she leaped to her feet. "Oh!" she exclaimed. "It is so stuffy here. Let's go for a walk. Do you mind just walking a bit with me? I've been standing around all afternoon, and it really has been boring."

Andrew listened and watched her talk, a little surprised at how suddenly this quiet appearing girl had sprung to life. She was still talking.

"I'd really much rather go for a horseback ride, but with this dress and all, I can't do that. But at least we can walk." She set her glass of punch down on the bench and took Andrew's left arm.

As they walked across the terrace by the round man and Mayor Turnwell, she paused. "I'm taking Lieutenant Greyson for a walk, Uncle," she said smiling. "His wound is stiffening up, and he needs to exercise it."

"Of course," said the mayor. "By all means. Take care she doesn't over exert you, Captain."

"Yes, sir," said Andrew. "I mean no, sir. I will take care, sir."

Andrew and Elisabeth left them, the mayor looking fondly after her; the round man looking after her, his mouth hanging open.

With Elisabeth's hand tightly gripping Andrew's arm, they walked briskly down the carriage drive that circled the yard of the house, Andrew having completely forgotten about any stiffness in his side. Neither spoke for a time, each perhaps not quite sure how the present situation had come about. At the junction of the carriage road with the thoroughfare they paused. "Just across the bridge over the river there is a path that follows along the edge of the water," said Andrew pointing with his free arm. "We could walk there. It leads upstream to just about where my company is encamped. It's quite pretty with some sheer rock walls behind and the water in front."

"Yes," said Elisabeth. "That sounds nice."

They turned right on the thoroughfare and came quite shortly to the bridge which they crossed, Elisabeth's heels clicking on the wooden planks. The river itself was not wide, but yet big enough to carry small barges or boats. They stopped to lean over the wooden rails and watch the water swirl against rocks on the shoreline and against the pilings of the bridge. This being perhaps the narrowest part of the river, the constricted water moved swiftly. It was picturesque, but by common consent they moved on, Elisabeth's hand having not let go of Andrew's arm.

They came to the end of the bridge and turned off on a gradually declining pathway to the water's edge where it joined a sandy path that came out from under the edge of the bridge. Here the path was wide enough to walk side by side if they walked close together, which did not seem to be a problem.

They had gone a short distance when, "Oh," said Elisabeth. "Stop. Stop for just a minute." She stooped down and quickly unlaced and removed both shoes. "I don't care if I ruin my stockings," she said. "This feels so much better." She wriggled her feet in the sand.

Andrew had watched, bemused by this seemingly impulsive person who seemed to follow her feelings before all else. It seemed a childlike trait to him, but rather than seeming immature, it seemed like the actions of an unaffected, perceptive person. Andrew had taken advantage of the pause to remove his too warm coat which he slung over one shoulder. Now he stooped down, picked up the two shoes, and tying their laces together, he also slung them over his coat. Then he offered his free arm to the woman, and they continued the walk.

Elisabeth's movements as she walked was a smooth gracefulness that enticed Andrew. He looked down on the shimmering golden curls; he could see the curve of her forehead and the long eyelashes. She was breathing in short, quick breaths, seemingly a little breathless, and Andrew could see her small nostrils flaring minutely with each breath. His eyes followed on down over the bare shoulders to the smooth curve of her breasts.

Just at that moment she looked up at him, eyes full of delight, and she skipped a little in exuberance. Andrew's heart lurched within him, and he had the confused feeling that this fairy that he touched could magically change from woman to child to woman at will.

Say something, thought Andrew. Talk or you are sunk. "Hmm," said Andrew. "Hmm, your name is Elisabeth Barrett? The name sounds familiar. How do the lines go? *'Let me count the ways.'*"

Elisabeth laughed brightly. "Of course," she said. "I was named after Elizabeth Barrett Browning, since I already had the Barrett part." She looked up at Andrew's face, an impish smile on her face. "Why didn't you quote the entire line? I'm sure you know it."

Andrew felt his face flush. "I know it," he said slowly. "I just didn't think…I didn't know if…I thought maybe you…" He stopped, quite flustered. Her hand tightened on his arm. "All right," he said. "I'll say them: '*How do I love thee? Let me count the ways.*'"

He was rewarded by a look of pure heaven on her face. Thus encouraged he quoted on:

> *"'I love thee to the depth and breath and height*
> *my soul can reach…*
> *I love thee freely, as men strive for Right;*

> ***I love thee purely, as they turn from Praising…***
> ***…I love thee with the breath,***
> ***Smiles, Tears, of all my life!'"***

"And so forth," said Andrew, his voice lowering and slowing as he quoted the lines. He felt a little embarrassed, but yet felt a rightness to the words.

"Those are beautiful lines," said Elisabeth quietly. She looked up at him. They had almost stopped walking as Andrew had concentrated on remembering some of the lines. It felt good to be dealing with poetry again instead of military matters. It felt good to walk alongside these rushing waters with this lovely creature beside him. He felt a wholeness and completeness that, he realized, he had never before felt in his life. He looked again at the woman on his arm, in fact, could barely refrain from doing so constantly. When she glanced up and their eyes met, he wondered if he was still breathing.

They walked on, the sand crunching slightly beneath Andrew's boots, whispering under Elisabeth's graceful feet. Each, perhaps, having much to say and ask, but each also not knowing where to start, or how to start, or if speaking was even necessary.

Elisabeth, realizing she was somewhat out of breath, opened her lips slightly to breathe. She felt a little faint, and said, "Is there somewhere we can sit and rest for a moment?"

"Yes," said Andrew, "just up a bit here is a break in the rock wall. There's a small opening we could go into. There are some flat rocks we could sit on, or we could sit on my coat on the ground."

"All right," said Elisabeth. She leaned against Andrew and they walked, a bit more slowly now, some small distance to where there was a broken opening in the rocks. It looked shady and cool in the room-like opening, a few tall shrubs and small bush-like trees having grown around the edges. "It looks nice in here," said Elisabeth as they turned around the corner into a shaded part of the opening.

The feeling was close and intimate. As soon as they were out of sight of the opening, Elisabeth turned toward Andrew and, standing on tip toes, threw her arms around his neck, clinging closely to him. He put his arms around her and held her. His coat and the shoes fell to the ground, but neither noticed.

There were some long moments, each aware of the other's breathing, Elisabeth's bosom pressed against Andrew's shirt front. Andrew put his face down into the golden hair of the woman and thought, the world could end right now, and I would be happy. Elisabeth clutched her arms ever more tightly around his neck and pressed her face against his neck.

"Take off my dress," whispered Elisabeth against Andrew's chest, but she did not relax her hold around his neck. Andrew hesitated. Where to begin? "The buttons in the back," whispered Elisabeth.

Andrew realized he had been touching those buttons ever since he had put his arms around her. They were round, pearl-shaped buttons, each buttoned through a small loop of cloth. And there are so many, Andrew thought. There could easily be fifty or a hundred. They ran all the way from the top of the dress on down past her waist, to where she would just about be sitting on them when seated.

He began at the top button and almost groaned aloud at the clumsiness of his fingers. It did not help that he could feel her breath against the bare skin of his neck. Finally one button came free. After more lengthy fumbling, a second came undone.

"Hurry," whispered Elisabeth, a slight gasp of breath against his throat.

Andrew's mind cleared enough so that he realized that some other course of action had to be taken. The undoing of those many buttons was an impossible task under these circumstances. With his right hand, he reached into his pocket and took out a clasp knife, a knife he kept sharp enough to trim his beard or to shave with. His left hand he slid, palm against Elisabeth's back, under the two undone buttons. With his right hand he guided the knife blade, and moving both hands simultaneously, they followed the curve of Elisabeth's back; and in a flowing cascade, the buttons fell to the sand, into the bushes, onto Andrew's coat, everywhere. Andrew tossed the knife aside.

With a sigh, Elisabeth relaxed her hold around Andrew's neck enough so that, one arm at a time, she slipped out of the shoulder straps of the dress, allowed the front of the dress to fall down; and as the dress fell to the ground, she stepped out of it. The next moment she again clasped both arms tightly around his neck.

"Lift my petticoats between us," murmured Elisabeth, and looking at her face as he did so, Andrew saw that her eyes were closed and that she was smiling, the corners of her mouth turned up.

She pushed against him with her hips, and almost in a frenzy, Andrew undid the simple buttons of his trousers, and with some quiet sounds in his throat, he moved against her. They held each other so, swaying a little, Andrew's feet planted apart so they would not fall. Then Andrew reached down, put one hand under her buttocks and lifted her enough so they would fit, and in one vivid moment, he was inside her.

"Ah," breathed Elisabeth.

"Oh," said Andrew.

They stood thus together, holding tightly to each other, their faces now at equal height, pressed side to side, feeling the searing surge of emotions flow through them. It could have been for only a second they stood so, or it could have been an eternity. Then in a smooth movement, as if they had practiced it a hundred times, Elisabeth's legs still clamped around Andrew's waist, still holding to each other; they sank to the ground where Andrew's coat had fallen.

Slowly the emotions eased to a warm glow. Andrew became aware of small bird sounds in the trees, of the rushing water outside the opening; he became aware of the fact that he was lying on some of the round buttons from Elisabeth's dress; but mostly he was aware of Elisabeth, her body and his, tangled intimately together.

He looked at the face so near his, her face now framed in an array of golden curls. Her eyes were closed, long lashes lay on her cheeks. Caught in the lashes the bright sparkle of quiet tears. On her face, a calm, quiet expression. And Andrew, looking, realized that he was committed, that his life would never be the same, that the remainder of his life would be in reference to this poignant moment.

Elisabeth opened her eyes, and Andrew felt awash in their deep blueness. She smiled, a small smile at first, then it became radiant in its happiness. Still no words, but words did not seem necessary. They both seemed to know and accept a bonding that was more than this moment. It included this moment, yes, but in their souls they knew it went far beyond.

Elisabeth's smile turned pixie-like as she looked into his eyes. She moved her hips just a fraction; tightened her legs around him just an iota; and so quickly Andrew felt himself growing big inside her. She gave an amused little laugh, a giggle, and they were swept off in a whirling, shuddering symphony of emotions; the ebb and flow of blood-rhythms, of heart-songs, of desired caresses.

Chapter 3

The following Sunday afternoon,Andrew Greyson led two saddled horses up the winding carriage road to the front of the Turnwell mansion. He was there as a result of some messages that had been sent back and forth between himself and Elisabeth, a request for her company for a horseback ride in the country, and a response that said simply that she would be pleased to do so.

Andrew was leading his own tall, bay horse, and another that was saddled with a side saddle. He had stopped at the stables at the side entrance to the Turnwell plantation to pick up that horse, a tall, gray gelding that pranced and strutted at each step.

Andrew was surprised when the groom at the stables had brought out the lively, gray gelding. "Is this the horse that Miss Elisabeth usually rides?" he asked.

"Oh, yes," replied the groom, a competent-looking black man. "She rides it all right," he said with a smile. He had brought out two saddles, one the side saddle with which he saddled the horse, and the other, a conventional English saddle which he put on the rack outside the stable door. He caught Andrew's curious look at the second saddle and said,"I could tell you the why fo' of thet saddle, suh, but effen you don' no mind, I'll let you see fo' you'sef."

"Fair enough," said Andrew. He like the looks of the man and the skillful way he handled the fiery, gray horse.

Once saddled the gray horse settled down a degree, and Andrew took the reins and was about to lead it away when he was stopped by the groom saying, "Now, suh, thet bay of yourn could use mo' grain feed. It shows some wantin'."

"Well, yes," said Andrew, "but we're a little short of grain at the regiment."

"Hmm," said the black groom. He was running a hand down the bay's chest and between its front legs. The bay swung its head and looked at him mildly. "I'll tell you," said the groom. "I'll have a bag of grain fer yeh to take when yeh comes back from the ride. It'll do dis one horse some good."

"Well, thanks," said Andrew. "I sure do appreciate it." He wondered briefly how the man had been able to keep a supply of grain. He knew that the army had caused some resentment among the populace by its rather high-handed way of seizing grain supplies for its own use and promising some future payment. Andrew had nodded to the man, and turned and led the horses up the roadway.

Andrew turned the reins of the two horses once through the ring on the hitching post, and, warding off the nuzzling of the gray who seemed to want something from the pocket of his coat, he walked across the terrace and veranda of the house to the large front door. The door swung open and was held so by an elderly black man wearing a white shirt and dark trousers.

"Good afta'noon, Captain," said the doorman.

Andrew took off his hat and stepped into the spacious room he had been in before. Just as he entered, he was delighted to see Elisabeth coming down the sweeping stairway to his right. She was talking amiably with a tall, young, black woman at her side, but when she saw Andrew, she stopped talking, looked directly down at Andrew, and smiled. Andrew felt his heart leap, and he knew he was smiling too. She is beautiful, he thought. The black woman had stopped a step below Elisabeth and was looking pleasantly from her mistress to Andrew to her mistress again.

Elisabeth was wearing a light brown, long dress and a red, woolen cape-coat. She wore a hat tied with a scarf, but golden strands of hair curled over her forehead. She came lightly down the stairs and held a hand to Andrew. "It is good to see you, Captain," she said, glancing at the embroidered captain's bars on the shoulders of Andrew's coat. Her tone of voice was just slightly mischievous.

Andrew had not known just what to expect in this second meeting with Elisabeth, and had, as a matter of fact, memorized a few pleasant social comments to make. He was not quite prepared for the physical feeling of pleasure he felt at seeing her again, and instead of a pleasant greeting he stammered, "Yes, the...ah, captain. Well, I thought I better accept the...the promotion." He felt quite the clumsy fool.

But he took her hand and, coming close enough to him so that her skirts touched him, she smiled demurely up at him. They stood looking at each other for several seconds while Andrew, his senses whirling, thought, does she know what she is doing to me? And Elisabeth, feeling that all her emotions were showing on her face, thought, does he know he affects me so strongly?

"Oh," said Elisabeth, tugging her hand from Andrew's grasp and whirling to her side. "This is my friend, Alexandra. I call her Lexie." And Elisabeth held out her hand to the black woman that had accompanied her down the stairs.

The black woman half-curtsied and looked at Andrew with just enough amusement in her face that showed she knew the unusual social situation her presence caused; but also with the deference in her manner to show she wished to cause no difficulty.

"Good afternoon, Lexie," said Andrew with a slight nod.

"Lexie and I grew up together," said Elisabeth, "and she came here with me when we had to leave upstate to come here. But the Yankee army caught up with us anyway, and now we are sort of stranded here." She smiled warmly at her friend to show they were comrades on this adventure together.

"Have a good time riding, Lissy," said Lexie, and she also looked at Andrew to show she included him in that wish. "Oh," she said. "Just a minute. Your picnic lunch." And she rushed out a door, presumably to the kitchen, and quickly returned with some large leather saddlebags. "Be careful with this," she said. "There's a bottle of hot tea in there wrapped in a towel." She handed the saddlebags to Andrew.

Andrew draped the saddlebags over one arm and held the door with the other. Elisabeth turned at the door and gaily waved goodbye. She put her hand in the crook of Andrew's free arm as they walked out on the veranda. At the steps between the veranda and the terrace she skipped lightly from the top to the bottom step, tugging at Andrew's arm.

Andrew, too, felt light and free. He looked down at Elisabeth's bright eyes and her smile. He could not help smiling, and when Elisabeth caught his smile, she held on to his arm with both her hands. "This is a happy day for me," she said.

"It is for me, too," said Andrew.

As they approached the horses, the big, gray gelding nickered a welcome, obviously for Elisabeth. "You big baby," she said as she rubbed his ears. The big horse closed its eyes and seemed to soak in the attention. "He acts so tough," said Elisabeth, giving the horse a gentle stroke on its nose, "but he's such a softie."

Andrew buckled the saddlebags behind the saddle on his horse and helped Elisabeth onto the saddle on the gray. She seemed light and supple, and perhaps he held to her hand a bit longer than needed. Elisabeth sat erect in the side saddle with a delightful smirk on her face. "Don't I just look like the perfect lady?" she said, tilting up her chin and daintily picking up the reins with her gloved hands. The big gray horse stood quietly.

"Ready?" she said, and Andrew realized that both he and the gray horse were under her spell. He swung into his saddle. He wasn't at all surprised when she took the lead and directed her horse in the direction of the stables.

The groom was waiting outside the stable door. "Good afta'noon, Miss 'Lisbeth," he said happily.

Elisabeth was out of the saddle and on the ground, holding the reins of the gray before Andrew could dismount. The groom changed saddles quickly—the regular saddle for the side saddle. He gave Andrew a knowing look.

"Tha' you is, Miss Lissy," the groom said. "Now you cin ride."

"Thanks, Howard," said Elisabeth. "And thanks for not telling." She swung up into the saddle, long skirts and all, with athletic grace, adjusted her skirts, and was ready to go.

"Ah would neva' tell," said Howard. "You knows that."

Elisabeth rewarded him with a big smile. She turned toward Andrew. "We can ride along the river for a short ways and then through some of the fields to some trees beside a small stream. It's so much easier to go riding now that the Union Army is gone. It was nice of you to send them away."

"It was my pleasure, ma'am," said Andrew, reining his horse beside hers.

They were riding through the plantation yard. To one side, their right, were the working buildings, some low barns, some tool sheds and storage sheds. On the other side were the weathered cabins of the workers—the slaves. These were small cabins, a window and a door facing the yard. Since it was Sunday, a day of rest even for the slaves, many of them were in or around their cabins. Some were sitting on the cabin steps, a few with small children.

Almost without exception these people greeted Elisabeth as they rode by, and Elisabeth returned their greetings, calling them by name. As they neared the end of the row of cabins, Elisabeth said to Andrew, "I've got to stop and see how Josie is doing," and she reined her horse toward one of the cabins. Andrew followed.

At the door of the cabin, Elisabeth slipped out of her saddle and handed the reins to Andrew who had also dismounted. She knocked on the door and entered. Andrew could hear voices inside. Presently, Elisabeth came out and smiled at Andrew. "Thanks for being patient," she said as he helped her into her saddle.

After they had gone a short distance, she turned in the saddle to look at Andrew. "Josie had a baby about a month ago," she said. "It was her first one. It wasn't very strong, and it died. And then to make matters worse, they sent Josie back to work too soon." Elisabeth smiled wanly. "I got in a little bit of trouble with my uncle by insisting they give her time to rest and recover." Elisabeth shook her head sadly. "She'll be all right now, but how tragic to lose your baby."

"You really care for these people," stated Andrew.

"Someone has to," said Elisabeth. Then she smiled. "It has gotten so that whenever I step into my uncle's office he looks up and says, 'now what?'" She laughed a delightful laugh. "But he usually gives in. I try to be helpful to the ones that are sick or need help, and if they would let me, I'd have a school for the children."

They rode quietly for a few minutes, when Elisabeth, riding beside Andrew, said, "I don't know what you think, but these people aren't going to be slaves forever, even if the war weren't going on. And we should be getting them ready for that life, or they're going to be worse off than they are now." Elisabeth spoke with the spirit of conviction in her voice.

Andrew looked at the determination in her face and thought, remarkable. He said, "I believe you are probably right."

Chapter 4

They were riding side by side on a wagon track that ran between fields. The terrain was somewhat rolling, so that the growing fields were often interrupted by hillsides of trees or ravines bordered by brush and small trees. Ahead of them were low hills that ran down to the river on their left.

Andrew had always been a good horseback rider—good enough so that riding was second nature, not something he had to think about. But now he found himself consciously sitting straight and riding with the motion of his horse, and he realized it was because he was aware of what a good rider Elisabeth was. She seemed to be part of the horse, and the directions she gave her horse, either by hand or heel or knee, were almost undetectable. Andrew enjoyed watching her ride, and was grateful when the wagon track divided into a one-track path, and Elisabeth rode in the lead.

They came presently to a shallow, gravelly stream that was flowing toward the river. Elisabeth turned upstream, and the horses stepped on sand bars or splashed through the shallows. They followed the meanderings of the stream for perhaps a mile before Elisabeth turned off the stream up a grassy slope that ran up under large, spreading trees.

"This is one of my favorite places," said Elisabeth. She turned her horse and looked back the way they had come. Andrew also reined in his horse and looked back. In the distance was the fold of land that held the river, and beyond that some smokey, hazy, low mountains.

"It is nice," said Andrew appreciatively. "A person could live here."

"We're at least going to eat here," said Elisabeth, and she swung down from her horse and led it to a level place under the trees.

They ate a lunch of cold chicken, slices of hearty bread, and tea, still quite warm from its wrappings in the towel. Andrew had unsaddled the horses, and they sat on one saddle pad, their backs leaning together against a convenient fallen tree, and used the other saddle pad as a spread on which to set their food.

"Next time we'll bring a blanket," said Elisabeth.

"Definitely," said Andrew. Actually, the thought of bringing a blanket had occurred to him, but he thought it might imply something that he did not want to make obvious.

Elisabeth took off her hat and sailed it toward the patient horses. The big, gray gelding took a step forward and nosed the hat on the ground. "Don't eat my hat, silly," laughed Elisabeth. The horse looked up at her, big eyes serious. "I love you," called Elisabeth, and the big horse nickered in reply.

Andrew and Elisabeth leaned back against the log, the warm sun on their faces. Presently his arm was around her, and her head was resting against his shoulder—golden hair in a swirl on his shoulder and chest. He put his face into her hair, closed his eyes and breathed softly. A song was playing in his mind that said, this is heaven, this is bliss…

"Hmm," sighed Elisabeth. She said, "I'm a little drowsy. It must be the ride, or the food, or the sun, or something." She wriggled closer to Andrew until she was curled up, knees tucked up, with her head in Andrew's lap. Andrew put his hand on the curve of her waist and hip. For a moment she looked up at him, deep blue eyes and long lashes. Then she closed her eyes.

Andrew was about to say something when he realized she actually was asleep. Her breathing was slow and deep, and her lips opened just slightly. Andrew, looking down at her, had a deep feeling that he would protect this exquisite being from all the world's dangers and cares. Meanwhile, he would hold her quietly while she slept. He felt he had never been happier.

Late afternoon shadows were lengthening as they rode back. Some bird songs sounded in the deeper thickets. The water in the stream flowed and splashed as cheerily as before. Just before they reached the stables, Andrew stopped his horse and turned to Elisabeth. "I must tell you something," he said. He paused. Suddenly he didn't know if he meant to tell her how much he had enjoyed the afternoon, or what a delightful person she was to him, or that his company, F Company, was shortly to be on their way to join Longstreet's army in Virginia.

"I…" he said. Elisabeth looked in his eyes. Her expression was serious, eyes wide. It was disconcerting to Andrew, to say the least.

"I must…I have to…I love you," he almost groaned.

Elisabeth blushed. She kept her gaze directly on Andrew's face. Finally she smiled, a tentative, small smile. "I know," she said, "but you don't even know who I am."

Andrew shook his head slowly. "Perhaps not," he said. "But I know what you are. I know that you are kind and generous to people around you. I know that you love creatures and the world around you. I know that you delight in life as a child does." Andrew paused again, feeling his emotions wash over him like an ocean wave. Finally he lowered his head and murmured, "You are the loveliest thing I have ever seen."

Andrew felt that if he tried to say any more, it would be unintelligible, gibberish, or perhaps a sob. He slumped in the saddle awash in a sea of feelings. Vaguely he heard a rustle of skirts as Elisabeth slipped out of her saddle and was suddenly on the ground beside Andrew's horse, holding on to Andrew, looking up at him.

Andrew swung his right leg over the neck of his horse and slid to the ground. He wrapped his arms around Elisabeth; and they stood there between the two horses, holding each other, not saying anything, feeling that they were meant to be here, now, together in this place.

Chapter 5

As evening dusk settled over the valley, Andrew was riding from the Turnwell house, riding slowly along the curved carriage road toward the river bridge. Elisabeth and he had stopped at the stables, and, much to the delight of the groom, had exchanged the saddle on Elisabeth's horse for a proper side saddle for the short ride up to the house. At the house, she waited quietly for Andrew to hand her down, and in the house, Andrew had stayed a polite interval and bade Elisabeth and her aunt a good evening and left.

Andrew was in a contemplative mood as he approached the bridge. He could hear the rushing water under the bridge, and a few swallows were swooping from under the bridge in quick flights over the darkening water. Andrew became aware of a figure at the bridge railing, and as he came near he realized it was Alexandra. Her stance at the railing suggested to Andrew that she was waiting for him.

She turned to face him as he approached, and Andrew reined up his horse, "Good evening, Lexie," he said.

"Evening, Captain," said Alexandra. They looked at each other. "May I speak with you, Captain?" Her voice was a low contralto. "I think it is important."

"Of course." Andrew swing off his horse, faced Alexandra, and waited.

"I wouldn't bother you, Captain, but it's about Elisabeth."

"Yes," said Andrew.

"We've taken care of each other for many years—since we were little children. She helped me many times. When her daddy died and I was to be sold, she put her foot down and wouldn't allow it. If anyone is mean to me, they know they have to deal with her. She taught me to read and write—as soon as she came home from school, she would bring her books and we'd go over all she did that day in school. She's been kind to all the black folk around here." Alexandra paused and looked earnestly into Andrew's face.

She continued. "And that's why I do all I can for her. I know many white folk would think it impertinent for me to call her my friend, but we are—we are good friends."

"I think I understand," said Andrew.

"That's why I have to beg you not to hurt her," said Alexandra. "You look and act like a gentleman, and I believe you are a good man. You must do the right thing by her."

"And what is that?" asked Andrew.

"I don't know," said Alexandra. "You and she have to decide that, but right now she's not thinking straight." Alexandra smiled, white teeth flashing in the evening light. "It surprises me, too, because she has always been very levelheaded about things like this. You know, she's twenty-two, the same age I am, and most white ladies are married by that age. She has turned down so many beaus—her aunt and uncle get so exasperated with her. And then you come along and she changes."

Alexandra smiled again. "But inside, she's still the same. My, but it was something to see when her aunt said she shouldn't go riding with you—that it wasn't proper. My, she just bristled. And her uncle took her side." Alexandra's tone was just a little bantering. "Well, you know, you are the big hero, and you've been wounded—and you are so modest—and handsome."

Andrew had to smile. He liked this woman who talked straight and who believed in friendship. "How do you know that I'm being levelheaded about this, Lexie?" he asked.

Alexandra paused, startled. "Heaven help us!" she said and shook her head slowly. "Heaven help us."

Andrew reached out a hand and touched Alexandra's sleeve. "I'll do my best," he said. "On my honor, I'll do my best." He looked in Alexandra's eyes. "I would die for her," he said. "I love her with all my heart and soul."

Alexandra looked at him. "I believe you," she said softly, and after a pause. "You must live through this war and come back for her." She turned and left.

Andrew watched her go for a moment, then stepped into the stirrup and sat in the saddle. After a moment he turned the horse and rode across the bridge.

Chapter 6

In the days that followed, Captain Greyson continued to lead F Company in its field training. There was no longer any doubt that two companies from the regiment, F Company one of them, was being transferred in a short time to the Army of Northern Virginia. Their places in the regiment would be taken by new companies being recruited in Tennessee. Andrew worked his company and officers hard to be ready for the move, and they responded well. They felt, after their battle of Little Hilltop, that they were a company set apart, destined for more glory.

"I'm sorry to see you leave my regiment," said Colonel Biddell when he broke the news of the move to Andrew, "but General Longstreet specifically asked for some experienced and tested soldiers, and your company is that."

In truth, Andrew was glad for the extra work. He was trying to resolve a turmoil within himself, and the demanding schedule of getting his men and equipment up to shape kept him busy. Could he continue to see Elisabeth and feel about her the way he did, without ending his marriage to Anne? He knew he could not.

There had been no letters from Anne since Andrew had ridden from their home in Milford. Andrew had been able to send two letters—dry, informative letters, about his life in the army; but that did not mention the Little Hilltop battle or his part in it. Now, on a late afternoon when the day's work with F Company was done, he sat in his office part of the smokehouse, lit a candle, and wrote two letters.

The first letter was to Anne, and in it he stated as unemotionally as possible, his belief that their marriage should end, and his reasons for the ending. The second letter he wrote to an attorney, a much older man that Andrew had met through a mutual interest in gun dogs. The man, besides his legal work, trained and bred English setters. Andrew had been planning to bring a young dog home with him when the war interrupted such plans. Andrew asked the attorney to begin divorce proceedings, and he instructed him to make whatever concessions Anne asked for. Andrew knew that Anne had considerable wealth from her own family, and he hoped she would not demand a large amount of his future earnings as a college professor; but he knew also that he was willing to give anything within reason.

Andrew put the letters into some makeshift envelopes and sealed them as best he could. He decided to carry them himself to regimental headquarters where the first sergeant collected letters and arranged for them to be carried toward their destinations by whatever transport or person was going in such a direction. He put on his coat and hat and stepped out into the late afternoon. It was cool, but a good walk would be refreshing.

At the company perimeter, he was startled by a voice calling out, "Stop, or I shoots!"

"What? Oh, it's you, Hatfield. How's the arm doing?"

"Yeh, it's me, Lieutenant, suh," said Hatfield, black eyes flashing with mischief. "My arm's all fixed. Lieutenant, how come I gets sentry duty so much? Some of them corp'rals never stand sentry."

"Some of us captains never do either," said Andrew.

"Well, shoot, suh. If I was in charge I wouldn' do no duty nuther. But some of these sargints and corp'rals are no smarter 'n me," Hatfield declared.

"Well, this is an army, in case you hadn't noticed, Hatfield, and that's the way an army works."

"What I really wants, Lieutenant," said Hatfield earnestly, "is to go on 'nuther night pateroll. If we could do thet more, I could like this army."

Andrew and Hatfield faced each other for a moment with no sense of rank between them. They were silent for the moment, and Andrew realized that if Hatfield and he were not in an army, he would have made some comradely gesture, perhaps a touch on the arm, or a handshake. There is something about being in a life-threatening situation that brings us together, thought Andrew. For those hours or days, life is trimmed down to bare essentials, and one of those essentials is the support of fellow human beings.

"Well, Hatfield, I'll leave you now. Carry on—and enjoy your sentry duty." Andrew turned and left as Hatfield casually saluted in perhaps as an unmilitary salute as Andrew had ever seen.

Chapter 7

On a balmy, almost springlike, Sunday morning, Andrew walked to church. The church was a small Presbyterian church close to the center of Clearfield, and the sanctuary was crowded, in addition to the regular congregation, with many uniformed soldiers. The inside of the church was divided, in the old traditional way, into family box pews; but with the influx of soldiers, these strangers were invited into any of the pews where space was available.

Andrew found a seat with a family with six young children. The youngsters squirmed together till there was room for him. They smiled shyly at him, four girls in flowery pinafores, and two awed boys. They whispered and nudged each other till the father, who had originally welcomed Andrew with a handshake and introduced himself as William Hammond, sternly shushed them into silence. The mother, a pretty woman with long, brown hair, smiled at Andrew, and he felt welcome and at ease.

The service had not started, so Andrew looked around as much as he could without seeming to be prying. The many uniforms were much in evidence. Andrew, himself, would have preferred to come in civilian dress, but he did not have with him any clothes except military. He had compromised somewhat by not wearing a hat, and by not carrying any sidearms or saber; the weapons, he felt, did not fit with his concept of a church-like atmosphere.

Andrew was pleased to spot the Turnwell family in a pew near the front, and, as a matter of fact, the reason he had chosen to attend this church was because Elisabeth had mentioned that they attended here. Andrew's anticipation of seeing Elisabeth, however, was dashed when he quickly saw that she was not there.

The organ prelude began, and as the congregation hushed, Andrew shut his eyes and thought of other churches he had attended, first as a small boy with his mother and father, and later at the chapel at West Point. His father and he had attended a chaplain's service together in Virginia when he had visited his father just before the battle that had ended his father's life; and Andrew thought of his father and missed his steady presence.

The organ continued its soft music, and for the first time Andrew thought of how proud his father would have been of his son's role in the Little Hilltop battle. Yes, he missed his father very much.

He was startled out of his reverie by a nudge at his arm, and he opened his eyes to see a hymn book held in front of him by one of the bright-eyed, young girls in preparation for the singing of the first hymn.

The organ prelude was over, and Andrew thought, that was well done; and for the first time he looked up to see if he could see the organ player. The organ, a fairly small instrument, a reed organ rather than a pipe organ, was on a slightly raised platform to the side of the front of the church. The performer, sitting sideways to the congregation, bent slightly forward, perhaps concentrating on the next music to be played, was a young woman. Andrew stared. He caught his breath. It was Elisabeth.

Andrew tried to join in the singing of the hymn, but time and again he found his gaze drawn to the front of the church where Elisabeth's profile was outlined against the stained glass window. He admired the blue dress she wore. It showed an elegant neck and slender arms. When Andrew began singing the fourth verse, the little girl at his side pointed to verse three and suppressed a giggle with a hand over her mouth. Andrew decided he would pay closer attention to the service so that he would not embarrass himself or his hosts in the pew.

The minister, a dignified, white-haired man that looked just like a minister should look, was standing behind the pulpit. "I have a serious announcement to make," he said, a somber look on his face. He paused, looked down and shook his head slowly. "Much to my regret," he continued, "at the General Assembly of the Presbyterian Church of America, it was decided to sever relations with the churches in the northern states.

"I had hoped," he said, "that our church denomination, spread across all the states, both north and south, could be an agency of compassion to the suffering caused by this war on both sides. We might have been able to assist in the exchange of prisoners, or supported families divided by the war, or, through intercession, been able to prevent the destruction of certain religious or cultural locations of significance."

The minister paused again. The congregation waited in utter silence. He shook his head sadly. "In the end, it was self-righteous men on both sides who refused to bend. I fear it will be a hundred years before we repair such a rift between our churches."

The minister bowed his head, and by common consent the congregation rose to stand in prayer. Andrew, though he did not consider himself an overly religious person, felt himself drawn into the sense of tragedy—of loss. He bowed his head with the rest, and thought again of the loss of his father. He looked up, over the bowed heads of the congregation to see Elisabeth, head bowed, eyes closed. Andrew felt a sudden jolt of fear course through him. If war can destroy churches, what all can it destroy?

The next moment he felt a thrill of joy as he looked up, and over the bowed heads of the people, their eyes met. Elisabeth's hand came up to her face in shocked surprise, but the delight in her eyes warmed Andrew. Even at the distance that separated them, he could see the blue in them.

The remainder of the service was probably long, but Andrew did not mind. He followed the promptings of the bright-eyed, little girl at his side in following the proceedings, and quite enjoyed his views of Elisabeth. Several times he caught her stealing a glance at him, and each time his heart surged within him.

At the end of the service, Andrew rose and thanked his hosts for their hospitality in sharing their pew. The father, a man perhaps a few years older than Andrew, rose with the aid of a cane to shake hands with him; and though neither spoke of it, both understood the sacrifice this man had already made for the Confederate cause. For a moment, Andrew envied him; he no longer had to face what Andrew knew was surely ahead for him.

Andrew turned to the delightful family that he had shared the worship service with. "Thank you, so much," he said. And to the oldest little girl, the one who had shared the hymn book with him, he said, bowing slightly, "You have a beautiful voice." The little girl, perhaps ten or eleven years old, beamed and blushed. She looked up at him, an adoring smile, and whispered a goodbye.

The pretty mother smiled at him, and Andrew lifted a hand to his forehead in deference to her. As he stepped out into the aisle, Andrew turned back to the father and said, "I envy you, sir. Goodbye."

In the aisle of the church, Andrew waited as people moved by him, many of them greeting him; in fact, some of them seemed to know him and called him by name, Captain Greyson. Andrew returned their greetings and accepted their well-wishes, but all the while he was aware of Elisabeth standing at the organ, picking up her sheets of music, and finally, as the throng cleared the aisles, coming toward him.

Andrew, walking up the aisle to meet her, felt right, felt complete. They paused as they came near each other. Finally Andrew said, "It's nice to see you."

"Yes," said Elisabeth, her eyes alight. "You did surprise me, but I like such surprises."

People moved by them as they stood in the aisle. Elisabeth smiled up at Andrew and clutched her portfolio of music to her bosom. Andrew felt her arms brush the front of his shirt. "You didn't tell me you were an accomplished musician. You didn't say you played the organ here at church." He touched her arm. "What else haven't you told me?"

"I haven't had time," said Elisabeth.

"No," said Andrew, "we haven't had time. And now time is getting short."

"It's true then," asked Elisabeth, "the rumors that your company is leaving?"

"Yes," said Andrew. "Yes, I'm afraid it's true enough."

"Oh," said Elisabeth in a small voice, and Andrew, looking in her eyes, had a premonition for perhaps the first time of the pain of leaving a dearly, loved one. They moved down the aisle slowly. At the back of the church, in the foyer, Elisabeth found her long coat, and Andrew happily helped her with it. They stepped out into the open air, a cool day, but bathed in bright sunlight.

"I came early to practice," said Elisabeth. "I have my horse and buggy. Will you ride with me?"

"That would be my great pleasure," said Andrew.

They walked slowly down the sandy churchyard past the row of horses and buggies and carriages. They came abreast the carriage in which sat the family that had shared their pew with Andrew. They greeted each other again with a nod and a brief wave of the hand, and Andrew and Elisabeth moved on.

"Wait!" cried a small voice behind them, and Andrew turned to see the little girl, his companion of the hymn singing, standing up in their carriage, calling to him. "Wait," she called again. She seemed almost in tears.

Andrew and Elisabeth turned back and approached the carriage. "Yes?" said Andrew.

The girl seemed too overcome with emotions to speak. She gasped, and finally blurted, "My papa has to take your picture."

"What do you mean, Liselle?" asked her mother.

The little girl reached forward and put her arms around her father's neck. "Papa," she said, "when you were gone to the war, we didn't have a picture of you. And I couldn't remember what you looked like. I tried very hard to remember, but I couldn't." Her voice choked in recollected pain. "I thought if I couldn't remember what you looked like, you would never come back." Tears glistened in her eyes.

"Please," she whispered in her father's ear. "Please take his picture so he will come back. Besides," she said with a flash of womanly wile, "he is almost as handsome as you are, Papa." And she smiled shyly at Andrew, a tear still held in her pretty eyelashes.

The father cleared his throat and brushed his eyes. He looked at Andrew. "Well, Captain," he said. "Shall we do the lady's bidding? You see," he went on, "when I came back from the battle at Bull Run with this quite shattered leg, I knew I could no longer work at my old occupation as a farrier, so I began a photography business—a portrait studio. It's a new business," he continued, "but I saw it done at battle sites, and it looked quite interesting. I've been successful," he said with some pride. His wife at his side put a hand on his shoulder.

"And," he said with a look at Liselle, who beamed at him, "I would be pleased to take your portrait."

Andrew was touched. His first inclination had been to decline, to not impose, but when he saw the pleading look in the little girl's eyes, and saw, when he turned to Elisabeth, a look of longing—a wish, he knew he must accept. He turned to Mr. Hammond. "Of course, I'll have my portrait taken," he said, "on condition that I pay for the pictures, and," he paused, "on condition you also take a portrait picture of Elisabeth and one of Liselle. Those are two pictures I would dearly love to take with me when I leave."

"Oh, good!" cried Liselle. "You will have our pictures, and we will have your picture, and then you will surely come back."

"I must come back," said Andrew. The family in the carriage and Andrew and Elisabeth looked at each other for a moment. They felt they had mutually agreed on a solemn pact.

"Well then," said Mr. Hammond clearing his throat, "I suppose you are quite busy with your company. When could we arrange to have you and Elisabeth come in?"

Andrew and Elisabeth looked at each other and could not help smiling. "I'm not sure," said Andrew, thoughtfully.

"I have a suggestion," said the photographer. "We could take advantage of this beautiful sunlight if we met this very afternoon at my shop. As a matter of fact," he went on, "the afternoon sun is best. My shop windows face west. Today at perhaps four o'clock would be an excellent time—that is, if you could manage."

"I'm sure we can," said Andrew after a glance at Elisabeth. He was relieved. He knew that after today, his days would be quite filled with preparations for the movement of F Company to Virginia.

"My shop is a half block past the courthouse," said Mr. Hammond as he picked up the reins of his horses. "I look forward to seeing you this afternoon."

"We shall be there," said Andrew, putting an arm around Elisabeth's slim waist. "Goodbye, Liselle. Goodbye, Mrs. Hammond." And he saluted the ladies, a casual hand to his forehead.

Elisabeth waved as the carriage moved off. "What a bright girl," she said. "And how well she put her feelings into words. I must say, I think they express some of my feeling also. I'm so glad you agreed to have your picture taken. Thank you."

And Andrew, as they walked toward Elisabeth's buggy and gray horse, felt again the rightness of things.

Chapter 8

The gray gelding perked up his ears and nickered at them as they approached. "He remembers me," said Andrew. He gave Elisabeth a hand up into the small, covered buggy and went to unhitch the horse from the hitching rail. The horse laid back his ears and rolled his eyes at him. Andrew swung the reins over the gray's head, walked back and sat beside Elisabeth in the buggy. For some reason, he was not surprised when the horse refused to go, and by prancing around and blowing air through it nostrils, seemed to be threatening mutiny.

"What's with this horse?" asked Andrew. People were looking at them and the scene the horse was causing. Most of them seemed quite amused at Andrew's embarrassment at not being able to handle the horse. Elisabeth, also, had an amused smirk on her face.

"All right," said Andrew, "so he doesn't like me, but he can't possibly know which one of us has the reins."

"Oh, no?" said Elisabeth. She took the reins from Andrew's hands. Immediately the horse calmed down. He shook himself vigorously, and stepped out smartly when Elisabeth flicked the reins on his back. "Good boy, Sunny Boy," said Elisabeth.

"I think," said Andrew quietly, "that Sunny Boy and I do have something in common. We are both in love with the same woman." Elisabeth smiled.

"Where to?" Elisabeth asked as they came to the turn onto the roadway. She looked sideways at Andrew. "I don't intend to take you home," she said. "I'm not inclined to share your company with anyone. We don't have that much time left together."

Andrew agreed. He felt that sitting in a parlor making conversation with family was not something he would enjoy. "All right," he said. "But we do have to eat. I could invite you to F Company's chow line, but Sergeant Grant would be quite upset with me if I brought you there without letting him know ahead of time so he could make something special." He smiled at the picture in his mind of Elisabeth in line for dinner with F Company. It would cause quite a stir.

Elisabeth had stopped their horse and buggy letting other rigs pass by them. The gray horse swung his head around to look at them.

"I could take you to the regimental officer's mess, but then I'd have forty or fifty officers looking you over," said Andrew. "They would all want to be introduced to you. No," he shook his head. "I'd rather not."

Andrew continued. "I've heard there's a roadhouse about a mile up the river road that reopened since the Union Army left. It's a tavern, really, but I guess they clean it up for Sunday and serve some good food."

"That sounds interesting," said Elisabeth. "Let's go there."

"All right," said Andrew. "We've got till four o'clock." He was very pleased that Elisabeth was willing to try something out of the ordinary. Elisabeth waved cheerily to the Turnwell family as they went by in their carriage, then turned the buggy north up the road and the gray gelding began an easy trot. They quickly passed the Turnwell carriage, and Elisabeth waved again.

Andrew nodded at them and saluted. "Don't you have to let them know you're not coming home for dinner?" he asked.

"They know I'm with you," she replied happily. "They're used to me doing things on my own."

"I'll bet they are," said Andrew, watching, with an occasional side glance, Elisabeth competently handling the reins.

They followed the road winding along beside the river past the turnoff to the bridge that led to the Turnwell plantation. Just to their left and below them was the rocky gorge with the sandy path beside the river. Andrew looked there, then turned to look at Elisabeth. She was looking at him, delight in her eyes.

"This is a beautiful place," said Andrew.

"Yes," murmured Elisabeth. They moved closer, if it were possible, together, and Sunny Boy shook his head and snorted through his nostrils.

A short distance farther up the road, Andrew pointed to their right. "My company is camped just over there," he said.

"I know," said Elisabeth. "I rode near there yesterday."

A half mile out of town they arrived at a low building set under some large trees. "McCormick's Tavern & Eatery" proclaimed the sign that swung over the door. Several horses were at the hitching posts, and some horses with buggies were at the side of the building. Elisabeth guided their rig in beside the other buggies with a warning to Sunny Boy, who was looking the other horses over. "You behave, Sunny." Sunny Boy pranced into place, knees lifting a bit higher than usual.

To Andrew, Elisabeth said, "I'm glad you're not one of those men who assumed women can't do anything and says, turn here, and do it like this, or like that."

Andrew was amused. "No," he said, "you are quite good at everything." He held a hand out for her to step out of the buggy. "But I do like to help you do some things, like this."

"Of course," she said, smiling.

The tavern grounds were dirty, mud off buggy wheels, horse droppings. Elisabeth looked around with some dismay. "I should be wearing my boots," she said, holding up her skirts.

"Allow me," said Andrew, and picking her up, swung her up into his arms.

"Oh!" exclaimed Elisabeth, and held on, her arms around his neck. With her face close to the side of his face, she was tempted to kiss him, but she merely nuzzled him with her nose.

"Hmm," murmured Andrew. He carried her to the door of the tavern, delighting in holding her, and, pushing the door open with his boot, he carried her over the threshold into the dimly lit room, rather startling the guests and the proprietor. He set her down with a flourish and straightened up.

"Thank you," said Elisabeth, adjusting her skirts. Her face, with a few stray curls of blond hair hanging over it, was a little flushed. There were some appreciative glances from the men at the long table at her trim ankles and legs, momentarily visible as Andrew had swung her to the floor; and Andrew was startled to see a group of high-ranking officers, among them his regimental commander, Colonel Biddell.

"Good day, sir," said Andrew, and the colonel nodded.

The proprietor, a short, wide, powerfully built man, approached them. Over rough clothing he wore an apron that was quite clean. "Good day, folks," he said. "You came for dinner?"

"Yes, we did," said Andrew. The man led them to the end of the long plank table that ran the length of the room, the opposite end from the other officers, and bade them be seated.

He looked closely at Andrew. "Aren't you Captain Greyson?" he asked. "Aren't you the Captain Greyson?"

"I don't think I am the Captain Greyson," said Andrew, "but I am a Captain Greyson." He was puzzled at what the man was driving at.

"Ah! But you are the Captain Greyson that drove the Union Army out of here. You won the Little Hilltop battle." He pointed out the window. "Just a ways up river. This place," he swept his hand around the room, "taken over by their officers. Bad manners. Always demanding." He smiled slyly. "I showed them. I sold them bad whiskey—watered down. And you drove them out. Good! We both did our duty."

Andrew smiled. He did not know quite how to respond to this. Certainly, he was not going to boast about his part in the Little Hilltop battle. A little embarrassed, he looked at Elisabeth. Perhaps it had been a mistake to bring her here. But no, she was enjoying this. She was smiling, listening to the man. She was really an extraordinary person.

"And now," Hugh McCormick, their genial host, was saying, "the menu today is venison stew with many vegetables cooked in with it, and corn bread."

"That sounds delicious," exclaimed Elisabeth. "I'm famished. I do like to eat," she said with a look at Andrew.

"Yes, that sounds very good," said Andrew.

"Excellent!" McCormick said, wiping his hands on his apron. He seized a towel that had been draped around his neck and briskly wiped the table top. "Will you be seated here, miss?" And he pulled back a chair for Elisabeth. Andrew had at the same moment taken hold of the other side of the chair, so Elisabeth, with a quick smile to each of them, seated herself at the table. Andrew sat across the table from her.

"And now, Captain, sir," said Hugh McCormick, beaming, "we want you and your lady to accept, at no expense to you, in appreciation for your heroic exploits, this fine meal. It is our honor to have you."

Elisabeth clapped her hands in delight. Andrew smiled at her and nodded to the man. "Thank you. Of course, we will accept your offer. Thank you."

The meal quickly arrived. A black iron kettle with three small legs was set before them. It was filled with steaming stew. Two deep, wooden bowls, a pan of hot corn bread, butter, some shakers of spices: these McCormick set in front of Andrew and Elisabeth and bid them enjoy their meal. As they were eating, he could not refrain from coming to their table at intervals to be sure they were enjoying their food.

"This venison stew is truly delicious," complimented Elisabeth. Hugh McCormick almost blushed with joy.

Andrew was mopping his bowl with the last of the corn bread. "This is excellent," he said. "Quite better than army fare. By the way," he added with a raised eyebrow, "you haven't considered joining the army, have you?" He felt he was being a bit disloyal to Sergeant Grant, but nevertheless he added, "We could use a good cook and food like this in F Company."

"Oh, no, no!" protested Hugh. "I am much too old, and besides, I have a severe case of flat feet. I could never walk sentry duty. I am only a good cook." He threw his hands out, palms up to show how badly he felt about not being able to do more. "And now," he said, "I have no coffee, but I do have tea—an herbal tea made from plants we pick ourselves. May I bring you some while we clear the table, and you can finish your meal by leisurely sipping some hot tea."

"It sounds like just the thing," said Andrew.

"Oh, yes," said Elisabeth.

The tea was good, and the time spent together was good. They sipped the tea and looked at each other, and looked at the others in the room—and looked at each other again.

After a quiet moment, Andrew said, "Will you tell me about yourself, where you were born, about your family, what you were like as a child, how you became what you are?"

After a pause, Elisabeth said, "Yes, I'll try."

"I'd like to know as much as I can about you," said Andrew, "so that when I am gone I can feel you are real. Our friendship till now has been so very beautiful that, I'm afraid when I am gone, I will have a difficult time believing it really happened."

"I am real," said Elisabeth. She reached a hand across the table and Andrew held it with his hand. When Elisabeth reached across with her other hand, Andrew held them both in his cupped hands.

"Your hands are as beautiful and graceful as swans," he said sincerely. Hugh McCormick, who had been about to approach, stopped and withdrew. It was not a moment that he wanted to interrupt.

Chapter 9

They were back in the buggy with Sunny Boy at a slow walk back toward town. The gray horse had reluctantly allowed Andrew to handle the reins after Elisabeth whispered something in its ear. Andrew had folded the top of the buggy back, and it was a leisurely, enjoyable ride in the warming sun.

Elisabeth touched her finger to Andrew's lips. "Now you must not laugh as I tell you about myself," she said.

Andrew could not help chuckling a little at that. "Of course, I won't laugh at you," he said, "but I may smile now and then when I hear something especially intriguing."

"All right," said Elisabeth. "It's not that I'm ashamed of my life, but it has been quite different than most Southern young women."

"I have already surmised that," said Andrew, "and I have appreciated it tremendously."

"My mother died when I was born," said Elisabeth. "She was about the age I am now. We have no picture of her, but my father said she was very pretty."

"I'm sure she was," said Andrew.

"There were no other children. My father was quite a few years older. I was turned over to a slave woman to raise—a woman who had given birth to a baby girl just a day before I was born. You may have guessed that that was Alexandra's mother, and the baby girl was Lexie."

Andrew smiled.

"You're smiling," accused Elisabeth.

"Well," said Andrew, "you must have been quite a sight—you as blond as can be, and Lexie quite dark."

"Yes," said Elisabeth. "People thought it very interesting, but some thought it was just terrible, of course. Lexie and her mother moved into the big house, and we grew up almost like twins. We sucked the same milk, we were bathed together, and we slept in the same cradle together. You can see why we are such good friends today."

"How was your father getting along?" asked Andrew.

"Not very well, from what I've been told," said Elisabeth. "He was devoted to my mother. He was a very lonely man after she died. You see," she said, "we were sort of the poor relations. The plantation we lived on is about fifty miles northwest of here, and compared to these places, it was not at all big or grand. People thought my mother had married below herself—she was the youngest sister of my Uncle Turnwell where I am staying now.

"But my father was a sensitive, caring person—a real gentleman. I can see why my mother fell in love with him. It was from him I learned to like music and beautiful horses, and animals.

"At any rate, the plantation was not doing well—perhaps my father was not a good manager. He was always more interested in music and literature. He was very easy on his slaves, though there were only four or five, and people say you can't make a plantation pay off that way."

Elisabeth paused and said a bit sadly, "I'm afraid he got to drinking more than he should. That was after my mother died. But he never got angry or hurt anyone. I can remember him, sitting at the table with a lamp lit nearby, reading aloud poetry from Edgar Allen Poe; and with tears in his eyes he would read, *'Quoth the raven, nevermore.'*

"That was when I was about five or six. They say he paid practically no attention to me till one day when I was three, I climbed up on the harpsichord bench, opened the keyboard, and began to play some notes. He taught me to play it after that, and also the violin. But he was still very depressed. I wish I could have helped him more."

Elisabeth was speaking quietly and at that point she paused. For the moment she could not go on as she thought of the lonely life that her father, James Barrett, had lived. "I can't imagine anything lonelier than living on after someone you loved completely, dies."

Andrew held her hand. We all live with our losses and our regrets, he thought. The gray horse, whose pace had been slowing down, realized that no one was paying any attention to him, so he came to a gradual stop at the side of the road.

Elisabeth smiled briefly, tentatively. "He did tell me, at one time when he was ill in bed, that it was worthwhile—that the few years he had with my mother were worth any price—that he had been a lonelier person before he met her. And I have to believe he meant it and that it was true.

"Somehow—I didn't know how he managed it then, but I found out later he was getting funds advanced from my uncle against the property—he arranged for me to attend boarding school in Richmond. That was for three years when I was fifteen, sixteen, and seventeen years old.

"Some people call it a finishing school," Elisabeth smiled, "and that is a little presumptuous, but I did learn a great deal. They had a piano there, shipped over from Germany. I loved to play on it. We also read a great deal—poetry and literature. And, of course, they taught us everything that a proper young lady in Southern society should know. Some of it was rather stifling and occasionally I had to do things out of the ordinary in order to let them know what I thought of it."

"Yes, I can see you doing that," said Andrew.

"The last year I was there, we were permitted to bring our own servant, so, of course, I brought Lexie. They stayed at a sort of dormitory nearby and we were supposed to be learning how to treat them. Of course, Lexie and I got to giggling and the headmistress, on more than one occasion, gave me a very severe talking to. I was being much too friendly, too informal with a black slave, according to her.

"I, of course, had no intention of treating Lexie like a servant. I brought her along so she would have the chance to see some of the world. She did help with my clothes and things the way they were supposed to, but I read all my lessons to her, poetry and such.

"The year ended tragically, though. Mammy got real sick—a heart situation. When my father got the word to us, we both cried and felt very guilty about the good times we had been having. I quit school and went home with Lexie, because, of course, she couldn't travel by herself on the train; and besides, Mammy was the only mother I had ever known, so I had to go."

Elisabeth leaned into Andrew's arms. "It was a sad time for us. Mammy lived for a month after we got home, but she was partially paralyzed. Either Lexie or I stayed with her all the time. For a while it was agony, watching her slowly die; but then, you know what we did? We read poetry to her. We read Emerson and Holmes and Whittier, and any poetry we could find. We borrowed books and read the poetry in them. Some of it was pretty awful stuff, but we read it all. What do you think of that?"

"I'd like someone to read poetry to me if I were dying," said Andrew. "Especially if it were you."

"Well, Mammy liked it," said Elisabeth. "Some of the poetry was sad and some was glad. Some of it made us laugh, and some of it made us cry, and though it didn't change the sadness of the time, it did give us some good times."

They sat quietly for a time. Sunny Boy turned to look at them when the talking stopped, but seeing that nothing was required of him, he settled himself into a half-doze. Andrew and Elisabeth sat comfortably, accepting and sharing the losses life had given them. Andrew thought of his mother, but that was so long ago, he scarcely could bring her to mind—only the small boy's image of a sweet, serene presence. The death of his father, scarcely a year ago, was more poignant. He thought of some poetry lines and he quoted them to Elisabeth. "'*Ah, love, let us be true to one another...*'" Elisabeth smiled, sighed, and settled closer into Andrew's arms.

"Matthew Arnold, Professor?" she asked.

"Yes, 'Dover Beach'," said Andrew.

"May I be a student in your class sometime?" asked Elisabeth.

Andrew smiled. "Yes, but you must not distract the teacher," he said.

After a moment Elisabeth said, "Will you read poetry to me, after the war, when we can be together?"

"That will be my pleasure," said Andrew, "and perhaps I will write poetry to you; certainly, I will think poetically of you; but of one thing I am quite sure. None of the poetry I could ever read or write or quote comes even close to matching the poetry that you are."

When Andrew looked down at Elisabeth's face, her eyes were closed, but she said, "It's lovely to hear you say things like that, and I know you mean it; and it makes me feel good."

A carriage drawn by two horses went by them on the road, and Sunny Boy awoke from his dozing. He snorted loudly through his nose to show that he had been alert all this time. Wasn't it time to be moving on? He turned the buggy back on the road and started in a slow walk. Neither Andrew nor Elisabeth seemed to notice that they were moving, since neither picked up the reins that were wrapped around the whip post. For a time the only sounds were of Sunny Boy's hooves on the road—a slow, steady rhythm—and the wheels of the buggy crunching on the gravel.

Elisabeth said, "I have to tell you about my father. For whatever faults he had, he was a good man—a kind, gentle man. He died three years ago of consumption and pneumonia. Once he got sick, he didn't seem to have the will power to get better. Toward the end he was quite depressed, thinking that he hadn't left me a large, prosperous plantation to live on, but I assured him he had left me much more—a love of beauty, a love for the outdoors, an appreciation for music and art and poetry—and a compassion to fellow creatures and all people—including black slaves."

Elisabeth looked into Andrew's eyes, and Andrew smiled. "I believe you," he said. "You have described the sort of man I admire. I think I would have liked him."

"In the end, I think he died a contented man," said Elisabeth. "He knew that I was all right and could take care of myself. My uncle and aunt, the Turnwells, took me in, and, of course, by then the property pretty much belonged to my uncle. I would have liked to stay on the plantation, but I couldn't make it pay for itself. Of course, now," and she smiled at Andrew, "I'm glad I came."

"I am too," said Andrew.

"There were only three slaves left, and one of them was Lexie. They came too, and three of my best horses, including Sunny." Elisabeth added thoughtfully, "When I realized that I owned Lexie, I tried to make her a free Negro, but she begged me not to. She said, what would she do? Go up north? How would she get started? And life for a free Negro down here is very difficult. She said, maybe later, but for now she wanted to stay with me—and to tell the truth, I was very glad about that."

They were in town now, and Andrew had picked up the reins, much to Sunny Boy's annoyance. A few vehicles were on the main street, and some people were walking the sidewalks. They turned the buggy toward the portrait shop.

"Eventually the slaves will be freed, won't they?" asked Elisabeth, "even if we win this war?"

"Yes," said Andrew. "No civilized country can continue such a practice."

"Are we going to win this war?" asked Elisabeth.

Andrew sighed. "No, I don't see how we can. We don't have nearly the industry they do, and they have the manpower, too. I think all we can hope for is to win a position from which we can bargain for concessions."

"I hope it doesn't last long," said Elisabeth.

Chapter 10

Liselle was standing in the open door of the portrait shop when they stopped at the curb in front of it. She was excited, fairly dancing for joy. She was wearing a green dress with a wide, white collar, and her brown hair framed her face in a cascade of ringlets.

"What a pretty sight," exclaimed Andrew, and he bowed gallantly to the girl.

"Why, thank you, sir," responded Liselle, and she curtsied. The next moment she seized Andrew's hand and hurried him into the shop. Elisabeth followed, smiling at the enthusiastic delight of the girl.

Will Hammond was busy setting up his photography equipment inside. He motioned to the back. "There's a basin of water in the back room if you care to freshen up," he said, "though," he looked at Elisabeth, "you look splendid. You could just brush the dust from your coat," he said to Andrew, "and we will be ready."

The picture taking went well, judging by the pleased manner of the photographer. He kept a constant eye on the sunshine coming in the window, and adjusted some reflectors to get the light on his subjects. First he put his daughter on a high stool where she sat, hands clasped in front of her, eyes sparkling.

Elisabeth was next, and Andrew thought she was simply beautiful, sitting with her back straight and head held proudly. After Hammond had snapped the shutter, he noted the color of her hair, eyes, and dress. "I tint the small miniatures with paint and brush," he said, "and I want to be right in the colors." To Andrew he said, "Now I think your expression should not be too stern. Pleasantly serious is more like it. And remember, you must hold still for eight seconds."

"If you tint my picture," said Andrew, "you might just touch over this scar on my face." He touched it with his left hand, self-consciously. "I'm afraid it ruined whatever chances I had to be good-looking."

"Oh, no!" exclaimed Elisabeth. "You are really quite handsome even with the scar." She was near Andrew, and she reached up and drew her finger lightly along the scar from his ear to his jaw. The touch thrilled Andrew, and he thought that whatever pain the wound had caused him, it had been well worth it.

The picture taking was over, and Andrew stayed back with Hammond, who was putting his equipment into cases. Elisabeth and Liselle, talking amiably, almost good friends by now despite their age differences, had gone outside to see the last of the sun.

"Mr. Hammond, I must ask another favor of you," said Andrew.

"Yes," said Will Hammond. "And what is it?"

"You may know that my company and I leave soon," said Andrew.

"I've heard that some companies are leaving," said Will.

"Actually," said Andrew, "we leave the middle of the week, and I would dearly love to have those pictures of Elisabeth and Liselle with me when I go. Is that possible?"

"Of course," said Will. "It's a bit of a rush thing, but I'll have them delivered to you. Will Tuesday morning do?"

"Yes, and thank you tremendously," said Andrew. He continued to look at Will Hammond till Hammond straightening up with the help of his cane, looked at him keenly.

"Is there something more?" he asked.

Andrew took a locket and chain from his coat pocket. "I've been meaning to give this to Elisabeth, but now it would be a more meaningful gift if we could include a picture of each of us inside."

"It's a fine locket," said Will, taking the heart-shaped, gold locket from Andrew. He snapped it open. "Good craftsmanship," he said. "Yes, I can do that," he said. "It will take more time, however, to carefully reduce the pictures and tint them. If you wish, I could do so, and deliver it to Miss Barrett when the work is completed."

"I'd be very grateful," said Andrew.

Will continued to look at the locket. "I have a suggestion," he said. "Since it will take more time anyway, perhaps I could have it engraved with a name or initials. I know a man here who does such things."

"That would be just right," said Andrew. "Elisabeth's initials on one side of the heart, E.B., and mine on the other side, A.G."

"Done," said Will, smiling.

"I can't thank you enough," said Andrew.

"No thanks needed," said Will. "We veterans have to stick together."

The ride back to Turnwell's plantation in the gathering twilight was bittersweet for Andrew. He was deeply moved by the delightful person beside him who smiled at him, laughed, listened to him, and responded to him. Yet, he was aware of an ache within that said, soon you must part.

They delivered Sunny Boy to the stables and began the walk under the dark shadows of the trees back to the house.

"How will you get back to camp?" asked Elisabeth.

"Walk, of course," said Andrew. "It's not that far, and I think I'll rather enjoy thinking of this day with you as I walk. And I feel quite all right walking in the night."

"Oh, yes, you are the famous officer who can see in the dark and lead a company of men besides," teased Elisabeth.

They were walking just then in the deep shadow of an overhanging willow tree. Andrew said, "I do not need to see in the dark to feel that you are nearby."

"I am very near," said Elisabeth.

"You are…" began Andrew, but the words were crushed from his mouth as he held Elisabeth close. He kissed her upturned face, her forehead, her closed eyelids, her cheeks—and her lips.

Chapter 11

On Monday at morning formation, a messenger—a young private riding a jittery horse—hurried up to Captain Greyson where he stood to the side of the formation of soldiers. "Sir, the colonel wishes to see you at once," said the messenger with a salute.

Andrew was annoyed. He had meant to spend the day personally supervising all the preparations for the company to move. His horse was saddled and ready for him to use in moving about the company area. He casually returned the messenger's salute and said, "I'll be there as soon as I can find the time."

"But I'm to wait and accompany you to regimental headquarters, sir," said the private nervously.

Andrew raised his eyebrows. What could be so urgent? A change in plans? "All right," said Andrew. "I'll be right with you. Lieutenant Meeks, take over. I'll be back as soon as I can." He went to his horse and swung into the saddle. "Let's get this over with," he said and the private and he cantered off toward regimental headquarters.

As they passed the artillery guns on the front yard of the main house, Andrew was pleased to see Sergeant Holbrook out with his gun crews polishing the little mountain twelve-pounders. "Good morning, Brookie," he called across the yard.

Sergeant Holbrook looked up from his work. In an instant he was on his feet facing his crews. "Battery, Attensh...hut!" he commanded in a ringing voice.

The men at the guns dropped what they were doing and sprang to attention in front of their guns. When they were all at attention, Sergeant Holbrook did an about face, facing in Andrew's direction, and saluted crisply. "Good morning, Captain," he said. "Sir," he went on, "my battery is ready to move at a moment's notice if you have any more expeditions in mind, sir." He was grinning happily.

Andrew returned the salute. "Your battery looks sharp, Sergeant," he said. "My compliments to your men. I'll keep you in mind, Brookie."

"Yes, sir," said Sergeant Brookie. After Andrew had passed by, he turned back to his men. "All right, back to work men, and if you ever get a chance to serve under that officer, do it even if it is in hell."

At the door of the stable that housed the 11th Regimental Headquarters, Captain Greyson handed the reins of his horse over to the private. The door was open, but Andrew knocked sharply on it and entered. He saluted Colonel Biddell who was seated at a desk. "Captain Greyson reporting, sir," Andrew said.

Andrew knew immediately that it was not going to be a pleasant session. The colonel, who seemed to be absorbed in some papers in front of him, did not so much as look up. Around the room other officers and sergeants were working. A few of them glanced at him, but did not greet him. Captain Sanders, the adjutant, was at his desk, and he looked up at Andrew, and quickly looked away. Andrew stood at attention in front of Colonel Biddell's desk and waited.

"So, Lieutenant, what have you got to say for yourself?" said the colonel, glancing up briefly from his papers.

"Sir, I got here as soon as possible. I was in the midst of getting my company ready to move," said Captain Greyson.

The colonel shook his head impatiently. "No, no, that's not it at all. Surely you realize how impertinent you have been these past days."

"Sir," said Andrew, hesitantly. "I'm afraid I don't follow you at all."

Finally the colonel gave him his full attention. He stood up and glowered at Andrew. "Of course, you know what I'm talking about. Everyone knows all about what I'm talking about. How you have been going around claiming all the credit for defeating the Union Army and sending them out of here—of how you, and you alone accomplished all that."

Andrew's mind was racing as the colonel paused. What was the colonel talking about? He knew he hadn't boasted of his part in the battle. Praised his company, yes, but what commanding officer wouldn't be proud of such a company and its accomplishments.

The colonel's tirade went on about how he, Captain Greyson, had risked the annihilation of an entire company by his daredevil tactics, and of how the enemy had left the battlefield only when they felt threatened by his, the colonel's, rescue force getting ready to advance from Clearfield.

As Andrew listened, still at attention, he realized there was nothing he could say to answer such blatantly false charges. But he decided he would not give the colonel the satisfaction of apologizing to him. He would simply stand and listen, and leave as soon as he could.

The colonel was still talking. "It was just plain luck that pulled you through. If that mission had failed, I would have had to answer to General Bragg. And then," the colonel seemed to get a second wind, "you top it off by bringing a lady to that tavern yesterday—something no officer or gentleman would ever do. And carrying on with her the way you did for everyone to see." The colonel shook his head sadly. "And you, a graduate of the Point." His voice had died down to a sad whisper.

"Well," said the colonel, throwing his arms wide. "It's a good thing you're getting out of here. We can get back to work—back to routine. You know," he went on, "I had three officers come in last week asking to be transferred to your company. And the first sergeant has been getting the same thing from the enlisted men. Everyone, including my staff, seems to think that the way to win this war is to charge off in all directions on some meaningless little raids."

Colonel Biddell looked at Captain Greyson and seemed to want some response. "Yes, sir," said Andrew.

Finally the colonel seemed to have run out of words. He waved a hand at Andrew dismissing him. Andrew snapped a smart salute, did an about face, and went to the door. The colonel, seemingly remembering something called after him. "You have your company out of here and on the road to Chattanooga by Wednesday morning at the latest. Is that clear?"

Andrew turned at the door, ready to protest, but the glowering look the colonel gave him told him it was useless. "Yes, sir," he said. He took the reins of his horse from the private and was ready to mount when Captain Sanders came out the door. He had a sheaf of papers in his hand.

He gave Andrew a sympathetic look. "I've got your written orders here," he said, indicating the papers in his hand. "There's authorization here for you to draw rations for the company, and there's authorization for railroad transportation when you get to Chattanooga. There's no authorization for ammunition. We're short of that. You'll have to get some from Longstreet when you report in there."

"Hopefully we won't cross paths with any Union forces, or find ourselves in the middle of a Federal raiding party," said Andrew.

"Can you be ready to go by Wednesday?" asked Captain Sanders.

"We'll make it," said Andrew. "We'll make it even if we have to work through the night."

"Well, good luck." Captain Sanders reached for Andrew's hand to shake it. "Don't worry too much about the colonel. He got chewed out by General Bragg for not being more aggressive and dealing the Yankees a good blow while they were occupied by your battle on the hilltop. He's just passing it along. He hasn't been easy to work with of late. Maybe you're the lucky one to get out of here."

Andrew swung onto his horse, casually saluted the captain, and set off for F Company. Already his mind was churning with the details that had to be completed in order to leave by Wednesday, the morning after tomorrow. He raised an arm in greeting to Sergeant Holbrook as he rode by the mountain artillery battery and headed for F Company.

Chapter 12

Captain Andrew Greyson worked late into the night on Tuesday. In the smokehouse, by candlelight, he wrote his reports to the commanding officer of the 11th Regiment, and he wrote the last of his letters to the families of the men of F Company that had given their lives in the battle for Little Hilltop—a process somewhat delayed because he had found that the regimental headquarters had not kept an accurate record of many of the home addresses of the men, and Sergeant O'Donal had to find such addresses or hometowns by questioning their acquaintances in the company.

The letters by Captain Greyson, commanding officer of F Company, were not required by regulations, and were, perhaps, poor solace to the bereaved families, but Andrew felt that the families should at least know that their men had died in a brave and noble manner.

It was warm in the smokehouse, the candlelight flickering on the walls, and Andrew removed first his boots and then his shirt. He sighed as he finished the last letter. He had not known each of the individual soldiers very long, but mutual respect had been forged by the dramatic battle they had fought together.

He paused after the last letter, his melancholy mood deepened by the writing of the letters and by his disappointment in not having been able to get away to see Elisabeth for a last time. Tomorrow the company would be on the march for Chattanooga. It seemed as though much of what he had wanted to say to Elisabeth was yet unsaid.

After a pause, he drew another piece of paper toward himself and dipped his pen in the ink, intending to write to Elisabeth of his deep affection for her and of his resolve to return to her after his obligations to the Confederate cause were ended. But how to express such emotions in words? It seemed impossible.

At that moment there was a light rap on the door of the smokehouse. "Yes?" he said. "Come in." Did one of his officers or NCOs have some last minute problem? He lay down the pen.

The door opened just enough for a slight figure to slip in, and Andrew was startled to see Elisabeth—Elisabeth, who threw back the hood of her dark cloak and stepped close enough to the light for Andrew to see the impish smile on her face. She laughed delightedly to see his surprise.

With a quick movement, he was around the table and held her very close in his arms. Even then, he could feel the laughter in her body, but soon she lay her head against his bare chest and whispered, "I had to see you again."

"Hmm," he murmured, the surge of emotion so strong in him, he could hardly dare to speak.

"I meant to come see you," Andrew said, "but when that became impossible, I meant to write a long letter to you. But this is much better." He held her firmly in his arms. "But how did you get by my sentries?"

Elisabeth giggled again. "It wasn't so difficult," she said. "I simply slipped by them when they were distracted." And Elisabeth, her face and mouth against Andrew's chest, nipped his skin with her teeth.

"Ouch!" said a startled Andrew, and he released her enough so that he could look down at her face. "But…"

"No buts," said Elisabeth, laying a finger on Andrew's lips. "Let me explain, and then we can talk of other things."

"Yes," said Andrew.

"For a moment," said Elisabeth, "when your note came saying that you couldn't come, and that you were leaving tomorrow, I felt utter despair. But then I looked at Lexie—we were eating supper at the time and Lexie was serving—and we both knew what we had to do, and we knew it would be fun. We could hardly keep from laughing together. I went to my room directly after supper—said I was reading a good book and did not want to be disturbed. Lexie came as soon as she could, and we slipped out through the kitchen. By then it was almost dark.

"Howard had some horses waiting for us at the stable, and we rode off as quietly as we could. Sunny Boy almost gave us away when he caused a terrible ruckus because I didn't take him—I knew whoever would have to take care of him while I was here would have a difficult time of it."

Andrew smiled. He was beginning to like Sunny Boy even though he felt that probably Sunny Boy would not reciprocate such feelings. Andrew clasped his hands behind Elisabeth's waist so she could lean back from the waist and look at him. She put her hands on his chest. For a moment they looked in each other's eyes—then both smiled.

"You have to let me finish my story," said Elisabeth.

"Of course," said Andrew. "I want to hear your story, and I'm not doing anything to stop you."

"Oh, yes, you are," said Elisabeth, and almost blushed. "Now then," she said after a pause, "Lexie has some friends here at the nearest plantation, so we rode there and left the horses. Lexie helped me to get by the sentries. We both had on these rather dark cloaks—it was part of the plan—and she walked here with me. When we came to the sentry, she went off a ways in the dark and called to him; and when he went to investigate, I walked in just like that, knocked on your door, and here I am."

"You certainly are," said Andrew. And he thought, why does she continue to surprise me? By now I should know she is going to do the unusual.

"Lexie is staying at her friend's place while I am here. She will wait all night if she needs to."

Andrew was amused by her impulsiveness and touched by her loyalty. He wished to say something to express those feelings, but found, when he tried to speak, that a deeper, more fearful feeling—one that had haunted him all day—took over. He looked in Elisabeth's eyes and saw that, despite her cheerful manner, the same fear was in them. There was the glimmer of tears in them, and when his own vision became blurred, he realized that his eyes, too, were filled with tears.

For the moment he could say no words. All he could do was hold her close, and Elisabeth clung to him. "Andrew," she said in a small voice, "Will we ever see each other again after tonight?"

Andrew knew he had never faced a sterner test. He would give everything to be able to say, yes, with conviction. But, in truth, he could not.

He paused, tried to control his voice so he could speak without too much quaver in it. "Yes, my love, I believe so. But I cannot say so with certitude. I only know that if it is within my power, we will." His voice grew stronger. "Meanwhile, I can tell you that I will see you in my mind every day that I live. I doubt there will be a moment of my life that I will not be aware of the fact that you are somewhere in the world, alive and beautiful, and that you love me—and I love you."

Elisabeth put her head against Andrew's chest again. He could feel the hot tears touch his skin. "I'm sorry that I am crying," Elisabeth murmured against him. "I vowed that I would not so as not to spoil our last time together. But right now, I can't seem to help it."

"It's all right to cry," said Andrew. In truth, it was taking all his resolution not to weep himself. He put one hand gently on the golden head of Elisabeth and stroked it. In a low voice, with his mouth almost at Elisabeth's ear, he said, "I want to try to tell you, in this our last time together, what you mean to me."

He paused. Against his chest, he felt a slight nod of Elisabeth's head. "All right," she said.

Andrew said, "When I first saw you looking down at me from the terrace of your home, I felt you were someone special—someone I wanted to know. And you are, and it has been such a pleasure to get to know you just a little bit during this short time.

"You captured my heart before we even crossed the bridge on that first walk. You seemed so exquisite, I couldn't believe you could see anything in me.

"When I see you riding a horse, or walking, or moving in any way, in that style you have that is so full of life, I have this deep feeling that is a mixture of desire and passion and longing and humility—a feeling I can't clearly define—but a feeling that says you and I are part of each other." Andrew felt her arms around him, hold him just a little tighter, and he both heard and felt her sigh—a brief exhalation of her breath that seemed to be a sigh of contentment, of pleasure, of acceptance.

"What I am trying to tell you," said Andrew, putting his face into Elisabeth's silky hair, feeling its soft texture, breathing in its fragrance, "what I am trying to tell you is that I deeply, sincerely, completely love you. I know I've tried to say that before in awkward, stumbling ways, but now I am in complete control of my senses, and I say, I love you, Elisabeth."

Andrew stopped. He was surprised and somewhat chagrined to hear and feel Elisabeth giggle. "Complete control of your senses, are you, my love?" she said.

"Well, yes…I mean…" Andrew stopped, confused. Elisabeth was sucking on his left nipple, gently, but persistently. She was trying not to giggle as she did so.

"Oh, Elisabeth," murmured Andrew in a voice filled with some exasperation, much love, and great passion. He put his hands on both sides of Elisabeth's head, gently tilted it up till their eyes were only inches apart, their mouth less. "I love you, Elisabeth," he said, his lips brushing hers.

"I love you, Andrew," Elisabeth said. And now there was no teasing.

They stood thus, quietly for a few moments, and Andrew noted how good she felt in his arms. He touched her closed eyelids with his lips, and kissed her neck below her left ear. When he moved his head to look down the steps to his bed in the lower room, she felt it and nodded her head, yes.

He carried her down the steps, slowly and carefully, enjoying the anticipation. She is so easy to carry, he thought; and she, with her head against his neck, seemed to be humming a happy song.

Later, the candle in the upper room had sputtered out, and they lay in the darkness, arms and legs entwined.

"I shan't sleep all night," she said, sleepily.

So, in a low, clear voice, he sang her a lullaby—not an easy thing to do while one is lying down, lips so close they brush another's skin. But he had forgotten most of the words, so he hummed whenever he couldn't recall them.

"Hush-a-bye, my pretty one,
Go to sleep, Hmm, hmm, hmm.
Hush-a-bye, Hmm, hmm, hmm,
Go to sleep."

They both fell asleep.

Chapter 13

In the very early, still-dark morning, Andrew lit a candle, and Elisabeth dressed by the light of its flame. Whenever she swung a petticoat around her, or pulled the dress over her head, the flame of the candle would flicker back and forth and throw a mysterious, dancing shadow on the wall.

They spoke quietly, but little. Mostly they just looked at each other and smiled. Their mood was not one of despair at their soon-to-be parting, but rather one of gratitude for the time they had stolen together.

Elisabeth, sitting on the bed, pulled one long, silky stocking over an elegantly shaped leg. Andrew was entranced, so, briefly she stretched her leg out full length for his inspection. He shook his head in wonderment. She fastened the top to the garter snaps and reached for the other stocking. Andrew picked it up before she could get it and draped it loosely around his neck.

Elisabeth smiled. "That is very becoming," she said.

"May I ask a favor of you?" asked Andrew.

"Of course."

"Do you think you could get along without this stocking? I mean, could you get back to the house all right? I would very much like to take this stocking with me. I would wear it around my neck always."

Elisabeth smiled. "It's not exactly military. Would they let you do it?"

"Well, no, it's not very military," said Andrew, and almost laughed as he imagined how he would look with the stocking around his neck, "but I'm not really concerned about being military-looking; and who knows, perhaps it will start a trend. We will all march to battle with the stockings of beautiful women around our necks. Fearless F Company."

Elisabeth laughed delightedly. "You must take it, with my love," she said. Then she asked, a bit wistfully, "But what may I have of yours to keep till you return?"

Andrew went to his coat hanging on a peg on the wall and drew from an inside pocket a flat package about the size of his hand. He sat on the bed beside Elisabeth and, smiling while she looked on eagerly, he opened the neatly tied package.

"Oh! I love surprises," said Elisabeth, putting one hand up over her mouth to stifle a delighted exclamation.

Andrew continued to smile mysteriously while he undid the package. Inside were two sturdy cards of paper that enclosed between them two pictures—the photographs of Elisabeth and of Liselle. Andrew held them carefully near the candle so they could see them.

"Oh!" said Elisabeth. "Oh, I'm not really that pretty."

"Yes, you are," affirmed Andrew. "I think it is a very good likeness. I'm so pleased to have it with me. But do you see anything unusual about it?"

"Why, of course!" exclaimed Elisabeth. "The locket around my neck. I wasn't wearing a locket." She looked at it closely. "It's a pretty locket, shaped like a heart; but I was wearing simply a gold chain."

Andrew continued to smile quietly, enjoying Elisabeth's excitement and also the surprise that she had not yet hit upon. "But how did you do it?" Elisabeth demanded. "I don't even have such a locket."

"But you will," said Andrew. "Will Hammond delivered these pictures to me yesterday. I gave him this locket," pointing with his finger at the locket around Elisabeth's neck in the picture, "to deliver to you after I had left with our pictures inside and our initials engraved on the outside. It was his idea, after we left his studio, to paint the locket onto the picture as he tinted the photographs."

Elisabeth sat with her hands in her lap, quite speechless. Finally she said, "If I weren't so happy, I would cry. Thank you, so much for the locket. I know I will treasure it, and I'm so glad it is on the picture where you can also see it." She gave Andrew a swift kiss on the cheek, then she leaped up and swirled her skirt about her, almost blowing out the candle. Andrew caught her by the waist as she swirled by him and pulled her to himself.

There was a faint light in the eastern sky when Andrew and Elisabeth stepped out the smokehouse door into the cool morning. "How will I get by the sentry?" whispered Elisabeth. "Do I simply waltz by him and pretend that I am taking a morning stroll?"

"You could," whispered Andrew, "and I believe you could make it work. Or I could walk ahead and send him to the kitchen for a cup of coffee for me. Perhaps that is what we should do."

"Yes," whispered Elisabeth. "Then you could walk with me till we must part."

It was quickly accomplished, and too soon they had to say their last farewell. "Goodbye, my dearest," said Andrew.

"Goodbye, my love," said Elisabeth, and she turned quickly and walked into the twilight shadows of the morning. Andrew watched her till he could see no more, a choking lump in his throat. He turned his face to the sky and felt the tears in his eyes.

"How do I love thee," he thought? *"Let me count the ways…"*

Chapter 14

Before the sun was an hour over the horizon, F Company was on the march. Dew was still on the grass at the side of the road, and the marching of several hundred boots raised very little dust in the cool air. Captain Andrew Greyson rode at the head of the double column with his newly promoted executive officer, Lieutenant Meeks, riding beside him. The privileges of rank—riding a horse instead of walking—did not feel comfortable with Andrew, and he often walked, leading his bay horse.

The column of men, numbering a hundred and fifty-three, was in high spirits. They were on the move again, now for the second time, while the remainder of the 11th Regiment was still in camp. Carrying only their rifles and a light personal pack, they felt like they could walk all the way to Virginia if they had to. "We will let you'all know when the war is over," they called to the stay-behind companies, most of them still in chow lines. "General Lee needs us in Virginny to do some fightin'. Don't you'all forgit to shine yo' shoes."

Laughter rippled up and down the column, and some skylarking occurred, but through it all the column kept up a steady, rhythmical march. "Now thet we is gone, you gonna' haf 'ta fight them Yankees by youselfs." F Company was a battle-seasoned outfit, and even the replacements for the men lost at Little Hilltop felt the pride. They were the best outfit in the Confederate Army, and they did not mind letting people know it.

Ahead, a quarter mile up the road, were the surviving three men of O'Donal's scout brigade, walking point. "I know we aren't anywhere near the enemy," said Andrew to his executive officer, "but I like to know what's ahead." The three men should have been returned to their home companies after the battle, but they had adamantly refused to leave till the regiment resignedly transferred them officially to F Company.

Behind the column of marching men, and staying back just enough to avoid any dust from the marching, came the two wagons of Sergeant Grant's field kitchen. The sergeant himself held the reins of the first wagon, now and then tapping them lightly on the rumps of the two mules he had named Mac and Scotty—after the two reluctant, slow to get going, Union generals, McClellan and Scott.

Trailing last came the two baggage wagons, each pulled by a span of horses. Piled high in each wagon were the tents, the blanket rolls, the extra equipment of the men. Also riding on the buckboard seat of the last wagon was Sergeant O'Donal. Stationed there by Captain Greyson, his job was to make sure that any men that drifted back to ride in the baggage wagons were genuine hardship cases. Just knowing that the sergeant was back there, kept many a man going that would have allowed himself to give up.

The column was on a somewhat improved road that followed the east bank of the river in a mostly southerly direction. Several miles out of the town of Clearfield, it would veer east to go around some swamps. After that it turned southwest again toward Chattanooga, about a hundred and twenty miles away. As soon as the column had established itself on the road, Captain Greyson rode back along the column to see how the rear elements were doing. He rode beside Sergeant O'Donal in the last wagon.

"The men seem in good spirits," said Andrew.

"It's a good outfit," said the sergeant.

"No takers on hitching a ride yet?" said Andrew.

"Well, actually, sir, I had a few come to me with some minor complaints. I suggested they ask for a transfer out of F Company if they couldn't walk. Get in the artillery, I told them. Ride on those damn caissons loaded with gunpowder. Get yourselves blown up. They changed their minds."

Andrew smiled. He could count on Sergeant O'Donal to handle his jobs with efficiency and spirit.

O'Donal frowned. "Captain," he said. "Clarkson and Hatfield didn't show up for morning muster. I think they decided they didn't want to go to Virginia and took off."

"I guess that doesn't surprise me very much," said Andrew. "I'm not sure those two ever realized they were in the army." He paused, thoughtfully. "Sergeant," he said, "don't report them till after our first action in Virginia. Then report them missing. I think those two boys have done their duty and deserve a chance to grow older."

"Yes, sir," said the sergeant. "I'll do as you say."

Andrew cantered his horse up the center of the road between the two files of men who were marching on either side of the road. He reached the head of the column, nodded briefly to Lieutenant Meeks, and continued riding. The road here swung close to the river, and Andrew looked wistfully across the water to the trail on the other side that Elisabeth and he had ridden just a few weeks ago. A longing to see her just once more came over him. He thought of the picture of her that he had in his coat pocket, and he felt slightly comforted by its presence. And Liselle, he thought, bright, vivacious and pretty. I am leaving so much behind, he thought.

At that moment, a moving object across the river caught his eye, and he turned to see it more clearly. It was a figure on a horse—the horse galloping furiously, leaping over hedgerows, splashing through shallow streams, its tail streaming behind. The rider was leaning over the neck of the horse—a gray horse—the rider seemingly as one with the horse, cloak fluttering, the golden hair of the rider flying in the wind. It was Elisabeth, and Andrew's heart swelled within him.

A short distance behind the gray horse was a black horse with flashing white stockings, galloping as swiftly as the first horse. The rider was a slight figure with dark hair, also riding with more than ordinary skill.

By now the riders across the river had caught the attention of the entire column of troops, and all were marching with eyes right, as if on parade. "Lookit them ride," they said. "Ain't thet purtty?"

"Are you talkin' 'bout the horses or the girls?"

"Both," was the answer. "I ain't never seen nuthin' like it."

Andrew watched with profound emotions as the gray horse charged up a bluff on the bank of the river and slid to a stop just as it seemed it would leap into the current. The rider, Elisabeth, vaulted from the saddle, and with one hand on the horse's bridle, she stood beside the horse's head and looked across the river at the marching men. She seemed quiet now, composed, pensive. The black horse stopped behind the gray horse, and though the rider alighted, she did not come up to stand beside Elisabeth.

Andrew watched, all his soul crying within him to turn his horse into the river, draw his saber and fling it away into the current, and ride up and seize forever the figure on the other side. But it could not be.

When his horse came opposite the figure on the other side, Andrew raised his arm high, and held it high for perhaps ten or twelve paces, held it high in salute to the lovely and beautiful Elisabeth.

And Elisabeth held up her slim arm, did not wave, simply held it up—and Andrew believed he could see her face clearly, see her smile, see her blue eyes, see the freckles on her nose, see the beautiful, golden curls that framed her face. Then with something like a shuddering sigh, he brought his arm down and turned his face to the road ahead.

On to Chattanooga, he thought. On to Virginia. Shenendoah Valley, here we come.

A Brief Digression to a battlefield of the Civil War Chickamauga Creek, Georgia September 19 and 20, 1863

The Confederate Army sent General Longstreet with two divisions from the Army of Northern Virginia in the hopes that it would swing the battle at Chickamauga Creek in their favor. And it did. Longstreet's divisions arrived on the evening of the first day of battle, and stiff and weary from two days of riding on trains, having been served very few rations en route, they, nevertheless, marched at double time from the rail head and took up positions during the night in order to make the assault the following morning.

In the early morning, Captain Greyson, whose company was to lead the charge, was chagrined to discover that the full ration of ammunition had not been given to his men—they had been allotted only a half dozen rounds each. When the regimental colonel, in answer to his inquiries, said, "We expect you to use your bayonets," Andrew threw military protocol to the winds and demanded to see General James Longstreet, himself.

Longstreet was at General Bragg's headquarters tent when Captain Greyson barged in unannounced. The generals and their staff, leaning over a map on a table, looked up in surprise at the incensed officer. "Sir," said Captain Greyson addressing Generals Longstreet and Bragg, "I am Captain Greyson, commanding F Company attached to your Virginia Light Infantry Division. My men and I are to lead the charge against Rosecrans' Corps on our left flank. Sir, my men were only issued six rounds of ammunition per man, sir, and if that issue stands, sir, I will not lead my men into battle." Here Andrew drew his saber and laid it on the table before General Longstreet.

Here and there a staff officer's face grew red in anger at the brashness of this junior officer, but Longstreet and Bragg merely looked at him.

General Bragg said, "Are you the officer that led the night assault on that hilltop in Central Tennessee?"

"Yes, sir," said Andrew.

General Bragg said, "How many rounds do you believe you need for each man?"

"Thirty rounds per man," said Andrew.

"And you won't fight with less?" said the general.

Andrew considered. For a moment he thought he might agree to twenty-five, but then he thought, my men deserve every chance they can get. I'll not sell them short. "No, sir," he said. "We deserve the full ration of thirty rounds."

General Bragg turned to his staff supply officer. "Do we have the ammunition, Colonel?" he asked.

"I believe I can find some, sir," replied the colonel.

"See to it," said the general, "and you, Captain, see to it that your company does not fail us."

Just before noon, Longstreet's two divisions, led on the left flank by Captain Greyson's company, charged the Union forces. The ferocity of the charge carried them right through the Union lines routing General Rosecrans' army of three corps, sending them reeling back to Chattanooga. In a scant half hour of fighting, the company lost more men than they did in the Little Hilltop battle, although most of the original company had already fallen at Chancellorsville, Gettysburg, and Antietam. Andrew, himself, was badly wounded in his left leg and arm from an exploding shell, and Sergeant O'Donal was killed in the first few minutes of the assault.

The Confederate Army won the battle—they drove the Union Army from the field, but Bragg's Army of Tennessee, reinforced by Longstreet's two divisions from the Army of Northern Virginia, lost 17,800 men in the two days fighting. The Union forces, Rosecrans' Army of the Cumberland, lost 16,600 men in the same time. The Chickamauga Creek, called the "river of death" by the Cherokees, had lived up to its name.

Book IV

Georgia, Virginia, Tennessee
1863-1924

The Gentleman

Chapter 1

November 1863

Captain Andrew Greyson was slowly riding north along a wagon trail in Central Tennessee—slowly because the wounds on his left arm and leg were not completely healed—wounds that were the results of a close shell burst almost beneath Andrew's tall, bay horse. The horse, which had carried Andrew through so many campaigns, had taken most of the force of the explosion, but fragments had cut into Andrew's left leg and left arm; and one small piece had cut a furrow in Andrew's scalp. Both Andrew and the horse had gone down; the horse mercifully had died of its multiple wounds, and Andrew, stunned, was hardly aware that the charge that his company and he had led at the head of General Longstreet's two divisions had carried completely through the Union forces.

Andrew, struggling to regain his consciousness, had been able to sit up leaning back against his stricken horse. Lights seemed to be flashing on and off before his eyes so he closed them and lay his head back on the warm body of his horse.

He stirred once when a soldier who looked to be as badly wounded as he, limped up to him. "Is this your sword, Captain?" the man asked proffering the saber. Andrew nodded, and the man lay the saber down at Andrew's side.

Andrew closed his eyes again, and he may have slept, or lost consciousness. When he opened his eyes again—opened them to just bare slits—there were long shadows on the hillside casting in deep relief every object on the ground, and Andrew, eyes still partially closed as if he could not quite face reality, saw that the field was strewn with the bodies of men. There were so many, and they were so randomly scattered, that he could not have counted them even if he could have made the effort.

Andrew felt a great weariness—a great sadness. There may have been tears mixed with the grime, the sweat, the blood on his face. What a waste, he thought. How many times have I seen this scene repeated? He lay an arm outstretched along the flank of his fallen companion, the bay horse. "I'm very sorry, old friend," he said. "You and I have fought one battle too many."

And that was the gist of what, several days later, he told General Longstreet. Andrew was sitting on a low cot in a makeshift hospital tent when the commander of the two divisions from Virginia, making a visit to the wounded of the Battle of Chickamauga Creek, stopped to see him.

Andrew saw the general approaching so he stood up, slowly and stiffly with considerable effort. He was glad his cot was near a tent pole so that he could hold onto the pole for balance and support.

The general said, "I'm sorry to see you wounded again, Captain. Your company did splendidly, leading the charge. We drove them back all the way to Chattanooga."

"Yes, sir," said Andrew. He could feel no rise of spirit—no sense of victory. He only felt a tremendous loss, as if his soul had been cut from him.

The general paused, sensing Andrew's mood, but not understanding it. After all, hadn't they come all the way from Virginia, and hadn't his two divisions led the charge that routed the Yankees out of Georgia? There was plenty of glory to go around.

"You'll be back with us soon," said the general. "You will be happy to know, being a Tennessean, that we will be staying here attached to the Army of Tennessee, at least for a while to fight some campaigns here." The general turned to go.

"Sir," said Andrew. General Longstreet turned back. Andrew paused. At other times he had not minded facing authority when it meant the welfare of his men. But now, when he was resolved to ask for something for himself, he was unsure of himself.

"Sir," said Andrew again. "I lost my sergeant in that charge. I lost all my company except fourteen men. The remainder of those who came from Tennessee almost two years ago lie in graves scattered from Chancellorsville to Antietam."

"We have all lost much in this war," said the general. "We appreciate the sacrifices you and your men have made." He turned to go again.

And again Andrew stopped him. "Sir," he said, "I can no longer lead men into battle—to certain death. Sir, I wish to resign my commission as an officer, sir."

Everything became very quiet. Men lying on other cots in the tent looked on in awe. The general's staff, two colonels and a major, looked uneasy. Finally, Andrew had the general's full attention.

"You can't do that, Captain," snapped the general. "We are in a war. You can't just quit."

"Sir, if you call being wounded a half dozen times quitting—if you call writing a hundred and fifty letters of regret to the families of my dead men quitting..." Andrew held firmly to the tent pole. The tent itself seemed to be spinning around. All Andrew could see were white faces with eyes—all looking at him. He pulled himself erect.

"Sir," he said, "if you wish, I will carry a rifle as an infantry private. But I will no longer lead men into battle."

The general looked at Andrew for a long time, and Andrew met his look. There was no backing down now. There was no taking back. And he had no regrets. It was right, what he was doing. At one time he had been right to fight for this cause. Now it was right to end this part of it.

The general seemed to have reached a decision. He beckoned to the major, his aide. "Major," he said, "write Captain Greyson a letter, granting him a convalescent leave, to begin as soon as he feels fit to travel, and to end when he feels fit for duty again. And I'll sign it."

"Yes, sir," said the major. He wrote.

"Captain, you are on your honor," said General Longstreet. "When you are fit, come back to this army and report to me."

"Yes, sir," said Andrew. The major handed the paper on a board and the pen for the general to sign. The general signed the paper, folded it, and handed it to Andrew.

"Thank you," said Andrew. "Thank you, sir."

The general paused a bit longer, looking at Andrew. His demeanor softened. He nodded and almost smiled. "Good luck,

Captain. Perhaps when you rejoin us, the prospects for the Confederacy will look brighter. I happen to know that General Bragg is planning some campaigns to take back some of Central Tennessee. I hope we meet again." And he put out his hand, shook hands with Andrew, turned on his heels and left the tent.

Andrew, riding his horse along the grassy, seldom-used wagon trail, was riding slowly because of his wounds, but also because the horse he had would go no faster. A week after the general's visit, Andrew had left the hospital. At the division's quartermaster he had, with the aid of a quartermaster sergeant, gone through the stack of saddles picked up from the battlefield, and he had found his own saddle. It was stained with dried blood, some perhaps his own blood and much of it the horse's, but it was still useable.

Over the protests of the quartermaster sergeant, Andrew had insisted they issue him a horse. "I came with a horse, and I'll leave with a horse," Andrew told the sergeant.

"These horses are all assigned to officers," said the sergeant. They were looking over the retinue of horses corralled at the division headquarters.

Andrew had no intention of taking some soldier's horse. He knew what it was to have a favorite, faithful horse that you got to know and that you could count on. He looked the horses over. "How about that dun mare?" He pointed to a smallish horse standing by itself, obviously not getting its share of the feed. Its head was low, ears drooping. It seemed to be asleep.

The sergeant snorted. "Well sure, Captain. If you call that a horse. You sure can take that critter off our hands. We was about to shoot it. It refuses to go into battle anymore—just puts its head down and balks."

Andrew smiled. "I think we'll get along," he said.

The horse had looked at him suspiciously at first. But Andrew talked to it as he saddled it, gave it some grain in a feed bag over its nose, and it seemed to understand that they were not headed for a place where cannons roared. When Andrew swung a leg over its back, it seemed quite willing to go; however, it had its own speed—a slow, easy walk.

This pace suited Andrew fine as they headed northeast out of Georgia toward Central Tennessee. He could walk at about the same pace as the horse preferred, and this he did for short intervals in order to get his body back into a state of physical competence. His leg seemed to be coming along in good order; he could use it without discomfort, but his arm was slower in healing, and he usually wore it in a sling.

His boots, he noted with satisfaction, were scuffed and worn with creases on both boots from rubbing against the stirrups, but were yet in excellent condition. They had been resoled and re-heeled just before the last campaign. If he ever got back to Milford, Andrew thought, he must surely compliment the bootmaker on the fine boots he had made.

Tied behind his saddle was a quite large bundle containing several blankets, some food the quartermaster sergeant had issued to him, some bandaging material, and some personal items. His revolver, uncomfortable to have on his waist, was in a holster on a belt and looped by the belt through a strap on the saddle. A bag of grain for the horse rode back almost on the horse's rump.

The surgeon who had given him the bandages and had dressed his wounds for the last time had said, "I can understand why you are anxious to get out of here—it's not the most pleasant surroundings. But you have got to keep these wounds clean. If they develop a redness or swelling come back, and we'll lance and clean them. You may still have some small pieces of metal in some of these cuts. We did the best we could."

He looked at Andrew keenly and said, "I have a feeling you don't plan to stick around here. Do you mind telling me where you are headed?"

"I don't mind," said Andrew. "There's someone I have to see in Central Tennessee—in Clearfield."

"Hmm," said the doctor. "That part of the state is out of our hands. I'm from Knoxville and I can't go there. The Union Army doesn't occupy every small hamlet, but they do control the larger towns, the roads and the railways."

Andrew nodded. "That's true," he said, "but it's a rather wild country. I think I can get by all right."

The surgeon nodded but said, "Just remember you are still handicapped by these wounds and bandages. Your left arm, particularly, will be awhile recovering. Don't overdo it."

"I appreciate your concern," said Andrew.

But the doctor wasn't finished. He sat down in a canvas chair facing Andrew and said, "We have been getting casualties and refugees from that area caused, not by the Union Army, but by renegade guerrilla bands that are taking advantage of the situation. They loot homes and villages, and burn them, and, worst of all, are actually murdering some of our populace."

Andrew stared. He hadn't heard of such dangers. His concerns for Elisabeth, for Liselle and her family, for others he knew in Clearfield suddenly increased. "Who are these people?" he asked.

The doctor looked at him without speaking for a few moments. Then he said, "Regrettably, they are ex-soldiers of our own Confederate Army. That's why you don't hear about it officially. When Vicksburg fell to the Union Army last summer, General Grant turned loose about thirty thousand of our soldiers he had captured, on condition they not fight any more. Unfortunately, some of the more ruthless ones did not go home. They drifted north from Mississippi to the wilder lands of Tennessee and the border states, and now they are outlaw bands preying on the people. As if it isn't enough to fight the Union Army." The doctor shook his head. "This war has just about made me lose my faith in the human race. How I wish it would end."

Andrew sat quietly, but a terrible dread was seizing him. He stood up. "I must go," he said. "Thank you, Doctor."

"Well, good luck," said the doctor, "and take care of those wounds." Andrew thanked him and left.

Chapter 2

Therefore, Andrew, who longed to return to Elisabeth as soon as possible, was riding slowly also because he was in Union Army occupied country; and he had no intention of being captured as a Confederate soldier, or worse, being shot as a spy. He proceeded as cautiously as he could along back trails, along wooded valleys and remote country, avoiding main roads and all villages.

The horse had turned out to be an unexpected asset. From its recent experiences it had developed a keen suspicion of soldiers whether they be Confederate or Union. On one occasion it had stopped and, ears forward and nostrils flaring, stared up the trail they were traveling on. Andrew had taken the hint, got off the horse and led it into some thick brush in time to avoid meeting a Union patrol. The horse, beginning to trust Andrew, had stood stock-still, rolling only it eyes expressively as they waited for the patrol to pass.

The nearer they came to Clearfield, the more anxious Andrew became, and he had to remind himself to not throw caution to the winds and ride as swiftly as possible to be with Elisabeth. Her picture was still in his inside coat pocket, wrapped and re-wrapped so many times that its edges were frayed. The picture of Liselle was there too, the shy appealing smile still there. How Andrew hoped that they were all right.

In the somewhat more than a year and a half that Andrew had been gone he had received two letters from Elisabeth. Mail was so haphazard with no organized mail service, that Andrew was sure there was many a letter that just hadn't made the connections to reach him. Likewise, he was sure that few of his letters had reached her, particularly during the last half year that much of Tennessee had been occupied by the Union Army.

The two letters from Elisabeth had been the brightest spots—perhaps the only bright spots—in his time with the Army of Northern Virginia. Those letters were also in his coat pocket, the pages beginning to come apart at the creases. How he had treasured those letters as he read and reread them. How he had marveled at the beautiful, flowing handwriting. He could see those hands, in his imagination, writing those letters.

Once, just before the battle at Gettysburg, he had awakened in the dark from a dream in which her hands were touching his face, soothing his brow, caressing his cheeks. For a while, there in the dark, the dream had seemed so real that he could almost still feel her hands on his face. Then in his great loneliness, he had wept…and wept.

"I must not despair," he had whispered to himself. "I will be with her again." But as the men around him fell in battle, it was not easy to remain hopeful. Now he was finally on his way back to her.

As Andrew moved through the country, it seemed to him that he was so much more skillful in woodcraft than he had been when he first led F Company into their first battle at the Little Hilltop. It seemed to him that he was quite aware—could sense what was over the next rise, or turn in the trail. He recognized where danger might lie, where he would be exposed to others before he could be aware of them; and he meticulously avoided such situations.

He wondered if he had become as skilled as his one-time scouts, Clarkson and Hatfield. He thought often of those two likeable boys, now that he was nearing their habitat, and he hoped they had survived whatever war had swept through their territory. He hoped their families were still safe there in the deeper wilderness of the Tennessee hills.

Andrew remembered Danny Clarkson's mother, what a remarkably beautiful, gracious person she was. In the short time he had been in her company, he had known he was in the presence of one of those unique persons that one does not meet often.

For night camp, Andrew would look for a particularly brushy area well off whatever trail he was traveling, or he would detour up some isolated ravine. Over a small fire he would boil some water for tea, and in a small pot he cooked a grain cereal.

One evening he watched a covey of quail go to roost in a brush patch, and by stealthy, careful maneuvering after darkness had set in, he was able to seize two of them. Usually he left the circle of light that the fire sent out, but that night he roasted the small birds held over the fire between green willow sticks. They were delicious.

Each night, once the darkness was complete, Andrew would get his blanket roll from behind the cantle of the saddle and go to some preselected spot well away from the campfire. There he would roll up in the blankets beside a log, or under an overhanging ledge and sleep.

He did not think he was in a great deal of danger from Union patrols, which he did not believe were out much at night; but the renegade soldiers that he had been warned of, though he had seen no evidence of them, concerned him. If they were outlaws, they might well travel at night, he thought. And he did not think his captain's rank would do him much good even to the ex-Confederate soldiers. In fact, the officer's rank might well incite anger from these disillusioned men. He was quite sure that meeting with such men would be disastrous.

The temperatures were quite cold at night in this winter season, and Andrew needed the two blankets he had for warmth. He took off his well-worn boots, but he kept his clothes on, and he would sleep with his revolver at his side under the blankets.

He did not tether the horse, the dun mare. He felt that if someone crept up on them, the horse might well give warning before he was aware of the danger; and in case of some sort of attack, the horse deserved the chance to flee. Each morning as Andrew came back into the camp, he would find the horse standing behind some thick brush—standing so still and so camouflaged by its dun color against the drying foliage, that it was not immediately evident when he looked for it.

And each night as he looked up at the stars, he would consider how much closer he was to Clearfield, and he would wonder if Elisabeth were looking up at the same stars and thinking of him. Perhaps she would sense that he was coming near. If sleep escaped him for a while, he would hum the lullaby that he once sang to her. "*Hush-a-bye, my pretty one. Go to sleep.*"

Despite Andrew's cautious mode of travel, he had one scare that he could not quite figure out. It was noonday, and Andrew was traveling through some hilly country quite covered with bushes and trees. He happened to glance back after he passed a particularly dense clump of bushes and saw the face of a man looking at him through the leaves. The face was low, as if the man were lying on the ground.

The two men looked directly at each other, neither making any gestures nor saying anything. Andrew was startled and quite chagrined that he had not seen the man before he passed by him, but he kept his composure and merely looked back at the face in the brush.

Andrew's trail took him around a point of a hill, and as soon as he was out of sight from the watching face in the bush, he turned his horse off the trail. He dismounted, took his revolver from its holster on the saddle, stood behind his horse and waited.

When there was no pursuit, no alarm, Andrew led his horse laboriously cross-country over a range of hills into another valley, and then turned north again.

When Andrew puzzled over the encounter later, he surmised that the man must have been a deserter from either army, that did not know quite what to make of a Confederate officer so far from any Confederate Army units.

After eight days of riding Andrew came to the river that ran south out of Clearfield. He did not know quite how he knew it was the right river, but he was quite sure it was so. He had been keeping a constant awareness of direction and distance as he rode, so that he was quite sure of his approximate location.

Tomorrow he would be in Clearfield. By noontime, he thought, he would be there, depending, of course, on how careful he would have to be when he got close.

He camped that night beside the river, lying down to sleep in the shadows of some large boulders on a ledge above the river. He could hear the water as it swirled through rocks near the shore, and as it got dark, he could see the stars above and their glimmer in the water.

Tomorrow, he thought, I will be there. Tomorrow, he thought, I will see Elisabeth. Tomorrow, he thought, this war will be over for me. Tomorrow, he thought, my life will begin again. Tomorrow, he thought, tomorrow...tomorrow...

He dreamed as he slept of Elisabeth—dreamed of her fleetingly as images wafted through the windows of his mind. He dreamed of her blue eyes, and of her golden hair flowing in a cool breeze. He dreamed of her smile, yet there seemed to be a sweet sadness to that smile. When he reached out to comfort her, she was gone.

The night air was cool, and Andrew woke. He heard the river water nearby, and could feel the mist that rose off the water touch his face. An owl called from across the river, hooted three more times—who...whoo...whooo—and was silent. For some reason that he could not explain, Andrew felt a deep loneliness. He pulled the blankets closer around himself and slept.

Chapter 3

By early morning Andrew was on a height of land on the east side of Clearfield, looking over the town with his field glasses. He could not see all of the town, but what he could see showed no sign of an occupying army. He was dismayed to see that some of the buildings in the business district were only charred remains. The courthouse, however, was standing, and it appeared that the bridge crossing the river was still there. As he watched, he saw a few people moving along the streets. It seemed that the war had passed through Clearfield and was gone.

Andrew came into the outskirts of Clearfield riding the horse on a wagon trail that became a gravel covered residential street. Houses with fenced in yards were on both sides of the street. Andrew rode slowly, watching the houses, watching the street ahead, not sure what the situation was. Many of the houses seemed uninhabited; and some, seemingly the ones that had once been the finer ones, were burned to the ground, the fireplaces and chimneys standing starkly amid the ruins.

Some of the homes were occupied; the yards looked tended, and at one, where the house was close to the street, a very old woman with a knit shawl over her shoulders rushed out onto the porch and down the steps toward Andrew. Andrew came off the horse and stood waiting for the woman to arrive. She was excited, waving her arms in the air.

"You're back!" she shrilled. "Thank God, you are back."

"Yes, ma'am," said Andrew, touching the brim of his campaign hat.

"I knew you would come back," said the old woman, standing in front of Andrew, smiling up at him. "Did you bring Luther with you? Is Luther in this army?"

"No, ma'am. I don't think so," said Andrew.

"Luther is in the Tennessee Volunteers," said the old woman proudly. "Do you know where they are?"

"Well," said Andrew, "no, I really don't. Really, ma'am, I'm just..."

"Oh, no need to explain," said the woman, brightly. "I know how these things are. Military secrets. I know all about them."

"Yes, ma'am," said Andrew.

"Now that you're here, maybe those dirty, awful men will go away," the woman said. She pointed to the charred remains of the corner house. "Burned that last week, they did. And the Phillipsons have been gone for nearly a year. Went to Atlanta, as I recall."

Andrew looked at the burned out house. He shook his head sadly. "Who did this?" he asked, perhaps not expecting a valid answer from the old woman.

"Pirates," she answered fiercely, her eyes angry, her hands quivering. "Pirates," she said again. "They come and they go. They shoot guns along the street. No one goes outside to see them. We only peek out the window, and if they see you, they shoot the window." The old woman's speech was faltering, but she said confidently, "Now that you are back, they will go away."

Andrew did not have the heart to tell her the truth—that the Confederate Army was not back—probably never would be back. As he left the old woman, he was both sad and angry—almost angry enough, he thought, that if he knew where the Union Army was located, he would ride up to their headquarters and demand that they control the outlaw element in the territory they occupied. He smiled grimly at the picture of himself doing such, riding into a Union camp while in his Confederate uniform, and demanding to be heard.

When he looked back, riding on down the street, the woman smiled cheerfully and waved. Andrew saluted, and rode on, not feeling very good about the alarms the old woman's words had started in his mind.

Andrew carefully rode the horse around the main business section of the town. If there were elements of the Union Army in town, that is where they would likely be, he thought. Particularly, they might be in the courthouse. Perhaps that was why that building was still standing.

Andrew found himself riding through the area on which his once famous F Company had been encamped—and that seemed so long ago. He noted that the smokehouse that had been his office and living quarters was still standing, looking as weather-beaten, but durable as ever. The main house and the stables that had been 11th Regimental headquarters were burned. As Andrew rode across what had once been the front lawn of the house, he remembered Sergeant Holbrook and his mountain howitzer-guns. Where was Brookie now?

Going west, Andrew came to the road that followed the river. To the north was Little Hilltop, quite visible from this vantage point. Andrew turned south and followed the road to the bridge. He met no one along the road and began to hope that he could get to the bridge and across it without attracting any attention.

Feeling very exposed, very vulnerable, Andrew got off the horse and led it across the bridge. Some of the railings were damaged, but the bridge seemed sound; and the water swirled through the pilings below as swiftly as ever.

Andrew turned up the carriage drive of the Turnwell mansion. The place seemed deserted. The house, itself, was standing, but was gutted by fire—part of the roof gone, black soot streaks marking all the windows, the grand veranda sagging, and the terrace gardens grown tangled and wild.

Andrew, still leading the horse, stopped, dismayed. He looked to the stables where Howard had once taken such good care of the horses. It, too, looked empty and forlorn, doors swinging open.

And where is Elisabeth? thought Andrew. The bleak windows of the house stared hauntingly back at him.

The working buildings and the slaves' cabins were in a yard stretching off behind the stable, and there Andrew saw a thin trail of smoke coming from one of the cabins. He turned and led the dun mare in that direction.

Once Andrew got close to the cabins, he could see that not only were they occupied, but the sheds and barns had occupants in them. There were people watching him from almost every doorway and window. The open sided sheds held numerous people who were slowly leaving their work benches and collecting at the open front to watch him. Children who had been playing in front of the doorways caught the mood of their elders and stood in small groups watching the man in a Confederate Army uniform, leading a horse, coming closer.

It occurred to Andrew as he walked up the space between the cabins and the barns and sheds—cabins to his left, barns and sheds to his right—that this large collection of people, all black, were refugees. These were the slaves who had come up to meet the advancing Union Army, or had been swept along by that army's campaigns. And suddenly Andrew was quite sure that if anyone had been responsible for these people gathering here, if anyone had been trying to help them begin a new life, if anyone had been doing all they could to take care of them, it would have been Elisabeth. This is where she would be. Any minute now she would come out of some doorway and come running to him. And he would hold out his arms…

But it wasn't Elisabeth who burst out of a doorway and with a cry of despair came running, arms held up, face turned to the sky in some agony of emotion.

It wasn't Elisabeth—it was Alexandra. Alexandra calling, "Captain! Captain!"

Andrew watched her come, tears on her face, broken words, choking sobs. What could be the cause for such deep grief in Alexandra? In an instant of clarity, of terrible reality, Andrew realized the answer. It could only be for Elisabeth.

Andrew wanted to close his eyes—shut out this scene. Though Alexandra was speaking, he heard nothing, only a terrible, roaring, rushing sound in his ears, in his mind, as if a sea was going to overwhelm him. Strength slipped from his body; he dropped the reins of the horse and managed to remain standing only because some unconscious reflex kept his knees from buckling. A loud, keening groan escaped his lips, a sound such as a person might make if their heart were pierced by a long knife.

Alexandra threw her arms around Andrew, and the two of them held each other up, since neither seemed to have the strength to stand alone.

Is there any greater pain than the knowledge of permanent separation from a dearly loved one? Certainly physical pain does not approach it. When the dearly loved one is merely separated from the person who loves that one, though the separation be for years or perhaps a lifetime, there is yet always that consolation, that hope, that at some future time the separation will end. But when the absence of the loved one is for always, then the lover must resign all hopes for a reunion, and rely instead on the strength of memories.

Chapter 4

When Andrew became aware, again, of his surroundings, he found himself on one knee, head bowed, elbows resting on the raised knee, in an attitude of prayer or meditation. Alexandra was kneeling in front of him, her hands covering her face. Around himself, Andrew heard the low murmur of voices, and he looked up to see that many of the people had come in closely. There was sympathy in their eyes. They seemed to be offering consolation.

"Dat Miz Elizbet, she one fine lady," said one older woman. Others said, "She he'p us when we wuz sick an' hungry," and "She wuz an angel from heaven." "We had no place to go, an' she come to he'p us."

Andrew began to understand how much these poor, black people, frightened by the turmoil of life the war had brought, revered his beloved Elisabeth. She had died five months previously—died of an influenza that was sweeping through the refugees. On a morning she had been nursing the sick that needed her. By evening she had a severe fever, and by morning she was gone.

"When you feel able, I'll take you to her grave," said Alexandra, "and I'll tell you all I can of her life while you were gone."

Andrew nodded. He was seated at a table in one of the open sheds being served a cup of hot, herbal tea—served in an elegant teacup salvaged from the destroyed mansion. Andrew tried to react to all the kindness being shown him, but often he found himself staring at nothing, his mind seeming to alternate between a sharp, cutting pain and a dull, cloudy haze.

It was with some relief that he agreed to go when Alexandra suggested they do so. He felt a need to be away from others, to face the excruciating reality of the day, to give way to emotions. Presently Alexandra appeared leading a gray horse, and Andrew recognized his fellow devotee, Sunny Boy.

He put his arms around Sunny Boy's neck, and holding back tears, he murmured, "Sunny Boy, Sunny Boy, we have both lost too much." The big horse lowered his head and nuzzled against Andrew's coat. When Andrew put his arms around the big head and hugged it against himself, the horse stood quietly.

They rode south on the river trail, Alexandra on Sunny Boy, Andrew following on the dun mare. Alexandra said very little; they were both alone with their thoughts of Elisabeth. They followed the trail that Elisabeth and he had once traveled together, the same trail on which he had last seen Elisabeth riding with the wind in her hair. He soon realized that they were heading for the high bluff where they had held their arms high in farewell, and he thought, yes, this is appropriate.

At the bluff at the edge of the river, they stopped. "There, under that small oak tree, we buried her," said Alexandra. She stayed back, holding the reins of the two horses. As Andrew walked forward, Sunny Boy nickered.

How to express Andrew's emotions? He walked forward, erect, firm steps, head held up. He stopped under the oak tree, some of its branches—leafless at this season—spreading out over the mound of earth beneath them. Andrew stood quietly looking down. After a moment he looked off across the river and saw himself, riding with F Company—and raising his arm in salute to the beautiful woman who had stood here—and was now buried here.

He knelt down on one knee and put both hands on the ground—on the earth that covered Elisabeth. "I am here, Elisabeth," he said.

He looked up at the sky, and at the trees around him; and he looked at the water of the river flowing by. He stood up, stood straight, and looked up. Through the branches of the oak he saw the sun coming out from behind a small, white cloud.

"Elisabeth, my love," he said, "I accept that what we had together is all that we will ever have together, but it is enough. Much of my life is buried here with you, and that will not change. I will always be with you, as you will always by with me. The sorrow I feel is less than the love and joy and delight you were and still are. I love you, Elisabeth."

Andrew took from around his neck the long, silk stocking that he had worn there for so long. He tied one end firmly to an overhanging branch. He looked at it thoughtfully for a moment, then tied two knots in the stocking close together. Finally, he tied the free end of the stocking to a branch so that the silk stocking swung between the branches like a small cradle. He looked a moment longer, and turned and walked back to Alexandra and the horses.

They rode back quietly. When they were near the plantation buildings, Alexandra pointed to a saddle path that went toward the big house and reined the gray horse into it. Andrew followed. They rode by the big house, looking at it, feeling its emptiness and desolation.

"The Turnwells left more than a year ago," said Alexandra. "When it seemed a sure thing that the Union Army would come here, they closed the house and went to Atlanta."

"And was my battle at Little Hilltop in vain?" asked Andrew. "We paid such a dear price."

"No," said Alexandra. "Something of such courage and sacrifice is not in vain. The world is different because of it."

Andrew nodded. "Yes," he said. "I believe it was the right thing at that time."

They came around the front of the house and at the grown over terrace, Alexandra stopped the gray horse and got off. She began to uncinch the saddle. "There is still much I must tell you," she said, "but first, take your saddle from that mare and put it on Sunny Boy." When Andrew hesitated, she said, "Elisabeth wanted you to have Sunny, and from the looks of your horse, Sunny will do a much better job of taking you where you have to go—and perhaps will be able to keep you from harm if you have to go into battle again."

"I'll take good care of him," said Andrew as he exchanged the horses' equipment. He finished the exchange by replacing the big Navy Colt .44 revolver in its place on the saddle.

Alexandra smiled briefly. "You have no idea how much work we went through to save him. First we hid him from the Union Army which was taking all able-bodied horses, and then we hid him from these raiders or deserters, or whatever they are." She looked keenly at Andrew. "They are more dangerous than the Union Army. They have no scruples."

Andrew nodded. "So I've heard."

Alexandra said, "They are the ones that burned this house. They came down there," she pointed at the refugee camp, "but by then we had all faded into the woods." She patted the velvety nose of Sunny Boy. "We finally hid him in a root cellar, walked him down into that dark place every day and brought him out at night to graze and exercise. He didn't like it much. But life will be better for him with you."

"Thank you," said Andrew, "for taking care of him and for giving him to me. We'll get along together." He stroked Sunny's neck, and the horse looked at him with a resigned look in his eyes.

"There are other things I have to talk to you about," said Alexandra.

"All right," said Andrew.

Alexandra took a folded paper out of a pocket. She handed it to Andrew and said, "Even at the end Elisabeth was concerned about me. She wrote this letter in which it states that I am a free Negro. I don't know how effective or legal this paper is, and now, with Lincoln's proclamation and with the way the war is going, it may not even be necessary."

Andrew looked up from the paper. "If it came to that, I could vouch for what she wanted for you," he said. "But I think you're right. It may not be an issue."

Alexandra looked at him earnestly. "The thing is, we tried to plan for what I should do, where I should go. And it all seemed so complicated and impossible. Finally, Elisabeth said to ask you when you came back—and so I'm asking. What shall I do?"

Andrew leaned back against the gray horse, and the horse braced himself to take the weight. Andrew thought for a moment and said, "Well, a big part of this is what you want."

"I know," said Alexandra, "but I've been so busy working with all the people coming in that I've not given it much thought. Besides," she added, "I miss Elisabeth so..."

Andrew nodded. "Yes, I understand," he said. He thought for a few moments more. "I think," he said, "that you have already made your choice." He looked over in the direction of the refugee camp. "It is helping your people in some way."

"Why, of course!" exclaimed Alexandra. She thought for a moment. "But how? In what way can I best help them?"

"Hmm," said Andrew. He took some paper and a pen and a small bottle of ink from his saddlebags. "A teacher of English is never without writing materials," he said with a hint of a smile. He began to write, the paper on a smooth part of his saddle, and dipping the pen into the ink bottle that Alexandra held for him.

"What I am writing here is a letter to a very good friend who is an English professor at Bloomington Normal School in Bloomington, Illinois." He wrote busily for a moment. "John Bailey was a classmate of mine at the Point until he had an accident while riding a horse. He still walks with a cane. Actually, I had a letter from him less than a year ago. How the letter got through from Illinois to my unit in Virginia, I'll never know. He wrote to assure me of his friendship despite the war between our people."

Andrew continued writing and said lightly, "I addressed him as Doctor Bailey just in case he has a doctor's degree by now, and if he doesn't, he will know that I consider him a good friend and don't mind taking a little jab at him."

He finished the letter and folded it. He carefully wiped off the pen tip with a bit of felt, and he corked the bottle of ink. These he stowed in the saddlebags.

He turned back to Alexandra. "I asked him to take you under his wing and to help you get an education. They train teachers at Bloomington Normal, and I believe not only that you could be an excellent teacher, but also that it is the way in which you could most help your people. I hope you believe, as I do, that education is the key to improving all our lives." He stopped talking for a moment and looked directly in Alexandra's face. "How does all this sound to you?"

"Captain," said Alexandra, "you are making some of my dreams come true—to go to school and learn. This is such a clear direction to go after these last very discouraging months." She paused and added wistfully, "Elisabeth and I had so much enjoyment reading and learning together."

Andrew smiled. "Elisabeth told me about that," he said. And he added, "Now, of course, you can read the letter for yourself, but I told him that you were very intelligent, were eager to learn, could read and write well. I also told him that as soon as the war ended and we could communicate, I would be supporting your education there financially." When Alexandra opened her mouth to protest, he held up his hand. "No," he said. "I know you can work and perhaps some work would be all right, but I hope you can really concentrate on your studies, and perhaps even have time to read some poetry."

When Alexandra still seemed hesitant, but did not quite know how to express her reluctance, Andrew said quietly, "I want to do this for Elisabeth. Please let me."

And Alexandra smiled and said, "All right. Let's both do it for Elisabeth."

"For Elisabeth," said Andrew, and he reached out and touched Alexandra's hand. "Now," he said, "we've made these plans, but I really don't know how we will get you to Illinois. I'm afraid I would be stretching my luck a bit if I rode with you that far north."

"But we send people north almost every week," said Alexandra. "It's not as risky as it used to be, but we still use much the same routes and techniques the underground railway used before the war—many of the same people are still helping us.

"You probably aren't surprised to know that the people in the North don't really want us to come up there—at least not in large numbers." Alexandra smiled. "That's a little ironic when you think how many men have died over the issue of slavery."

Andrew handed the letter to Alexandra. "When you are able to, write me a letter. I will be very interested in knowing how you are getting along. By the time you can write to me, I will probably be back at Albers College in Milford, Tennessee."

"All right," said Alexandra. "Now that I have a direction in my life, I'll go as soon as I can arrange for someone to take over my role here at the refugee camp." She paused. "Thank you, so much, Captain."

Chapter 5

There was a pause between them. Andrew went to the horse, the gray gelding, and adjusted the saddle straps and his blanket roll behind the saddle. The gray horse was somewhat larger than the mare.

Alexandra said, "I have more to tell you. Some very important things."

"Yes?" said Andrew.

"I must tell you about Elisabeth," said Alexandra. "I must tell you about her, not only because she wished me to, but also because I need to talk about her to someone who loves her as I do."

Andrew nodded. "I need to talk to someone about her, too," he said. "I don't know if it is possible for me to express the impact that her life made on my life. I divide my life into two phases—the before Elisabeth phase and the after Elisabeth phase. Even though she is gone, she continues to be the single most moving part of my life. I wish she were here, but the fact that she is not, does not change my devotion to her."

Alexandra looked earnestly at Andrew. "Come," she said, "let's sit on this old bench."

"All right," said Andrew. He looped the reins of the horses over the railings of a low fence, and sat down beside Alexandra. He waited quietly for her to go on.

Alexandra said, "Elisabeth was my sister as much as if we were really sisters." She paused and looked at Andrew. "I hope you don't think it is presumptuous of me to think of her as my sister."

"No," said Andrew. "I think she was very fortunate to have a sister like you for a friend. I'm sure that is one of the reasons she did not follow the usual pattern of women in this Southern society."

"She sure was an independent one," said Alexandra. "Some things she did just because she did not want to follow the usual way. Did she ever tell you why she spelled her name with an "s" instead of the usual "z"? Well, it was because her namesake, Elizabeth Barrett Browning, spelled it with a "z". One day when she was eight or nine she told her father that she wanted to spell her name in her own way, and that was that." Alexandra smiled at the memory.

"That's Elisabeth," said Andrew.

"What I was getting at," said Alexandra, "is that we were very close. I know how she felt and how she thought. And that is why I can say to you that Elisabeth loved you very much. There were no reservations in her love for you. It was not a blind infatuation. It was a real commitment to you. And there were no regrets on her part when things turned out as they did."

Andrew nodded his head slowly and perhaps a bit sadly. "I believe you," he said, "and thank you for reminding me of that."

Alexandra nodded and sat quietly. She shut her eyes and leaned her head back against the back of the bench. Andrew could see the tears in the corners of her eyes. He waited patiently.

Alexandra spoke so quietly that Andrew had to lean toward her to hear. "Andrew," she said, "Elisabeth gave birth to a baby nine months after you left for Virginia." Alexandra's smile, mixed in with the tears in her eyes, seemed a strange mixture of happiness and grief. "You are the father of a very beautiful baby girl, Andrew." Alexandra tried to go on, but couldn't. The tears trickled down her temples, down the sides of her upturned face, and she seemed too weary to brush them away.

Andrew waited. So many, many emotions and questions crowded in on him. A wild surge of joy—there was still something of Elisabeth left. Where was this child? He must see her. Then he thought of Elisabeth. Had the birth brought her pain? The thought of having missed seeing Elisabeth with their child in her arms almost brought a sob twisting out of him. He had a fleeting vision of a child with blue eyes and blond hair.

"Alexandra?" said Andrew.

"Yes," said Alexandra. "I wish you could have seen them together. Elisabeth was so proud of that baby. She was a fine mother."

"Tell me first if the baby is all right somewheres," said Andrew. "And then tell me as much as you can how it all took place."

"The baby, her name is Andrea, is a healthy, happy child. She is, let's see, eight months old—a very pretty baby. And—you probably guessed it—she has blue eyes and quite blond hair." Alexandra smiled at the picture in her mind of the child.

"Is it possible for me to see her?" asked Andrew.

"Let me explain some things and then you can decide," said Alexandra. "That is what Elisabeth asked me to do—tell you what the situation was, and she said she would trust you to do what was right.

"By the time the baby was born, the war situation here was in a turmoil. The Turnwells had long been gone; they tried to take Elisabeth with them, but she would not have any of that, and they never knew Elisabeth was going to have a child.

"A good doctor, Dr. Joseph Friedman, took care of Elisabeth before and during the birth, and he and his wife, Sara, are good people. They did not ask any questions of Elisabeth, and they asked to take the baby for their own if she could not manage it. They are quite a bit older and have never had children of their own, and they said they would so much love to have a child.

"And that is where Andrea is now—at the Friedmans. That was Elisabeth's decision at the end. She knew it wasn't possible to keep a white child in our refugee camp. There would be serious questions and trouble. She had no way of getting the child to you, and she knew the doctor and his wife would give Andrea a good home."

Andrew nodded. "I understand," he said. "Andrea...Andrea...," he mused. "It is a pretty name."

"Yes," said Alexandra. "Elisabeth thought that if the child couldn't have your last name, at least it could have a first name similar to yours. So she named it Andrea."

Andrew's emotions, near a breaking point since before these last words, almost broke. "This is a little overwhelming," he said quietly, and Alexandra, seeing how it was with him, stood up and put her arms around him—a black woman, by heritage a slave, comforting an officer of the Confederate Army.

"I have lost my best friend; you have lost the woman you love," said Alexandra. "For you, the child is some consolation; for me, my new life is a consolation. But she was much too precious to ever forget. She will be with me in my new life, and I know you will often think of her wherever your life takes you."

Andrew was dabbing his eyes with a handkerchief. "I'll go see Dr. Friedman and, hopefully, Andrea," he said.

"I think you will be impressed with him," said Alexandra. "He is a good man and a good doctor. He comes here to the refugee camp when we need a doctor." She looked closely at Andrew. "Are you all right, physically, I mean? I could see you were moving somewhat stiffly. Have you been wounded?"

Andrew nodded. "Yes, I'm afraid it goes with the occupation. I have a number of punctures and cuts on my left side. Some of them are not doing as well as I had hoped."

"A good reason to see the doctor without immediately stating your other reason," said Alexandra. "You'll go tomorrow. It's almost evening. You'll have a better chance to see Andrea in the morning. You can stay at the camp tonight. No one resents you there, partly, of course, because they remember Elisabeth's kindness to them."

Chapter 6

That evening Andrew ate fried grits made of a combination of ground together grains. He drank a pale, hot tea and was at ease in the company. Although no one tried to make conversation with him, yet there was a friendliness and a respect in the way they looked at him.

After dark he brought Sunny Boy to one of the low, open sheds, tethered the horse there, and rolled out his blanket roll. He lay down on the blankets, revolver under his blanket as was his habit, and slowly let his mind wander through the events of the day.

Part of his mind said, she is not gone. She cannot be gone. And another part of his mind said, yes, it is so, but don't face it all today. Wait for it to become a part of you, this knowledge that she is no longer here.

And another part of his mind said, a child, a child with blue eyes. I must see her. And another part of his mind said, be patient. Do what is right for the child. But how about me? his mind said, and she is part of Elisabeth. Yes, that is true, answered another part of his mind, yes, that is so.

Later in the night, after Andrew had slept briefly, he was awakened by the sound of singing. He could see the flicker of lights and shadows on the walls of the shed. He got up, pulled on his boots, and walked to the center of the field where many were gathered around a fire.

The gathered people were sitting in a circle around the fire, the flames lighting up the faces in the front row, and flickering high to touch the faces in the circling ranks. It seemed that most of the people in the camp were there, many with a blanket around their shoulders, and some holding a child warm against themselves. Andrew saw Alexandra in the front row, sitting amidst a gathering of her people, in the place that had been the gathering place of people since time was known to them, the campfire.

Stories were being told, and songs, mostly hymns lined out by a lead singer, were being sung. But the speaker or the singer did not rise and stand before the group. Instead, he spoke or sang from his place in the ranks.

The mood of the gathering was happy, but not light-hearted. There was some brief, amused laughter at a story now and then, some "amens" during the singing, but much of the speaking and singing was of the pain and travail that had been the lot of these people.

Andrew, standing on the outer fringe of the group was moved by the scene, the sense of communal sharing, the feeling of brotherhood, the strength of spirit that bonded these people together. He became aware of what he had at first thought was the undertone of people talking but what he now realized was an undercurrent humming of voices that never ceased. The pitch of the humming rose and fell, trailed off and returned louder. There was the deep timbre of bass voices moving like a river current, the medium voices blending in, and the occasionally high, but subdued, soprano voice touching the ethereal notes of a descant.

Andrew felt an urge to join in, to blend his voice with the rest, but just as quickly came the realization that he was not part of this. All of the human race has suffered, but these more than others. These black people, bonded by the river of suffering they had come through, were just now catching a glimpse of the far, safe shore. Andrew listened quietly.

There began then a song that Andrew had never heard before. Most of the songs that were sung, he had some familiarity with, but this was a bold, strong, almost militant song of hope and optimism. Andrew listened as the voices around him blended in the triumphant words of the song, and the song played itself in Andrew's mind for days afterward.

"Mine eyes have seen the glory
Of the coming of the Lord.
He has trampled out the vintage
Where the grapes of wrath are stored.
He has loosed the faithful lightning
Of his terrible, swift sword.
His truth is marching on.
Glory, glory, hallelujah…"

Chapter 7

Andrew woke before dawn. He lay under his blankets in the darkness, eyes shut. He heard Sunny Boy breathing on the other side of the railing. There was a small rustling noise on the floor of the shed, probably a mouse. When he opened his eyes, and it was still as dark as when he had them closed, he thought, the world is empty for me. And he thought, how many mornings will I wake and my first thought will be that Elisabeth is gone? He thought, how many years can a dream live in a man's heart? He thought, in a half-century from now I will know.

Sunny Boy stirred, and Andrew got up. Pretty much by touch and feel, he saddled the horse and got his belongings rolled up in the blankets and tied behind the saddle.

The only ones astir in camp were three women getting a fire started in an outside stone and iron stove. When they opened the stove lid to put in more wood, the light from the fire lit up their faces. Andrew, as he rode by, touched the brim of his hat, and though it was probably too dark to see, they smiled.

On the near side of the bridge, behind some screening trees, Andrew stopped the horse. He got off the horse and, leaning against the warm neck and chest of Sunny, they waited for the first pale light to come over the hills around Clearfield. When there was enough light to see, he carefully scanned the opposite side of the river. It is possible, he thought, that the Union Army may have gotten word of a Confederate officer in the area. He did not know if his capture was a prize worth the trouble of taking, but he did not want to take the chance. He had the directions to two places he hoped to see, Dr. Friedman and Will Hammond, the photographer; and since both locations were on the east side of the town, he hoped to pass by the main area of town before full light.

After a dozen minutes of watching and seeing no sign of an ambush, no movement except one sleepy worker plodding his way to the business district, Andrew reined his horse to the bridge. They crossed without incident.

Dr. Friedman's house was on the outskirts of the town with some acreage in the back, a small orchard, a garden, a one-horse pasture, and a stable. Andrew had waited in a wooded lot down the street from the house till a time when he could assume the occupants were up and about. He saw an older man, bareheaded, hair turning to gray, go out to the stable and return to the house.

Andrew rode his horse down the street, and almost stopped at the front hitching post, but a thought occurred to him that a good horse tied in front, in a country in which good horses were becoming scarce, might look suspicious; and he dismounted and led the horse around the back and directly into the stable. A tall, dappled horse, busily eating grain in a manger box, looked up startled, then continued eating. Sunny Boy allowed himself to be tied up in an empty stall.

As Andrew walked back toward the house, the back door was opened by the man Andrew had seen earlier. "Come in, come in," the man said pleasantly. "I don't have the office open yet, but we might be able to get something hot to drink here in the kitchen."

"Good morning, sir," said Andrew, removing his hat as he entered a cozy kitchen.

A pleasant woman, quite tall, dark hair tied back loosely with a ribbon, turned from the stove. "Good morning, Captain," she said. She indicated the small table by the window. "Would you have some tea?"

"Thank you, ma'am, I will," said Andrew.

"This is my wife, Sara," said the man. "I'm Dr. Friedman, and I believe you are Captain Greyson."

"Why, yes, I am," said Andrew, surprised that the doctor knew who he was.

The doctor smiled. "I recall you from a reception at the mayor's home several years ago. You, I believe, had just astounded the military strategists by taking a difficult objective by a night assault."

Sara, at the stove, just picking up the teakettle, laughed delightedly, and to Andrew's surprise, was also blushing. The doctor, with a twinkle in his eye, looked at his wife, then at Andrew. "I'll tell you why my sweet wife is blushing so beautifully." He paused and before he could go on, Sara interrupted him.

"I'll tell him myself, Joseph." She turned to Andrew. "I said to my husband—we were in the reception hall when Colonel Biddell introduced you—I said that you were handsome enough to be a general. So there," she said, flashing a smile at her husband.

The doctor shook his head in mock despair. "If only she would act her age," he said looking adoringly at his wife. "Here we are, both of us old enough to be grandparents..." As he spoke the last word, both of them fell self-consciously silent, and Andrew, too, knowing what meanings the word had brought, was also silent. He raised his cup and sipped the hot tea.

The doctor cleared his throat. "Actually," he said, "we knew someone like you might be in town. One of my patients, Mrs. Winslow, was telling everyone that she had seen the Confederate Army marching into town." The doctor shook his head. "Poor woman. She has lost a husband and both her sons to this war. When her last son, her youngest, Luther, fell at Antietam, it seemed too much loss for one person to bear." The doctor shook his head again, sadly. "I have no cure for such grief. Perhaps time will heal." Sara nodded her head sympathetically.

And Andrew, sitting in that warm kitchen with sunlight coming through the window, listening to this warm couple expressing sympathy for someone else's loss, suddenly found he could no longer control his own emotions. He set down the tea cup. "Have to check on my horse," he choked out as he headed out the door.

In the stable he put his arms over Sunny Boy's shoulders, his face against the rough mane of the horse, and wept. Anguish that seemed to come out of his deepest soul poured out of him. Mouth against the dark mane of the horse, he moaned out a grief that he could no longer keep inside himself.

After a time, he realized that he was quiet and that Sunny Boy had turned and was nudging him with his head. Andrew sighed, breathed deeply, and went to the watering tank where he washed his face with the cool water. He dried his face with a handkerchief, and he brushed back his hair with his fingers.

When he came back into the kitchen, everyone was deliberately casual. A cheerful looking black woman was kneading bread at the table. "This is Julie," said Sara Friedman. "She has come to help since we had an addition to the family."

"Yes, suh," said Julie. "I was in thet refugee camp over the bridge, an' the doctor asked me to come work here."

Andrew's cup of tea had been refilled and set on the sideboard. He picked it up and turned to the doctor. "I came to have you look at my wounds, if you would," said Andrew to the doctor. "I'm afraid they're not doing as well as they should be."

"I noticed you were favoring your left some as you walked," said the doctor. "Let us go to my office at the front of the house, and we'll have a look. May as well bring your tea."

Andrew removed his shirt and trousers, and the doctor carefully examined each one of the dozen or so wounds the shell fragments had caused. "Hmm," the doctor said several times. "Basically, these cuts are doing all right," he said after a moment, "but there are several here that I'm going to open and disinfect with alcohol. Of course, they would all heal more quickly if you would rest yourself for a week or two. I don't suppose I could get you to do so." He looked at Andrew.

Andrew smiled. "No, I really can't stop. I'll do what I can about keeping them clean."

"Good," the doctor said. "I'll send along some clean bandage material." He finished cleaning the cuts on Andrew's arm, and as Andrew reached for his clothes, he said, "Now, before you put on your clothes, there's a hot bath waiting for you down the hall. The women have been heating some water. I dare say it has been a good while since you have enjoyed a bath." The doctor led the way down the hall to a bathroom where, exceeding Andrew's expectations, was a real bathtub with hot water in it, steam rising off the water like a dreamy mist.

"This is really too much," said Andrew. He, as a matter of fact, could not remember when he had last had a hot bath in a bathtub. There had been some washcloth baths out of a bucket of water heated over a fire, and there had been quite a few hurried baths in cold, running streams—but hot water in a bathtub!

"Take your time," said the doctor. "Here are soap, towels, and a razor if you care to shave, and also some small scissors if you want to trim your beard."

At the door Dr. Friedman turned. "When you finish your bath," he said, "come into the kitchen. We'll have a breakfast for you and," he paused, and went on, "you will want to meet our daughter. I'm sure she will be up by then."

The bath was luxurious. Is there anything else in life that equals a hot bath? thought Andrew. Of course, there is, he answered himself, but just now this feels wonderful. He shaved and took special care trimming his beard and mustache. As his eyes met those in the mirror, he realized with some amusement that he was trying to appear as good as possible in order to impress an eight-month-old baby girl. With a damp cloth he wiped the dust from his coat and trousers, gave his worn boots a quick brush, and he was ready.

His daughter was beautiful. A symmetrical, oval face, wispy, yellow hair, alert blue eyes—and exquisitely formed little hands. Sara Friedman was sitting in a rocking chair holding the child when Andrew entered the kitchen. The child noticed his entrance at once, and followed him with her eyes as he walked forward.

The doctor was standing at the opposite doorway, leaning against the door jamb, appearing very casual. Sara proudly holding the child, looked expectantly at Andrew. "This is Andrea," she said.

Andrew sat at the table and bread, cheese, and a sweet jam were set before him, but he could not keep his eyes from watching Andrea. And the little girl, already having accepted her position as the center of the universe, saw that here was a stranger who must be approached, charmed, and eventually brought into her retinue of admirers.

She squirmed out of Sara's arms. As soon as she found herself on the floor, on hands and knees, she looked around to get her bearings. There he was, the tall stranger with the interesting face, and she crawled as swiftly as she could directly toward him, little arms and legs churning furiously. When she reached his boots, she stopped, reached up one tiny fist to hold onto his trousers, and pulled herself up to stand looking up at his face.

Andrew had watched with fascination this small creature approach him. When she grasped his trousers with the incredible hand strength those small ones have, he looked down at her.

Their eyes met, and what happened then, Andrew could not explain. The look in her eyes was all-knowing, confident, and proprietary. She knows who I am, thought Andrew. They looked at each other quietly for a moment—a moment in which Andrew felt almost as if he were in some sort of hypnotic spell.

"Ga-baa," she said, and let go of his trousers and held up her hands. She would have fallen, but Andrew quickly put his hands down and picked her up and set her on his lap facing him.

She inspected his face for a moment, then put out her hands and explored his beard, his mouth, his nose. All this time Andrew thrilled to this little one's touch even though she may have pinched his nose a bit more than was comfortable.

After more wriggling around the child settled herself in Andrew's lap, sitting quietly, and Andrew knew it was time to go. He carried the baby back to Sara. "You have a beautiful daughter," he said as he placed her in Sara's arms.

Perhaps there were the beginnings of small tears in Sara's eyes as she held Andrea. "Yes, I believe we do," she said. "We are very proud of her, and we are going to take very good care of her."

"I know you will," said Andrew.

Dr. Friedman accompanied Andrew out to the stable. "Thank you for everything," said Andrew. He and the doctor shook hands. Andrew led Sunny Boy to the door where he stopped. "As soon as this war is over, I'll be back at Albers College in Milford. You can always get in touch with me there, if for some reason you need me."

"I'll keep that in mind," said the doctor.

"I may just wander back here to Clearfield now and then," said Andrew. "If I do, I'll drop in to say hello."

"Do that," said the doctor. "You are always welcome."

Andrew swung into the saddle, looked down at Dr. Friedman, and said, "That is a remarkable little girl."

"She certainly is," said the doctor and smiled. Andrew raised his hand in salute, the doctor did likewise, and Andrew rode off.

Chapter 8

Andrew and Sunny Boy followed a winding wagon trail that circled the outskirts of the town and was headed northeast to where Will Hammond and his family lived. Andrew knew he should not relax his watchfulness, but his mind was drawn irresistibly back to the little girl that had looked so deeply into his own eyes. As he rode he mused, if the war was over and if I was out of the army—but he immediately knew that was not realistic. No, Andrea was in the right place now. Actually, she was in an almost ideal situation—growing up as the daughter of the doctor and his wife. There was no doubt in Andrew's mind that they loved the little child and would do their best for her. She would be in a stable situation with many opportunities. Yet, Andrew remembered how good it felt to hold the baby and look at her and know she was the child of Elisabeth.

There was also no doubt in Andrew's mind that, though no one had mentioned or questioned, the Friedmans knew his relationship to the child. They were fine people, he thought, and they would do what was best for Andrea.

Andrew came presently to a blacksmith shop, a shed, open to the road. The Hammond's house was set back from the road with a small bridged stream between the house and shop. From the shop came the sound of hammering on metal. Andrew stopped at the open door.

"Captain!" There was genuine pleasure in Will Hammond's voice. He had dropped his work on the bench before him, and he held out a hand. Andrew could see that Will was standing inside a frame that allowed him to lean against the sides and still accomplish blacksmiths' tasks. One of the small boys that Andrew had met in church several years ago, and grown bigger, was working the bellows to keep the fire glowing hot.

"It's good to see you again, Will," said Andrew shaking hands.

"And you," said Will warmly. He shook his head sadly. "Captain, I can't tell you how sorry I am." Though neither mentioned Elisabeth, both knew what they were speaking of. "My wife, particularly took it hard," said Will. "She thought you were a good man. We are so sorry."

Andrew nodded his head. He knew Will's sympathy was genuine.

Will Hammond turned to the boy. "Curt," he said, "best run ahead to the house and let them know Captain Greyson is back." Will turned back to Andrew. "Carrie likes to tidy up when company comes, and, of course, we had better give our Liselle some warning of your return."

"All right, Pa," said Curt, the boy. He looked at Andrew. "That's a fine horse you have, sir. Isn't that the horse from Turnwell's place?"

"Yes, it is," said Andrew.

The boy inspected the horse closely as he went by it, and Will said to Andrew, "That boy knows every horse in the county. He sure likes horses, and is quite good with them." Will waved a hand at the workshop around him. "I ran out of photography supplies quite some time ago. Can't get any now, of course, so I'm back at my old trade, blacksmithing and shoeing horses. Couldn't do it without Curt's help. He does the running and holding and brings the work to me."

"How are things for you and your family?" asked Andrew.

"We make do," said Will. "The Union Army brings me some horses to shoe—the officers do when they want a better job than their own smithies can do, and they pay good." Will paused. "These renegades roaming the country are a different story. You've heard about them, Captain?"

"Yes," said Andrew.

"They're plain scoundrels," said Will. "There's one gang of four led by a man with one dead eye. They've been by here a few times. I keep my family inside when they come, but I may have to shoot that one some day."

"Are you set with powder and ball?" asked Andrew. "And a dependable gun?"

Will opened a drawer of his work bench and held in view an old Wesson and Leavitt revolver. "Found it at one of the old Union Army campsites," he said. "I rebuilt it. It shoots where you point it. I can make my own ball ammunition, of course, but powder is another matter."

"You're short of powder?" said Andrew. He opened a saddlebag and drew out his issue container of gun powder. "Will this help?"

"It most surely would," said Will. "But what about you? Won't you be needing it?"

"My revolver is loaded and I have a few extra cartridges," said Andrew. "I'll get more when I get back to the division."

"You'll be going back, then?" asked Will.

"I'll see it through to the end," said Andrew. "If things had been different, I may not have, but now it doesn't make much difference."

They were interrupted by the sound of running footsteps on the footbridge from the house, and the back door of the shop was flung open. It was Liselle. Liselle who hadn't stopped to change to better clothes, or even to brush her long brown hair. Liselle, breathless from her run, bright tears in her eyes. She ran to Andrew, but stopped just in front of him. "Oh, Mr. Captain, you're back," she gasped.

"Yes, I'm back," said Andrew.

Liselle stood for a moment. "I still have your picture," she said.

"And I have yours," said Andrew touching his coat pocket.

"I prayed and prayed that you would be safe," said Liselle.

"Thank you very much," said Andrew.

Quite suddenly Liselle's face contorted in anguish. "But..." she said. "But..." she said again, her lower lip quivering. "I forgot to pray for Elisabeth, and now she is gone...gone," her voice trailed off in despair. She tried again, "I could tell you loved her so much, and...if...if I could I would change places with her so that you could be together. Oh..." she wailed, falling forward into Andrew's arms and burying her face in his shirt front.

Andrew held her in his arms for several moments as he worked very hard to control his own emotions. He glanced at Will, but Will was looking off into the distance out the open door of the shed.

Andrew thought, young ones like this should not have to carry the burdens of the world on their shoulders. They should be free to play and to dream. Life itself can be cruel, and then we make such things as wars to make it worse.

"Liselle," he said, "listen to me. I'm sure you didn't forget to pray for Elisabeth. I don't think you have to kneel or fold your hands to pray. I know you thought of her and hoped she would be happy. I think that is the same as praying—maybe even better because it is part of your living."

"Do you think so?" asked Liselle. She looked up hopefully, face still streaked with tears.

"Yes, I do," said Andrew, having convinced himself.

Liselle was somewhat consoled. "I think you're right," she said. "God would think of something like that. But I'm still so sad about Elisabeth."

"Yes, I understand," said Andrew.

Liselle stepped back. "I'm going now to help Mama. She is putting some biscuits in the oven. You're to come up for some in a short while. You'll come, won't you?" She smiled.

"Yes, I'll come," said Andrew.

"We'll be along shortly," said Will.

The fire in the fire pit was burning low and Will Hammond raked the coals apart so they would die down. Andrew closed the large shed doors, and they turned toward the pathway to the house. "Best bring your horse," said Will. "As my son Curt says, that's a fine horse. Just the sort those scalawags would like to take. I've been hoping the Union Army would catch them at horse thieving and hang them. They deserve worse."

Andrew led Sunny Boy as they moved on the pathway to the house at Will's cane-assisted pace. Andrew said, "They sound depraved enough to harm your family."

"I've no doubt they would," said Will. "I've drilled the family in what to do in such a contingency—where to hide, what to do. Pray God it may never come about, but I'll give my life before I'll let them touch my family."

With Sunny Boy tethered in the back, they entered the house to be greeted by the smell of fresh baking. Caroline, Will's wife, greeted Andrew warmly. "I'm so glad you stopped in," she said. "You coming back gives us hope for the future." She had brushed her long, brown hair and looked as pretty as ever.

Liselle came into the room just as they were sitting down at the table. Wearing her best dress, a soft green one, and having brushed her hair, she looked quite grown up, and was a bit self-conscious about it.

Will could not help teasing her."Your hair is as long and pretty as your mom's, and you're almost as tall as she—and you only fourteen yet."

"Oh, Pappa," said Liselle, but she blushed as she sat down at the table, all eyes on her. The other children smiled and seemed as cheerful as when Andrew had last seen them at church, some two years ago.

When Caroline passed out the biscuits, warm and brown, she also passed around a pot of honey to put on them. "Curt found a bee's nest back in the woods," she said. "He roams around a lot, and we worry about him, but he does come home with food—sometimes rabbit or quail, and once a small deer."

"I'd bring home more food if Pa would let me take a gun," said Curt, obviously bringing up a topic of prior discussion.

"And invite the Union patrols to shoot at you?" said Will. "And you only twelve years old? No, we can't do that."

Curt smiled a small secret smile and rejoined mildly, "I'm better in the woods than they are."

The talk around the table was friendly and cheerful. The young voices of the children was music to Andrew's ears. He had not heard any such in quite some time. As the talk quieted, Will asked, "How does it go in Georgia? Are we still in the game?"

Everyone listened soberly as Andrew said, "I'm afraid there's no chance for the Confederate cause, Will. They've reelected Lincoln up there, and he means to carry this through. If the opposition had won the election, we might have hoped for a change of policy."

He paused and looked at his hosts and at the children around the table. "The best thing now would be to end it as soon as possible. There would be less men dying for a lost cause."

He finished quietly. "You would not believe the carnage at Chickamauga. I am going back, but I have already informed General Longstreet that I will not—I cannot lead men into battle."

As they stood up from the table, a picture on the mantle of the fireplace caught Andrew's eyes. It was the picture of himself that Will had taken. He went and stood, looking at himself for a few moments. Briefly he remembered how happy he had been on that day. He turned around to see the family, concerned, looking at him.

"You will be careful, won't you?" said Caroline.

"Yes, I will," said Andrew seriously. He looked at Liselle and touched his hand to the breast pocket of his coat. "I still have your picture, Liselle. Some day, when I get home, I will put it on my mantle to remember you by."

Liselle nodded, eyes bright. "Goodbye, Mr. Greyson. You must come back." She came toward him and when Andrew leaned down, she put her arms around his neck and kissed him on the cheek.

Andrew shook hands with Will, and waved a hand to the rest of the family as they stood at the back door to see him off. When he got to Sunny Boy, he found that the horse had been given a ration of grain in a nose bag, and the horse was standing there looking rather smug.

"I gave him some oats. He is a fine horse," said Curt. "I'll walk Captain Greyson to the road," he said to his family, and he fell into step with Andrew as they walked the footpath toward the shop and the road. When they had walked around the shop, Curt said, "I have to tell you something, Mr. Greyson."

"Yes?" said Andrew.

"I have a gun," said Curt. "I found it on the edge of a battlefield. I keep it hidden in a hollow tree just back of our place. I don't want Pa and Mom to worry, but if I have to, I'll shoot some of those bad men if they bother us."

"Hmm," said Andrew. "That's how you got the deer?"

"Yes, I told them I found it wounded. You won't tell Pa?" asked Curt.

"No," said Andrew, "but I have an idea he knows and is waiting for you to tell him."

"I don't know," said Curt.

"I think you may be able to make a deal with him about when and how to use the gun," said Andrew. He counts on you a great deal. I think I would be honest with him."

"All right," said Curt. "I'll think it over, but I'll probably tell him. Thanks, Mr. Greyson."

"Now you take care, Curt. I can see that you are very capable for a boy your age. Take care of your family, and if you have to shoot, make absolutely sure that first shot counts."

"I'll do my best, sir," said Curt.

Andrew got into the saddle, and with a backward wave of his hand, he was off down the road.

Chapter 9

Riding east with the intention of circling around Clearfield before he turned south, Andrew found himself on some of the same trails and ridges over which he had once led F Company to their memorable battle. At one point he actually got a glimpse of the small hilltop on which they had fought so gallantly.

He stopped and looked at the hilltop. Late afternoon sun turned the ridges into dark shadows. It looked distant, mysterious, and foreboding. I'll come back some day to go over it, walk on it, he thought.

So much has happened in my life since the night I walked up that hill, he thought. So much. Would I ever have met Elisabeth if I hadn't gone up that hill? If that is what that hill gave me, then it gave me the greatest dream of my life.

Do dreams ever become a reality? he thought. That dream is behind me, but it is still part of my life. Part of that dream did come true, he thought, and I'm going to live my life with that reality.

Andrew turned Sunny Boy back to the trail. There was a fork in the trail ahead, and he stopped again to consider which way to go. Just as he was about to heel Sunny forward, he caught a glimpse of some movement down the trail ahead. Was there a figure in the shadow of the trees ahead? Andrew wasn't sure, but he meant to take no chances. He reined Sunny Boy to the right on a faint trail that seemed to lead into a ravine. The trail came to a small clearing and seemed to fade out. He stopped the horse.

"That's right, Cap'n," said a harsh voice behind him. "Stop right there."

Andrew turned in the saddle. Advancing toward him from behind some large trees was a big man in dirty clothes, clothes that seemed to once have been a military uniform. The man was holding a rifle pointed at Andrew, and it looked as if he meant to use it.

When Andrew glanced to his front and to his side, he saw other men, all armed, coming toward him.

The first man laughed. "That's right, Cap'n. You is surrounded. Hah! You fell for our decoy up the trail and turned right into our trap here." Again the man laughed, arrogantly, very pleased with himself.

Two other men were coming through the trees, and a third was coming down the trail behind him. Taking the speaker to be the leader, Andrew turned Sunny Boy to face him, and as he did so he saw that the man had only one good eye. This must be the group that Will had mentioned.

"Hands up!" snarled the one-eyed man. "Hands up, and no tricks. Git down from thet hoss." He motioned with his rifle.

Andrew hesitated. Once he was on the ground, he would have lost the advantage that Sunny Boy's speed gave him. But the horse could not outrun the bullets these men obviously seemed capable of firing. Andrew slowly got down from the saddle.

"Thet's right, Cap'n. Now you is bein' smart. Stand right there."

Andrew looked at the men who now encircled him and Sunny Boy. All were likely deserters from some army unit. It was not likely they would feel kindly toward an officer that probably represented what they hated from whatever army they had been in. Yet, sometimes a common cause, a common plight, brought men together. It was worth a try, thought Andrew.

"What outfit are you men from?" asked Andrew. "Are any of you from the Army of Tennessee?"

The leader glared at him with his one seeing eye. "This ain't no social event, Cap'n. You orficers is all alike. You think you cin order men around. The army never did me no good. It gave me this," and he lifted a hand from his rifle to point to his face. "And did I get any thanks from the army? Hell, no! I say, damn the Confederacy."

These are hard men, no doubt, thought Andrew. He began to consider how far they would go. By reputation, they had killed without compunction. Stay close to the horse, he thought. It's my only chance. Also, his revolver was holstered to the saddle, but the time it would take to get it out of its holster and fire it effectively was much too long against four armed men.

"My this is a nice horse. We sure cin use it," said One-Eye, and one of his men moved toward Sunny Boy. Sunny Boy laid back his ears and slashed at the man with his teeth. The man leaped back, stumbled over his own feet, and fell to the ground.

Sunny Boy would have pressed the attack except for Andrew who stopped him with a sharp, "Whoa!" The others whooped in merriment at their fallen comrade, who, still on his knees, gave Andrew a look of malice. I made no friend there, thought Andrew. His situation, he decided, was becoming more desperate.

"We bin followin' you, Cap'n," said the one-eyed man. He seemed to enjoy gloating over the plight of Andrew. "I allus thought I was as good as an orficer, an' I guess this proves it." He waved his rifle at Andrew. "Git back, now. Don't let him grab your gun," he warned one of his men who had stepped in closer. Indeed Andrew had just been considering such an attempt.

"Tell you what we goin' ta do," said One-Eye. "We gon' ta' take this hoss, an' we is gon' to' ride up to your friend, Hammond's house, an' we is gon' ta' pay his family a visit." He spit at Andrew's boots.

"You orficers think you is so high an' mighty. You think you cin go up and lift yo' hats to the pretty girls an' say, howdy ma'am. Well, we is gon' ta' go up an' pay a visit to Hammond's pretty girls an' his wife." He leered at Andrew. "What does you think of thet, Cap'n?"

At that moment Andrew decided, cooly, that he would kill the man. Somehow he must do it. Let these others shoot him, but this man would die first.

The man came a bit closer. "You is shakin' in yo' boots, ain't you, Cap'n."

Goad him on, thought Andrew. Make him so angry he'll do something stupid. He can be had. This is just between you and me now. The others don't count.

"Just look at you," said Andrew in a low, penetrating voice. "A poor excuse for a man. Dirty, filthy slime. Bet you were worse as a soldier—ran at the first shot. I've seen your like. You're a disgrace to any army. Thank God you weren't in my outfit. We'd have turned you over to the Yankees, if they'd have you."

"Why, goddamn you," snarled the man. He sputtered, wordless for the moment.

Andrew half turned to the other men and raised his voice. "You follow a man such as this, do you? What holds you back? He's less than half a man. You can see he is all bluff. Why he shoots left and he has no left eye. You could all outshoot him."

"I see your game," snarled One-Eye through clenched teeth. "You think you cin talk your way outen this. Jist like an orficer." He took one hand off his rifle and drew a long knife from a sheath at his belt. "Don't move at your hoss, Cap'n. I knows you hev' a pistol up there."

Any moment now, thought Andrew. Dodge under Sunny and draw the revolver and get off one good shot. If the others just hesitate a second, I'll have him.

"Shoot him if he goes to the hoss," ordered the man to his men, but his eye did not leave Andrew. "I'll show you I don' need no gun to finish you, Cap'n. All I need is my sharp friend here." He lay the rifle on the ground, eye on Andrew, knife pointed up in a knife fighter's stance.

Andrew crouched slightly. He thinks I'll fight him, he thought, but when his foot is raised for his second step, I go for my revolver.

The man laughed nastily. "So, Cap'n, is you ready?" He shuffled forward one step.

Andrew tensed. The man stepped forward again, and Andrew leaped toward his horse, saying loudly as he did so, "Hold steady, Sunny!"

Two shots almost simultaneously rang out. Andrew, under the horse and up the other side, was aware that One-Eye was down and another man on his side of the horse went down with a cry, his rifle flying from his hands.

Andrew had the revolver out of the holster and in his right hand. He thumbed back the hammer and shot the man behind the horse, thumbed back the hammer a second time as he leaned under Sunny Boy's belly, and shot the remaining man standing on the other side, still so surprised he hadn't moved.

One-Eye was struggling to get to his knees. Andrew shot him in the face. He looked at each of the other three men. The two he had hit were down for good, but the man who had taken one of the first shots in his chest was sitting up. Nothing to do but finish him, thought Andrew, which he did.

It was over. He walked to Sunny Boy, who had not bolted but was milling about, and calmed him. He leaned against the horse, and wondered who had fired the first two shots. Someone, or two persons at the least, were nearby. I'll let them come to me, thought Andrew. He wished he could reload the spent chambers of his revolver, but knew that his hands were not steady enough just now, that the reloads were behind the saddle in one of the saddle bags, and that whoever had fired the shots could easily shoot him. So he waited.

He looked up the sides of the ravine to where he thought the shots had come, but could see no one. He looked at the men, now dead, on the ground and realized he felt no sympathy for them. They gave up their identity as humans when they began preying on the weaker and helpless humans around them, he thought. If they were dangerous animals on the loose, ready to harm others—which they were—I would not hesitate to destroy them. I would like to get a message back to Will, he thought, to let him know that these, at least, he does not have to be concerned about anymore.

He was musing on these thoughts, when he heard, "Psst! Captain, it's us." He knew who it was before he turned around, and when he did turn around, it was, of course, his two truant soldiers, Clarkson and Hatfield. They were standing not twenty feet behind him, gleeful smiles on their faces, dark eyes sparkling with merriment, and he had not heard their approach. Both boys carried long rifles.

He could have hugged them, it felt so good to see them, but they, though obviously happy to see him, seemed shy, holding back. Clarkson spoke up. "We bin follin' you, Captain, but we didn' know if you wanted to see us, since we skipped out on you on your expedition to Virginny."

Hatfield spoke up. "When we seen these rascals follin' you, we thought you might need ar' he'p."

Andrew shook his head and looked fondly at his two former scouts. "I can't tell you how happy I am to see you. You came just in time. You saved my life, I'm sure. Thank you."

The smiles on the boys' faces broadened, white teeth gleaming. "You gonna' fergive us fer not goin' ta' Virginny with you?" asked Hatfield.

"Well, I'll tell you," said Andrew. "Officially you are both dead, so nobody is going to come looking for you as deserters. Just don't show up at any Confederate Army celebrations when this war ends."

"We is daid?" Both boys thought this hilarious. They looked at each other in common amusement. "We is daid," they repeated. This was too much. Clarkson leaned against a tree. Hatfield sat on the ground. They laughed till tears came to their eyes.

Hatfield looked at Clarkson. "You is daid," he said. "How does you feel?"

Clarkson felt the sides of his head with his hands. "I feels fine," he said. "How does you feel?"

"I feels fine," Hatfield answered, "considering that I bin daid for near two years." And both boys broke down in uncontrolled laughter again.

Andrew smiled as he watched the two boys. Here were two young men, obviously well acquainted with violence, but still as human and naive as could be.

Finally the two boys were up and stood in front of Andrew, still as slouchingly graceful as they had been two years previously when they had guided Andrew and F Company up to the Little Hilltop.

"We could have shot two of 'em soon as they hed you surrounded," said Hatfield. "But we didn' know what you 'ud do with them other two. We figured you would make a move, and we concluded to shoot two of 'em when you did thet."

"My, you sure kin shoot when you gets started," said Clarkson, pointing to the bodies on the ground.

Andrew shook his head. "I'm not particularly happy to have to do that. In this case, though, this gang is the one that threatened a family I'm acquainted with in Clearfield, so I'm relieved to remove some of their fears." He looked around at Clarkson and Hatfield. "I wonder if you could manage to get a message to Will Hammond, the blacksmith, that this bunch won't be bothering him anymore?"

"We cin do thet," said Hatfield.

"We knows where he is," said Clarkson. "We'll do it."

"You ain't stayin' then, Captain?" asked Hatfield. "We thau't meybe you was organizing 'nother expedition like we done fer Little Hilltop."

"If you was, we'd jin up agin," said Clarkson.

"No," said Andrew. "I'm headed back to Georgia now."

The captain and the two boys looked at each other, mutual regard for each other showing. "Well," said Clarkson finally, "you is the best captain I ever seen. If you needs somethin', you let us know."

"Thet's the truth," said Hatfield.

"Yes," said Andrew, "and you two are the best scouts I ever hope to see. After the war, if you can use some help from me, get in touch with me at Milford in Eastern Tennessee. Just ask for Professor Greyson."

"Perfesser!" both boys exclaimed. "You mean like a school perfesser?" asked Hatfield.

"You alus did talk like you read a lot of books," said Clarkson.

Andrew was amused. "There may not be much a professor can do for you two, but if there is..." He put a leg into the left stirrup of the saddle and swung onto Sunny Boy's back. He lifted a hand in salute and farewell. The two boys, laughter gleaming in their eyes, stood at something resembling attention, and saluted—after a fashion—their captain.

"Goodbye, Captain," they said.

Andrew, in response, sent them a sharp West Point salute that left both boys grinning. Just before a bend in the trail, Andrew turned in the saddle and again lifted his arm in farewell. Clarkson and Hatfield, lifting their arms in response, held them aloft till their captain turned the trail's bend, then they turned and faded into the trees.

Chapter 10

Virginia 1865

On the 9th of April at Appomatox Courthouse, General Lee surrendered the Army of Northern Virginia to General Grant. A day later, Lieutenant Colonel Andrew Greyson packed the few personal belongings he had into saddlebags and a blanket roll and began the long, melancholy ride home to Milford, Tennessee. The war was over for him and for the Army of Northern Virginia, as well as for the Army of the Potomac which, though it lost more battles than it won, had finally won the war for the North. Andrew was thankful that the conditions of the surrender allowed Confederate officers to keep their sidearms and sabers, and their personal horses. And so, Andrew, who had been on General Longstreet's staff for the final months of the war, mounted on the big, gray gelding, Sunny Boy, headed west toward Tennessee.

Andrew, though low in spirit, sat erect in the saddle. His uniform was rather worn, and hand stitches repaired tears or worn spots. His boots, worn every day for three years, were perhaps beyond repair, but Andrew brushed them and they looked presentable. Both his revolver, the Navy Colt .44 caliber his father had given him, and his saber were buckled to the saddle.

He traveled alone, at his own almost leisurely pace, preferring not to be in the company of other men, who, like him, were returning to their homes. He preferred to ride quietly with his own thoughts and reflections.

On the first afternoon of riding, Andrew had come up on a regiment of Union cavalry camped along the roadside. Andrew had expected some remarks, some catcalls, and had steeled himself to bear them with dignity. Instead he was surprised to hear, "Good morning, sir," from several troopers nearest the road, and a courteous salute from a young captain.

A quarter mile down the road, Andrew was startled to hear a galloping horse behind him. He reined up Sunny Boy and waited for a young trooper, uniform and equipment sparkling, to pull up to him.

"Are you Colonel Greyson, sir?" asked the trooper saluting.

"I am," said Andrew.

"In that case, sir, I'm to inform you, sir, that General Sheridan requests the pleasure of your company for some afternoon tea and coffee." The trooper smiled. "He's just down the road, sir, and thought he recognized you as you rode by."

"By all means," said Andrew. "Coffee would be fine for someone who hasn't had any in some time. Lead the way."

"Yes, sir," said the trooper, smartly reining his horse around, and Andrew spent an hour visiting with an officer he had worked for just after he had graduated from the United States Military Academy at West Point.

General Phil Sheridan, the flamboyant cavalryman, dark hair and dark eyes, flaring mustache, was seated at a small table under a canvas tent fly when Andrew rode up. The general stood up to greet Andrew. "Afternoon, Greyson. It's been a dozen years, but I thought I recognized you as you rode by."

"Good afternoon, sir. It's good to see you." Andrew saluted, then shook the extended hand of the general.

Sheridan looked at Sunny Boy, the gray gelding. "That's a fine horse, Greyson. You should have been a cavalryman. You always knew horses and rode well."

"Thank you, General," said Andrew.

Sheridan pointed at a magnificent, black gelding, saddled, tethered just outside the fly. "What do you think of my black beauty, here? My Rienzi?"

Andrew said, "I've never seen a finer horse, sir, and I'm pleased to get a look at him. You may not know, General, that your horse was as well-known as you among your Confederate foes."

Sheridan laughed in good humor. "So you heard of me, now and then?"

"Oh, yes, General. Perhaps a bit too often for our comfort," said Andrew.

Sheridan looked keenly at Andrew. "Well, Greyson, I'm a bit sorry we wore different uniforms during this war, and though I'm not sorry we have finally won, I must say that you and your officers, and especially your fighting men, have my greatest respect."

Andrew nodded. He accepted the sentiments as sincere. Indeed, the glances of Sheridan's officers and of the troopers he had passed as he rode into this camp had all been courteous and respectful.

"Now, then," said the general, "sit down and we will have coffee or tea, whichever you prefer, and satisfy my curiosity. I heard of some West Point graduate who led a company of men at night up a hill in Tennessee, and then held off two regiments of Union forces. That wouldn't have been you, Greyson?"

"Yes, sir," said Andrew. "That was my company of Tennessee volunteers."

"I knew it!" exclaimed Sheridan, and slapped his hand on the table. "When I heard of that exploit, I thought it had all the earmarks of the work you did for me as a young lieutenant." He shook his head and smiled at Andrew. "By gosh, Greyson, all loyalties aside, I wish we could have worked together in this."

Coffee arrived and Andrew sipped the hot liquid appreciatively. "It's good of you to remember me, General. I'm not sure just now what I think of our cause. Perhaps it is something that had to be done to burn out some of the aspects of our lives here in the South. It is encouraging to be able to come into your camp here, and not feel as though I were some sort of traitor to be hanged. I fought out of a sense of loyalty for the country I was a part of, and I now wish to go back and rebuild what we can."

General Sheridan nodded. "I was in Washington just a few weeks ago. Those are President Lincoln's wishes and his instructions to Grant—that there should be no recriminations or accusations. There may be some politicians that will get in the way of that, but if it were left to us, here in the field after the battle is over, I believe we can salute each other in mutual respect and good will."

Andrew rode west for four more days, and just at dusk, with the last light of the day, he saw a ridge of smokey, blue mountains ahead. Just a day and a half later, Andrew rode the winding road up the sloping mountain side and over the Cumberland Gap pass—and he was in Tennessee.

It was spring at the higher altitudes, and for two days Andrew rode through a land scented by the blossoms of flowers. The war seemed far away and long ago. With the cool breezes blowing off the mountain tops, Andrew felt the discouragement and disappointments of the war washing out of himself. The flowers, the pine trees, the fresh grass seemed to represent a new beginning, and Andrew felt his spirit rise with their messages that life was good.

As he came near small villages, folded into the valleys along the road, the scent of blooming lilacs from bushes planted at many home sites would reach him before he would see the dwellings of the town. Forever after, for Andrew, the scent of lilacs brought memories of that long, bittersweet ride home. So many, many men had died, a cause had died, lives and families had been tragically disrupted, but there were still life and hope ahead.

Chapter 11

On a late afternoon of a Sunday, Andrew and Sunny Boy came to Milford, Tennessee. The sunlight slanting over the mountains caught the red tile roofs of the buildings on Albers College campus across the river, and that is what Andrew saw first as he came near the town. As he came over the last hill, the town lay out before him, the houses, the small business section, the river, the bridges, the mill, and the college campus. The town seemed quiet, serene. It was obvious that harm had bypassed the town. It was untouched by the ravages of war.

Andrew rode down streets that he knew well to the modest house that he had once called home. He rode Sunny Boy through the front gate and he felt a tremendous weariness. He did not see the flowers that climbed the gate posts and the flowers that lined the walk that led to the front door. He did not see the startled faces in the window, the faces of the ladies aid society who were having tea on that Sunday afternoon. He saw the house as a white haze before him, and on his face was a vacant, rather fearsome look that sent the poor ladies scurrying out the back door, leaving Anne alone to deal with the returning unknown. Andrew sat in the saddle, meanwhile, and waited for his fatigued mind to tell his equally tired body what to do.

When Anne came out the front door, Andrew said, "I'm home."

"Welcome home, Andrew," Anne said.

"It's good to see you, Anne," said Andrew, and they embraced.

"Are you wounded?" asked Anne, looking closely at her husband, who had been gone for more than three years.

"Not really," said Andrew.

"But this scar on your face," said Anne.

"Oh, yes," said Andrew. "I'd forgotten about that."

They looked at each other for a moment. "I'll take care of my horse," said Andrew, and led Sunny Boy across the neat flower beds, around the house, and out the back gate to the stable in the back yard.

Andrew unsaddled Sunny Boy. "Thanks, my friend," said Andrew as he briefly rubbed down the horse. "Thanks for these many miles."

When Andrew came into the house, Anne offered him some supper. "If we have coffee, I'll have a cup of that," said Andrew. "I'll put off eating till tomorrow. I'm just too tired."

"Of course," said Anne.

And so Andrew Greyson returned home after the war to take up his role as a professor of English at the college. The letters of divorce that Andrew had initiated almost three years previously were never mentioned between Anne and Andrew, and their relationship picked up just about where it had left off some years before.

In the morning, Andrew, feeling much recovered, visited the dean of students at the college. He found the school in session, but almost empty of both teachers and students.

The dean was happy to see him. "So glad you're back, Greyson," said the dean. "We have a lot of rebuilding to do. We almost ran out of teachers and students, but Mr. Albers at the mill said, 'if you can't find male students, bring in the young women who are qualified,' and we've done that. We're pleased with how well that has worked out and we intend to continue to encourage women to attend even after we regain our usual male enrollment."

Andrew nodded. A positive development, he thought.

"Despite the war," the dean went on, "Mr. Albers' investments have paid off. The mill was in full operation and Mr. Albers' investments, he confided to me, were made overseas and even in the North. He is completely committed to the college, and so we shall have funds to build, to procure a first-rate staff, and to provide a fine education for the students who come to us. We're glad you're back, Professor Greyson."

Chapter 12

1866

In the years that followed, Andrew devoted his time to his work as a college professor of English. When he paused to reflect on it, he felt that he had found his place in life. He believed he was working with young people that would make the world a better place. He enjoyed the challenge of teaching his students the value of literature and the arts in their lives. His classes became known as a place of open discussions of provocative and life-related topics.

He would feel particularly pleased when he could get a spontaneous discussion going in his class, when students would raise their hands or jump to their feet to speak, eager to get involved. Students often stayed after class or stopped him in the hallways because he would give them his full attention, making each of them feel worthwhile.

Occasionally at the end of a class on a sunny day, he might say, "This afternoon I am going to take a walk along the north boundary path to where it crosses the stream. A good place to read some Wordsworth, I think. If any of you care to join me, please do so." And teacher and students would enjoy an informal session of sharing poetry, inspired perhaps by the sounds of trickling water, the sight of flowers swaying in the light breeze, or the music of birdsongs in the trees overhead.

One fall opening day of school, as the students were milling about the campus, some nervously starting their first class as freshmen, others eagerly anticipating their return as upperclassmen, they were surprised to see a graceful, speckled dog following at Professor Greyson's heels as he walked to his classroom. The dog settled unobtrusively under Andrew's desk, and over the years the setter became an accepted fixture in the classroom.

Occasionally the dog would emerge during the professor's lecture and wander between the desks of the students, slowly wagging his tail, looking earnestly at the faces of the students. When he saw the hint of a smile, or an empathetic look, he would lie down beside the desk of the friendly student, place his head on his front paws, and look up at the professor biding him to go on with his lecture.

On late afternoons, when Andrew walked down the steps of the First Academy Building after a day of work, he felt a glow of satisfaction, feeling he had been a part of something positive this day.

Once each summer during the break of classes, Andrew went to Clearfield for several weeks. His purpose, he told Anne, was to visit the site of the battle on Little Hilltop and perhaps write a historical treatise on it. She always declined to accompany him.

He did visit the site each summer and relived the bittersweet memories of that time—the victory won there, but also the tragedy of lives lost there. As he walked on the hilltop, he could almost see the faces of the men who had fallen there, and the words of the dying, young soldier haunted him. "I done my best."

For years he wrestled with questions about the battle in his mind. Were the deaths of those many soldiers worthwhile? After all, the war was lost, and even the impact of that small battle had been quickly erased by the losses in larger battles. But yet, hadn't these brave men fought at gallantly as any before or after? Hadn't their sacrifice been just as great?

It was only as he became older, gaining the perspective of years of searching for meanings, that he was able to understand that the backdrop against which each person lived their life didn't matter. It could be in war or peace, in disaster or turbulent times. It mattered only with what courage, how much giving to others, how much sacrifice they endured, with what deeds they lived their lives. In that final balance, one single sacrifice of a life on a battlefield equaled any achievement of a life's work.

Of course, the real purpose of Andrew's visits to Clearfield each year was to see how Andrea was doing. He had thought, at first, to simply visit Dr. Friedman and his family each year; but when he realized how much the child looked like himself, he thought it might become awkward, so he observed more discreetly.

On Sundays, he attended the church where the Friedmans did, the small church where he had once been surprised to see Elisabeth playing the organ. And each time he attended services there, though it were years afterward, he would look up at the small organ on the raised platform with the stained glass windows behind it—and just for a moment—a micro-moment—he would expect to see Elisabeth there.

He watched children at play in the school yard at Andrea's school at recess time. He attended school programs and musical events in which Andrea participated. Each year he was able to get a good sense of how Andrea was growing and progressing. Each year he was able to feel a secret pride in this bright, delightful person that Andrea was.

Usually if Andrew happened to meet the Friedmans, he and the doctor would simply nod and go on their way. However, one year when Andrea was seven, Andrew happened to meet the Friedmans just as they were coming to the entrance of the small church. The family was dressed in their best, and Andrea wore a pretty yellow dress and a small flowered hat. Walking between her parents, one hand in each of theirs, she was a pretty picture.

Andrew stopped, raised his hat to the little girl and Mrs. Friedman and said, "Good morning, ladies."

The little girl, in a clear voice, said, "Good morning, sir," and smiled.

Andrew was charmed. Dr. Friedman paused just long enough to say to Andrew, "She has been our greatest joy and pride. She has made our lives complete." Andrew nodded, touched and proud.

Chapter 13

For several summers, Andrew visited the Hammonds, Will still working as well as he could in his blacksmith shop, Liselle growing up but still showing a child's delight in Andrew's visits. Liselle was excelling in the schools that Clearfield offered, and Andrew encouraged her to consider going on to higher education, possibly even at Albers College. Will Hammond, proud of all his children, but having a special spot for Liselle, agreed to consider it when she was old enough.

"The college has scholarship funds for promising students," said Andrew. "Liselle certainly qualifies."

"She shall have the chance," said Will, and a number of years later, Liselle, a mature, young lady, eager to learn, arrived on the college campus on an autumn day, enrolled as a freshman student with major interests in literature and the arts.

And Andrew was eventually privileged to have Liselle as a student in one of his poetry classes. "You're getting old, Professor Greyson," Liselle teased him after class one day. "You have some gray in your hair."

"Ah, yes," sighed Andrew. "It is my students who do this to me. Particularly these pretty, bright coed students who are the epitome of the poetry we are reading."

"I think that was a compliment," smiled Liselle, "and I must tell you that even though you are old, that scar on your face makes you look very dashing and mysterious, and, I must say, quite handsome."

"Tch, tch," said Andrew. "Young lady, are you flirting with me?"

"Of course," said Liselle, "I've always flirted with you, and I've enjoyed it tremendously, especially since I was old enough to know what I was doing."

Andrew could not, at that moment, think of a rejoinder to that.

The Hammond family, meanwhile, had moved to Rochester, New York, for a position that had been offered to Will in a photographic products company. The opportunity and salary were such that he could not refuse, and though Andrew missed seeing Will and Caroline and their family, he was pleased for their good fortune.

One Hammond stayed in Clearfield—or rather, the country around Clearfield. Curt, the boy who as a twelve-year-old had helped the family survive the war by bringing in food from the woods, could not bear to leave those woods and the hills of Tennessee. In addition to that, even as a teen-aged young man, he was beginning to be known as an expert on horses. In postwar Tennessee, good horses were difficult to come by, and it was a situation that was open for a good horseman.

On one of Andrew's walks to Little Hilltop—taken this time in broad daylight and on the most direct trail—he chanced to meet Curt Hammond. Curt was, by now, a tall, handsome young man with blue eyes and long, tawny hair that he tied back with a short length of rawhide leather. Curt was riding a tall, well-muscled horse that kept stamping its front feet as if it could not bear to stop.

"It's good to see you, Curt," said Andrew, shaking hands. "What a fine animal."

"I brought him down from Kentucky," said Curt, "from up around Lexington. They are breeding some fine horses there."

Andrew stopped and considered. "I'll be needing a good horse soon," he said. "My gray gelding is getting into years. If you see a horse you think I could use, make arrangements for me to get it. I'll trust your judgement on the matter."

"All right," said Curt. "I'll do that. To tell you the truth, horse trading and horse breeding is what I would like to get into. What do you think of that?"

Andrew thought for a moment. "I think you would do very well, Curt. You know horses very well. It would be the active sort of life you enjoy."

"Of course," said Curt, "I might just spend my life running around in these woods. I enjoy doing that."

Andrew smiled. "Yes, you could," he said, "but eventually a person has to look at himself and ask, am I making my life count for something."

"I think you're right," said Curt seriously. He thought for a moment. "Another thing I might get into on the side is carriage and buggy making. I would put to use some of the blacksmithing skills I learned from my father."

"Well, Curt," said Andrew, "it's obvious that under that devil-may-care air that you have, you are a thinker. It seems to me that all your ideas have merit."

As they were talking, the two had started up the trail in the direction Andrew had been going, and they continued on together, talking companionably about Curt's plans.

Chapter 14

The first summer that Andrew returned to Clearfield he did not go to the river bluff where Elisabeth was buried under the small oak tree. Nor did he go the second year. Whenever he thought of going there and imagined the scene in his mind—which he did often—he felt he could not bear the emotional pain that would be made more poignant by being there.

On the third year, however, he rode, one early morning, across the bridge to the Turnwell plantation. He was still riding Sunny Boy—aging some by now—and when he reined the horse up the carriage drive to the house, Sunny Boy perked up his ears and quickened his pace. Andrew reached forward and patted the horse's neck. "Don't expect too much," said Andrew to the horse—and perhaps to himself as well.

The Turnwells had not returned from Atlanta after the war ended, perhaps realizing they could not make the plantation pay without slave labor. The terrace was an overgrown jungle of thorns and vines. Andrew got down off the saddle and led the horse through the vegetation on a path that looked like a trail made by some wild animals. He ducked his head and Sunny Boy pushed through the overhanging branches.

They stopped at the bench against a rock wall where Andrew had first spoken to Elisabeth. Andrew stood before it quietly, and Sunny Boy stretched out his neck to sniff at the bench still there and in surprisingly good condition.

They walked up the terrace to the veranda steps, the veranda sagging, some of the steps broken through. Andrew dropped Sunny Boy's reins and walked carefully up the steps, across the creaking veranda floor, and in through the large doors standing ajar. The big house was rapidly going to ruins. Daylight showed through holes in the roof, visible from the great front ballroom where Andrew stopped. Windows were broken and open to nesting birds. The sweeping stairway seemed intact, but much of the railing was broken. The furnishings had been looted, first by the raiders and later, perhaps, by transients or squatters who lived temporarily on the former prosperous plantation.

Andrew walked to the center of the ballroom and stopped. He looked around the room, turned and looked at the stairway, looking for what, he knew not. Perhaps I am looking for the past, he thought. Sometimes the past seemed more real than the present, certainly more real than the future which seemed, not empty, but vague.

Andrew walked out the house, his steps echoing in the emptiness of the house as he walked. He led Sunny Boy around the house and they rode slowly up the river trail. The trail, or wagon road, had kept its visible identity though quite overgrown with long grasses.

The day had turned into one of those days of rapidly alternating weather. The blue sky and occasional bright sun were interrupted now and then with brief showers. Streaks of rain clouds came leaping over the mountain ridges to the northwest, only to be followed by the bluest of skies.

Sunny Boy did not mind the weather, walking steadily through the tall, wet grass, rain streaking down his neck and shoulders. Andrew, as it rained, would pull his hat brim lower and raise the collar of his coat.

They splashed across the shallow stream and continued along the river trail till they arrived at the raised bluff overlooking the river. Andrew dropped Sunny Boy's reins and walked to the oak tree. Grass and some native, white flowers had taken over the ground covering the grave.

Andrew stepped carefully around the flowers and sat down beside the grave, back against the oak tree. After a few moments he put his hand out on the grave and left it there, put his head back against the tree trunk and sat quietly. Presently one of the brief rain showers passed overhead, cool drops of rain touching Andrew's face. He did not move.

The bright sun followed the rain. Andrew could feel the warmth on his face drying the wetness. The seasons come and go, he thought. There is a sadness and there is a goodness. There is still an ache for something, a longing for what could have been, but there is also an acceptance. It is good to sit here, quietly and remember. I will come back each year. He thought of the line in Keat's poem and quoted it over and over in his mind. *"Forever wilt thou love, and she be fair...Forever wilt thou love, and she be fair...Forever wilt thou love..."*

As Andrew returned in the following years, the oak tree grew larger. The grasses and flowers grew deeper and more bountiful each year. A casual passerby would not know it was the site of a grave, but might only comment, "What a pretty spot this is."

A number of years later, Andrew spent much of a day carefully carving, with a sharp clasp knife that he carried with him, on the trunk of the oak tree. He planed the bark smooth, slanting upwards so all could be read at a glance:

Elisabeth Barrett, 1840 to 1863
My Love, 1862 to Forever, A.G.

Chapter 15

Often when Andrew returned to Milford after his early summer trip to Clearfield, he would find a letter waiting for him at the school post office. These were letters from Alexandra, reporting her progress at the Bloomington school for teachers. It was obvious from her letters that she was doing well, that she enjoyed her studies, that she was looking forward to the work ahead of her.

Her letters were quite lengthy, sometimes discussing some topics from her classes that had caught her interest. She would relate some anecdotes from her school life and some amusing incidents that had happened, perhaps, in her classes.

Alexandra was not shy about telling of her triumphs—her good grades, a particular term paper that she had done well on, or some classroom discussion in which she had been able to make some significant points. Likewise, she wrote of her difficulties. "Why am I required to take this Methods of Teaching class?" she would ask. "I can't see that I'll use any of this. I'd rather be taking a class in literature."

Some of her difficulties also stemmed from the fact that she was one of only a few blacks on the campus. "I haven't seen much intentional prejudice," she wrote. "It's the indifference that sometimes gets to me."

Andrew corresponded regularly with his friend, John Bailey, the professor to whom he had first sent Alexandra. John Bailey's reports on Alexandra's progress were very complimentary. "The most remarkable thing about her," wrote John Bailey, "is that a person of her station could have all the background she does in reading, in music, in literature, in philosophical understanding. Where could she possible have learned all this as a slave?"

Finally, some five years after Alexandra had first left for the Bloomington school, Andrew received a letter from her that said, "I have accepted a position as a teacher at Stuart Mills Institute," she wrote. "I am eager to begin." Farther in the letter: "How can I ever thank you for your friendship and your financial support?" And: "Elisabeth would be proud of me, and that makes me happy, but I am also proud of myself."

In the years that followed, the correspondence between Andrew and Alexandra became one of good friends and fellow teachers.

Chapter 16

The railroads of the South, damaged by war, were repaired and rebuilt. By 1868, the Baltimore and Ohio Railroad, the Nashville and Chattanooga Railroad, and the Richmond, Fredericksburg and Potomac Railroad were operating again. Anne Greyson was able to again visit her family in New York State as she had done quite regularly before the war.

It was a three-day trip from Milford, Tennessee, to Highland Falls, New York, a town on the Hudson River about forty miles north of New York City. Andrew would escort her to her family home, visit briefly, and return to Milford. He did not mind the travel time as he could read, or talk to fellow passengers, or look at the country passing by the sooty windows of the train—country on which just a few years ago he had fought a war.

They would travel by coach to Chattanooga, then by rail eastward to Virginia, up to Baltimore, then eastward again through New Jersey, through New York City, and on to Highland Falls. Andrew would remain only a day before he would depart on the return trip, his presence at Anne's family not nearly as enthusiastically welcome as it had been as a young lieutenant graduate of West Point. His participation on the wrong side of the Civil War had been awkward for Anne, and was not easily forgiven by her family. After all, Anne's father, the Methodist minister, had prayed from the pulpit for the destruction of the Confederacy. Now here was Andrew, and not very repentant at that.

"I can't believe that you actually fought to preserve such a loathsome institution as slavery," the minister said on one occasion.

Andrew, determined not to get into a dispute, said mildly, "There are more forms of slavery than what we had in the South."

"And just what are you inferring by that?"

"Well," said Andrew, trying not to sound too self-righteous, "I've been in the industrial sections of New York and of Boston. I've seen the young children they put to work in their sweatshops. Perhaps their condition is not much different from what it was for our black slaves."

"But at least they are free to leave if they wish," argued the minister.

"Perhaps," said Andrew, remembering the dull eyes of a small boy, possibly ten or eleven years of age, that had looked back at him as he peered into the dingy window of a workshop near the rail yards of New York City.

"I'm rather surprised they did not hold at least you officers responsible for your actions during the war. Lincoln was much too soft on the Confederate leadership. They should have been punished. 'And eye for an eye'," quoted the old minister.

Andrew would return in several weeks to escort Anne, who at times seemed reluctant to leave, back to Tennessee. If the six or seven days required for the trip came while Andrew's classes were in session, he could usually arrange his schedule accordingly, but most often they were during the summer while classes were not in session. Andrew's only regret was leaving the cool climate of Tennessee's hills for the humid summer heat of lower New York State.

In midsummer Anne asked Andrew to accompany her on one of these trips. "Perhaps I can rid myself of this persistent cough I have if I return to my native climate," she said. "I would at least like to get Dr. Robinson's diagnosis of it."

Andrew readily agreed to go. He was building a log cabin on the mountain side above the college, skidding the logs with a pair of Percheron horses he had borrowed and with the aid of two college boys he had hired for the summer; and he could arrange his time to accommodate her trip.

"Send me a telegram when you are ready to return," said Andrew as he left Anne with her family. Anne looked pale and uneasy. "I hope this warm weather makes you feel better." Andrew himself had taken off his coat and was boarding the train for New York in shirt-sleeves. He waved to Anne from the steps of the train as it began to move.

Andrew returned to his work of bringing pine logs to the cabin site, peeling them, notching them to fit, and slowly building up the walls of the cabin. In the center of the cabin stood a large stone wall and fireplace, built the previous summer. Andrew quite enjoyed the physical work, beginning in the cool of the morning, taking some time in the middle of the day to rest—perhaps do some reading—and working till the mountains looked hazy blue in the evening twilight.

Several weeks after Andrew left Anne in New York, a telegram arrived, delivered to Andrew at the cabin site by a young man on horseback. "Telegram for you, Professor," the messenger said as he handed the envelope to Andrew. "I hope it's not bad news."

Andrew wiped the sweat from his hands and took the envelope. "Thanks, Jerome," he said. "We'll see you back on campus this fall, won't we?"

"Oh, yes," smiled Jerome. "I'll be a sophomore. I'm looking forward to it."

"Fine," said Andrew. He sat down on one of the long logs, slit open the envelope and read the message.

"It's not good. Please come," said the brief message. Andrew felt his heart sink. So the cough was serious, after all? Or had some other symptoms come up?

When Andrew arrived at the Shipley home in New York, he was shocked at the appearance of Anne. He could hardly believe her condition could deteriorate so quickly. Anne spent much of her waking hours sitting in a wicker arm chair in the warm August sun, often in the garden, and wrapped in a blanket. Andrew sat beside her talking, sometimes reading a book, or writing. Occasionally he read aloud to her if she seemed alert enough to listen.

The first opportunity Andrew had, he questioned Dr. Robinson, who visited the patient once a day, but said very little.

Dr. Robinson looked soberly at Andrew and shook his head. "Tumors," he said. "Growing in her lungs. They can be felt just at the bottom of her rib cage. That is what caused her cough, and that is what is sapping away her life."

"How could her condition change so rapidly?" asked Andrew. "She had the cough for quite some time, but now suddenly she is very ill."

"It is the nature of these tumors to suddenly accelerate their growth," said the doctor. "Something goes wrong and these bad cells multiply rapidly. Some surgeons I know have tried removing them surgically with limited success, but no one has ever done surgery in the lungs. There is just no way to control the bleeding in lung tissue. I'm afraid there's nothing to do but wait."

"Pain?" asked Andrew. He felt helpless. What could be done.?

"Some," said Dr. Robinson. "It may get worse. We've been giving her daily doses of morphine, and we can increase that if necessary."

A full time nurse was employed to take care of Anne, but Andrew carried her out to her chair in the garden each sunny day, then sat with her. It was a time of quiet introspection for both of them.

The physically inactive life was trying for Andrew. Sitting around the house in the evenings did not appeal to him. Conversation with the Shipley family had always been difficult, and now there was a new element in their attitude toward him. They seemed to be blaming him for Anne's illness. If only he hadn't taken her away from her native state to the uncivilized mountains of Tennessee. There were plenty of teaching positions nearby. If he had taken employment here, the entire Civil War thing could have been avoided, and Anne would have been happier.

Andrew developed a habit of going for long walks after Anne was asleep in bed in the early evening. There were numerous paths along the rocky shoreline of the Hudson River, and the twilight glimmered off the water with enough light so that he was able to make his way till quite late.

On an evening, almost three weeks after Andrew had come to Highland Falls to take care of Anne, he realized, as he walked, that the fall session would start at the college in two weeks. In the morning, he thought, I will have to write and tell them I will not be there to teach my classes.

But Anne died quietly in her sleep that night, and for the next two days Andrew meekly acquiesced to all the funeral arrangements made by Anne's family. In time of stress, he preferred to be alone, and the bustle about the house was disturbing.

On the afternoon of the second day, the day of the burial, he walked in the garden in the back of the house. Flowers were in bloom, neatly growing in their assigned plots. Andrew walked slowly through the garden and into a back field with a rock wall along its border. Growing out of the wall were some purple, long-stemmed, wild flowers. Andrew picked several, and on his way back to the house, he picked some white flowers in the garden. And these flowers, the wild and tame together, were the bouquet that he lay on the casket before it was lowered into the ground that day.

Chapter 17

A number of years after the Civil War ended, many of the small railroad companies in the South joined together to become The Southern Railway. Eventually spur lines were built to Clearfield, Tennessee, and several years later, to Milford. Andrew was able to, making transfers at Nashville and Chattanooga, travel by rail during his summer odyssey. He was able to get a horse, for the time he was in Clearfield, from Curt Hammond whose enterprise in horses and horse-drawn vehicles was doing well. Andrew and Curt were looking over the available horses one day in early summer, leaning against the top rail of a corral in Curt's yard.

Curt was proud of his line of horses. "I'm getting these horses from up in the bluegrass country of Kentucky," he said. "They are thoroughbreds. Note the long barrel of the body and the long, tapered legs. These horses can almost fly."

Andrew was impressed. "They look good," he said. He pointed to a spirited bay that was trotting across the paddock. "That gelding. Is that one for sale?"

Curt smiled. "I knew you could not resist them for long," he said. "This is a good lot, and he is the best of the bunch." The bay horse, as if he knew he was the subject of their conversation, wheeled in front of them; and with a flash of mane, tail, and hooves, and with a burst of speed, galloped away from them.

"Look at that stride!" exclaimed Andrew. "He's magnificent."

The horse put up a token resistance to being caught, bridled, and saddled, but once Andrew was in the saddle, its good training showed through. Andrew rode him down some grassy lanes and across a nearby field. The horse responded well, went through all the paces that Andrew asked of it, gracefully jumped a low hedgerow; and fairly flew when Andrew touched it to a gallop. This boy can run, thought Andrew.

An hour later they were in the small office room in the stables going through the paper work to make the horse Andrew's. "He's three years old," said Curt. "On paper his name is Bay Ram, but you can call him what you wish."

"The name is fine," said Andrew. He signed the papers Curt held out to him. "I noticed as I rode, that you have built a new house back in that grove of trees on the side of the hill. You really are settling down."

Curt broke into a wide smile. "That house is for my bride. I'm getting married in two weeks," he said. "And to the prettiest girl in the valley. Perhaps you know her, Andrea Friedman, the doctor's daughter."

Andrew's surprise stopped him for a moment, but he recovered quickly. "Congratulations, Curt." He grasped Curt's hand. "Of course, I've seen her on occasion, and I completely agree with you. She's the prettiest girl in all of Tennessee."

"Then you must come to our wedding," Curt said happily. "I want everyone to celebrate with us. I still can't believe my good fortune. Why she would choose me when she could have had any one of these young men around here. I'm a few years older than she. But not enough to make a difference," he added quickly.

Andrew smiled at Curt's enthusiasm and let him go on talking. Horses were quite forgotten for the moment. I couldn't ask for a better husband for a daughter, thought Andrew.

Curt was still talking. "You have got to meet her," he said. "She's a remarkable person. You know, she came here to see my horses one day—sometime last fall it was—and she bet me she could beat me in a horse race, using any two horses I would pick. Well, she quite outwitted me. I saddled a horse for her, and she held the reins while I saddled my horse; and when I finished she dropped the reins of her horse and took mine." Curt laughed happily at the recollection. "Of course, she beat me." He shook his head ruefully. "She can ride like the wind. No side saddle for her."

Of course, Andrew went to the wedding, having also received a particular invitation from the Friedmans, when he met them at church, to sit with them at the wedding. He greatly admired his daughter as she came down the aisle, moving quite slowly to accommodate the aging Dr. Friedman whose arm she held. Mrs. Friedman wept happily, and Andrew passed his handkerchief to her—though at times during the ceremony he felt he could have used it himself. He tried not to think of the similarity between Elisabeth and Andrea, but such thoughts kept coming to him.

After the ceremony, at a dinner under the trees in the city park, Andrew shook hands with Curt and took Andrea's hand in his to congratulate her. When she swept her eyelashes up to look at him, Andrew, momentarily visioning Elisabeth in his mind, thought for a moment that his knees would give way.

"Oh, Professor Greyson. How good of you to come." Andrea smiled, a picture of the happy bride. "You always seem to show up for my special days." She leaned close to Andrew for a kiss on her cheek, and as he kissed her, he saw around her pretty neck a beautiful gold chain with a heart-shaped locket.

"I hope you are both very happy," murmured Andrew, shook hands again with Curt, turned and left.

Andrea put her hand through her husband's arm and watched Andrew leave. "I think he's nice," she said. "Why do you suppose there were tears in his eyes just now?"

Chapter 18

The years that followed were golden ones in many ways for Andrew. His work at the college as a teacher of literature was a source of a great deal of satisfaction for him. He felt that students could learn much about themselves through the study of literature, and now he was seeing writings by American writers, such as Mark Twain, Herman Melville, Ralph Emerson and others, reflecting the uniquely American character. It was easier for his students to relate to them than to the European authors they once studied exclusively.

He saw some of his students become teachers of literature, and that was gratifying. Occasionally he was able to recognize that potential in young students and guide them in their endeavors. But perhaps even more satisfying to Andrew was when he was able to awaken in students who were not majoring in literature, or any of the arts, an aesthetic sensitivity for literature. The light that came into such students' faces and eyes when they first caught a glimpse of the possible depths and meanings of literature, also lighted Andrew's life.

Andrew believed he had achieved what life was meant to be: happiness in a vocation that he was good at, and the respect—and sometimes the affection—of his students, his fellow staff members, and his fellow citizens of the community. He felt fulfilled in that he believed he was making a worthwhile contribution to the world he lived in.

When Andrew was in Clearfield on his summer visits, he stopped in at Curt Hammond's horse stables as often as he could without being intrusive. He would talk horses with Curt, and whenever Andrea noticed he was at the stables, she would come out to talk. Often she would bring out a pot of coffee, and the three of them, Andrea, Curt, and Andrew would talk.

"You're a college professor?" Andrea asked at one time.

"Yes, I am," said Andrew.

Andrea looked thoughtful. "Do you suppose that when you come next summer you could bring me some books to read? Some good books? I can't seem to get them here."

Andrew smiled. Actually he was thrilled. "Andrea," he said. "Books are my specialty. I'd be pleased to bring you some books."

Andrea's warm smile was all the reward Andrew needed. "You can't wait till next summer, though," he said. "I'll send you a package of them as soon as I get back to Milford."

Andrew had no intention of ever revealing his relationship to Andrea. He could see that her life was quite complete. She had a loving husband, devoted parents, and a fulfilling life. It would be quite wrong to interject himself into that. If there were a real need for me in that capacity, he thought, I would. But as it was now, he was content to watch from the sidelines.

Only in one instance, in all those years, did Andrew do anything that directly influenced the life of his daughter, Andrea. Curt and Andrea had been talking enthusiastically about expanding their business. Curt wanted to build a large, open-ended shed in which to build carriages. Getting the shed built, getting the materials for building carriages, and hiring two skilled craftsmen would require a financial outlay quite beyond their resources.

"I'll go to the bank tomorrow for a loan," Curt declared at one of Andrew's coffee time visits. Curt smiled a bit sheepishly at Andrew. "See how she has changed my life—for the good," he quickly added. "I would never have considered asking for a loan, or going to a bank, except maybe to hold it up," he joked.

Andrea smiled at him. "You're not as wild as you pretend to be," she said, putting her hand in his.

"No, I'm not," Curt answered. "You're the wild one, really—the way you ride some of these mustangs we get in here."

Andrew sat quietly, listening to the talk, watching two people he loved.

Curt turned to Andrew. "Have you seen her with these horses I bring in? They come in wild and scared; and she goes in with them, talks to them—probably sings to them—and first thing you know, they are eating out of her hand." Curt shook his head fondly as he looked at Andrea. "In a few days she's riding them. She really is something."

Andrew nodded. He agreed.

"Will you go with me to the bank?" Curt asked Andrea.

"I'll go with you," she said.

Andrew found it necessary for himself to be near the bank the next day. He saw Curt and Andrea go into the bank, and he also saw them come out, discouraged, disheartened. It was plain what had happened. They had been turned down.

Andrew went into the bank and asked to see the president, a Mr. Cosgrove that Andrew knew slightly. "I'm a friend of both their families," Andrew told him in the privacy of his office. "Is there any way I could guarantee their loan without them being aware of it? It's not likely they would accept my help if they knew about it."

Mr. Cosgrove was thoughtful and serious. "I believe it could be arranged," he said. He apologized somewhat for originally refusing their loan. "Horse business, you know," he said. "It's not a dependable business."

Andrew did not agree with him, but he did not see the need for open disagreement.

And so the next day, the Hammonds received a note from the bank asking them to come in again. After some checking around, some new considerations were being made. The directors of the bank were now looking very favorably at the loan request made by them recently.

Andrew's reward was the happiness and enthusiasm he saw in his friends as he watched them plan and work on their project. And no problems ever came up as a result of Andrew's intervention. The loan was paid off as Curt's business continued to grow.

For a dozen years or more, though, of course, he never mentioned it, Andrew wondered if Andrea and Curt would have children. It seemed quite natural that they would. They were obviously a devoted, loving couple. Andrew was pleasantly surprised, as he arrived one June morning, to see that Andrea was quite apparently going to have a child—and soon.

Andrea was in the corral, patiently working with a coal-black filly, black mane, black tail, black hooves—not even a white mark on her face—a beautiful animal that showed great promise. Andrea was sitting cross-legged on the ground in the corral, a saddle on the ground a few feet from her; and the horse was edging toward the saddle to smell of it. Andrea saw Andrew watching at the rails and smiled, but did not move.

The horse, black flanks gleaming in the sun, was satisfied the saddle was all right, so Andrea held out the bridle. A few cautious steps by the horse and an outstretched neck to sniff at the bridle. Well, there was nothing to fear from those, and the horse took one more step to nuzzle at Andrea. When Andrea did not respond, the horse pushed at her with its nose; and Andrea, feigning reluctance, slowly stood up, saying, "Well, if you insist, of course, we'll put on this funny, old saddle and this silly bridle."

In a few minutes she was walking the horse, saddled and bridled, around the corral, now and then draping her arm over the horse's neck or leaning deliberately against its side. She led the horse to the rails where Andrew stood. "Isn't she a beauty?" she asked Andrew.

"That she is," said Andrew. "You two make a pretty picture." He wanted to say, but did not say, do you think you should be doing this in your condition? The concern showed on his face.

Andrea laughed. "You men are all alike. Curt keeps telling me I've got to stop working with these horses. Don't worry. I'm not going to ride her. That will have to wait till after."

"Yes," said Andrew. "I'm extremely happy for you and Curt." And for myself, he thought.

Andrea flashed a happy smile. For some reason, though most people did not speak of childbirth on a familiar basis, she did not mind talking about it with this old man whose kindness showed through his eyes.

"It might be a boy, and then it might be a girl," Andrea said.

"I hope it's a girl," said Andrew, "but I know you will be happy with either."

And so, in July of 1898, Lisbeth was born.

Epilogue

1918

Lisbeth was waiting when the professor opened the door of the faculty lounge. She leaped to her feet and rushed to meet the professor, her eyes sparkling with excitement. The professor smiled to see her so happy. She has figured out some of what I have to tell her, he thought. Whatever hesitations the professor had about the course he had chosen—the decision to explain to Lisbeth the source and identity of the locket—were gone.

Lisbeth came quickly to the old professor and almost threw her arms around his neck, but at the last moment she seized his arm. "It's you, isn't it?" she said. "I know it's you. Once I had you in mind when I looked at the picture, I could see the resemblance. I thought at first that there was a blemish in the picture on the face, but then I remembered this scar on your face." She touched the left side of the professor's face with a finger tip.

"Yes," said the professor. "It is I." He looked at Lisbeth and smiled again.

Lisbeth opened the collar of her coat. The locket was around her neck, and she picked it up, turned it to face herself, and with a finger nail deftly opened the catch on the locket. Looking at the picture in the locket, and at the face of the old professor before her, she nodded her head. "Yes, it's you," she said.

She turned the locket over to look at the engraving. "A.G.," she said. "I didn't know your first name, but I looked it up in the college address book. It all fits."

"Yes," said the professor. Lisbeth turned the locket back over and looked at the woman's picture. Andrew waited.

There was a silence for a few moments. Lisbeth looked up from the picture to face the professor. "I've discovered something about this picture, too," she said.

"Yes?" said the professor.

"Well," said Lisbeth, and she blushed a little. "It looks like me—but, of course, it isn't me, but that's why it looked so familiar to me all these years. Doesn't it look like me, Professor?"

"She looks very much like you," said the professor.

"E.B.?" said Lisbeth. "I don't know any…"

The professor held up his hand. "Let's sit at this table," he said, seating himself. He reached into an inside pocket of his coat and withdrew an envelope.

"You sit," said Lisbeth. "I'll stand here beside you. I know you have more to tell me and I can hardly wait."

The professor lay on the table the picture of Elisabeth—the picture he had kept for so many years, frayed around the edges, faded somewhat, but still showing the remarkable beauty that she had.

"Oh!" exclaimed Lisbeth. "It's her. It's the same person as the locket." She paused, thinking, perhaps trying to make some connections. She put a hand on the professor's shoulder. "She is so beautiful—much more than I, even though we do look alike."

Lisbeth sat down in a chair beside the professor and turned to look at his face. "Why do you look so sad? Is this someone you lost?" She took his hand in her hands. "I'm so sorry."

The professor tried to smile and managed a faint one. It's more than a half-century, he thought. And I still long for her—and probably more now than ever as I sit here and talk with this girl that looks so like her.

"You loved her very much," said Lisbeth. She put an arm around the professor's neck and lay her head against his. Both their eyes were again drawn to the picture on the table before them.

After a moment, the professor heard a small gasp from Lisbeth. She sat up, put one hand to her neck and picked up the locket at her throat. With the other hand she placed a finger tip on the locket in the picture. "Are these the same?" she asked in a small voice.

The professor cleared his throat. "They are the same," he said. "The initials, E.B. stand for her name, Elisabeth Barrett. She was a woman I fell in love with during the war. I gave her that locket, and we had these pictures taken just before I left Tennessee for the war in Virginia."

Lisbeth looked intently at the professor. Her eyes glistened with small tears of sympathy. She took the professor's hand in her hands again.

After a moment the professor went on. "When I was finally able to get back to her, it was too late. She was gone…she died while I was gone, and…" The professor paused again. Lisbeth waited quietly.

"We had a child, a girl." Lisbeth squeezed the professor's hand, but could say nothing. "We weren't married," said the professor. "We were just in love." The professor sighed. "And that baby girl, Lisbeth, was your mother, Andrea." The professor stopped. There would be so much to tell later. But for now, this was all he could manage.

Lisbeth looked the professor in the face, tears of emotion in her eyes and on her cheeks, the corners of her mouth quivering just a little. She said, "Then you are…you are my grandfather." She surprised both herself and the professor with a happy giggle. "You are my grandfather," she said again, emphasizing the word "my." She shook her head in amazement. "Somehow," she said, "I just knew there would be a happy ending to all this."

But, of course, it wasn't just an ending. It was also a beginning. It was the beginning of a friendship that brought together the past and the present, the old and the young, and Andrew Greyson and his granddaughter, Lisbeth.

Lisbeth wanted to know the story of Elisabeth Barrett's life, and the story of Andrew Greyson's life, and part by part, in the meetings that followed, the professor told her the story the reader has read.

"It's awfully romantic," Lisbeth said when the professor told her of his first meeting with Elisabeth.

"Why, that's Aunt Liselle; she was my favorite aunt," she exclaimed when the professor told her about the little girl at the church that insisted they have their picture taken.

"You were very brave," Lisbeth said when the professor told her some of the story of the battle of Little Hilltop. She touched the scar on his face, and the professor shut his eyes, remembering other hands that had touched him just so.

Lisbeth wept when the professor told of his return to find Elisabeth gone. "I'm so very, very sorry," she said. "Now I know why you could understand when I was so worried about Peter in France."

"I want to see the grave," said Lisbeth, so they went by train to Clearfield, which was, after all, Lisbeth's hometown. They drove a small buggy out to the bluff to see the grave site, overgrown by a profusion of wild, deep pink roses. "It's beautiful," said Lisbeth, and she also said, "This is your place, your place alone. I won't come back with you again, but I'll remember what a lovely place this is."

Perhaps Andrew Greyson's proudest moment was when he walked Lisbeth down the aisle of the church at her marriage to Captain Peter Morgan.

"Is it a military wedding?" he had asked. "Are the men wearing uniforms?" Yes, they were, the bright blue, dress marine uniform with the red stripe on the trouser legs. "Then I should also wear a uniform," the professor said, and on the day of the wedding, wearing his old, gray Confederate uniform—carefully repaired and pressed by a skillful tailor—with saber at his side, he walked straight and proud with the equally proud—and immensely beautiful—Lisbeth at his side.

At the front of the church, he kissed the bride and turned to the waiting bridegroom. Instead of shaking hands, he saluted as sharp a salute as was ever made by a West Point cadet, and Captain Peter Morgan returned the salute with as precise a salute as was ever made by a United States Marine.

The old professor grew older, but he still walked the college grounds each day with the gentle dog, Sally, and the proud thoroughbred, Thor. He continued to attend football games, track meets, basketball games, concerts, banquets, and other student activities. If, perchance, he was absent from some event, someone would say, "Where is the old professor?" Someone else would remember, "He's gone to visit his grandchildren. He'll be back next week."

For holidays, now, he would sometimes travel to Jacksonville, North Carolina, where Peter Morgan was stationed at a marine base; and later to Quantico, Virginia, where the family lived while Peter studied at the marine corps schools there.

And it was a family now. There were two boys, the oldest named Greyson. Lisbeth would meet him at the railroad station, running to throw her arms around him, with the two boys trailing behind. The professor always felt quite welcome.

Lisbeth, each visit, would always have some questions, either about her mother or about Elisabeth. She wanted to know as much as she could about their lives, and gradually the professor told the whole story. "I'm writing it all down," said Lisbeth. "It's a very interesting story, and someday if I have a daughter, she will want to know."

Peter, in the evenings, quite enjoyed discussing the history of the Civil War and military tactics with the professor, particularly the battle of Little Hilltop. "This battle isn't in any of the history books," said Peter, "and it should be. It's the sort of smaller unit tactics that battles are coming to. It's not feasible, anymore, with massed artillery, to move in regimental formations."

Peter was studying at Quantico at the time, and he got the professor to agree to come and lecture to his tactical planning class. For an entire afternoon, with some breaks, the professor talked to a roomful of interested marine officers about the Little Hilltop battle, demonstrating some of it on the blackboard. Later the class adjourned to the officers' club, a plantation mansion that had been remodeled to accommodate its new use, and over drinks the professor was plied with numerous questions by the officers.

"I'm very impressed by the professionalism of these officers," the professor told Peter afterward. "If they are an indication of what sort of troops you have, then you have some good forces, indeed."

"We think we are the best," said Peter.

"Only one thing," said the professor. "You really should have some poetry reading in your military tactics classes."

"We're not quite ready for that," said Peter.

The professor got along nicely with the two boys, Greyson and Peter, Jr. Young as they were, they loved to go horseback riding. Horses were always available at the marine base, and the professor carefully picked mounts they could handle, and he brought them along in their riding skills. After the ride, they would rub the horses down—the little boys rubbing as high as they could reach. The grooms at the stable offered to take care of that task, but the professor said, "No, a man has to take care of his own horse. Right, boys?"

"Right!" the boys responded as they rubbed down the horses' legs or belly.

One day they talked Lisbeth into riding with them. "I used to ride with my mother when I was quite small, and when we still had the stables in Clearfield. But I was awfully small. I'm not sure I remember how to ride."

The professor smiled. He remembered the two-year-old Lisbeth hanging on the broad back of a gentle horse. Shortly after, her father had died in an accident and the stables were closed.

To the boys' delight—and to the professor's—Lisbeth rode very well. Near the end of the ride, when the boys said, "Let's race to the gate," she had to hold her horse back in order to allow the boys to win.

"And now," said the professor to Lisbeth, "I'll race you to that tree in the pasture and around it back to the stables."

"All right," laughed Lisbeth, and she took off at once, momentarily leaving the professor and his horse standing in the dust. But he followed her at a gallop noting how she leaned forward in the saddle riding with her legs, her body in accord with the running horse. Of course, she rides well, thought the professor. How could she not?

Some evenings the boys asked for stories, and the professor would comply. "Tell us how the bandits captured you," they would say, and the professor would retell the story, leaving out the parts he thought they were too young to hear. "Wow!" they would say, their eyes shining in excitement when he told how he was rescued by his scouts.

The professor particularly enjoyed reading stories in poetry form to them, poems such as "The Charge of the Light Brigade," and "The Highwayman," and "The Cremation of Sam McGee," and "Abdul Abulbul Amir." The professor would become dramatic as he read, and he would begin quoting from memory till one of the boys would say, "Gwamp-papa, you're supposed to read, not say."

"Oh, yes." He would obediently hold the book in front of him, careful to keep his eyes on the pages, or the boys would accuse him of cheating again.

Those were enjoyable visits for the professor, but he would return gladly to his cabin on the mountainside, his English setter, his horse, and his beloved college and students.

On a wintry day in 1924, a group of students, a foursome, out for a walk in the brisk air, saw the professor seated on a bench near where the pathway crossed over a clear, running stream by a footbridge.

"There's the old professor," said one of the girls. "Let's stop and talk."

The old professor did not seem to hear them coming. Sally was lying quietly at his feet, and Thor stood behind the bench, his head near the old man's shoulder. The professor sat, an open book in his hands on his lap.

Just as the students were about to hurry forward, to call a greeting to the professor, one of the boys held up his hand. "Let's go easy," he said. "It's awfully quiet—and peaceful—here." As they came closer, Sally stood up, slowly wagging her feathery tail, and lay her head on the old man's knees.

And that is how they found The Old Professor. He had died quietly, in dignity, as perhaps most would prefer to die when it becomes necessary. He had seen it coming, and put the book down in his lap instead of dropping it—and if anyone had thought to take note, it was a book of Robert Frost poetry, and the professor's finger lay on a line in a short poem titled "The Pasture." Perhaps the professor had just read the last line: "*I shan't be gone long.—You come too*."

After the funeral, after she had walked quietly behind the wagon with the casket, Sally went to live with Lisbeth in Virginia—and in her old age was lovingly adopted into their family. Lisbeth made sure there was a rug to lie on in the kitchen, and one in front of the fireplace.

Thor did his duty nobly—walked with pride beside the wagon that carried the casket to the burial site. But he was impatient. He couldn't understand why the old professor did not come to ride him, lead him around the campus, give him treats, rub him down. He would allow no one to ride or exercise him. Finally, on a night in which a scattering of snow fell, his restlessness got the best of him, and he leaped the rail fence.

The stable boys who tried to find him the next morning saw his tracks where he had landed on the outside of the rails, followed his tracks in the thin snow as Thor had wandered along the campus paths where they had so often walked, and they saw his tracks go up to the cabin on the mountainside. From there, his tracks became indistinct in the rough terrain, and eventually the followers had to give up. Thor had disappeared into some hidden, deep, mountain recess. No one ever saw him again.

If perchance, you visit the campus of Albers College today and follow the pathway around the outer perimeter of the grounds, you will come to a spot on a sunny slope where a clear stream runs nearby, and you can just get a glimpse of the smoke-hued mountains beyond a deep and blue valley. There you will find a monument put up by donations from students, from fellow staff, from alumni of the college, and from townspeople. On the slab of granite is a bronze plaque which reads:

Here rests our teacher and our friend,
Andrew Taylor Greyson
1832 to 1924
Scholar, Philosopher, Writer,
Soldier, Patriot, Outdoorsman,
Horseman, and always a
Gentleman.
"Seek beauty, for in the search,
you will find truth."—A.G.

A Final and Brief Digression
1925

Born to Peter and Lisbeth Morgan of Quantico, Virginia, at the Naval Hospital, on May 10th, 1925, a daughter, eight pounds and six ounces, named Elisabeth Andrea Morgan. Mother and baby are doing very well. Attending doctors and nurses agree that the baby girl has shown a unique vivacity for life, that she has bright blue eyes, and that she has incredibly fine hair that looks like spun, silken gold.

The End